"This just in, sir." The officer placed a folded message on Colonel Lawrence's desk.

*Situational change is hereby ordered. Immediately terminate maneuvers. An unknown illness has been discovered in a community near your location. You are ordered:*

*A: To inform your men they are no longer on a routine exercise.*

*B: To institute procedures for the segregation of the remains of the victims.*

*C: To locate a site suitable for the eventual cremation of those remains.*

*D: To take the above instructions into consideration in the discretionary briefing of your command.*

What incredible nonsense, Lawrence thought. He had two duties and he knew it. One was to help in the control and, if necessary, containment of a particularly nasty bug. Another was to keep his superiors looking productive, in charge, and definitely—God, yes, above all—not responsible.

*What the hell*, he thought. *Occupational hazard...*

"WELL THOUGHT-OUT...
INTRICATE!" —*Publishers Weekly*

# THE JULIET EFFECT

## JESSE SLATTERY

**ST. MARTIN'S PAPERBACKS**

THE JULIET EFFECT

Copyright 1988 by Jesse Slattery.

All rights reserved. No part of this book may be used or reproduced in any manner whatsoever without written permission except in the case of brief quotations embodied in critical articles or reviews. For information address St. Martin's Press, 175 Fifth Avenue, New York, N.Y. 10010.

Library of Congress Catalog Card Number: 87-16142

ISBN: 0-312-92185-3

Printed in the United States of America

St. Martin's Press hardcover edition published 1988
St. Martin's Paperbacks edition/June 1990

10  9  8  7  6  5  4  3  2  1

To Jessie Slattery,
my mother,
this book is yours.

# ACKNOWLEDGMENTS

TO THOSE WHO LEFT ME ALONE, BUT NEVER, EVER, allowed me to be alone, I express my gratitude.

There would have been no *Juliet* without the faith and support of Don Cleary, my agent at the Jane Rotrosen Agency. There would have been none without the extraordinary patience of Tom Dunne, and the help of David Hirshfeld, both at St. Martin's Press. I owe a great debt to Elisa Petrini, whose pointed red pencil makes me appear a better writer.

There would have been no *Juliet* without what I'll call the "logistical support" of Jonathan Bristol.

There would have been none without the meticulous assistance of Kathy Tate. My thanks to Lisa Steinbaum, the sailor.

Thanks is due to friends at Yesterday's, where much plotting was accomplished, and to The Office—which I occasionally used as one.

I owe a great deal to professional colleagues and friends far too numerous to list.

Finally, there would have been no *Juliet* without Dr. Jonas Leifer . . . but then again, without him, there might not have been an author.

To all of them, my thanks.

# PROLOGUE

PETER BRANDES RIPPLED HIS FINGERS ACROSS THE bottom of a test tube, mixing solutions. Clear liquid dripped slowly into it from a calibrated buret.

Another drop. To the inexperienced eye, nothing had changed in the test tube, but Brandes stopped the buret, read the level of the reagent remaining in it, made some calculations and wrote 94.9 on a slip of paper next to *chloride*. To him, after years of laboratory work, the sudden color change to a slight pink had been obvious.

Despite the late hour, Brandes surged with adrenaline-induced energy, enthusiasm—the euphoria of success.

Success still confined to the laboratory, yes.

*Damn that nagging voice of practicality*. Sometimes it seemed there was a small imp residing somewhere within him whose sole function was to tell him things he didn't want to hear.

*Total* success, for Brandes, would depend a great deal on his prowess *outside* the lab, with his sponsors. He most certainly would not enjoy their scrutiny; equally certainly, he must face it. He looked for a long time at the nearly invisibly pink solution, postponing accepting that his laboratory work was completed and that what was for him the hard part of his project still lay ahead.

He ran his hand through his brown hair. At thirty-eight he still had virtually all of it, though all his life, its fine texture had implied incipient baldness.

The laboratory phase of his work had consisted of more than a year of torturously delicate labor, almost all of it at night after the technicians had left. Not that their absence mattered much; none of them worked on this project. There had been a few eyebrows raised when some of his new equipment had been installed—no one could see a use for most of it—but his employees knew better than to interfere or even to ask questions. Only Linda had come close to gleaning a hint about the project—and barely that.

But then, Linda was not just a lab assistant.

For the technicians it had been a psychological setback when engineered organisms had been released in California to help strawberries withstand cold. *Their* work applied only to citrus crops; they knew the strawberry project was not a competitor. It was just that the "berry-frost" program had been the first to release man-designed biological material into the environment.

Brandes knew his people at Futures Labs had wanted to be first, a point of view he well could understand. But his technicians did not know about the much more important project their efforts *were* supporting.

*Maybe they'll never know.*

In truth, at the beginning there had been times when he doubted his ability to achieve his goal. He'd even wondered if it was attainable at all. His sights had been set high, for the potential rewards were high—a fact his sponsors recognized. He and they might differ in their opinions of what was "momentous," but the results would be nothing less than that.

For him successful completion of his project could be a gateway opened. As it would be for them, he knew. *Just a different one.*

He sighed and leaned forward, bracing himself with both hands on the edge of his work counter.

"Everything will be all right," he mumbled. *The hell it will,* his little inner voice said. *And you know it.*

The fruits of the project would have to be handled very carefully. Very carefully. His backers, though, had always seemed men willing to take enormous risks for commensurate gain. Perhaps *they* would not immediately like everything about his product. *They'll learn; they will come to appreciate it.*

*These are the things I must remember: I can give them something even more valuable than what they wanted. Because of that alone, I'm secure. They are businessmen.*

Still, there was so much to tell them, and Brandes had not yet decided just how he would couch his description of his accomplishment.

*These people frighten you. Admit it.*

*No!*

*It's just dealing with people,* he thought. *I'm not that good at it. That's all.*

But at some point, a buret's reagent *always* would yield the pink color he had sought. It would do it again and again and again. The certainty was his anchor—he needed that. He needed predictability.

"Fingerholds" never had been enough for Brandes. He needed broad ledges, the security of *knowing*. People—especially businessmen or bureaucrats (or God forbid, both)—always were minor toeholds in friable, shatter-prone rock.

Often Brandes envisioned his movement through life—or as his brother would have put it, "from the chute to the shroud"—as inches gained on the sheer face of a cliff. He'd never told Alex that, of course. His brother would have grinned and pointed out that no one ever made it over the top. The fall was inevitable.

But then Alex had pretty much settled on not bothering to "climb" anymore at all. He'd belayed where he was and waited for something to sweep him into his shroud. Sometimes Peter despised him for that; sometimes he envied him. Alex's cynicism—which Peter had always met with his own brand of satire—might be necessary now, he thought.

Peter Brandes had created precisely what his sponsors had ordered; they would see it work. Earlier in the evening he had notified Rachek that he had succeeded, promising delivery the next day. His fulfillment of the order was all that mattered. He'd just added . . . a bit—as a demonstration of what *could* be. It was his masterpiece.

Brandes considered himself an artist as well as a scientist. Instead of pastels, oils, or acrylics, though, he used a much more delicate and sophisticated medium. A palette of glass tubes and reagents. A canvas unlike any painter's.

He worked with the material of life itself. More subtle than any hue, more demanding than any brushstroke, more rewarding than any static work of art. Amino acids and their nucleic acid templates lay at the foundation of his art. Twisting three-dimensional linkages were formed by his mind, his hands, in ways nature had not contemplated.

Nature had, however, provided the ground rules that made his art possible and infinite in its possibilities. An infinite number of combinations, linkages, could be arranged according to his model.

He created organisms totally new to the world. Each had its own characteristics, its own potential. And each had its own dangers.

Brandes was aware that some of those potentials could be disastrous if his creations were allowed outside the laboratory. But others could be extremely beneficial. The day would come, he felt certain, when a man-mutated organism could be injected into a human being and selectively destroy cancer cells, leaving the rest of the host whole and healthy.

He would be there. He would be the one.

That was the work—the goal for which he most would need his sponsors' helping hand. What he'd done so far was preliminary, but already he had refined techniques that would be useful in the project that lay ahead.

That truly would be his masterpiece.

He rose and walked across the large main lab to a massive steel door. He tapped out a combination on the wall-mounted touch pad. Only he and Linda knew the code.

It was the laboratory's second-stage airlock; Brandes did not like to take chances. The inside of the main work area was maintained at an atmospheric pressure slightly lower than that outside—should any leaks occur, air would rush in, preventing any potentially dangerous organisms from escaping. And in his private lab, Brandes had taken the extra precaution of keeping the pressure even lower than that in the main lab.

There was a hiss of air as the seal cracked and the door silently swung open at his touch. The room beyond was small, but it was the heart of Brandes's private project. He walked to a high workbench and picked up a metal box. Inside were a half-dozen vials of a slightly blue liquid and three that were totally clear. The differences in viscosity of the substances were apparent as he gently removed the test-tube rack from the box. He looked for a few moments at those tubes and then just as carefully returned all his specimens to safety.

The more viscous solution contained the colony whose creation culminated the year's labor—once the colony in the pale blue vials had had time to act upon it. *That* colony also had been produced by late nights, many tests—and, in turn, had produced many explanations.

And much euphoric anticipation.

And—*admit it*—much fear.

A soft buzzing alerted him; the lock to the outer lab had been opened. Out of habit, he had closed the inner lab's door behind him and been reassured by the sound of the compressor reestablishing the negative air pressure.

His eyes darted around to make certain the specimens were secure—he knew they must be since he'd barely touched them but the habit was reflexive—then he opened the door and peered out, suddenly cautious. It was Friday night, late. No one should be anywhere near the lab.

Outside the building, security usually was effective—but he knew it was minimal. His was not a government installation, and the guards were privately contracted. So, much of the real work was handled by standard electronics. More security simply would have attracted attention. After all, Futures Laboratories never was involved in anything secret. At least not until now. And no outsider knew that.

He waited for the tell-tale sound of the compressor in the outer lab to engage. It didn't. He heard footsteps.

*Damn,* he thought.

The idiot had not closed the lock. Brandes was not really worried. The outer lock to the main lab had to be closed or the inner one would not have opened at all. Still, exposure of the inside of the lock itself, where the disposable smocks were stored, should be kept to a minimum. He knew nothing was loose, but it was the principle.

He opened a cabinet and carefully pushed a small bottle of crystals far back on the shelf. He intended to place the vials in front of it.

"Who's there?" he demanded.

The figure came into view. Rachek.

He should have known. The man could be an imbecile. Sometimes Brandes thought he courted the impression.

"Doctor."

"Rachek. Damn it, you know the rules. Close that goddamn door."

"Some of your pets on the prowl?" he asked easily, but he walked back to the lock and sealed it. The compressor's note was a welcome sound to Brandes.

"It is not to be taken quite that lightly," Brandes said, his voice not quite as firm as he would have liked.

"The risk was minimal, doctor," Rachek said absently. "You, alone in here—you of all people—would not be likely to have anything accidentally floating around and certainly not outside your inner sanctum there."

"What are you doing here, anyway?" Brandes asked. It had just occurred to him that Rachek was a day early.

Rachek just looked at him for a moment. He was tall, very wiry. Brandes doubted he weighed more than a hundred and sixty pounds, and for his height that was not much. He had black eyes, the darkest and most penetrating Brandes ever had seen, and closely cut black hair.

"You have completed the project." His voice was even. "So I've come to get it. We're very eager to test it."

Things were not going as planned. Brandes was a meticulous man, a tidy man who loved the order the laboratory gave his life.

"There it is," he gestured. "You're welcome to it." He did not know why he said that—the petulant statement of a child. "Of course," he said quickly, "that's if you're stupid enough to take it out of here alone at night and without any security at all." He folded his arms and smiled triumphantly.

"I think that's just what I'll do, doctor."

"You're crazy," Brandes said in astonishment. "You don't even know how the organism works." He realized he was gesturing wildly and saying more than he wished.

Rachek simply held up a hand to silence him and with the other picked up the metal box.

"It is enough to know that it does work. Our employers have decided that even if testing is not one hundred percent satisfactory, the material is sufficiently developed for any able scientist to refine it. In other words, if it's good enough for someone as . . . distinguished . . . as you, it's good enough for them."

He should have sensed it coming, Brandes thought.

*Part of you did. You knew . . . you knew . . . Alex wouldn't have trusted them this far. You knew . . .*

"You intend to get out of the grant commitment," he said dully.

"Oh, that . . ." Rachek laughed. He was at the door of the inner lab, still chuckling. "A mere detail," he said.

Brandes looked at him helplessly for a few seconds and then moved forward. As he reached the door, Rachek surprised him by pushing him hard.

Brandes slipped, his head striking the counter's edge as he fell to the floor. He could feel the wetness of the blood on his head. His vision blurred.

As his grip on consciousness loosened, he saw Rachek, who

continued to find the whole thing very amusing, almost casually remove one of the vials from the box and toss it toward Brandes. It sailed passed him into a corner under the counter—and smashed.

Brandes screamed, the sound covering the sound of the door closing, locking, and that of the compressor.

He knew he was dead; still, the importance of that fact did not penetrate his sense of confusion about what was happening. His workers would find him—days later—and he would be pronounced dead. Consciousness slipped, but finally he was beginning to realize that these were the last moments of his life.

Fear began, then that inner voice of practicality spoke up—for the last time. He *had* known it all along, hadn't he?

*Yes. I did. I did.*

He had taken at least minimal steps in case something like this ever should happen. But would they be enough?

*Alex, you'll have to climb again.*

He cursed the self-imposed blindness of his desire. *You knew, you knew. No more shit in your eyes now*, the imp's voice said. *You knew.*

*At least that gloating voice dies with me.*

His eyes fluttered; his ebbing mind grew clinical, detached. It didn't matter whether the head wound was serious. It was enough.

His masterpiece—especially through exposure at this level of concentration—would do the rest.

# ONE

LUNCHTIME CROWDS SURROUNDED AND OCCA-
sionally jostled him. The weather was oppressively warm, though
it was not the temperature that was irritating, but the suddenness
with which the heat had appeared. Very probably, Allenberg
thought, the next weekend would be cool enough to warrant a
sweater. It was New York's treacherous season, no longer spring,
not yet summer. The skirts on the young women around him
seemed if not *unseasonally* then somehow *unconscionably* high.
Age, he thought.

Seemingly monolithic glass and steel towered over him.
Allenberg's eyes swept the scene around him, caution resulting
simply from years of caution. Still, caution hardly could be out of
order.

Only a handful of times had he been summoned to such a
meeting. And since he had *called* this meeting—it was the first
time he'd done that—unusual prudence seemed all the more
appropriate.

Allenberg was about to attend a meeting of directors of an
organization incredibly pervasive in its influence, in its interests,
in its raw power. Nowhere, at any time in the past, had such an
assemblage of power existed.

Nearby stood the famous statue of Atlas balancing the world. Once, on the way to another meeting, he had made the psychological error of passing the statue and actually *looking* at it. Now, at sixty-three—a reasonably healthy and robust sixty-three, but with the mileage gradually winning—he knew that *no one* had shoulders like that.

Walking north, Allenberg veered away from the stream of people and entered the building just to his left. The spinning doors seemed never to stop at that hour of the day.

Several blue-clad guards stood behind a curved desk near the banks of elevators. Men and women streamed passed them after having signed the large log book on the countertop.

Allenberg approached the sole guard wearing a white shirt. He was the only one armed; he wore lieutenant's bars.

"I'm Allenberg."

The other man held out his hand and took what looked like an American Express card from Allenberg. He inserted it into a machine under the counter, looked up at Allenberg, nodded, and returned the card.

He gestured to a casually dressed man near the entrance. "Sir," the guard said to Allenberg when the second man reached the desk, "this man will escort you."

"Thank you," Allenberg replied. He followed the waiting man outside to an empty taxi; its "off duty" light was on.

Allenberg settled into the back seat, and the cab began wending its way across traffic and then turned east toward Madison Avenue. Allenberg knew their route would be circuitous, and he was pleased knowing that his own agency could match the security expertise of the much larger and more experienced organization. He'd provided much of that capability himself.

After all, the agency itself had not existed for *that* many years. It was a shadowy extension of Congress's oversight function (and certainly a potentially unconstitutional one, considering that only the "redundant" congressmen—even they joked about their continual reelections—even knew about it). Allenberg's agency was what he himself would consider a transient manifestation of Washington's subculture of people-watching-people-who-watched-people. It might just evaporate, fade away—possibly when that long-overdue balanced budget amendment passed and funds no longer flowed so easily.

Then he would be moved. He might even once again find himself associated with NSA or Langley, within the administrative branch. He knew he never would find himself involuntarily out of work—and that was more than congressmen, or presidents, knew.

It was not a surprising development that "selected" members of "selected" committees of Congress had seen fit to create their own intelligence service.

Keeping such an operation funded and functioning hadn't been too difficult under Carter, who hadn't seen much beyond events on the White House lawn. It had been touchy under Reagan, though not critically; yet it might soon prove unsupportable. But then, it had never existed, had it? Allenberg would go on. Others like him would go on.

Particularly, Allenberg would. His membership in the organization transcending any government in power, in subtlety, insured that.

In its nearly forty-five years of existence, *this* organization never had handled a problem with anything less than potentially global impact. Nor had it ever failed. Sometimes results were less than optimal, but never could they be defined as failure. And ultrasecret it had remained, confounding all odds. Even his own agency didn't know of it, except of course for the agency's director—himself. Allenberg, who had been a member of its board for eight years, did not know everything about it, of its members or all of its activities.

He doubted any one man did.

Yet he was as much a part of it as any of its founders. That had been made clear at the time of his recruitment. The organization did not have "second generations." Each man was considered in every respect an equal of the men who had created Uisce Beatha.

The cab had completed much of its winding path, Allenberg noticed, when he refocused his mind on the present. Already it had crossed to Fifth Avenue and was moving south. The driver turned just before Grand Army Plaza and looped through Central Park's East Drive.

Most of the remainder of the trip would be relatively straightforward, Allenberg knew. The cab went back to Fifth and eventually crossed to Park Avenue. A few blocks further it stopped at 101 Park.

Both Allenberg and the driver got out and crossed the large flat plaza leading to the lobby. Once inside, the driver took him to another armed security guard and nodded.

"Good morning, sir," the officer said. He handed Allenberg a key and motioned him into an open, empty elevator car. Allenberg nodded thanks and once inside unlocked the car's mechanism. He rode to the 53rd floor and relocked the elevator before stepping out.

The corridor was, he knew, substantially the same as every other one in the building: clean, diluted orange carpeting, off-white walls; small signs facing the elevator giving directions to those who sought particular office numbers.

Allenberg turned without hesitation to the right and walked to a door near the end of the passage. It was nondescript.

He did not knock. He used a key—a very special key with invisibly embedded magnetic zones—to open the door.

Virtually invulnerable as locks went, all the same it was changed at irregular intervals. He had received his replacement keys in some of the damnedest ways. Someone either had imagination or a sense of humor or both, he'd often thought.

He was not greeted by a receptionist as he entered. Rather, he faced a palely illuminated wall, the light a gentle green.

The wall spoke. "May I have your name, sir?"

"Adrian Allenberg."

"Have you an appointment, sir?"

"Of course. I made it yesterday afternoon."

That should, he thought, give the analysis machinery enough to work with.

There was a short delay, long enough for Allenberg, as usual, to feel foolish standing and talking to a wall. Still, that wall was as far as most members of Uisce Beatha ever got to the heart of the organization. They got their assignments there and carried them out. Considering what some of them were, their success was astonishing.

He remembered the story of an attorney who had been—perhaps still was—a member. He had reported to the wall and had been told to become the vice-president of a major New York City bank. He had complained that he had no experience, that he'd never be accepted.

The wall, the story went, almost seemed to chuckle as it said, "Don't worry about it. Apply. You'll get the job."

The man had.

Soon the feminine voice returned. "Please enter the door to your left, Mr. Allenberg."

Allenberg entered a well-furnished conference room. Four other men were present. The council had other members, but it was seldom that every member could attend a meeting: it was sufficient that "enough" could.

Paolo Cerva was the oldest member of the group. Soon, Allenberg knew, Cerva would vote for his own replacement.

Naturally Fitch was there, too. Fitch was a White House aide, though the White House, of course, knew nothing of his position in Uisce Beatha. Allenberg hoped—and he had no reason to believe otherwise—the White House did not even know of Uisce Beatha.

It was touchy enough, he thought, that through Fitch the White House even knew of CI, but he never believed Fitch would allow his knowledge to survive his tenure. Fitch was more than American, more than White House; he was Uisce Beatha.

Every member was in the same sort of situation. All were somehow prominent in some branch of their countries' governments, yet at least in theory, the nationality of members was

5

inconsequential. Allenberg reflected that it might be considered ironic there were at present no Irishmen on the council of the organization, which bore an Irish name. *Uisce Beatha* loosely meant "whiskey" in Irish. The members took its literal meaning more seriously—"water of life."

The goal of Uisce Beatha was simple. It had been established to make war simply unthinkable, though it did not seek "peace." The distinction was subtle, and peace would be an offshoot, a by-product of its efforts, of course. But it was an established belief of the organization that there was only one way to avoid war—by making it unprofitable.

Fitch looked up as Allenberg entered. "Hello, Adrian," he said calmly. Allenberg nodded and took a place next to Anton, a ranking member of France's government, deeply involved in its economics. It had been Anton who had persuaded his government not to allow American planes to pass over his country's airspace when they bombed Libya. He had no affection for the Libyan regime but his country was not ready; Uisce Beatha was not ready.

Across the mahogany-finished table was Georgi Neuschoff. Neuschoff was seven years Allenberg's junior—slim, well mannered, and certainly well-dressed.

Finally, at the far end of the table, sat James Albert, of Great Britain. He was a calm man, more than usually cautious, and a direct blood descendant of one of the organization's founders.

Those "founders" had been somewhat naive, Allenberg thought. In more modern times, he knew, no one could be trusted totally to subjugate the interests of his own country for a "greater good."

All that was required of the directors of Uisce Beatha was that they try.

"Adrian, it's your show. Maybe we shouldn't wait . . ." Fitch cut off as the door opened and a gray-haired man with ramrod bearing entered. Allenberg was glad that he had been able to attend. It had been nearly three years since he had seen him.

The South American—Carlos Ryan—nodded wordlessly and took a seat.

6

"We do not have to wait any longer," Fitch said.

"I'm not late," Ryan said and smiled. "You're always so damned early."

Allenberg grinned back.

"We have a unique problem facing us, according to Adrian," Fitch opened. "I'm not entirely sure it's any of our business at all. I know something of it only because of the . . . juxtaposition . . . of our offices."

Now Allenberg moved to the head of the table. *He* was convinced that what he brought Uisce Beatha was of possible global concern. Also, he knew that it was something different for the organization. Oil cartels, labor manipulations, currency fluctuations—these had been the means, methods, and reasons for the existence of Uisce Beatha. But the world was changing. What concerned him, and what he would have to express, was that the world's "inhabitants" also were changing—sometimes terrifyingly.

He placed his palms flat on the table's surface.

"It's a health hazard," Fitch continued. "It is outside the purview of Uisce Beatha."

Allenberg was slightly taken aback by the seeming belligerence in Fitch's tone. Indeed, something about the man's appearance always had bothered him, he thought. Fitch was no more than five-feet-five—in itself not so bad except that his frame supported a good two hundred pounds. It was the face, though, Allenberg always had felt. The lack of lips, the thinning hair, character-proof eyes—definitely the lack of lips.

Carlos Ryan spoke. His accent was an indescribable nearly British form of American English with a Spanish overlay. "What is it? Where is it? Is it confined? And"—he paused—"perhaps most important, is someone responsible for producing it?"

"That—here I understand Mr. Fitch's position—is what would conceivably make an illness an Uisce Beatha concern. Even then . . ." Ryan trailed off, looking directly at Allenberg. His eyes were not challenging nor hostile; Ryan reciprocated respect. If Allenberg thought there were reasons for this meeting,

Ryan would listen. That alone was a relief to Allenberg. When Carlos listened, he knew, everyone else at least *listened*.

Fitch tried to smile at Ryan.

"Thank you, Carlos," Allenberg said. He doubted Ryan and Fitch liked each other but knew that would not interfere with their performance. "I can only partly answer your questions, and then only some of them.

"In a relatively small community in New Hampshire there has been a disproportionate number of cases of an unidentified flulike disease." He paused. "It appears to be one hundred percent fatal."

The silence that followed was contemplative. Members of Uisce Beatha were not given to shock nor numbness.

"It, so far, is localized there, but the president has authorized a military quarantine."

"Much must be explained here, Adrian," Ryan said. "The president of the United States does not so quickly give such authorization. You remember Legionnaire's Disease? No quarantine then in Philadelphia. No military."

Allenberg replied, "That leads to why *this* might be of concern to our organization."

Ryan nodded, cupped his chin in his hand, his eyes slitted, his mind active, and his ears not missing a word. The fact that what the *president* did was closer to Fitch's territory was not lost on Ryan. He raised an eyebrow, turned almost imperceptibly toward Fitch and then back to Allenberg. The speed with which the White House had reacted could only fuel speculation that the illness was caused by an American experiment gone awry.

*Perhaps Fitch should have called this meeting?*

Allenberg knew that and even more so understood that unless he made his position clear—very quickly—the directors would look upon the situation as one of internecine rivalry between Fitch's superiors in the White House and Allenberg's in the legislature.

That, above all, he could not allow. For one thing, Uisce Beatha and what it hoped to achieve meant too much to him.

"There is no evidence that the disease is not natural," Fitch barked. Tension was palpable.

"No one *suggested* that," Neuschoff said—of course, intentionally raising the possibility that the disease was *not* natural.

"Well, there are many possibilities." Fitch's face tightened.

"Enough," Ryan said firmly but quietly. Everyone understood and visibly tried to relax. To have the Russians and the Americans accusing each other of carrying on biological warfare experiments would hardly do anyone any good.

"The disease is there and it seems to have at least a high mortality rate," Allenberg came back. "That, gentlemen, is all we need concern ourselves with now."

"Not quite," Albert said, speaking for the first time. "It matters if it is manmade simply because that might determine just how it must be fought."

That line of discussion, Allenberg thought, was better.

He was pleased that it had not been necessary to cover preliminary ground concerning whether or not such an outbreak concerned Uisce Beatha. He should have more respect for his fellow members, he thought. People traveled. Food traveled. Goods traveled. Much of that commerce was due to the efforts of the organization. Where things and people traveled, so did disease.

"It is contagious and not contracted from exposure to a common element?" Ryan again.

Allenberg nodded. Fitch seemed uncomfortable still and his discomfort appeared to Allenberg slightly out of proportion.

Ryan threw up his hands. "What are *we* to do?" He shrugged off impending comments and continued. "Oh, I know such a thing *is* as much a problem as almost anything else these days. My country also is experimenting with artificially created organisms—you all know that.

"It isn't a secret. The Matto Grasso will be the world's newest 'breadbasket,' if we don't kill ourselves first. That is why I have chosen to listen to Adrian discuss what a decade ago Uisce Beatha would have considered no more than a local health problem.

9

After our jungle *becomes* that breadbasket, we will have new problems. For one thing, it no longer will produce so much of the world's oxygen. Gentlemen, we are connected in ways more extensive than even our founders understood—and, for their time, they were fairly farseeing.

"I mean, *we* are not equipped for such a thing, though." He paused, looking thoughtful. "Or are we? Do we have microbiologists now?" His query was sincere.

"Perhaps we should develop the capability," Allenberg said. "Perhaps we should have before."

"We develop this capability at a time when it is already *needed*?" The question was Anton's.

"Do we have a choice? Or was I being silly? *Do* we have microbiologists?" Ryan waited. "Since no one is volunteering any information, I think we can assume we don't."

Each member briefly considered the segmentation of the organization—so necessary to its secrecy—and how it could be such a damned nuisance that no one held all of the pieces of Uisce Beatha.

For Allenberg, the problem was somewhat refreshing even if it was terrifying. He had headed a scientific section once; when he was honest, he would admit that the financial problems sometimes bored him, even though he recognized their importance.

"Lyle, New Hampshire," he heard. His head jerked up. Fitch had been responding to a question from Albert.

Lyle.

"Population of about five thousand," Fitch continued. "About three hundred miles from the New York metropolitan area. Despite its relatively small population it is spread out over a considerable area. There are many farms."

The directors looked slightly off-balance for once. They glanced from Fitch to Allenberg, who himself was slightly surprised by Fitch's knowledge, even though he was fully aware of the president's sudden and precipitous interest.

Fitch turned to Allenberg. "After all, we *do* know about it, Adrian. I only was concerned with how appropriate it was to bring before this board."

"I'm glad," Allenberg managed. "I still think that—no less than Qaddafi or the PLO or the Baader-Meinhof gang—disease that can spread globally is of interest to this organization."

"Quarantine will be difficult even for the military," Neuschoff said. His sudden interjection was as welcome as it was unexpected.

"The president has authorized adequate troops," Fitch replied.

Allenberg looked at Fitch and saw him avert his gaze. Fitch *knew* where *he* was leading. "For the military alone, yes," Allenberg said. "We did discuss, once—"

"That's irrelevant," Fitch cut him off.

"That was an internal problem . . ."

"Horseshit," Ryan said, his lilting accent dampening the harshness of the interruption. "If there is disagreement between two of our directors on something being Uisce Beatha's business—well, that *makes* it Uisce Beatha's business." He looked back and forth between Fitch and Allenberg. "Of course, this had better *be* Uisce Beatha's business."

"I believe it to be," Allenberg said calmly. No one else spoke until Ryan nodded his head and said, "I shall respect that judgment. Tell us of this other thing."

"We had some difficulties with an agent—an ex-agent of Adrian's service," Fitch said reluctantly. "He was from Lyle."

"And he was a research biologist," Allenberg added.

"Irrelevant?" For the first time Ryan actually raised his voice. "You know of an agent from that area who is by coincidence a medical scientist? I do not like many of the possibilities developing here, gentlemen . . ." he paused. "On the other hand, there are others I like very much."

It was everyone else's turn to be confused. Patiently, Ryan explained, "The worst is that he had something to do with it. The best is that we may have found a man on which to build our needed new capability. Gentlemen?"

"Neither is likely," Allenberg said sadly.

"And why?"

"Before I even answer that," Allenberg said, his voice calm and noticeably cool, "I think there are a few more things you

11

should know." He looked at Fitch, who clearly did not like the turn of events.

Ryan looked expectant.

"The man, Alex Brandes, had a brother," Fitch said, in a monotone. "He also was a biologist. And he did research in Lyle."

"This smells," Ryan said. The comment, in his accent, at another time would have made Allenberg smile. "Why are you using past tense?"

"Peter Brandes is dead," Fitch said. "He was one of the disease's first victims."

"The stench is becoming far too strong. For God's sake, Fitch, is there anything else you are reluctant to tell us?"

"No," Fitch said. "That's all of it."

"I hope so," Ryan said. "This last bit of information, it seems to me, makes it imperative we recruit Adrian's ex-operative if only to keep an eye on him." There was a murmur of agreement from everyone except Allenberg and Fitch.

"What's the trouble, Adrian?" Albert asked quietly.

"As I said, getting Alex might not be possible." They waited. "His position with us was overt," he explained. Each man knew the type of work. Professionals were recruited from many fields by intelligence agencies. They were not cloaked in secrecy but did not advertise their affiliations either.

They attended conferences around the world and returned to report back on the capabilities of foreign scientists. It was part of the game. Everyone did it; everyone knew it.

"One of the men he filed a report on was killed," Allenberg said. He hesitated. Everyone present could probably finish the story for him. "He blamed the agency. He blamed himself, of course, too.

"He became useless to us; he left us with a bitter taste and a large 'settlement,' which he used to buy a boat. He's been on it ever since. Three years."

"He won't come back," Fitch said. Allenberg shot him a curious look, but he had to agree.

12

"It's not likely," Allenberg said.

In his very best tone of sensible calm, Ryan concluded the discussion—and, in essence—the meeting.

"Gentlemen," he said. "I am in favor of allowing Uisce Beatha's resources to be tapped on this for several reasons. One is that I believe that scientists tampering with some of these organisms *do* create the potential of a threat that transcends national boundaries and interests. Researchers on my own continent might equally have been guilty of creating such a thing.

"I do not like the appearance *here* of something that looks like a purely American squabble over who does what." He gestured toward Allenberg and Fitch. "We appear, though, to have available—at least, from the point of view that the man *exists*—someone who might be of use to us.

"My other reason for believing we should get involved is nothing more than subjective and intuitive: I trust Adrian's judgment in determining that something is happening that comes within the purview of Uisce Beatha.

"As far as this other man's willingness or lack of willingness to help us"—he spread his hands and shrugged—"the choice cannot be allowed to be his."

# TWO

BRANDES CENTERED DENEB IN THE CROSSHAIRS OF his sextant, made a final check of the instrument's alignment, and locked its mechanism.

The star was visible only for moments at a time.

Even a dozen or so miles off the American Northeast coast, there was a surface-hugging mist that blotted visibility to near-zero most of the time. Only occasionally did the breeze lift the moist blanket up in swirls, giving a glimpse of faint demarcation between sea and sky. Brandes took full advantage of those seconds and the momentary gaps above him to catch a glimpse of a star, identify it, and take a measurement. He enjoyed the extra challenge of navigation on such a night.

No doubt, he thought, smiling to himself in the cockpit of the *Siege*, his newly found friends a half-mile astern were certain he was relying totally on his late-model Loran-C receiver to fix their positions. They would have been unnerved to know that he was depending to *any* extent on celestial navigation on such a night. They had, after all, attached themselves to him *because* of their own doubts about being able to plot and to follow a course.

Not that Brandes took unwarranted risks. If conditions worsened to the point that he no longer could see a navigational star, he would without hesitation switch to the electronic beacon. But as long as he felt it unnecessary and not dangerous, he would enjoy the night as he wished.

If the fog was the product of a storm system seaward, Brandes estimated it was far away. The sea around the boat was soothing and calm, its soft susurration gentle against the hull of the thirty-four-foot sloop.

The *Siege* had been Brandes's home for nearly three years. He stood a moment longer in the cockpit, glancing at the mainsail, and enjoying the fact that his seamanship kept the canvas taut and well-filled, even in the light night breeze. He hadn't rigged the jib, and unless he changed course or the wind shifted, he would not have to trim the main. Brandes liked sailing at night. In fact, he'd found that quite often he performed best—at any activity—after the sun had set.

He swept his eyes astern, across where the horizon would have been in clear daylight. Eventually a momentary break in the mist let him clearly see the running lights of the *Charon*, the smaller sailboat manned by the vacationing Lombardis and Connors.

Brandes had been properly polite when they had visited the docked *Siege* in the Chesapeake earlier in the week. The usual pleasantries between "boatmen" had been exchanged.

John Lombardi was the owner and nominal captain of the *Charon*. Brandes had learned the limitations of "Sunday sailors," however, and did not assume that ownership of a craft was equivalent to being its most competent master. In this case, though, it was so. The others on board had no experience at all at sailing. Lombardi actually was not that bad, Brandes thought. He was intelligent, and more importantly and more impressive to Brandes, he was intelligent enough to know where his abilities ended and when it was time to seek the aid of someone more knowledgeable.

Lombardi's recognizing that he had reached his limits had prompted the jolly vacation-buoyed foursome to visit him. Brandes quickly had developed a fine reputation among other sailors. Lombardi had heard of it and had learned that Brandes intended to make for Long Island, and he asked if the *Charon* might trail behind.

It was the type of request not easily refused. But it was the people's willingness to put their lives in his hands that bothered Brandes. He did not need that, he'd thought. He did not *want* that.

He breathed deeply of the damp air. He also had recognized the ambivalence of his feelings. There was a part of him—a part he wished he could deny—that did like the idea of having human contact again.

But they remained an intrusion; there also was a part of him that recoiled from their attention and companionship.

At least, he thought, he successfully had fended off their further attempts at neighborliness. No afternoon cocktails, with dinner heating below . . .

He went below to the galley and mixed a gin and tonic. There were times when he worried that he was drinking more frequently and times when he worried that he simply was making them stronger—and there were times when he didn't worry at all.

He'd also begun to feel that he needed something to worry about. Anything.

He gulped at the drink, letting the warmth of the gin and the coolness of the tonic compete, feeling content with the final result. He moved to the navigator's station, with its charts and radios, and concentrated on his jotted readings of the position of Deneb. Calculations kept him occupied for some minutes—which he minimized because he wanted to spend as little time as possible away from the cockpit. A small lift to the corners of his mouth, too often set arrow-straight across a handsome face, showed he was pleased with his navigation. He made a small mark on a chart.

*Loran could not have done better.*

*Face it, it hadn't.*

Brandes had used his equipment along with his "old-fashioned" navigation methods fairly regularly. In addition to the navigational and depth-sounding equipment, he had installed VHF and all-band amateur radio transceivers. He was licensed to use them all. Chances, at sea, were thrills for fools. *What the hell. I could have done it without the Loran.*

He switched his hand-held microphone to the citizen's band radio nestled into the other electronic gear of the station. "John," he called, and waited.

Lombardi answered, "Alex?"

"No one else," he confirmed. "How's things?"

"Fine," Lombardi replied. Brandes did not miss the slight tremor that said that everything was not all right.

He couldn't blame the man for being more than slightly uneasy about trusting someone else's navigation on such a night, Loran or not.

"The girls are catnapping. Henry's out cold. It gets a little lonely sometimes. I don't know how you take this all the time. Not only sailing at *night*. The . . . loneliness." It was a comment to which Brandes did not intend to make a response. "Talk to me more often, Alex. There's nothing out here but fog."

"Can you see me at all?"

"When there are breaks, Alex. Sometimes I can see your lights, but not for very long."

"We're on course," Alex reassured him. "I just finished plotting our position. We're making good time."

Brandes was certain that fourteen miles offshore was as far or farther than Lombardi ever had taken the *Charon*.

"Henry won't have much of a watch, I guess."

"Maybe a little," Brandes said. "I'm not that tired yet. By morning—even if we do stop for some sleep—you'll be in sight of Fire Island."

"Great." The lack of heartiness in Lombardi's voice was noticeable. Brandes's good reputation aside, he was having second thoughts, Brandes knew, about having followed this far into the unfamiliar.

"Can you see us?" Lombardi asked.

17

"Every once in a while. Don't worry. Between the radio and your compass you'll be all right. Everything will be fine."

"Oh . . . I know that. We're all still glad to have run into you, Alex. I doubt I could have done this even with Loran and everything."

Brandes smiled. He sighed and sipped. He replaced the microphone. It was to be expected that the *Charon* would bring memories to the surface. It had been a long time since his actions could literally mean life or death to someone. But then, at least, *this* time he had known the consequences beforehand.

He finished the drink and mixed another.

The chart of the waters around him drew him into a timeless-spaceless place where thought could be suspended.

For long moments he didn't really see the chart spread on the navigator's desk. He simply stared. Soon, he thought, he would have to switch charts, using a larger scale as he approached the shore where the sea hid most of her myriad dangers. The approach to Fire Island Inlet and its negotiation could be particularly hazardous. At one point the only deep water lay not in the middle of the broad beckoning bay but in a small channel hugging the shore. Treacherous.

He wanted to sleep, but he also wanted to complete the trip. He was certain that his estimate of a morning arrival was accurate if weather conditions remained the same. There was no guarantee, of course, because, as usual he was determined to make as much of the passage as possible under sail and not to use his auxiliary diesel. And then, he thought, it would be: Goodbye vacationers. They, no doubt, would be jubilant at the sight of land. His own reaction would be ambivalent.

He leaned back in the swivel chair and took a small sip from his glass.

Perhaps Henry would have a chance at at least a short working watch on the *Charon* after all. And at the end of the trip, *they* would be home. He would be where he intended to spend the summer, no more. Home was the *Siege* and wherever she was.

Suddenly he looked up and around him. Instinct.

He went up into the cockpit. Peripherally—as though an insect had passed at the edge of his vision—he became aware that something in the night had changed. He had seen nothing, heard nothing. But the fabric of the night had a different texture.

He looked about, straining to pierce the thick cloud that simply diffused or bounced back light. He listened for the tell-tale flapping meaning a wind shift, but it did not come. The sail remained full.

He was certain they were too far out to have a chance encounter with another pleasure boat. Even the possibility of crossing courses with commercial shipping was remote, since he was still far away from the relatively narrow channel leading from the Ambrose Light and into New York Harbor. Still, it was a chance, and he did not like chances at sea. And like any good sailor, he did not dismiss any possibility out of hand. The sea itself was a mystery, and stranger things had happened on her surface.

He swept his eyes across the line where sky should have met water. He could see nothing but the occasionally reflected green and red of his own running lights. He might have to switch to Loran, he mused.

Then there was a sound.

It had the quality of a heart beating to exhaustion. He noticed a clammy sweat, a feeling not at all made more pleasant by the night's dampness. He scanned toward starboard, where the sound seemed louder. But sound, almost as much as light, was diffused by the fog. He could not be certain.

Still, the sound grew louder, its volume increased with each passing second. There could be no doubt about it. There was another boat out there.

Somewhere.

Twin screw, he guessed.

His mouth opened slightly as he realized something else. The other vessel sounded like it was damn near and running at full RPM. *Damn*—what kind of idiot would run at such speeds on such a night, on any night for that matter?

He had to see that boat. The engine pitch and loudness told him without question that it was coming closer and undoubtedly now from starboard, from seaward.

He reached down into the cabin, straining his arm, and grabbed the microphone.

"John?"

"Yes, Alex? I think I hear something, Alex. There's another boat out here. But I don't see a damn thing. I'm a little nervous about this, Alex."

"Take it easy," Brandes said to Lombardi and to himself. He was nervous but knew better than to give in to pure, clear panic. That, he was sure, was something he could leave to Lombardi very soon. "Can you see any running lights, John?"

"There's nothing, Alex. But the sound—it's getting louder. It's waking up Henry and the girls. It's getting *loud*, Alex." The panic was there.

The mystery boat was getting closer to the *Charon* than to the *Siege*, Brandes thought. He hoped *someone* on either the *Charon* or the other boat would see running lights before the impossibly improbable happened—a meeting in the middle of a fog-shrouded nowhere in the middle of the night. And a collision. Brandes knew what that would mean.

If struck broadside, the *Charon* would be cut in half, shattered into fiberglass splinters. And in the damnable near-zero visibility, survivors, if any, would be nearly impossible to find.

"Alex. It's got to be pretty close. I'm going to hit the strobe."

Damn, why hadn't *he* thought of that sooner. The bright-as-the-sun light mounted atop the *Charon*'s mast would be visible for a half-mile around, even if diffused by the fog. Before Brandes could agree, John's voice again crackled over the radio.

"Alex!" Lombardi was openly panicking. "I see it. Christ, Alex, it's big and it's coming right at us.

"It can't be more than a hundred yards away. It hasn't any lights at all."

"You just mustn't be able to see them," Brandes said lamely.

Hell, he could picture many a half-assed Sunday sailor making mistakes—but not one like running a night fog without lights.

"No, Alex. I'm sure. I should be able to see them. Damn, I can see the outline of the damned thing when the strobe goes off. He *has* to be able to see us."

The plaintive ring lingered, looking for reassurance.

"John, get everyone into life jackets," Brandes snapped.

"No time," Lombardi's voice was ragged, coming in gasps. Brandes guessed Lombardi probably was trying to turn the *Charon* and knew that only firing the boat's diesel could avoid spilling needed wind from the sail and effectively stopping the *Charon* where she was.

In his panic Lombardi continued to hold the microphone open—even if Brandes had had orders for him, Lombardi could not receive them. The terror simply froze the man's hand.

"It's coming," Lombardi screamed. "No time. No time. Too late, Alex."

"Come *on*, Henry," Brandes heard Lombardi scream. The roar of the oncoming engines was pummeling Brandes both over the water and through the radio. Brandes knew that the other boat must be right on top of the *Charon*. "Get the girls out!"

Suddenly there was a shrieking and screaming that made Brandes stand cold, numb, in his cockpit as he strained his eyes astern, trying to pick out the *Charon*—knowing that even if he did, it was hopeless. All he could do was curse the stupid bastard causing a needless tragedy.

A patch of mist blew away, like a curtain rising, making the *Charon*'s running lights momentarily visible. Brandes's stomach turned when he saw that its green starboard light was drastically lower than the port's red. She was not on an even keel. A fraction of a second later, the rending, screeching sound of disintegrating fiberglass reached the *Siege*. He no longer could see the *Charon*'s lights, but he thought he heard one loud and very distant woman's scream mingled with the sound of destruction.

The strobe light was the last to disappear.

Brandes shook himself from his stupor and went below to change frequencies to call the coast guard.

There would be very little they could do until daylight, when the sun burned off the fog, he knew. But he was virtually certain that any search for survivors would be in vain.

The lights of the cruiser came on. Green. He was looking at the starboard side of the killer boat. It slowed. Brandes saw a spotlight sweeping the water. *At least the stupid son of a bitch was looking for survivors.*

Then, astoundingly, the lights went dead and the engine note deepened and the vessel disappeared, vanishing quickly into the darkness, fog, and mist.

# THREE .

TOMAS WATCHED IN FASCINATION AND DELIGHT.

He had known the sea and ships and, inevitably, the men who were part of both, for nearly sixty years. He had retired from merchant shipping, recognizing with sober dignity that such work required younger and more resilient muscles.

Years earlier, after a local restaurant's lease on the dock at Kismet on Fire Island had run out and the township of Islip on Long Island had assumed control, Tomas had been offered the job of managing the summer crowds of pleasure boaters who berthed in the small manmade harbor.

It was surrounded on three sides by concrete covered with wooden planking. On the fourth side of the square, on the edge nearest the bay, was a wooden walkway.

He eagerly had accepted the job. It did more than keep a retired man occupied. It kept him near the water.

Only a twenty-foot gap between the walkway and one of the concrete walls permitted entrance from the bay.

Taking charge of the dock and the boats was a task of love. The boats' owners could be something entirely different. He never had tried and never had had the inclination to involve himself in the activities of the people themselves—unless those activities involved "his" dock.

Some of the "boatmen" made him want to weep. He'd seen some, with boats whose beams were half the width of the opening, try for an hour to aim properly and to get into the calm waters. Many not only failed but gave up altogether. The summer before he had seen one man surge through the gap with a forty-five-foot twin diesel. After colliding with the side of the dock and narrowly missing a nearby sailboat, the "pilot" had barreled straight into the opposite wall, sending chunks of planking and splinters flying. Of course, he'd pay for it, he'd told Tomas. The dockmaster reassured him that he indeed would pay—and also could immediately take his very expensive weekend toy to some other dock.

His realm might not be large; still, here Tomas ruled.

What he was watching now both pleased and awed him, as it had for several years—ever since Alex Brandes had first come to the island and to Kismet for his summers. Other sailors—even good ones—prudently would have lowered sail far out in the bay and used their auxiliary engines to negotiate the entrance. The first time Tomas had seen Brandes bringing the *Siege* in under sail he was certain that disaster was imminent. Now he knew better.

Gauging precise angles by sight, by feel, estimating currents and winds, Brandes used only his sail to shoot the large boat through the entrance, and Tomas would have sworn that there were identical clearances on either side of the boat. The man was incredible, he thought. Brandes waved to Tomas in the early morning light and the older man waved back.

Once inside the open area of the lagoon, Brandes quickly lowered his remaining sail and looked to Tomas, who motioned him to Slip 17. Only then did Brandes use his engine to back into the narrow docking space. He didn't even touch the pilings used to secure the already docked boats. No one more than Tomas could appreciate the difficulty of backing a single-screw craft that large into such a space. He walked quickly over the narrow walkway and grabbed the lines Brandes threw to him.

"Hello, hello," he yelled. "Glad to have you back."

"Hello, Tomas," Brandes said, grinning broadly. He liked the old sailor, and some nights while the young weekend vacationers crowded the two bars in Kismet, he would sit on the *Siege*'s afterdeck with Tomas and listen to his stories of days at sea and of faroff ports.

Brandes jumped ashore, shook hands with Tomas, and handed him a box with a bottle of Jim Beam inside. Tomas smiled and said, "It is always nice to have friends who remember—and nicer still to have friends to share it with." He lifted the bottle.

"My pleasure," Brandes said.

"Is there something bothering you, my friend?" Tomas asked. He looked deeply into Brandes's eyes.

Brandes wondered how much, if anything, ever got by the man.

"There was an accident," he answered. "A collision."

"I know. I heard of it on the coast guard radio. I didn't know you were near there."

"I was *right* there, Tomas. I was leading another boat—"

"The *Charon*?"

Brandes nodded. "Some idiot came out of nowhere, Tomas. I couldn't do a damn thing."

"There are many people who do not know how to handle their vessels," Tomas said sadly. "But no boat comes out of 'nowhere.'"

Brandes looked at the old man for a moment and tried to see if he was leading up to something. Tomas just shrugged and turned to securing the spring lines.

No doubt the coast guard still was circling the disaster area in both cutters and helicopters, Brandes thought, but he knew there were no survivors. The last pieces of wreckage of the *Charon* he had seen had been its life jackets. Empty.

Earlier in the morning, as he approached the inlet, a cutter had come alongside as arranged, and Brandes had given a brief formal statement to the officer in charge of the search and the accident investigation.

The necessary red tape delayed him slightly, but he accepted that the way he accepted the deaths. At least at first.

They all were dead. There was a part of him—some self-destructive impulse he believed was embedded in everyone—that wanted him to accept some of the guilt for their deaths. But even with that impulse he could not feel responsible.

Once, in the past, guilt had overpowered him; it would not again. The couples had chosen to tag along; they had been sunk in a freak accident more than a dozen miles at sea. Perhaps, he thought, familiarity with that impulse could be a shield.

"Is the restaurant open?" he asked Tomas.

"For breakfast. I didn't think you'd grown so tired of your own cooking." Almost impossibly, more lines creased Tomas's face. He dropped plastic bumpers between the *Siege* and the dock.

"I've had breakfast," Brandes answered, grinning; the old man's good humor never failed to rub off on him and break into his darker moods. He was glad he'd chosen Kismet as his summer "home." During the winter months, he moved from marina to marina along the coast. Nowhere else had he established a relationship like the one he had with Tomas.

"Unlike some retired people," he said, "I don't sleep all day. This is the middle of the day for me. Maybe even time for a nap."

"Humph," Tomas laughed. "I've been up since five. The restaurant . . . I had to wait four hours for the first cup of their coffee. Which was not worth the wait.

"Anyway, it's open now, and maybe they made another pot and you'll be lucky." He looked at Brandes sidelong and shrewdly. "Or is it enough of the middle of the day to have an afternoon drink instead of a nap?"

"Only if you join me," Brandes smiled.

"And if I refuse?"

With mock sadness, Brandes answered, "Then I guess I'll have to have one for you, too. I hope you need it, Tomas." He tapped

26

the older man lightly on his shoulder in affection and walked the narrow boards that led to the island.

Brandes was pleased and flattered when the bartender greeted him by name and was slightly embarrassed when it took him a few seconds to remember the other, younger, man's name. Bob.

At this hour on a weekday, Brandes knew, Bob probably was not only the bartender but the waiter and possibly the cook as well. There were no other customers.

Brandes smiled. "Hello, Bob. Tomas tells me you have coffee." It was Bob's turn to smile.

"Yeah, what would you like?"

"Screwdriver."

Bob laughed and moved away to fix the drink. Brandes exhaled slowly and relaxed, easing his back against the bar chair.

He'd found similar moments of relaxation in other parts of the country, even other parts of the world. To be alone, in the fresh morning, in a public place. Sitting, breathing. It was a kind of contentment.

And, as he momentarily saw Lombardi's features—or those he could remember—in his mind, he thought it might be time for more than one drink. Perhaps, he thought, he might even try to fit into the crowd later, small as it would be on a weekday.

Not likely.

One of the few times he had ventured into one of the Kismet bars filled with weekenders escaped from New York City, he had seen Bob—obviously off work—with a sheet wrapped around him as though it were a toga. He was completely, obliviously drunk and was dancing and plainly enjoying himself.

Brandes had envied him. He hadn't remained long in the bar but quickly had worked his way through the crowd and outside and then back to the relative quiet of the *Siege*.

Bob slapped down a paper napkin and put Brandes's drink on it. "How have you been?" Brandes asked.

"It was a tough winter. Damn cold. But here I am, ready again for summer and, I hope, all that goes with it. I don't get to ride out the winters, like some people I know."

27

"Where do you spend the winter?"

Bob raised an eyebrow. "Oh, I thought you knew. Right here in good old Kismet. It's quite a bit different in the winter."

"I can imagine. I didn't know you turned Eskimo after the sun and sand season."

"Yeah. Most people never think of anyone living here year-round. It's an experience. Actually there are quite a few of us. You've got to live someplace, and in a weird sort of way, I enjoy it. It's quiet."

"I'm pretty sure I understand. Living on a boat . . . You know, someday I might try staying here."

"Don't get me wrong, Alex. I *like* it here in the winter, but *anytime* you feel like trading for a season, I'm your man. That is one hell of a beautiful boat."

"Maybe I'll let you know."

Bob looked as if he were daydreaming. "With a boat like that . . . My God, they'd have to have ushers to keep the lines of women from rioting . . ."

Brandes only smiled and grunted. He tried to remember; it seemed that only Tomas had ever spent any time with him on the *Siege*. He ruefully admitted to himself that he'd not thought much about women for some time—far too long, he guessed.

"Quarter?" he asked Bob. The younger man absentmindedly was lining up bottles in early anticipation of the lunch that would lead to happy hour and eventually to dinner. He stirred and looked at Brandes.

He smiled as he straightened and moved to the register drawer. "You going to get the habit again?" He dropped four quarters on the bar.

"I wouldn't have to if you didn't shut off the electricity every year and wipe out my high score."

"Gives you a chance to compete with yourself."

"Yeah."

He scooped up the coins. Two pinball machines stood against the wall in the far corner of what now was a restaurant. In the evening, the machines would be partially disabled to cut down

28

on noise during dinner and then reactivated after the floor was cleared of tables and opened for dancing.

He took almost childish delight in waiting for the last possible second before hitting the buttons controlling the flippers, sending the metal ball winging again into the maze at the top of the machine. He concentrated as he played, using the machine to help him cover the past hours.

He was sure he'd beaten his previous year's record and the game was not yet over. He was totally absorbed. Bells, lights, a little body motion—not enough to cause a tilt. Finesse. He wanted to leave an anonymous challenge for the vacationers—one they couldn't beat.

Brandes was unaware of the approach of another man.

The newcomer remained silent for a while, watching the man and the machine. Then, partly because he knew Brandes well, he realized he might be standing quietly for quite some time, and time was a factor.

"You've already won," he said quietly and calmly.

Brandes froze, looking at the blinking score—his highest ever—and let the ball fall, ending the game. That was what *that* voice meant anyway. The end of a game.

"Hello, Alex."

"Hello, Adrian." Brandes did not turn.

Allenberg, he thought. By coincidence in a nearly empty bar in a small resort community off the coast of Long Island on an off day. Coincidence. No use in even trying to convince himself of that.

"No," Brandes said.

"No what?"

"Don't give a shit, Adrian. Whatever it is, the answer's no."

"So much for old times' sake."

"You *really* want me to think about old times, Adrian?"

Allenberg hesitated, then said, "No, I guess not."

It wasn't fair, damn it, Brandes thought. Three years of hard work just getting *away*, and this one man had the ability to make it all worthless with a few words . . . with just being there. Carefully layered armor, gone to hell.

"You'll have a drink, won't you?" Allenberg asked.

"If it's on you and not on your expense account."

"That *is* a hard bargain." Brandes turned; Allenberg, facing him then, smiled. Brandes wished he hadn't. Goddamn it, he *liked* Allenberg and always had. He'd had difficulty believing the man was behind his troubles with the agency. He almost accepted Allenberg's word that he wasn't. But the thing was too big, too big. He couldn't trust any of them.

Allenberg gestured to a table. Brandes wondered how long he had stood and watched him play pinball. And what he might have learned from watching.

Allenberg was a man who always learned *something* from watching *anything*. Brandes could not help but admire the ability, even when he was the subject. "Screwdriver," Brandes said. And now to find out what the hell it was all about.

Bob dropped off two drinks and went back to the bar, glancing over his shoulder once, knowing that *something* he did not understand was happening.

"We need you, Alex."

"No, Adrian."

"Yes, Alex." He sighed. "Definitely, yes."

# FOUR

THE REST OF THE MORNING AND THE EARLY AFTER-noon passed swiftly. Brandes had planned to take a nap to help recover from the rigors of the night and, more recently, his encounter with Allenberg. Instead, he found himself reading. And thinking.

More often than not pages remained unturned and paragraphs were read two and three times with little comprehension. He thought about Peter, about the possibility Allenberg had raised that he might somehow be involved in the epidemic. His belief in Allenberg was tempered by a certain amount of suspicion—but he found his suspicions invariably touched by elements of trust. A difficult man to understand. Peter, however, never had been that complex—not to him. While they were never close, he felt he'd known his brother fairly well. He could not imagine Peter having purposely created a deadly virus or bacteria. Allenberg had not used the word *purposely*.

*It had to be an accident. If Peter had indeed created the organism.*

Brandes was not surprised by how calmly, unemotionally, he had accepted news of Peter's death. But he was curiously surprised by how intensely he had defended his brother.

Brandes had known that his brother was engaged in recombinant DNA research. He himself was considered something of an expert in the field, and he had attended many conferences on the subject while he worked for the agency. All that meant, he thought, was that he knew how dangerous it could be. In fact, he was very much a reluctant expert; the research terrified him.

Brandes was not the type of man afflicted with the notion that man was invading God's realm. In fact, Brandes considered that attitude to epitomize man's unbelievably colossal ego.

He was terrified simply because he doubted man's ability to handle his newly developed techniques and their products. Even if the scientists were 100 percent thorough in their adherence to their safety procedures, it would not be enough, Brandes knew. Unlike his fellow "experts," he also was a man who had seen much of how the world really worked.

The contractor who wanted to save a few percent on the lab's construction. The bored and bitching worker who screwed up a critical weld just to twist the knife in the boss. The hard-hatted cocaine sniffer or pot smoker who figured, "What the fuck. A gasket is a gasket."

Brandes did not believe it *could* happen.

He knew it *would*.

Or, more likely, already had. Anyone who followed the news of nuclear reactor scandals—just *how* the hell could someone be crazy enough to fuck around with a nuclear reactor, he'd always wondered—would be as certain as he that the same fate awaited the genetic labs that were springing up as quickly as their own creations reproduced.

When it happened, though, the results would make the atomic threat a trifling annoyance. A shattered reactor spewing radioactive death might get a few million people or so. But an organism no earthly creature could have immunities against because the damned thing never before had existed on Earth—ah, that was something different. That *was* perhaps putting a finger into what had been one of God's monopolies—that of universal destruction.

He thought about Allenberg's insistence that *he* was the best person to go to Lyle and investigate. Partly, he suspected, that was vintage Allenberg puffing a recruit's ego. Partly, it was Allenberg's way of saying that there was too much coincidence. The new disease was of paramount importance, he knew, whether or not Peter had been involved.

Then, too, there was the grim prospect of seeing his father in Lyle. Peter's death had not made it less awkward, Brandes's talking to him—their first conversation in several years. After their brief phone call, Brandes had endured what he supposed was a psychologically classic moment of wondering if his father would have preferred him dead and Peter alive. The suspicion had been brief; he'd never thought that his father hated or even disliked him. He did know that he had been a great disappointment to the older man, however.

Peter, while not going into medical practice, had at least used his medical education in "medicine." Alex had not, strictly speaking, done that; but then, he'd told himself, he never had asked for the education either.

Brandes had one more great concern, born from his experience in working for the agency. If he did discover a virus or a bacterium that his brother had created—and he was far from convinced that that was the case—he never could be sure that the agency wouldn't add it to an already bristling arsenal of unthinkable horrors.

His own emotions confused him. Perhaps he *could* help. It had not escaped him that the illness striking his home town would affect people he knew.

But what if he did go back?

Even if he could put aside his three-year effort to divorce himself from humanity, could he really help?

Or would he simply once again be a pawn of the agency?

It seemed he had been put in a position of deciding which type of guilt he would rather bear.

Footsteps interrupted him.

He put aside the book and rested on his elbows in the narrow bunk. The *Siege* had been built to his specifications, and the master's stateroom was aft of the main salon, below and slightly aft of the cockpit. He looked through the porthole and just caught a glimpse of a man's shoes passing before he heard a rapping on the stern.

"Who's there?" He was alert. The porthole was open to an early summer breeze; the man could hear him. "Can I help you?" A knot formed in his midsection. He had not expected Allenberg to begin applying pressure so soon.

A deep, resonant voice called from above. There was an unmistakable element of amusement in its tone, of friendliness. Killing me with kindness, he thought.

"I was just wondering how you knock on the door of a man who lives on a boat, without going aboard."

Brandes had to smile. "You just call out something—usually incomprehensible—and then you ask for permission to come aboard."

As if nothing had preceded their exchange, the stranger's voice took on a serious timbre. Then he shouted, "May I have permission to come aboard?"

Even if Allenberg was behind this visit, Brandes thought, at least he'd chosen a cordial course of seduction. He expected he would like the man. Then he sobered; of course he would like him. Allenberg's planning—when it came to manipulation—always was the next best thing to perfection.

Almost immediately he felt the slight dip of the *Siege* as the man stepped aboard. Brandes left his cabin and walked into the salon. He decided to fight cordiality with cordiality.

"A drink?" he asked even as the man's head cleared the deck.

"Rules say I'm never to drink on duty. They also say I'm always on duty. Scotch and water, please."

He was tall and handsome, and his smile did not at all seem forced. Brandes stood straighter; the man was about his height. And if the smile beneath the brown eyes and the matching hair was phony, it was the damn most convincing false smile Brandes ever had seen.

"Jim Kracke," the man said, stepping forward and ducking slightly before straightening. Like Brandes, he was able to stand totally erect only in the salon proper, though he moved like a gymnast, his body possessing that certain fluid grace.

Brandes shook his hand. It was dry, strong, and not overbearing. Brandes sensed that viselike power was there—it just was not used lightly.

"I guess there's no need for me to introduce myself or you wouldn't be here," Brandes said. He handed the man his drink, mixed one for himself, and motioned to a table on the salon's starboard side.

"Thank you." The smile remained in place. Either something was amusing Kracke or he had a propensity for smiling.

"I told Allenberg I wanted nothing to do with his organization," Brandes started. *Might as well get it out.* Kracke said nothing for several moments, seeming only to immensely enjoy the flavor of the twelve-year-old liquor.

"I'm not from the agency. Not exactly."

How the hell many ways were there? This was a day—these last two days—he gladly would have foregone.

"All right. You're from Allstate. Putting me in good hands."

Kracke lost his smile. "Why did you say that?"

Brandes was caught offguard. "What? What do you mean?"

"The insurance joke."

"Yeah. *Joke.* What the hell *are* you talking about?"

The smile rekindled. "I guess I just like people to be intuitive to a degree."

"You're losing me."

"Good. You see, in a sense, you weren't far off. About the insurance angle."

Silence. Kracke could be disconcerting, confusing, and fascinating all at once. Brandes was sure this all would have made perfect sense to Allenberg. By then melting ice marginally had weakened his drink; he used refreshing it as an opportunity to gain time and order his thoughts.

Kracke sipped and said nothing, but Brandes noticed that his eyes flicked occasionally here and there—and, without fail, at regular intervals toward the open cabin door.

"You didn't come here to get a lesson in boat etiquette."

Kracke's smile broadened. He finished his drink in a gulp and made an unabashed gesture for a refill. Brandes poured, knowing that Kracke asked for one simply because he wanted it; he needed no respite.

"I told you my name," he said. "Incidentally, it's my real name." He said that in the tone of someone who had just accomplished something noteworthy.

"You're here to try to convince me to return to the agency when Allenberg couldn't." Brandes's voice was monotone. When Kracke matched it, the voice froze Brandes.

"I'm here," Kracke said, "to save your life."

*He's good*, Brandes thought.

Brandes's stomach tightened anyway. "Who would want to kill me?"

"You are a unique person in a unique position possibly to handle a unique situation. There're always people around ready to kill someone with those qualifications."

"Hell of an answer, that. Who?"

"I can't tell you. I really mean I *can't*. I don't know that. Yet."

"And the why of it?"

"It would be pure guesswork."

"One hell of a bodyguard, you are. Well informed. Damn good beginning."

"I'll tell you what I do know," he said. His smile didn't slip a bit, but it somehow hardened. "You have been living on this boat for two years and seven months.

"You have been trying to bury some old and bad memories and haven't had any real success.

"You are bored to death, and I think that you're tempted to help us not so much because we need you—and we really do—but to pull your own ass out of a rut that is slowly killing you."

"Finished?" Brandes knew he had reddened.

"No."

36

"Finish."

At first Kracke said nothing. Then he finally said, "Not every night someone tries to ram your boat, right?"

"What the hell do you mean?" Memories of the misty night flashed by. The strange behavior of the unknown captain— searching a moment and then leaving. Running into a strobe light at full speed. Not, if Lombardi was right, displaying any lights of his own. But this? . . .

Brandes felt he was perspiring, didn't know if it was true, would not give Kracke anything by wiping his forehead to find out. *This is not possible.*

*Anything is possible. I choose not to believe.*

"How many meanings you get out of that? I know what happened last night."

"It's been on the radio."

Kracke sighed and said, "Whether you know it or not, Alex, we were really able to talk to each other for a moment there. I very much would like to get back to that."

"Go on," he said.

"There's not much else to say. That ramming was meant for you." He held up a hand. "Don't ask me how I know. I'd have to lie to you, and I don't intend to do that."

"Well, there's got to be something you can add to that. If we're talking now, keep talking. You're more interesting than I am— *meant* for me?"

"Well, you were right about my being more interesting, anyway."

Kracke smiled, and Brandes fought, trying not to slip back gently into fellowship with the man.

"Yeah, meant for you," Kracke continued. "Only no one knew you were shepherding a flock of sheep, for Christ's sake. Who would have guessed there'd be more than one boat at that point and at that time in that fog?"

"No . . ."

"It was very intentional and very professional—at least to a point. I mean, they *did* get the wrong boat. But they used a

37

heavy, old, double-planked wood boat to get an edge on the fiberglass."

"You do know more about it."

"I know less than I'd like to. So far."

"There'll be an investigation?"

"Coast guard only, I'd expect."

"You've got reason to believe four people were murdered, and there only will be an accident investigation?"

"Nothing is done about a lot of murders. Damn it. *Those* people were killed by mistake. *You* were to be murdered."

"Shit."

Kracke shrugged. "Your conversation still lacks."

Brandes thought of another possibility.

"Was it Allenberg's idea to take advantage of the accident, to try to frighten me into coming back? Or was it yours?"

Kracke waved his dismissal of Brandes's comment.

"You've got a real problem, Alex," he said. "We didn't have to invent one. There might even be people who will wonder whether you and not your brother was involved in making this damn thing."

The idea stunned Brandes. "That's stupid. I'm the one on a boat, remember?"

"Yeah, and you're also the one who worked for an intelligence agency."

"You don't think I did it, do you?"

"Of course not. At least, uh, you're on the low end of the probability scale."

"Thanks."

Kracke grinned.

"If what you say is true, could those be the people after me?"

"Could be. Someone could want to stop you from developing the thing further. Someone may want to stop you from curing it. We don't know."

"It makes sense then for me to stay here, doesn't it? It might convince whoever it is that I'm not joining you in any way and I'm harmless. Makes sense, right?"

"Sure, to you. To these people, Alex, you deal with a danger while it's a possibility and don't wait for it to prove to you it's a danger."

"Great. Anything else?"

"Yes. There's more. We can't keep guard on you if you're not working with us on this. We don't have the manpower for luxuries like that."

"I'll let you know."

"Don't wait too long, Alex. I'll be in the motel just one night. I leave tomorrow."

"Go ahead. Finish me off."

Kracke's eye lifted. "Oh, if you don't sign up and you have no protection, I won't have to do that, Alex. Someone else will. I really believe that."

Brandes really didn't.

He did not know that Kracke didn't believe a word of it either.

# FIVE

BRANDES LISTENED ATTENTIVELY TO THE PEACE-
ful slapping of the water against the *Siege*'s hull. Events around
him appeared unformed, amorphous, much like the mist of the
previous night. Someone else was pulling the strings, and
Brandes suspected he was not the only puppet.

Small comfort.

He was a piece in a game already in motion, to be sure. The
question was: Could he successfully remove himself from the
board before someone else did . . . permanently?

*But Kracke is lying. They all lie.*

And did he really want to be removed, in any case? Kracke had
touched some truth in his machine-gun analysis. But only
some—did he feel all *that* much like he was in a rut?

Kracke's world, where you might eliminate a man on the mere
possibility that he *might* do something you'd prefer he didn't, was
alien to him. Or almost alien. Certainly he was reluctant to
become part of it again, in any way.

*Then there's Lyle. There's Peter.*

He decided he needed to walk, to think. Darkness already had
begun to settle over Kismet; sunset on the island was a beautiful
but brief affair, but while night stole the daylight with shocking

swiftness, it almost always replaced it with star-filled splendor—
to Brandes it was a more than equitable exchange. There was
slightly less than a quarter-moon; little light was shed between the
widely spaced lamps on the island's paths.

It only was a few hundred yards at that point from the bay side
of the island to the sea. The sea and the night surf sound would
help him; it usually did.

He put on rubber-soled, canvas-topped deck shoes and left the
*Siege*. No one was in sight. Hardly anyone was in either of the
bars, and the music coming from their jukeboxes was turned low.
One "streetlight" illuminated the end of the dock area near the
Kismet Inn. Spotlights shone into the small harbor itself. He
could see that several other boats had arrived since he had. Their
sailors probably were in the bars or enjoying their vacations in
their salons.

He expected the beach to be empty. Even if it was not, Brandes
knew he would have privacy; in all likelihood, that also was what
was being sought by any other person there at night.

Brandes walked the narrow catwalk to the island proper and
then kept going on one path. It was concrete and narrow. He
knew that a garbage truck did manage to make its rounds on Fire
Island, and he had wondered how until he noticed how little
foliage grew on either side of the walkway. The truck straddled
the path.

The garbage truck was one of the few vehicles on the island.
Private cars were prohibited, except for a small parking area on
the tip of the island. Occasionally a police Jeep would pass—very
occasionally. In winter, he knew, the few year-round residents
used a Jeep with a snowplow to clear their own way, taking turns
as each storm came and went. With those exceptions transporta-
tion either was by bicycle or on foot. Brandes liked it that way.

Ahead was a light, but it was barely sufficient to illuminate the
walkway except for the area immediately beneath it. Brandes
walked slowly toward the beach, wondering how much of it had
been lost since last summer. Each year winter storms attacked
and ate away at the fragile strip of sand. The appetite of the ocean

41

was insatiable, slowed only by efforts of residents and some government aid.

Growing things, be they weeds, flowers, or trees, were encouraged, their roots helping to hold together the soil and sand. On vacant land, plant life was allowed to grow rampant. The primary sin—even weekenders observed the taboo—was to walk on and to disturb the remaining sand dunes on the ocean side of the island.

Brandes found comfort in the darkness. He luxuriated in the stillness of the night. On weekends, he knew, the same pathways would be filled with boisterous crowds of young singles who had bought shares in the summer houses. That was their world, he thought.

As he approached the beach, the path became steeper. He was near a narrow cut in the dune, leading down to the shoreline. He topped the rise and saw it was low tide. A hundred yards, perhaps less, of the beach lay before him. The line of seaweed, showing him where the last high tide had stopped, was only slightly more than twenty yards away.

His shoes filled with sand as he stepped off the concrete and onto the downward slope of sand leading to the water's edge. In the faint moonlight he clearly could see the surf, breaking very gently. He stepped across the seaweed line and then turned to walk parallel to the water in the direction of the Fire Island Lighthouse.

Silence. It was beautiful, lulling, peaceful, unlike the world he was being asked to reenter. He looked up and could see the brighter stars directly overhead, dimmer ones as he swept his eyes across the horizon line.

With the soft purring of the sea helping to clear his mind, he decided he had three choices. He could rejoin—but would do so only on his own terms and even then would not trust the agency. He knew that, if he did go to Lyle and did find the cause of the disease, he would have to make his own private arrangements to guarantee that the organism stayed out of the hands of the agency or the military. *Just in case they like the damn thing.* He didn't know how he would do that, but he knew he would have to.

Secondly, he could remain in Kismet and hope that Kracke's "competitors" got the message that he intended to do nothing. Kracke *could* be wrong, he told himself.

Finally, he could set sail and vanish. Then he thought of the ease with which he'd been found once, in the fog, at night, miles from shore. *If I believe Kracke.* A vast ocean in which he never would feel safe. *He's poisoned it, just by the suggestion. I don't have to believe it.*

Even if he succeeded, he knew, he would spend many days and nights wondering what kind of world he had helped create by inaction. If that disease broke free—and no matter how tightly the quarantine was woven he knew it would be a fragile control . . .

He admitted as he started back toward the pathway that his life of nomadic sailing was over, at least for now. It was surprising how easily that admission came and a shock how easily and swiftly and almost subliminally the decision had been made.

He climbed the dune cut to the concrete path, aware of his straining calf muscles and how little they were used in his life aboard the boat. He reached the top and started for the dock area. A five-minute walk.

He turned back for a last look at the ripples reflecting moon- and starlight and the white surf pounding and the beach itself. Then, as the path sloped downward, the view was cut off. He continued.

The beach would be gone someday. So what? Something else would replace it. Something always filled every niche. Even those left by men.

Brandes was tired.

He passed the first of the two pole-mounted lights between himself and the dock, sliding into intervening darkness.

He thought he heard a sound behind him and credited himself with a *grand* case of paranoia. Kracke had gotten to him after all, he thought. Brandes had no doubt that Kracke was a man of many secrets and probably had his own troubles and conflicts, but he had an undeniable strength and purpose. Kracke was a man, Brandes thought as he continued slowly walking, who considered what he did *now* to be important *now*—and always knew that whatever he did probably wouldn't matter a hell of a lot in a thousand years.

How many of any man's works survived that long? Certainly Brandes didn't expect to be remembered in the fourth millennium. The thought made him chuckle and he could see why Kracke might employ such a technique to keep his perspective, to get things done.

He stopped laughing when he thought about the disease. It could be remembered in a thousand years.

Brandes was about halfway between the beach and the dock area when he paused, again thinking he had heard something.

No. There was no question. There *had* been a sound. A cat lucky enough to have survived the forbidding Fire Island winter and now foraging? He wanted to keep looking straight ahead.

The *Siege* was in view in the distance, lazily riding the barrier-quieted waters. *Straight ahead. Walk. Think about tomorrow.* Then he would have to act on his decision. Change was coming. For the first time in a long while, that thought did not frighten him.

Brandes became aware that as nearly silent as they were, his own footfalls were coinciding precisely with the sound he knew to be behind him. It definitely was not a cat.

Well, he could either give in to paranoia and turn around or take the consequences of ignoring the sound. It was a test, he thought.

He would have to face it. Pulling a blanket over his head had worked very effectively at dispersing monsters when he was eight years old. Then just getting his feet off the floor had provided perfect refuge. He was not eight anymore.

He stopped suddenly.

The sound stopped. A sound he almost wanted to hear.

Brandes spun around fast. A man stood not a dozen feet away. He could see him only as a slightly bent silhouette.

"Mr. Brandes?"

The man's voice sounded dusty, dry. Brandes's own throat felt dry. Damn, he thought, for all he knew it could be Bob or Tomas. *I know better than that.*

The black shape remained still for the moment. Brandes managed a small sound and then suddenly cut it off. From the shadows, from the foliage of a vacant lot beside the path, another figure emerged from the darkness. It came closer. So also did the first, but then the second leaped pantherlike and there was a soft sighing as though someone had let the remaining air out of an already flaccid balloon. The first shape slid to the ground.

The second straightened, and Brandes knew the man was looking at him. Brandes was frightened, very frightened. Perhaps as he never before had been.

Until the chuckle. Then it was all right. Almost.

"Alex. You okay?" It was, of course, Kracke.

"In a way."

"Good. Sorry to have to interrupt your evening stroll, but then . . . you can see that someone else had intentions of doing that anyway."

Kracke reached into the shadows near the ground and picked up what must have been the other man's silenced revolver.

"I don't belong here," Brandes said quietly, his voice barely audible. As Brandes backed into the last light's puddle of illumination, Kracke came forward.

"I know that, Alex. I'm sorry you have to be here." He gestured, seemingly unaware of the stiletto in his hand. "But you can see that you are here whether you like it or not."

"You really were sent to protect me." Brandes's voice was dull.

"I don't do things like this for fun, Alex." Kracke bent, wiped the blade on the other man's slacks. He straightened and took Brandes by the arm, turned him, and began leading him toward the dock, closing and pocketing the knife as they walked. "I have to make a call to have this cleaned up," he said. They stopped at one of the two telephone booths at the end of the walkway.

Brandes's mind seemed determined not to center on any one thought for any length of time, seeking safety in drifting. Kracke calmly spoke into the telephone. Brandes couldn't hear through the door and wasn't sure he wanted to. Briefly he wondered what number one called to have a person's body taken away in the dead of night on an island.

Kracke finished and again took Brandes by his elbow.

"I know it's hard for you, Alex."

"Hard?" He felt a sudden rage. He was not aware his voice was louder.

"Quiet," Kracke hissed, and Brandes subsided. "At least let us have half a chance of getting that guy out of here. Things are simpler that way."

Brandes felt properly chastised for his childish behavior in this all-too-adult world.

"Yes, it's hard," he said, more subdued. "It's hard for someone like me to think that I'm such a threat to someone that they think I'm worth killing."

"Not much on self-esteem, huh?" The words were lightly, jokingly said. But Brandes sensed a seriousness to them. Kracke did not like low self-esteem in a person.

"Maybe. But maybe a hell of a lot more of it is due to the simple fact that I am flat-out terrified."

"*That* is as it should be."

"How long will I be in danger?"

"How long will that epidemic last?"

"I see."

"I think you're beginning to."

They had reached the well-illuminated stretch of the dock and the walkway that led to the *Siege*. "You'll only be here until tomorrow?" he asked Kracke.

The other hesitated. "Yes. You mean that you haven't made up your mind *yet*? Hell, man, you almost gained the weight of a piece of metal!"

"That's the damnedest part about it." He looked curiously at Kracke. At least Kracke thought the expression curious.

"What?"

"Well, I *had* made up my mind to leave tomorrow for *Lyle*." Kracke looked dumbfounded and confused.

"And now?"

"I know it doesn't sound like it makes sense. I guess it doesn't. I'm so shit scared now that I'm seriously considering doing something I'd ruled out."

"What?" Kracke asked warily.

"Running. Just fucking running. Taking my chances." He paused. "Face it, Kracke. Be honest with yourself, too. You know goddamn well that you can't be with me every minute I'm in Lyle. You *can't*. And when you're not . . ."

"Try to get a good night's rest, Alex." Brandes was surprised by the sudden flatness of the tone. "Make believe it was all a nightmare. Make believe anything."

Then Kracke was gone.

Brandes immediately felt very vulnerable, even more afraid. He'd read that fear reached a certain point and numbness set in. He didn't believe it.

But Kracke was professional. If he felt Brandes was in no further danger that night, he'd have his reasons. Brandes had to trust the man.

Brandes stepped onto the *Siege* and, for the first time in memory, fastened his cabin door behind him as he let himself down into the salon. Certain he wouldn't sleep, he didn't bother removing his clothes. He moved into the master's cabin and lay down, having taken off only his shoes. He was asleep within minutes.

He wondered, just before sleep came, if he would call Allenberg in the morning.

Two hundred yards away, the "body disposal team" did its work.

The "body" of the man who had followed Brandes simply got up from the path and began to walk to his room in the motel, wiping the "blood" from himself as best he could. He knocked twice on Kracke's door to let him know that he was back. He heard an irritated "Goodnight" from inside and wondered what he'd done wrong. He shrugged and continued to his own room.

Hell, nothing could have gone wrong.

# SIX

LYLE'S NOON STREETS ALMOST WERE AS EMPTY AS they would be at midnight. No children played; none went to school. Adults as well rarely were seen, visible only as they moved from one store to another or from a store to a car. Such incidences were the only noticeable evidence that the few small businesses even were open. Indeed, little except staples were available in town. Most residents shopped in the malls that had sprung up recently in neighboring communities that had greater access to the larger highways.

Often the vehicles that did pass had flashing emergency lights or were painted a drab green. The latter were new to Lyle; there was a good deal of curiosity about the choice of the area for military maneuvers.

No one connected the presence of troops with the flu that recently had settled on the town.

Lyle had grown slowly until its population reached five thousand, scattered over the large countryside or concentrated either here in the town's center or in the much smaller and just developing business district a few miles away. Still, despite its relatively large area, there was no doubt Lyle was a small town.

Like many good New Hampshire towns, it had been founded around the middle of the 1700s, on a site that was a compromise between a valley and a mountain slope. One side offered a spectacular view of rolling hillside that suddenly steeply mounted into a fair-sized peak. Yet from the same vantage, facing the opposite direction, an observer would see a valley below, crisscrossed with furrows and with some land allowed to rest fallow while the remainder produced the local farm goods—mostly corn.

Lyle's farmers, as did most others in that area of New England, grew their crops right up to the narrow roads that often marked the farms' property lines. They were not concerned that passing motorists who knew the sweetness of ripe raw corn straight from the husk often stopped to take an ear or two. Often they smiled at these petty "thefts," which to them were a form of flattery. It was difficult to harvest that near the road anyway, and the corn that grew there probably would have been wasted.

Their attitude was typical of the area. Nature gave; it was better to allow the gift to make someone momentarily happy than to waste it. Besides, no one ever took much.

It was that kind of town—a place many Americans who lived in cities thought existed only in stories of older times.

Locks rarely were used. Shoppers for real estate often simply drove up to an empty house that was for sale and went inside to look around before even calling a broker. Copper pots and pans and brass lanterns adorned those houses; it just seemed unthinkable to the people of the area that anyone would even consider stealing them.

For the most part the system worked.

People were much closer than they ever could have been in a city, even though physically they lived so much farther apart. Yet in that intimacy lay danger for Lyle and for all other towns near it—or for that matter, for any other small community of caring, trusting people.

Lyle was a community: Community inadvertently can kill just as effectively as it can help make life worthwhile.

* * *

Dr. Jonathan Shortell had come to New Hampshire to get away from the pressures of New York City and still not be too far from the city itself. Like many urbanites, he was unable to totally give up the sound and pace of the city. The City. To Shortell, who had traveled considerably, New York was the only place that deserved the title. Shortell at least had to know that the bustle was only a fifty-minute plane ride away, on a small Beech 99 flown by a pilot whose uniform consisted of a tie loosely worn under a V-neck pullover.

Still, the pressures he found at that moment in Lyle were such that, for the first time, he wondered if he had made the right decision.

A soft-toned chime sounded overhead and a voice calmly called "Code-E" in a reassuring, feminine tone. Evenly spaced speakers in the corridors' ceilings made certain that the voice penetrated most of Lyle–Mount Saint Sydney Hospital. Despite the softness of the overhead voice, the message was not calming or reassuring.

Someone had stopped breathing; a heart had stopped.

Shortell stepped to one side of the corridor and leaned on the rib-high reception desk of the nurses' station. Three other white-coated persons, faces grim, clattered down the hall pushing a two-shelved stainless steel cart. It contained the wide variety of medicines and equipment, from adrenaline to electrical paddles, that might help the doctors to bring the newly dead back to life.

Shortell had little hope that the "crash" cart crew would succeed this time, and even if they did, he doubted the patient would continue to live for any significant length of time. Another code would be called and the process repeated—until a doctor finally decided that the case truly was hopeless and wrote the cryptic, often compassionate words *no code* on the patient's chart.

It was not an advertised practice, and most often physicians consulted families before writing those words. More often the word *slow* would appear on the chart. Nurses and technicians would respond, but not quite with the enthusiasm he had just seen.

Codes recently had become routine, and not one of the recipients of the most advanced technology and the most honed of medical skills really had been given another chance at life.

It had been Shortell who only a few days earlier had alerted the Centers for Disease Control in Atlanta that something was happening. A hell of a scientific evaluation, he knew, but he could do no better.

The symptoms were consistent—shortness of breath, a slight bulging appearance to the eyes as the patient's labored lungs tried and failed to oxygenate the blood and to remove waste. The muscles were flaccid. Patients alternated between high fevers and cold sweats. Body systems failed like falling dominoes. Death followed.

Keflin was administered intravenously, as were other broad-spectrum antibiotics, even though Shortell suspected neither these nor others would prove effective. If the disease was a virus, the antibiotics would be useless as a weapon, but they would stem invasion of the weakened patient's body by secondary bacteriological infections such as a pneumonia.

None of the fifty-seven persons admitted since the beginning of what appeared more and more to be an epidemic got pneumonia. Shortell would have been glad if they had; since it would have meant they had stayed alive long enough to catch something he could understand and treat.

A disheveled nurse in her mid-thirties approached the station as Shortell watched. She had not yet seen him; her head hung tiredly as she walked.

"Who?" he asked, and she looked up as she entered the station and began rotating a large circular file containing the metal-sheathed charts of the patients on her floor.

"Harlson." Her voice left no doubt about the outcome of the attempt to revive Sarah Harlson. The nurse, Jeannette Pierce, pulled one of the charts from the carousel and sat down. She

51

flipped it open and made a notation. She replaced it and turned to Shortell. "Anything from the pros?"

"They're down in Pathology, I guess. Some are, anyway. One or two are interviewing patients, and I know that at least two of their epidemiologists have gone over to Futures," he said, referring to Brandes's lab. Shortell hoped that whatever was invading Lyle had not come from Futures. He knew little of the work that went on there—only enough to know that it involved recombinant DNA research.

Shortell had met Peter Brandes several times but never had become socially friendly with the scientist. There hadn't been many opportunities, and their work had little in common—Shortell, at least, had supposed that there was little or no overlap. Now he wasn't so certain.

Of course, he knew that the facilities of Futures would offer the CDC team a better environment for its search for a causative agent. The pathology laboratory of the hospital was not geared to that type of work on a large scale. Shortell tried to reassure himself that CDC was using the only lab because of its superior facilities and not because it was suspected of producing the illness. As different diseases were ruled out, however, more and more attention would be paid to that possibility.

"Have you talked to them lately?" Jeannette asked.

"Not since yesterday. They're busy collecting samples. I'd imagine they will be sending some soon to Atlanta. I think I'll drive over to Futures soon. Offer my services." He grinned. "My talents don't seem to be doing much here."

"Don't think I wouldn't like to reassure you, doctor." Her clear eyes looked straight at him. "It probably comes from Futures, don't you think?"

"I'd rather not."

"Then why is the army sealing off this place? Or are you buying the maneuvers line that colonel handed out?"

"No," he said. "And I doubt that the people around here are going to buy it much longer either. They're not blind—it's only because things have happened so fast that no one's noticed that people coming in here aren't leaving.

"I give them another two days," he concluded.

"Maybe. How many total so far?"

"Thirty-eight, I think."

"The morgue only holds six."

"I understand Colonel Lawrence has commandeered a spot for temporary burial. The bodies will be released to families later, after the cause is isolated. And the cure found."

"Cure?" Her voice was sharply cynical.

"Oh, there'll be one," he said, proud of how confident he sounded, even to himself. But she was not to be outdone.

"Sure," she said. "You can get rid of wheat rust, too. All you have to do is get rid of all the wheat."

Shortell didn't say anything. He straightened and walked to the elevator bank. He intended to see some of his patients on another floor—ones who were there for more prosaic illnesses. He hoped the visit would cheer him up and grimaced at the macabre quality of the idea.

Later he planned to stop by Pathology. He had more than the obvious reason. One of the CDC epidemiologists was one very stunning woman. At first he told himself that now wasn't the time to think about such things. As the situation worsened, though, he decided that the present was looking like the best time for just about anything.

Dorothy Jenner took care to allow the screen door to close quietly behind her. She walked to the edge of the porch and stood next to Emil, her husband. Both were quiet. Emil, a strong, self-reliant man, looked down the gentle slope that led from the comfortable farmhouse to the fields below, to the soon-to-be corn.

"How is she?" he asked, not moving, barely turning his head at her arrival.

"No fever now," Dorothy answered.

"Good."

They lapsed into new silence, and she became aware of his deep, regular breathing. To Doro his breathing seemed louder, more noticeable than she had remembered.

*He's worried*, she thought. *No matter what he says or does, he's worried, anxious—frightened*. She had to help, if possible. *But I'm frightened, too* . . .

Nancy, their ten-year-old daughter, was all either thought about. She'd become ill late two nights earlier, high temperatures alternating with sudden perspiration that left the bedsheets sodden.

Far down in the field Jenner watched Jim Harlson climb into the driver's seat of the tractor. A sudden puff of dark smoke, followed seconds later by a loud *crack*, indicated the starting of the diesel engine. The tractor lurched deeper into the field, its tracks churning into the earth.

The small figure waved when he saw the Jenners watching him. Emil raised a hand wearily and allowed it to drop back to his side.

"Should we take her to the hospital?"

"I don't know, Doro."

"Jim took Sarah."

"Yes. I know. But we don't know that Nancy has the same thing. Not yet."

"If she does? If she gets worse?" There was an anxious edge to her voice. Jenner felt uncomfortable.

"Then we'll have to, I guess. You know I don't like hospitals."

"Yes." They became silent again, the sound of the working tractor reaching them lazily in the still air.

Emil Jenner was an engineer by training, and an intelligent and sophisticated man. He also was a careful man, who thought everything through before reaching any conclusions—a quality his wife appreciated greatly and admired. And, for a man who had no formal education in medicine, he was remarkably knowledgeable on the subject. Having been a patient a few times in a hospital, he had come to the conclusion that it was an

54

excellent place to *catch* diseases. A doctor friend had agreed with him once at a dinner party.

"You aren't far off, Emil," Shortell had said. "Sometimes I think that if you stay long enough in any hospital you'll develop everything everyone else has. I get my patients out before they get really sick," he'd joked—perhaps.

"But we will take her there if she gets worse, Emil."

"If we have to, Doro, we'll take her any place we have to. I think I'd prefer to take her to a different hospital, though, if it comes to that."

"What's wrong with Lyle?"

Jenner didn't want to frighten her any more than she already was. She was well aware that several friends and neighbors already had checked into Lyle–Mount Saint Sydney. *He* was aware he had seen none of them since.

"Nothing, I guess," he said. He wished he hadn't said anything at all about another hospital. He added, "I've just heard a lot of good things about a few doctors not with Lyle."

Both were quiet again. Jenner moved to a swinging bench on the porch and motioned his wife to join him. Both were attuned to the open door behind them and any noise Nancy might make.

The Jenners liked life in Lyle; a bequest had brought Emil Jenner there when he was a child. His father had been an engineeer; his grandfather had been a farmer. Emil had been named for his grandfather.

He'd always had great respect for both men. His grandfather, more progressive than many of his own era, had not in the least minded when his son had elected not to become a farmer himself but to move to Boston and establish himself as an engineer. "He told me I made the right decision," Emil's father had recounted. "'Go be an engineer,' he said, and I knew he meant it when he wished me well. That's the thing to keep in mind, Emil. He really meant it. Your grandfather always seemed to know something no one else did. And damn it, he usually did.

"But," Emil's father continued, "he said, 'Remember this: I

intend to hold onto this piece of land. And the day will come, I promise you, that the land will call you. You'll come.' He was right, you know."

Emil never had regretted his father's decision to return to Lyle. He himself was a hybrid of the two men. He loved the land, but he was not a farmer. He had compromised. The farm still was productive—the thought of land not being permitted to produce was anathema to him, as it had been to both his father and his grandfather—but it produced for a tenant who received favorable terms.

Emil had followed in the footsteps of both men. He lived on the farm *and* had become an engineer. He had a business based in Lyle.

It was a good life. Or had been.

Normally, Nancy's illness would not have bothered him unduly. Children become sick. But the rumors in the town, the army—all of it added up to a very disturbing picture. Jenner said nothing about that to Doro. He might be very good at adding two and two, but he wasn't the type of man to jump up and shout "Four!" without reason.

The sound of a cough made both parents look up. It stopped, and Jenner put his hand on his wife's arm and settled her back onto the bench. "She's all right," he said.

"No, she isn't, Emil. I'm frightened."

"So am I," he said finally. "Look," he turned and lifted Dorothy's face gently until their eyes met. "I promise you. I'll do whatever I have to do to make sure she gets well. I promise."

His wife nodded, relaxing a little, letting herself at least try to respond to her husband's strength. She knew him to be a very resourceful and capable man. There *was* comfort in knowing that.

"What about this army thing? You were in the army."

"I was in the engineers," he said. "These aren't engineers." He didn't add that most were infantry and that he'd noticed more than a sprinkling of medical and signal corps personnel.

"I was talking to Bob Torre in the general store," she said. "The army people were there just before I was."

"What for?" he asked, not sounding very interested.

"They bought all his ammunition," she said. "You'd think they would have their own, wouldn't you?"

"I'm certain they do, Doro." Jenner felt himself straighten, his back and stomach muscles suddenly rigid.

# SEVEN

BRANDES HAD LEFT THE *SIEGE* IN THE CARE OF Tomas. The older man had asked no questions, but he had looked concerned. It was not like Brandes to leave the boat and its equipment and not say when he would return.

The concern in Tomas's eyes could have been a reflection of that in Brandes's own. Brandes had not yet gotten over Kracke's assertion that the sinking of the *Charon* had been no accident. But neither Allenberg nor Kracke—and certainly not Brandes himself—could say who had done it or why. Even more so, he had not yet fully accepted that an attempt on his life the previous night had occurred at all. That one, though, he could not deny.

It was late morning, and he had left Fire Island early. The trip was multilegged and tiresome. First he'd taken a ferry to Bayshore and then a train to Penn Station in Manhattan. From there Brandes had gone to the Port Authority Bus Terminal and had taken a bus to Newark Airport. He preferred to fly from Newark. Although it was a very busy international terminus, Newark did not have the hurried and confused atmosphere of the city's airports. Finally, the twin-engine Beech. As noon approached, the small plane entered its landing leg over Lyle.

Touchdown was smooth, and the pilot gently taxied to a small airport building. The steps were dropped; Brandes was the last of eight passengers to leave. Waves of heated air rippled before him, rising from the sun-warmed concrete.

He had one suitcase; a seasoned traveler, he never packed more than a few days' supply of anything and very few toilet items. What could not be washed could be replaced.

A car rented by Allenberg would, he knew, be parked nearby. The agency would have rented the car in the city had he wished, but long, nonstop driving did not appeal to him; despite the changes he had had to make, he preferred his ferry-to-plane route.

He'd played some games in his own mind, wondering if hidden there was another reason for the circuitous route. He had, after all, been damned tiresome to follow, if anyone had tried. He'd shrugged that off, though. *I just didn't want to drive.*

He passed through the small terminal's lobby, signed for the car, and went to the parking lot. More than half of the building was taken up by a restaurant; he intended to drive back there for lunch if possible. Certainly for dinner. Only those who had lived in or frequently visited Lyle seemed to know that the best place to eat out was the airport.

He noticed an army van parked nearby. The side door was open, and Brandes could see two men inside. They sat on small folding chairs, with a card table between them. One, Brandes noticed, occasionally glanced at the airport through field glasses while the other made notes on papers stacked on the table.

They evidently were caught up in an infrequent spurt of activity as the plane passengers left the terminal and walked to their cars or to cars where relatives or friends waited to pick them up.

It would not be long, Brandes thought, before people in Lyle began to feel that something was wrong here, that these troops were not on a training maneuver. Allenberg had not been too informative about the situation; Brandes knew he liked to give his operatives an outline of their assignments and little more. But

Brandes did know that these soldiers were poised, waiting for an order that would clamp a quarantine hard and fast around Lyle.

He also knew that wouldn't be easy because of the size of the town and the distances separating the farms.

Brandes only hoped that if that time came, the people would accept it. They would be terrified, of course. Some would think of escape, and they were resourceful New Englanders. Establishing an enforceable quarantine might not be all that easy; Brandes hoped there would be no violence.

The army would move on its own, if ordered. But Allenberg also had arranged to give him authority to spring the quarantine.

He had grown up in Lyle; many residents were friends or at least more than nodding acquaintances.

Brandes planned to do everything he could to avoid putting those troops into action—and to avoid having them put into action by someone else.

His car was an old Grand Prix—at least, old by any rental agency's standard. Brandes guessed it was at least six years old, but it appeared to be in excellent condition. He put his suitcase in the trunk, checking as a matter of habit that there was a usable spare tire and a jack. Both were there, along with several flares and a small tool set.

He got into the car and checked the odometer—slightly more than thirty thousand miles. Brandes did not care how the agency had managed this; he assumed it was standard to keep inconspicuous, well-maintained vehicles available.

Brandes started the engine and rolled back the sunroof; he preferred the breeze to air conditioning. The center console was filled with a selection of cassette tapes; he chose "Rhapsody in Blue," put the car in gear, and eased past the army truck. It was only a matter of time before he was identified and the commanding officer notified that he had arrived.

Several more army vehicles were parked on the side of the road about two miles from the airport. Two men worked on a parabolic antenna atop one truck while an officer looked on. Passing motorists could assume what they wanted—that it was a signal corps exercise or an effort to pirate Home Box Office—the army didn't care. The two enlisted men who counted were those who sat nearby with clipboards, making a second note of license plates.

There was no more visible army presence for the remaining three miles to the Lyle Tower Hotel. It didn't matter. Either the force was hidden or it could be called at a moment's notice.

The bustle just outside and in the lobby of the hotel was unlike anything Brandes ever had seen there before. The Tower was a small hotel, deriving most of its income from tourists who came during the fall when New England became a wonderland full of autumn color.

Brandes liked the hotel. It was eighty-five years old and had had only three owners. There was a friendly atmosphere that could never be rivaled by any city hotel or ordinary roadside motel.

"Johnny," he said quietly, after he made his way through the busy, small lobby to the registration desk. A harried-looking man about his own age looked up; he said nothing for several seconds before he recognized Brandes.

"Alex! It's good to see you." He hesitated. "I'm sorry about Peter."

Brandes nodded. "Thanks." He changed the subject and waved his hand. "Busy?"

"Crazy. Been like this almost two days. There's . . . Oh, I guess you know about it, right? The flu thing or whatever. Or did you come because . . ." He trailed off.

Johnny Avery hadn't changed, Brandes decided. He welcomed the man's disjointed sentences and tendency to blush; they made things more real, more acceptable. He smiled. "No, I didn't come just for Peter," he said. "I'll try to help out here if I can."

Avery was a canny New Englander. "Do you think it came from the lab?"

"I honestly don't know, Johnny. I may not even be of much use. These CDC people know their business."

"Oh, I know. And they're nice people, too. Polite. It's just that

61

we would welcome any help we can get, Alex. I mean, we're a little concerned. The lab and all . . ." He started to flush again and quickly tried to recover. "I don't want to make us sound like the villagers in a Frankenstein movie, but . . ." He stopped again, realizing his comments were not leading him where he'd intended.

"It's okay," Brandes reassured him. "I don't think you should worry too much." Avery nodded. "Now, how about a room?"

Avery straightened and steadied; he was relieved to be occupied once more with things he understood.

"I got a call saying you'd be coming, Alex. Good thing, too. I don't know how many of these people will wind up here." He winked. Brandes smiled.

"Can I leave this here—" he gestured toward his suitcase— "while I get a drink and relax a minute? It was a long trip."

"No problem," Avery said. He reached around and moved the piece of luggage into the small office behind him. "Glad to see you again, Alex."

*You don't look glad.* Brandes smiled acknowledgement, recognizing the several levels on which Avery meant the comment and understanding all of them. He walked through a wide, walnut-trimmed doorway and into the bar.

There were several tables, all occupied. Voices were soft, a murmur only occasionally rising enough to allow a word to be understood. The lighting was dim, the lounge cool. Brandes relaxed.

He walked to the bar and took a stool. He stayed away from the light of the window but still could see outside. Lyle from that perspective was much as he'd remembered it. The street was quiet. Cutting along his vision was a line formed by the high backs of rocking chairs on the Tower's wide porch. Near the edge of the window he could just see the light blue canopy that covered the steps leading to the hotel's first floor.

"Manhattan, up," he said to the man behind the bar, someone he didn't recognize. The drink was well-made. He breathed deeply; he would have to get to work soon and was not quite certain where he had best start.

He had to visit the lab, of course. He expected he would spend a considerable amount of time there. But he also wanted to go to the hospital and talk to someone in Pathology. Then, of course, there was the army—eventually. And—as "eventually" as he could make it—unless he decided just to get it over with, he would have to see his father.

Brandes put that thought out of his mind as best he could. He would deal with his father when he had to, and if he could manage it, he would make sure that "when he had to" would coincide with "when he was best able."

A hand settled gently on his shoulder. *Shit*, he thought. *Uncle Sam wants me . . . already.*

He turned. It wasn't a soldier. For a fraction of a second he couldn't place the man—and then felt as foolish as had Johnny at the registration desk. He hoped he didn't blush.

"Mr. Wismer," he muttered and then caught himself and smiled. "Gerry." It had taken him years to be able to use his former teacher's first name; he doubted he ever would become comfortable with it. He wondered if anyone ever felt he had "grown up." He could remember the first time someone younger had called him "Mister" and how he had done a doubletake.

The older man smiled. "Welcome home, Alex." Brandes was fond of him. He had loved working in the high-school chemistry and biology laboratories under Wismer's direction. They had become good friends with the passing of years; Brandes regretted he had not kept in touch more. But the last few years had been a time of adjustment he couldn't share—not with family, not with friends, not with anyone.

"Join me," Wismer said. He gestured across the room to a small table, now empty except for a glass and a bar napkin. Brandes realized Wismer had been there all along and that he had not seen him in the dimness of the room. Brandes picked up his Manhattan and followed Wismer to the table. He sat in a chair with his back to the wall.

"I see you haven't changed in some ways," the retired teacher chuckled. Brandes always had taken a good amount of joking about his "paranoia." In public places he *had* to sit so he could see the door, preferably with a wall at his back. Now, of course, he had more than ample reason for wanting to have no strangers behind him.

"Force of habit. How are you?"

"Nothing much new," Wismer said. "Until now, of course." Brandes tried not to show any emotion. He knew Wismer and his perceptive abilities. He knew better than to underestimate him.

"Not the best of reasons or times to renew old friendships," Brandes said and sipped at his drink, swallowing more than he'd intended. He looked up to see if anyone was waiting on the tables. No one was; he was grateful. He could gain a few minutes "adjusting time."

"Be right back," he said. "What are you drinking?"

"Tanqueray, tonic."

Brandes nodded and went to get the drinks. Wismer was a hard man to put off, but Brandes could tell him so little! He wished he *could* open up to the older man. It would do him good. But he knew better. He knew better than to get *anyone* involved in his life, particularly a person for whom he cared.

He picked up the drinks and returned to his seat.

"So, are you going to tell me anything?" Wismer opened.

"Oh, a few tidbits here and there."

"Did it come from the lab, Alex?"

He was taken aback by the directness of the question.

"I really don't know, Gerry. Really." He paused. "I hope not."

Wismer appeared to accept that. He nodded. "I hope not, too. I've never felt comfortable about this biological tinkering." He held up a hand to stave off comment. "Don't get me wrong. I was a scientist before I was a teacher or I wouldn't have been any good as a teacher. And I was good, Alex. As both teacher and scientist." It was simply a factual statement.

"I know this research has to be done." Wismer went on. "God knows it offers too much to be ignored. Cures for cancer, diabetes—name it. Who knows where it will end?" He paused. "That, I guess, is also my real worry. Where *will* it end? And where will it take us in the meantime?"

"I'm just as scared as you are, Gerry. But you knew Peter."

"Yes. It's the only thing I can cling to for reassurance. I know he wouldn't make something like this on purpose. And"—he paused again and smiled mischievously—"I also know he was very careful in the lab. More careful than his more gifted brother ever was."

Brandes grinned. "I only made a few mistakes," he said.

"Someday you'll convince me all of them were mistakes." They both laughed, but the seriousness of the topic at hand quickly returned.

"He *was* careful. And he'd never want to kill anybody. I sometimes think he had trouble sterilizing equipment because he didn't want to kill the bacteria."

"People do change, though."

"Yeah. I know."

"What do you intend to do?"

"I haven't really figured it out yet, Gerry. I'll get settled in first and I suppose I'll have to feel my way around while I get brought up to date."

"You know the CDC people?"

"I don't think so," he said. "I haven't met with them yet."

Wismer said nothing for several moments.

"So," he said at last, "you're not here with CDC. I'm counting on it not being idle curiosity or an intention to protect the family's good name."

Damn. He'd fallen into that. He should have known better. "The government has more than one organization concerned with health research," Brandes said lamely.

"Tooth fairy."

"Huh?"

"Oh, I know it does. But somehow I think you're trying to sell me a tooth-fairy story."

"If there was anything I could . . ."

"I know."

Brandes was getting slightly irritated. He was very fond of the man—truth be known, more so than of his own father. But it was

65

because of their friendship that he most resented Wismer's probing.

"Gerry . . ."

"Alex. Really I do believe you. I hate doing this; I hate playing on a friendship. But to be honest with you, I'm scared."

*You don't look it.* "So far the disease is limited," Brandes began.

"For Christ's sake, Alex." He kept his voice low and even. "The goddamn *army* is out there."

Brandes only could stare. He hoped not many of Lyle's residents were as alert and analytic as Wismer. He knew better than to play dumb.

"Yeah," he said. "I know. I guess I'll have to go see them soon, too." There was no sense in denying it. He would keep what he could from his former teacher, but he knew that he couldn't hide everything.

"They haven't done anything much yet. I wonder . . ."

"Gerry, there are some things I just cannot discuss. Try to understand that."

"Okay, my turn to buy."

Wismer got up and went to the bar. Brandes sat back and looked around. He didn't recognize anyone else in the lounge. Most of the tables were occupied by pairs or threesomes. Only one table had a lone drinker. His back was to the light, and his face was shadowed. Brandes couldn't see his features. Suddenly he felt uncomfortable, but there wasn't much he could do about it if the man *was* watching him.

The real question, of course, was that if the man was observing him—on whose behalf was it? Allenberg's? Or his mysterious enemies'?

Wismer returned shortly. Idly he glanced over his own shoulder; Brandes hoped he was not picking up his momentary preoccupation with the lone stranger. He could never explain *that*.

"After this one," Brandes said, "I'd better be going. There's a lot of work to do, and right now the biggest part of it for me is finding out just what I'm supposed to do." *Foremost: Peter's notes.*

Wismer nodded. For a few minutes they sat and drank in quiet, and then they spoke briefly of other things—things not connected with any crisis. "Have you got any ideas?" Brandes asked suddenly. It only then had occurred to him that all the while Wismer had been quizzing him he never had volunteered any information on his own. Brandes was not about to let that pass. Wismer was a very capable scientist in his own right; he wanted to know what that, coupled with the old man's perceptive powers, had produced in the last few days.

"Yes and no. It's most likely airborne; people who wouldn't be kissing each other seem likely more often than not to be candidates for each other's vectors.

"It's fast. I don't know, but I'd guess the incubation period is no more than a day or two, possibly less.

"And it kills, Alex. It kills everybody."

"You, I trust, have not been pointing that out around town, have you?"

Wismer snorted. "Such silliness you get away with once." He paused. "I think you should go to the hospital first. Talk to a doctor named Shortell. He's a nice guy, but he's up to his ass in something that's beating him, and he doesn't like it. He was the one who called in CDC."

"Sounds like a good idea. I think I'll unpack and head over there."

"Unpack? Where?"

Brandes was confused. "What do you mean?"

"You don't think you're staying here, do you? I still live alone in one godawful big house. Unless, of course, you're going to stay . . ."

"No. That's out."

"Well, then it's my place."

"No, Gerry. That's out, too."

"Afraid I'll keep picking? I promise to poke as little and painlessly as possible. But you may find that tossing some things around in the evening can be helpful."

"It's not that, Gerry." Damn! He couldn't let Wismer get involved. Christ, no. He thought of the Lombardis and the *Charon*.

"Damn right it's not." Wismer's voice was barely audible but had a sudden sharp edge to it. Brandes looked up at him. "Look at it this way. If you *have* got a shadow over there"—he jerked his head curtly over his shoulder toward the strange lone drinker—"then the one thing you need more than anything else is a back door. I've got three."

*Hell.* "Gerry . . ."

"Stop it. Listen," he said more reasonably. "You may have noticed I'm not blind. I wasn't always a teacher in a nice New England town."

"What?"

"What what? I didn't say a damned thing."

Brandes was thrown completely off-balance. Vague curious thoughts were beginning to form, vague questions not ready to be asked. *Nuts*, he thought. *Wismer, my high-school teacher . . .*

"You'll keep your room here, of course."

"What?"

"Don't fall apart on me, Alex. Keep the room here and keep up appearances. My back doors are just as useful for getting into the house."

The idea had its appeal. He felt certain Allenberg would approve. Protection would be much easier without the bustle of the hotel's guests. But then it was Allenberg's business to involve innocent people in dangerous things if it served his purposes.

"It's just that . . ." He stopped and nodded his acceptance.

"You don't have time to argue, Alex. Look." Brandes followed Wismer's pointing finger to the window and beyond. An army Jeep had pulled up. "I'll see you later. After you're drafted."

# EIGHT

"I THINK THE COLONEL EXPECTED YOU TO HAVE checked in by now," the young lieutenant said.

Brandes rumbled in his throat, said nothing. Heat struck him as he left the Tower's lobby and walked down the steps to the Jeep. Even though it was not air conditioned, the hotel's interior was much cooler than the streets. The sun had just passed its zenith, the day's heat neared its maximum.

*Half the day gone,* he thought as they got into the Jeep. *And nothing accomplished except a long trip and a reunion with a high-school teacher and . . . will I be able to accomplish anything here? Will I be permitted?*

*Why had he left the* Siege *and Fire Island?* He was afraid and had reasons to be afraid, but he knew there was more. Parts of himself best left unexamined until later. Yet even without soul-searching there was Lyle, Peter, Futures Labs, Allenberg, the *Charon* and the Lombardis, a lethal disease, murderers—all, together, more than enough parts for a jigsaw. He hoped that the colonel would not prove to be an additional piece in perhaps yet another puzzle.

"You did arrive a few hours ago," the lieutenant continued, seemingly determined to inflict guilt.

"Yes."

"I guess you just wanted to check in, huh?"

"That's all. That and to get a drink."

"I'm sure the colonel will have refreshments."

"I met an old friend." He debated whether he wanted to shock his disciplined young companion. *What the hell.* Quickly, before the officer could comment, he said, "You *will* take me back to the hotel to get my car, right?"

"I, uh, I'm sure the colonel . . ."

"If the colonel doesn't," he said pointedly, "you can let me out right here." They barely had traveled a hundred yards from the hotel and were stopped at a traffic signal.

"I'm sure you'll have no trouble, sir." The lieutenant seemed less eager to talk; Brandes first decided that he liked him that way but then wondered if he should not try to be friendly and possibly learn something.

"Oh, I know," he said. "Sorry I was short. It was a long trip."

His driver relaxed marginally. "We *could*, I guess, have gotten you here directly. I mean, if you'd wanted that."

"I appreciate the thought, Lieutenant. But I don't think it would have been seemly for me to arrive in an army helicopter." *Seemly, hell,* he thought. *Allenberg would have collapsed.* "I mean, you are keeping a low profile here, right?" *You may be trying; these people won't close their eyes forever.*

"Very much so," the lieutenant agreed. "We don't even go into town very often. Everybody's more or less scattered." He waved at the horizon before them as he put the Jeep in gear and accelerated slowly. "Even drive carefully."

"Good. Wouldn't want to scare these people."

"No. It's complicated enough."

"In what way?" Brandes wasn't sure what he was pursuing; he felt the question to be "right."

"Well, the quarantine. You don't want to scare them, and if

70

you do scare them, you can't even tell them there's nothing to be scared of. Kind of tricky, isn't it?"

Brandes nodded agreement but remained silent, digesting what he just had learned—the lieutenant knew that the army was there preparing to spring a quarantine, yet thought there was nothing for the quarantine to contain. Just an exercise. And he thought Brandes was part of it.

"How far do we have to go?" Brandes shifted the subject.

"Another mile. Our headquarters is in an empty farmhouse that's for sale. You know," the officer offered, "I like this area. I like that house. I wouldn't mind owning something like that someday."

"It is a nice area. Nice people, too. I grew up here. Matter of fact," he added, "the people are so nice here that I'd hate to see them frightened at all."

The lieutenant said nothing. Brandes added in a low voice, "Certainly not by something they shouldn't be worried about anyway."

They drove the rest of the way in silence.

Brandes did not recognize the house. It was old, rambling; additions had been made over the years, probably in step with a growing family. The land around it was not being farmed. Tall grass stretched away behind the outbuildings. A small stream near the house emptied into a culvert. Large boulders embedded where they'd lain for millennia led down a steep slope from the house to the stream.

Brandes briefly looked at the road they'd traveled. It was empty. Silly, he thought. Whoever the man in the bar was, there'd been no need to follow him to keep Brandes on a leash. He obviously been headed here; it was a good assumption he would return.

An uncomfortable aspect of that thought was that only one of his enemies would have behaved that way. Anyone sent by Allenberg wouldn't want just to know where he was but would want to be near him.

Which left two possibilities. The stranger was an enemy—or Brandes was overworking his imagination, and the man had no interest in him at all.

The lieutenant held a door for him, and Brandes entered. The farmhouse was even cooler than the Tower; a large tree shaded practically the entire house.

The colonel was not an imposing or exceptionally large man. He sat behind what had been the kitchen table and looked up, rising immediately and smiling as he opened his hand.

Brandes took it and nodded. The colonel waved to a chair; both sat.

"Colonel Mitchell Lawrence. Good of you to come, Dr. Brandes. I hope I didn't interrupt your schedule."

"I was on my way to the hospital."

"I'd like to reassure you that there is plenty of time, but as you know, I really can't."

"I know. I didn't want to waste any."

The colonel digested that with a small nod; here, Brandes thought, was a man who seemed to understand him. He didn't like that, not really.

Lawrence handed a paper to the lieutenant with a small smile, and the younger officer left. They were alone.

"I understand you're not exactly under my command."

"I understand I'm not under it at all."

"Well, I've always believed that in a real crunch situation, 'Might makes right.' But we're not going to have a crisis here."

"You seem certain." Brandes decided he might forgo his usual practice of postponing decisions about people he just met. He didn't like Colonel Lawrence. Maybe he would later if he ever saw the man in action; for now, no.

"By no means, Doctor. By no means." His tone was serious, his voice's volume easily audible but low. "Particularly with something like a disease. And most particularly"—he paused and locked his eyes with Brandes's—"with diseases that men create like so many Tinker Toys."

Brandes would not be badgered into defending his brother—or

science. He kept his eyes on the colonel and equally quietly said, "And which Tinker Toys the military just loves to play with."

"There's that," the colonel said and eased back into his chair.

"These things aside," Brandes said, "why am I here? I *am* busy, and time *is* short."

"Just getting acquainted," the colonel sighed, looking wistful. "Lieutenant!"

The young officer entered. Brandes said nothing.

"Take the doctor to the hospital . . ."

"To the hotel," Brandes corrected. "I want to get my own car."

The colonel nodded. "Take him back to his hotel." He paused, then asked, "You *are* staying there, right? I mean, I know you have family here."

"I'm not staying with my family." He rose and headed into the now-afternoon sun. He turned back just in time to see the colonel beckon to his junior officer. He couldn't hear the colonel. Within seconds the lieutenant joined him, and they walked together to the Jeep.

"Get along all right?" The officer was positively cheerful as they pulled out and headed toward town.

"Fine. We definitely have an understanding."

"You know," the lieutenant said, "I like to see a little competition now and then between services and such. It is mostly for fun. At least I always thought so. I get the impression you guys are taking all this seriously."

"I get the impression you are talking a lot more than you did on your way here. Tell you what. You ask me what the colonel wants to know, and if I can tell you, I will. Make your job a hell of a lot easier."

"Thanks. Am I supposed to tell him how tricky I was getting you to talk, too?"

"He didn't."

"He didn't what?" The officer didn't understand.

"When he was a lieutenant," Brandes said, "and someone put him in the place you're in. He didn't tell how he found out whatever he did."

They swerved gently around a curve. "I like these roads," the lieutenant said. "I'd like driving them better on a motorcycle."

"You should take Myers Road," Brandes said. "Nice scenery."

Up ahead Brandes saw an army truck leave the roadside and place itself across both lanes of traffic.

"What's going on?" Brandes said. He felt a knot in his stomach. It *couldn't* have started already, he thought. He hadn't even had a chance.

"Nothing to worry about," the lieutenant said. He looked at his watch, but said before he could see its face, "Must be two P.M." He looked at Brandes, smiled, and began to explain. "The units do this every day at two P.M. for about a half hour."

"Do what?"

"Watch." He looked into his rear-view mirror and pulled off to the shoulder to allow a car to pass. Then he bounced back up to the highway and followed it to the roadblock. "Watch closely," he told Brandes as they pulled alongside the stopped car. Two soldiers walked up to it, grinning, their weapons held loosely.

"You again?" one asked a woman in the car.

"Me again. I tried to beat you to it this time. Got stuck at a light. How long?" The woman, pretty and in her mid-thirties, asked.

"Same as usual," one young enlisted man said. She seemed to enjoy the man's attention. "You can take the detour, or"—he smiled more broadly—"you can join us for afternoon tea and biscuits."

"My husband would never understand," she bantered back. "I'll take the detour."

The soldier saluted, the woman waved. She backed up a few feet and then swung left, quickly crossing the oncoming lane and mounting swiftly up a hill and into a side road. Brandes said nothing; he intended to say nothing until the lieutenant spoke.

The enlisted man approached the Jeep. "Lieutenant, sir," he said. "I'll have this out of your way in a minute."

"No." The officer shook his head. "We'll take the detour."

The soldier nodded and saluted at the same time. The

lieutenant returned the salute and turned up the steep slope that quickly curved, leaving the road hidden behind scrub bushes and small pines.

"I took the detour on purpose," the lieutenant said. "I don't know where that Myers Road you mentioned is, but I do know this one. A lot more scenic than the main route, and it won't take more than a few minutes off our time."

Brandes knew that to be true. "I'm not sure I'm following all this," he said.

"Nothing to it. The colonel's idea. Every day at two P.M. exactly, all roads in and out of Lyle are blocked by our people. We've turned it into a game—like you just saw. People are *used* to stopping. They figure it's part of the game, and they're willing to play along. Most people are pleasant, I guess."

"You mean you're telling them you're practicing for a quarantine?"

The lieutenant snorted. "'Course not. We tell *our* men that. And then *they* feel they're putting something over on the civilians when they them tell it's practice for flood emergencies or other natural disasters."

Brandes rolled his eyes. "Wheels within wheels."

"Yep. And so far, all of them spinning along nicely."

Brandes didn't trust himself to comment on that. "So when the exercise calls for the quarantine to go into effect," he asked, "no one will make any fuss or think anything is out of the ordinary?"

"Right."

"Interesting idea. Of course, it would be quite a bit different if it ever was the real thing."

"How do you mean?" The officer actually was curious.

"Those pleasant people you were talking about?" The officer nodded; Brandes continued, "They wouldn't be so pleasant."

They drove on in silence for several minutes.

# NINE

THE DETOUR HAD NOT COST THEM MORE THAN
ten minutes, and Brandes had welcomed the extra time spent on
the more scenic road. Now, from a distance, as the Jeep
approached the hotel, Brandes saw several persons walking up its
covered stairs. Each carried one or two cases. Outside, three cars
and one minivan pulled away. Brandes guessed he was seeing the
arrival of the rest of the CDC team.

"They're really going all out," the lieutenant commented.

They pulled up in front of the hotel. Brandes stepped out.

"I'll tell the colonel we're terrific buddies by now," he said.
"Next time I see him."

"I didn't get anything from you," the lieutenant said, looking
hopefully at the doctor.

"Don't bullshit a bullshitter, Lieutenant." Brandes was becoming annoyed.

The sound of footsteps on the stairs to the upper two floors of
the Tower were the only sign of the new arrivals as Brandes
entered the hotel lobby. He walked to the desk.

"Johnny," he said. "Business still is improving."

"Yeah. I could do without it. Well, I'm not really complaining. You know what I mean."

"Yeah." He asked the hotel owner for his single suitcase, took the proffered key to his room, and left by the side entrance.

His room was in the annex, fifty yards away, on the rear edge of the hotel's property. When he entered, he almost regretted that he hadn't taken a room in the main hotel. Its rooms might be dated and he probably would have had to share a bathroom, but the annex was sterile—a modern motel in every sense.

The double bed covered in a textured blue spread dominated the room. There was a foldup rack for unpacking luggage, one chair, and a nightstand. Across from the foot of the bed was a television; atop it was a small box that controlled the cable selections. There was a bureau and a small closet and a bathroom with both tub and shower.

He wanted to get to the hospital. Already his—he felt—unnecessary visit to Lawrence had cost him lunch. He wanted to begin to get a grip on the situation and to be free for dinner. He already had decided to take Wismer to the airport restaurant.

The motel room depressed him, so he was glad he'd decided to accept Wismer's offer of lodging.

Brandes picked the white plastic liner out of the trash basket he found in the bathroom. He opened his suitcase and dumped many of its items into the bag.

He closed the case and put it on the floor of the closet. He straightened, hesitated, and then decided that, whatever the situation, it would have to wait a few more minutes. He was tired from his roundabout trip and his meeting with Lawrence. He needed a fast shower and a change of clothes.

Much of the afternoon already had passed by the time he had dried himself and dressed casually in jeans and a sports shirt—long-sleeved, despite the heat. The temperature did not make Brandes uncomfortable, and somehow he'd always found short sleeves distasteful. He wore no T-shirt beneath the lightly striped shirt. A medal, silver, was barely visible at the neckline. It had been given him by his grandfather, and while it was a religious medal, it had held no religious significance for the older man. It held none for Brandes, either. He wore it as a tribute to the close relationship he had shared with his grandfather.

His mother, when she was alive, had regularly checked the medal for tarnish. It was her contention that as long as it was shiny he was not ill. He'd never disputed her; once he'd begun medical training he would remember her periodic inspections and smile.

If only it were that simple, he had thought.

Those were the days when he had all the answers. As his education proceeded, though, he found himself less sure that his mother had been wrong.

She had had a similar medal—and an uncanny trait none of his studies ever really explained. *Any* silver she wore turned shiny, even if encrusted with black oxidation when she put it on. Obviously, it was some peculiar biochemistry. Curious as he thought about it, he took the medal out from his shirt and looked at it. His mother would have been happy; it was mirror bright.

Brandes tossed his plastic bag into the rear seat of his rented car and drove toward the hospital.

The road to Lyle–Mount Saint Sydney Hospital took him past the Futures laboratory.

He would go to the lab later, perhaps even the following day. While he was eager to start—and more so to finish—he knew speed in the lab would be artificial "progress." Some things simply could not be rushed. Bacteria and viruses grew at their own pace.

This bug, like any other, would show itself in its own good time. The frenetic activity at the beginning of an investigation accomplished only that—a beginning.

But the earlier the tests and cultures were begun, the earlier answers would be found. Speed in that phase *was* essential. The CDC people would move fast until they reached the point that nature set the schedule. Then, once the organism was identified and isolated, the pace would increase again as they searched for a cure or preventive technique.

Brandes's own work, he suspected, largely would consist of

watching and thinking. Allenberg had not sent him to Lyle to centrifuge serum specimens. He was there to determine if the disease was manmade. If so, he would try to find out if it was an accidental product or if its virulent sweep through its victims was incorporated into its design.

His job was to try to think like Peter.

Brandes pulled into the hospital lot, entered the building. An electric tension, unlike the usual low-keyed-but-hurried pace of a hospital, suffused the atmosphere. Or, he wondered, was he projecting more of his own feelings, adding another overlay to an already complicated situation that certainly did not need his help to become both frightening and depressing?

A young woman, her eyes deepset, somewhat haunted, stood behind the reception counter.

"Dr. Shortell, please," Brandes asked.

"He's very busy. Are you ill?" She looked frightened as he asked. No, he thought. He was not bringing any imaginary fear with him. It was here and it was real.

"No. I'm a doctor."

"Oh." She relaxed. "Are you with the CDC?"

"Something like that."

She shrugged and spoke into a telephone. "He really is busy," she said. "Would you go up to the fourth-floor desk, please? The elevators are just around there . . ." She pointed to a turn in the corridor that led from the reception area. Brandes nodded and walked.

A uniformed guard sat behind a small desk just in front of the elevators. Brandes noticed the sergeant's stripes on his sleeves—and noticed too that the man was armed. He couldn't remember when he'd seen a hospital guard armed.

"Sir?" The guard's eyes were hard.

"I'm Dr. Alex Brandes. I'm here to see Dr. Shortell."

"Have you identification, sir?"

Brandes could *feel* that he'd not be allowed to proceed if he didn't. No excuse would work here, not now. This hospital, he thought, was a fortress with its defenders not yet certain whether they were keeping invaders out or prisoners in. He produced a driver's license.

"Doesn't say here you're a doctor."

"No."

"You have something that says you're a doctor?"

Brandes thought about it and didn't like the solution. He had only an old agency ID—which identified him as a doctor with the National Institutes of Health. It was one of several the agency had provided him. He produced it.

The guard handed him a pass after initialing it. Brandes clipped it to his breast pocket and walked to the elevators. He was alone as he rode to the fourth floor. He'd never been in this part of the hospital; his domain when he'd worked here was in the basement lab areas. As he stepped out, to his right was an open doorway. He passed through it to a small lounge area. A plaque in memory of Myer Jacobson announced that it was the patients' convalescent lounge. It was empty.

A bleaker room in which to heal Brandes could not imagine. The chairs and small couches were a variety of pastel vinyls. Some were marred; the plastic was brittle. The window that was one wall would have been more cheerful as a mural. Brandes could not understand it.

The hospital was located in one of the most picturesque parts of the country, and some architect had placed a window looking out on the six-story smokestack of the hospital's central power station.

Brandes stepped back through the doorway. Patients' rooms were on either side of the hallway. He looked at the numbers and the white plastic hubs that protruded from above the doors. Several were lit, and as he watched, he heard two chimes and saw two more lights flicker on. Patients were signaling their need for nurses.

None came down the corridor; Brandes found himself almost hoping that the reason was that the hospital was short-staffed or had lazy nurses, but he didn't believe it. The nurses simply could not keep up, he thought.

He walked ahead about fifty yards to the floor's nurses' station. It was very busy.

The metal carousel holding the aluminum-clad patients' charts hardly ever was still. One nurse or another, one or another lab-coated technician, and occasionally a doctor kept the thing seemingly in constant motion.

For several minutes no one paid attention to him. Finally a young nurse, pretty with large green eyes and waist-length black hair, noticed him.

"Can I help you?"

"I'm Dr. Alex Brandes. I want to see Dr. Shortell."

"Oh." She looked lost and confused. "He's here, I know. Kathy, do you know where Dr. Shortell is?" she called over her shoulder.

"He's in Pathology," another nurse answered.

"I'll call him," the first nurse said. "Oh, I won't have to," she said, looking past Brandes.

Brandes thanked her and waited, then turned. He looked back the way he had come. He saw a man come out of the elevator and knew it was Shortell.

The other doctor was as tall as he, Brandes guessed. The speed of his forward motion seemed to push his shoulders ahead of him. He wore a black tie, and a white hospital coat flapped about him. He reached the counter and did not stop to look at Brandes until the nurse pointed at him.

He immediately came over, hand extended. Shortell's grip was firm, the handshake hurried. He had intelligent eyes placed well in a fine face.

"I'm glad to meet you, Doctor. I've been expecting you." Before Brandes could question that, Shortell said, "Gerry Wismer told me you'd be over. He also told me to call you Alex. And he told me you'd gone on to meet our very own colonel.

He grinned, and Brandes decided he liked Shortell. It seemed his day to make quick decisions about men.

"Right." Brandes smiled back. "All true, and I underestimated Gerry once again."

*This man knows or guesses—already—about the army.*

"Common occurrence," Shortell said. "You know, until all this happened, I think I underestimated him too."

"Don't worry. He used to be one of my teachers in high school."

"Hmm. I guess things like this sometimes bring out new sides of people. I know I'm seeing some new sides of *me*. I'm reserving judgment on whether I like them until it's all over."

"Which will be soon."

A light flickered in Shortell's eyes, and Brandes quickly held up his hand. "No," he said. "There's nothing new that I know of. It's just that a situation like this can't remain as it is very long."

"You mean it will either get better or . . . worse."

"Just that. Can we talk a minute?"

"Sure. Sometimes I think I run around just to feel like I'm doing something. I'm not, you know." There was a blank, childlike quality to that statement. Brandes would have liked it better had the man been bitter when he said it.

They went into the nurses' lounge area and sat.

Shortell poured coffee without asking and placed a jar of nondairy creamer on the table with some envelopes of sugar and Sweet 'n Low. Brandes took two sugars and some of the powdery creamer. The coffee was hot and not bad; he'd expected "gray" coffee.

"How much do you know?" Shortell began.

"Not much about the disease itself. You've been working with it."

"Let's say I've been working, anyway."

"I've seen CDC work before. They'll help. All local doctors feel a little inadequate in situations like this. Otherwise, we wouldn't need CDC."

"Oh, I know all that. It's one of the things I'm learning about myself. I'm learning I can feel one way and know things are different. I'm also finding out I'm able to feel 'wrong' and act 'right,' if that makes any sense."

"I think so."

"The incubation is very fast," he said, becoming efficient. "I think it's faster in children. There's no doubt that the *progress* of the disease is faster in children and in old people. First complaints usually are about burning eyes. Occasionally the first thing the patient notices is neck stiffness.

"Within a few hours there is pain in most joints; for some reason, the hands seem most affected. The patients always are flexing their hands; their faces show it causes pain, but they can't seem to stop.

"The fever sets in early in the development. We've recorded them as high as a hundred and six in two kids." He paused, making certain Brandes had absorbed that and continued, "There is a gradual fluid buildup, but it's not confined to the respiratory system. The whole body seems to retain fluid—sometimes it seems sudden, and the extremities become edematous.

"When the fevers start we put them on D5W and piggyback antibiotics, KCl, and multivitamins. The fevers never break, and we have to discontinue the fluids after the retention phase starts. I've tried large doses of Lasix IM, but it takes so much to reach a threshold that I'm afraid of losing too much potassium despite the KCl."

"Do the electrolytes usually hold up?"

"No. That's the other thing. Potassium usually is low to begin with. I tried Aldactone as a diuretic to spare the potassium, but it doesn't work. The kidneys don't seem damaged at all; it's not a renal shutdown in the normal sense. It's just that the people don't piss." He paused and grinned. "I'm getting tired of using nice, proper medical terminology all day."

"I don't blame you. They don't piss."

"No. We're sending out some specimens to check hormone levels, but nothing's come back yet."

"Next?"

Shortell shrugged. "They just get worse. In some of the cases, the pain in the hands has been so bad we've had to give seventy-five of Demerol and fifty of Vistiril. The respiratory fluid continues to increase. We've tried respirators and oxygen, but it doesn't seem to help. And that's a strange thing. Even with the respiratory system shutdown, blood gases aren't bad."

"That doesn't make any sense."

"Sure as hell doesn't. I got somebody barely sucking wind and his blood oxygen isn't dropping."

"Then they don't die from pulmonary failure?"

"Sure they do. Their lungs fill up, their hearts stop, their brain waves go flat, and their body temperature stabilizes at room temperature."

"And there's no shortage of oxygen in the blood."

"And no excess of carbon dioxide. Lovely little bug, isn't it?"

"Sure is."

They finished their coffees without speaking again. Shortell looked tired. His eyes, unfocused, gazed passed Brandes's shoulder.

"You want to see one of them?"

"Very much."

The men got up. Shortell left the room first and called to one of the nurses.

"Mr. Bertoli, please."

The nurse spun the carousel. It picked up speed, and she braked it with her fingers and pulled out a chart. It was thick. Brandes guessed just about every test imaginable had been done to Mr. Bertoli, whoever he was. Brandes did not envy him.

Hospitals faced with the unknown and staffed by uncertain doctors could be a chamber of horrors for a patient. The number of ways medicine had devised to prod, poke, and prick a person outdid the Inquisition's. At least the Grand Inquisitor never said, "This won't hurt," Brandes thought.

He flipped through the different-colored sections of the chart, skipping the general information about age and occupation. The disease didn't seem to care and so he couldn't see why he should.

The first section was general chemistry. The electrolytes—chloride, carbon dioxide, potassium, and sodium—were just as Shortell had said. Potassium was low. That, combined with a normal carbon dioxide level, was enough to throw the balance to hell.

Heart and liver enzymes were normal, but Brandes knew that even if Mr. Bertoli had sustained heart damage the transaminase associated with the breakdown of heart tissue would not show up in the blood serum for forty-eight hours anyway. Bertoli had only been admitted that morning. They certainly were rushing him through the tests!

Bilirubin was normal. He skipped to hematology and the blood count was normal. There was no attack on the red cells and little increase in the white count.

It almost seemed that the body was not recognizing the invader as an enemy and marshaling its defenses. Hemoglobin and hematocrit were normal—both in keeping with Shortell's puzzling normal blood gases in corpses.

"We didn't order any IVP on Bertoli," Shortell said. "No point in it. We've tested everyone else's kidneys and found no damage."

"They just don't piss."

"Yeah," Shortell said and smiled weakly.

"Let's visit." Brandes closed the chart and handed it back to the nurse. He led the way down the hall. They entered one of the rooms. Two men occupied it. Both were connected to intravenous bags containing the pale yellow of dextrose and water. Smaller bags with antibiotics were connected to the tubes where they left the large, one-liter containers, piggybacked to the main IVs.

Brandes walked nearer one and saw that MVI (multivitamins) and KCI (potassium chloride) had been mixed into the dextrose; nurses' felt-tip scribbling on the bags' sides told the story. He noted the rate of drip of the bag nearest him and guessed that the solution would be exhausted in about six hours. By then, though, if the patient followed the pattern Shortell had outlined, he would be retaining so much of the fluid that the IV would be removed.

It was a no-win situation; Brandes certainly did not envy Shortell.

"This is Mr. Bertoli," Shortell said. "Dr. Brandes."

Brandes resisted the impulse to put out his hand, remembering what Shortell had told him about the painful symptoms. Indeed, Bertoli was wringing and flexing his hands, his face reflecting the discomfort it brought him. The fear in the man's face was unnerving.

Bertoli knew he was dying.

He nodded, and Bertoli responded, "Hello, Doctor. You the new one who's going to fix me up?"

"Dr. Shortell's doing everything that has to be done. Your hands hurt?"

"Getting worse, too."

"When did you first notice that something was wrong, Mr. Bertoli?"

"Early this morning. Real early. About five. It was just getting light out. I opened the drapes, and even that little bit of light hurt my eyes. They started to burn like hell."

"They didn't burn until you saw the light?"

"No."

Shortell looked interested; apparently he'd not known that. Brandes doubted it was important.

They talked a few more minutes with the man and turned to leave. Brandes noticed that the man in the second bed was not conscious.

"Was the other one comatose?" He asked when they were back in the hall.

Shortell looked surprised.

"Only at the end," he said. "I didn't tell you?"

Brandes shook his head.

"That's one of the cute things about it. That man was asleep; he'd probably just been given a shot of Demerol. They're with it right until the end. *Then* they just literally *lose* consciousness, become comatose. *Then* they just . . . die."

"No particular warning? No crisis?"

"Not a damn thing," Shortell said. "I've been with some of them. They just look at you. One man was in the middle of a sentence and he just stopped talking. It was like someone just pulled a switch and turned him off. He never regained consciousness."

"That's the damnedest thing I've ever heard."

"No, it's not," Shortell said. He stopped and looked at Brandes. "Nobody outside of the hospital, the CDC, and Colonel Lawrence knows this, but since this whole thing began somewhere around a hundred people of all ages, sexes, and occupations—the numbers really are guesses themselves at this point—simply have *stopped functioning*."

"Had their plugs pulled."

"*That's* the damnedest thing you ever heard."

# TEN

THE LAND ALWAYS HAD SOOTHED ALLENBERG; THE scene now before him both calmed and excited him, the emotions complementary rather than contradictory. He had chosen more than a decade earlier to live—at least to have his residence of record—in the western part of New Jersey. He spent as much time there as he could.

Elsewhere in the country, the "Garden State" nickname of New Jersey was considered a joke. Oil refineries and some of the most densely industrialized areas in the nation were all many visitors saw. But in other parts, the northwestern counties in particular, the term certainly applied. Knee-high grasses, amber near the stalks' tops but maintaining a deep green cast overall, rose and rolled with the contour of the hills.

Allenberg sat quietly on his porch, enjoying the view.

What excited him was the sight of his fifteen-year-old grandson, mounted well on a chestnut horse, Gramps, speeding across those hills, scything through grasses that bent to allow passage and sprung back as if undisturbed.

Jason rode well. He also enjoyed and did well in school, and he'd shown an uncommon ability to make friends and—subtly—

to end up dominant in most social situations without offending anyone; a useful talent.

Jason neared the farm's boundary to the north. He turned and came toward Allenberg at a gallop. "He gets better every day," Allenberg said, turning to his daughter, Sarah. She sat near him on the porch of the large old renovated house.

"I wish I could keep up with him."

Sarah was a strikingly attractive woman. Her figure was not what it once had been, he thought. But her face was beautiful, with crystal-blue eyes and soft, dark brown hair.

Perhaps, he'd thought, she'd let her figure go after a disastrous fourth marriage simply to discourage a fifth. "My face is my fortune," she'd claim, and she was right. Sarah was co-anchor on a local television news show—the camera saw her only from the bust up. Below, where her desk cut the view, she sat in tattered jeans and sandals.

Her proficiency in her profession provided a good living for her and Jason. It never had bothered her that she did not work in the more prestigious and even more lucrative New York press corps. She could, if she chose, he knew.

He also knew that Sarah was a woman quite capable of change at any stage of life; someday she just might change her mind and enter the city's higher-priced and higher-paced arena.

The last thing the head of an intelligence organization would seem to want was a daughter who was a journalist. For Allenberg, that simply was not true. The president would stare blankly and eventually sputter apoplectically if he ever learned that one of his most trusted intelligence agents had a reporter daughter. Allenberg long ago had decided to defuse his daughter's curiosity and to discourage her poking. It was his *method* that would have upset the president—greatly.

He told her virtually everything.

Allenberg watched his grandson's approach and grinned. What *really* would give the president nightmares would be learning that Allenberg also told a good deal to fifteen-year-old Jason. He came in handy.

The boy and his mother often had keen insights that Allenberg carefully considered. It certainly made for a unique situation and a unique family-professional relationship.

He wished Sarah had been able to find happiness with some man, though men who could handle his daughter were not easily found. Her last husband had followed a pattern set by the two previous ones. At first he'd loved the idea of being married to a television personality. That wilted quickly enough with the realization that many men had an "affair" with his wife every night in the privacy of their own homes. That thought, coupled with the fact that Sarah earned several times as much money as he did, sent Michael—the last one—drifting down a road familiar to Allenberg and his daughter.

"You should practice more," he told her. "You used to be pretty good on a horse."

"That was twenty-five pounds and five years ago."

"The years you won't recover."

"I know, I know. The pounds I can lose."

"I've never said that."

"No." She looked at him thoughtfully. "You know, Dad, now that I think about it, you're the only person I can think of who can say, 'I never said that,' and even mean he never hinted at it. *Does* my weight bother you? I really don't know."

"Yes."

She nodded thoughtfully. She was accustomed to getting direct answers like that from her father; she welcomed his attitude, a quality she had sought but never found in the men in her life.

"I'll lose it," she said.

He nodded and said nothing. He knew his daughter; he knew if she decided to lose twenty-five pounds, she could and would do it. Sarah had inherited much of his strength; little of her mother was apparent either in her looks or mind. Elizabeth had been a "good woman." For him, that was sufficient description and summary of his ex-wife.

Jason dismounted, secured Gramps to a rail, and came up the porch steps.

"He's fast today," he said. Jason was tall and broad, his eyes bright with the excitement of the ride. Allenberg was very proud of his grandson, of the boy's zeal for life. Jason had not set career aims—or rather he'd set *too* many—but Allenberg was certain he'd succeed at whatever he tried.

"You certainly seemed to enjoy it," he said.

"Always do. I wish I could race him . . ." he looked slyly at his grandfather and then at his mother. Entering the horse in a local county race had been Jason's latest project. Sarah was not yet convinced; Jason openly was seeking an ally in his grandfather. Allenberg grinned; he did not doubt the boy eventually would have his way.

"Hmpf," was the only answer he got from his mother. Jason smiled. It was definitely a step up from "no."

"How long will you be here?" Jason asked him.

"Only today. I've got some business. I'll try to get back for the weekend."

The ringing of the telephone cut off a comment from Jason. "I'll get it," he said, and loped into the house, his arms swinging.

"I wonder when he'll get coordinated," his mother said. "He's still got arms and legs where nobody else does."

"You've seen him dance," Allenberg replied. "He's coordinated when it counts."

"You mean, when there are girls around."

"Like I said. When it counts."

"It's for you, Grandpa," Jason called. "Sounds like Mr. Kracke." Allenberg had expected that. The situation in Lyle was a pressing one; he hoped there was good news. It was all too easy to look at his daughter and grandson and at the gentle landscape and picture them in Lyle.

"Trouble," was all Kracke said at first.

Allenberg tensed. "Brandes?"

"No. Nothing like that. He's in Lyle and presumably doing what he thinks best. He's still looking over his shoulder a lot; maybe we scared him a little too much."

"Better to be sure we'd get him there. I don't like it, but Alex is probably our best chance for the serious answers. It would annoy him if I told him, but he's got a lot more potential as an agent than he likes to think. What's the trouble?"

"It's not clear," Kracke said. It wasn't like him to call with something indefinite. That alone Allenberg did not like. Kracke was an agent, of course, but more than that. He was one of the most capable people Allenberg ever had worked with—and right up until a policy decision had to be made, Kracke did work *with* and not simply *for* Allenberg.

"Tell me."

"Ten minutes ago I received an envelope by messenger. There was a key in it and an address in Greenwich Village. The only other word written on the note was *Lyle*."

Allenberg said nothing. The cryptic message and package practically announced that someone had intentionally set a disease loose.

Everything, he realized, had changed. Suddenly, simply, completely.

"What took you ten minutes?"

"Arranging a helicopter. It should be at your place within a half hour."

"You're that nervous."

"Yes."

"Get a team ready to go," he said.

"In the works. I don't like this very much."

"No."

"What do we tell Brandes? Or do we?"

"We'll have to. If someone is claiming responsibility for this thing, it could change the entire line of approach he has to take."

"I don't know just what he'll change, but like I said: he's got the instincts of a good agent. I trust he'll choose a proper course."

"You don't really expect him to come up with a cure, do you?"

"Of course not. I just wanted *him* there. It feels right."

Kracke never had questioned such a reaction from Allenberg and knew he never would.

"Don't call him yet, though. Let's see what's in the apartment."

"Should I plan to go to Lyle?"

"Are we still in contact there?"

"I don't think you have to go. Not yet. He still thinks he's in danger, so he'll be careful. And I'm sure that if he finds anything he'll get to us right away. But don't rule out a trip altogether."

"For both of us?"

"Let's see what that key leads us to first."

Allenberg hung up the phone and went back out to the porch.

"I'll be leaving in a few minutes," he said. "Jason, would you get me a beer, please?"

"Sure." The boy was gone.

"I take it your ride is coming?" Sarah tilted her head as she spoke.

"Yes. It will be here soon."

She nodded and said nothing. He knew that her mind must be whirling frantically and also knew she'd never ask about his business. It was tacit policy that the family only become involved at his behest.

The flight had been routine, the helicopter landing near Battery Park City in New York, where Kracke waited with two other men. Allenberg got into their plain blue car, and the driver without a word turned onto West Street, using the exit for the World Trade Center to cut across the oncoming traffic.

"Anything else?"

"No," Kracke answered. "We called local police in to seal off the block. They were ordered to stay away from the building."

Allenberg nodded. He wanted to get there and leave as quickly as possible. New York's press corps was *very* professional. A blocked street wouldn't go unnoticed long, and he didn't want reporters on the other side of the barricades, armed with press cards technically giving them the right to cross all police lines. He could, of course, delay that while they yelled and protested, but he knew they eventually would win.

The car soon passed into the fringes of the West Village, turning onto Tenth Street, heading east. The driver turned right on Seventh Avenue and again just past Sheridan Square. Allenberg knew the area, and he knew the block that was closed to motor and pedestrian traffic by sky-blue and white city police cars.

His driver stopped, and a police lieutenant approached the car. He studied their identification and faces and then nodded. All four got out of the car.

Kracke and Allenberg inched past the wooden horses the police had erected. The other agents took several items of equipment from the car's trunk and then followed.

When they reached the address, the agents took the lead. There were no police outside the building. Kracke had done his job well, as usual. The police had been asked—*ordering* the New York City police department could be counterproductive—to close the block; they'd not been given the specific building address. Still, Allenberg very much liked working with the city police, by far the most professional force he'd ever encountered. Privately he'd often admitted he preferred dealing with New York cops to working with other federal agents.

The building was a five-floor walkup. The slip of paper in the envelope had given 1-C as the apartment that the key presumably opened. One of the agents checked doorbells.

"Downstairs," he said. "It's a basement apartment."

All four men went to the rear of the dim hallway and turned into a stairway leading into even deeper gloom. Allenberg looked about; a naked lightbulb hung from the ceiling, but it was not lit. The apartment was at the end of the hall. There was no name on the door; there had been none on the upstairs mailbox.

Allenberg and Kracke stepped back, making way for the other men. Professionally, proficiently, they unpacked the cases they carried and began sweeping instruments over the door.

"The door is steel," one said. "Only the frame's wood."

One of the men, wearing headphones, moved a disk-shaped object over the door. "No metal other than the door," he said, "and the kind of reading you'd expect from studs and things in the frame."

Another carried a tapered probe connected to a plastic tube. He watched a meter on a hand-held black box as he moved the point around the door's outline. The meter did not register.

"Reads clean," he said. The mechanical "nose" had not sensed explosives.

The team, however, was not satisfied with that—only slightly less nervous.

The first man reached into another case and removed a small tool. He fitted it to the doorframe near the lock, flicked a switch, and braced himself as a steel blade ate quickly into the wood. Within a few seconds he had removed a chunk. The lock no longer engaged the jamb; the door was free to open.

The two waved Kracke and Allenberg back still further and then very gently began opening the apartment. Both swept flashlights around the growing opening. Finally the door was open enough to allow entry.

One of the men went first, then gestured to the second, who brought in a powerful electric lantern and set it in the middle of the room.

The "gift" key never was used. No one ever had even *thought* to use it, any more than anyone intended to flick on a light switch. At last one of the men came out and motioned for Allenberg and Kracke to join them.

There was no furniture in the single-room apartment. The men began in one corner and systematically examined the walls and floors, their hand-held lights augmenting the brilliant white given off by the lantern.

At least there is little to search, Allenberg thought. And little to find?

He and Kracke remained in the middle of the room, moving only to prevent their shadows from interfering with the other agents. Ten minutes passed.

"Nothing, sir," one man reported. "Shall we open that door

now?" He gestured to the only other door in the room. Probably, Allenberg thought, a closet.

"Yes."

The team once again used their equipment to test the door; again, when the results were negative they inched the door slowly open. They stopped when it was open only a few inches and stepped back.

Allenberg made to move forward; one of the agents motioned him back. He might be their boss under most circumstances, but here he did not challenge their judgment.

"What is it?"

"I don't know, sir. It's a damned funny noise."

Everyone was silent, and Allenberg thought he could hear something also. It was like whispering. "Open it," he said. "Carefully."

The agent nodded and placed both hands on the side of the door. The other man moved back also—there was nothing to be gained by risking more than one man.

The door swung open hesitantly, its hinges slowed by multiple layers of paint. The sound got louder, but nothing happened.

The agent who had opened the door swung his flashlight toward the interior. Allenberg could see his profile and could see a look of mild confusion on the man's face.

Allenberg and Kracke walked toward the door, to peer into what indeed was a closet. It was empty of clothing; its uniqueness lay where the light shone. Allenberg looked down at the floor.

There was none.

It took a few seconds to register, but where the floor should have been there was—a river. The rushing water was the source of the odd sound.

Kracke grunted. "I once was told there is still a canal under Canal Street," he said. "I didn't know about any rivers going under people's houses."

"Hell of a way to get rid of bodies," one of the agents muttered and immediately looked apologetically at his superiors.

Allenberg's attention shifted as the agent lifted the beam of his light. A tripod with spindly legs had been mounted over the hole. Suspended from its apex was the top half of an hour glass.

It was half-filled with what looked like sand or salt. A thin stream of it poured slowly from the glass and disappeared into the water.

Allenberg shivered. He motioned everyone back from the closet.

"Don't touch that thing," he told the agents. "And don't let anyone else touch it until I get a sanitary team in here." They nodded, said nothing. Allenberg knew they were uneasy. Faced with a living enemy they would be nerveless; this intangible potential threat was . . . different.

He led Kracke outside.

"Keep the block sealed," he told the police lieutenant who by then had come up to the building's entrance. "I'm sending in another team. When the press get here tell them it's a bomb scare." He turned to Kracke. "Let's get back to the car. You drive."

Neither spoke until Allenberg used his car radio to issue instructions.

"I guess that answers some questions," Allenberg said. "Some-one is behind Lyle's trouble."

"And is planning to give us more trouble."

"What next?"

"Keep yourself busy," he told Kracke. "Try traces on the key. When the contamination team is through, get Forensic in there. We won't find anything, but what the hell."

"You seem sure the cleanup people will give it a clean bill of health."

"They won't be able to on the spot. But I'm betting the lab clears what's in that container. Whoever planned this wants to *demonstrate* just how easily the disease could be introduced.

"The closet was an interesting touch. It certainly makes its point. They *can* strike *anywhere*. We always knew it, but that damned closet makes it something you feel. An effective psychological touch. They're professional, James."

97

"Yes. What do you think they'll do next?"

"Contact us, of course, when they're damned good and ready. They can't wait too long—the situation in Lyle won't allow it. They haven't got leverage if we find a cure. Whatever they want, they'll demand soon. But not too soon; we are to sweat a while."

"I think we should notify Brandes."

"Yes." Allenberg sighed. "I wish we didn't have to. He's a reluctant ally as is. This probably means that his brother had something to do with the bug. He won't like it."

"No."

# ELEVEN

THE SITUATION SHORTELL FACED, BRANDES thought, was not very much different from that encountered by doctors collating data on AIDS. Shortell had said that nearly a hundred people so far had died from this disease—a number that was largely guesswork. For all medical science really knew, the AIDS virus might have been around for years, its victims being classified as pneumonia cases or liver cancer cases or any number of things.

How many had died of *this* particular disease before it had been recognized as a "new" illness? Shortell only could guess. Brandes saw no reason, though, to question Shortell's estimate.

Few diseases could kill in such a way that it appeared the switch controlling someone's life force had been turned off, Brandes thought. *Few? Think of one . . .*

Assuming that the figure was correct, nearly one hundred persons had been "death processed." They had been pronounced dead, embalmed, viewed, buried, or cremated.

It wouldn't be more than a matter of hours, he thought—a day at the most—before the authorities would step in and start segregating the corpses of victims of the so-far unknown killer. Then all hell would break loose.

*What the hell could kill you by causing your respiration to stop and still not deplete the oxygen in your blood?*

Electric shock. And what else?

*Blank.* At least for now, he thought. *Blank.* And let it remain that way.

Brandes drove slowly toward Wismer's house. He loved the old place. It was enormous. It fitted the retired teacher the way a very large tin can would fit a very small marble. And yet, he thought, Wismer belonged in that house. Although he used relatively little of the available space, Brandes could not visualize the man in a smaller place. The idea amused Brandes, and he smiled as he drove. He preferred to think about a past Lyle and his old teacher than about the patients he'd just seen in the hospital.

Brandes looked forward to a relaxing dinner with Wismer. He wondered if he would get some questions answered. Their encounter at the Tower had posed some pretty big ones. Almost automatically now, he looked in the car's rear-view mirror. He was reassured by the empty road behind him and still not sure if that *should* be reassuring. It meant that the people intent on stopping him were not there; it also, however, meant that Kracke or his agents were not there.

When he reached Wismer's house, he parked the car and went to the rear door. Wismer's car was not in the driveway; Brandes was pleased to find, though, that the door had not been locked.

He walked in, passed through the spacious kitchen that still was equipped with a massive old black stove. Battered aluminum pots and pans hung over a central work area. He didn't know if Wismer cooked. The place just seemed too big for the preparation of morning bacon and eggs.

Brandes entered the living room. Like most of the house, it had a ten-foot high ceiling. A marble-façaded fireplace dominated the room; one wall was totally covered with books, and a small stool had been placed in one corner of the library wall.

Brandes went to Wismer's well-stocked bar and poured a gin and tonic. He looked around, spotted a very inviting overstuffed chair and relaxed, hoping that Wismer would not be gone too long. "People" coming after him dominated his thinking. One man, two, could come through the same door he had used, slip by the black iron stove and the battered pots, and quietly move into the living room.

He couldn't resist turning his head slightly; no one was at the kitchen door. He thought about locking the back door. Knowing it was there, open for anyone at all, was like a physical coldness on the back of his neck. Brandes's mind could, he felt, reach out through the kitchen and *touch* that open door.

Eventually he yielded. He got up, walked through the kitchen, and latched the door. He left the chain loose; presumably Wismer would have a key for the lock, and he wanted the man to be able to get in. It was, after all, his house.

He returned to the chair after refreshing his drink. Alone and not on the move for the first time that day, he tried to relax, to think. Instead, he remembered.

Brandes thought back to the small hotel in which he'd stayed in Tel Aviv. It was only one block away from the Mediterranean and only two blocks away from another hotel of similar size—or what had been a hotel of similar size.

Two weeks before his arrival for the scientific conference the agency had ordered him to attend, six PLO terrorists had landed on the thin strip of beach in a rubber raft. They had taken explosives, guns, and a single rocket launcher up the beach and had aimed it at the other hotel.

Brandes tried to picture the roiling smoke and ballooning ball of flame that must have erupted when the rocket hit.

Forty-three people, some Israeli but mostly visitors, had died. When Brandes had seen the place, it was a pile of rubble—reduced to dust in seconds.

The Israeli authorities had been understandably jittery at the time he'd arrived in Tel Aviv. They had provided what, only in restrospect, was an amusing introduction to the man he would grow to like—and then cause to be killed.

Brandes had just finished showering before dinner. Suddenly the lights in his room had gone out. He'd opened the door when he heard running feet. There were loud mechanical clicks; it had taken seconds for him to realize it was the sound of cocking machine guns. Then he'd begun to feel fear.

The blackout didn't last long, though. The lights had come on in another few seconds, and Brandes had found himself watching a bizarre tableau.

Four Israeli soldiers, all heavily armed, stood a few feet away. Their weapons were leveled at a disheveled, middle-aged man in a bathrobe and with wet hair. In his right hand he held a hair dryer. The damned thing, Brandes thought, looked for all the world like an outsized pistol of strange, even alien, design.

The scene had all elements of high comedy. A wet, middle-aged man was holding off four young, tough, trained Israeli soldiers with a ConAir.

One officer who spoke English talked to the man, looked at the dryer, began to chuckle, and issued an order. The other men began giggling, too. It was the kind of giggle that only the relaxation of intense tension can produce. They'd lowered their guns, turned, and left.

The wet man saw Brandes and grinned sheepishly.

"I was using a voltage converter," he said. "It started smoking and blew the lights out, I'm afraid. And then . . ." he gestured after the retreating soldiers.

"You wouldn't have stood a chance with that thing, anyway," Brandes said and smiled. He stepped forward and introduced himself.

And that was how he had met Ernst Hoeckle of East Germany.

Thinking about Hoeckle sharpened his memories of the men who actually had pulled the triggers. It sharpened his thoughts about the *type* of men who had killed Ernst. It sharpened his visions of what men like that now would be doing—with Alex Brandes as the target. And more than ever, the one thing that didn't fit into his picture of such men was the fact that no further attempt had been made on his life.

That they would know he had come to Lyle was a given. Shit, he thought, if they can find me in the middle of a foggy night more than a dozen miles offshore, they sure as hell know I'm here. Perhaps they had received new orders. Perhaps. But that, he knew, was not something to count on—ever. He had to continue assuming each step of the way that he was in danger. He had to hope there was a Kracke around to step in at the right moment.

Brandes looked at his watch. Six-thirty. He felt as though it were midnight—three days later. He doubted he'd have any trouble sleeping that night.

There was a scraping sound in the kitchen. Gerry Wismer, of course, he told himself, but the stomach knot was there anyway; he rose from the chair quietly, ready to move if he had to.

"Alex?" It was Wismer.

"In here. Sampling your bar goods." The knot took longer to relax than it had taken to gather itself together.

"Sample me one. Wild Turkey and soda."

Brandes moved to the bar and poured Wismer's drink, adding some gin to his own. Wismer came in the door, moved quickly to the chair Brandes had just left, and sat.

"Just as I figured," he said. "Nice, warmed-up chair. *Everybody* grabs this chair if I'm not here to grab it first or I can't lure them out of it."

Brandes smiled and handed Wismer his glass, condensation already making the outside wet enough to drip onto the carpeting. He sat on a nearby sofa.

"How'd your day go?" Wismer asked.

"Fast."

Wismer grunted.

"I met our colonel, and I met Jonathan Shortell."

"What did you think of Jono?"

"He seems competent, and I think that when he's not so hassled, he might even be a very friendly man."

"He is. He's a good man. Did you get to the lab?"

103

"No. It was too late, and I've had a hell of a day. All I want to do is get something to eat and relax as much as possible. Get some sleep. I'll get to the lab tomorrow morning and may swing back to the hospital and visit Pathology."

Wismer nodded and took a long drink.

"I went to the lab," he said.

Brandes raised an eyebrow. "Investigating on your own?"

"It's my ass on the line here, too. Besides, I didn't think you'd make it, and I figured that if there was anything worth knowing up there I could fill you in tonight."

"Is there?"

"Just work. Technicians playing with eggs and setting up incubators, and secretaries shuffling a lot of papers. One of the CDC people was going through Peter's papers. I doubt if anyone's found anything there yet. I'm not even sure they'd recognize it if they did."

"That's really the main reason I'm here, I guess," Brandes said. "Maybe I'll see something in what Peter left that no one else will."

Wismer nodded. "Have you decided when you're going to see your father?" he asked softly.

Brandes looked into his glass a moment, swirling what remained of an ice cube. "No. I know I'll have to if I can't find anything in the lab. But I always can hope, can't I?"

"Even if you do find something, Alex, you should go."

"I don't think he'll need my contribution of sympathy for Peter."

"We'll see. Let's eat."

Brandes rose gladly. He took Wismer's empty glass, drained his own, and went back to the bar. He rinsed both and turned them over on a towel neatly folded along the bar's edge.

"Good housekeeper material," Wismer said.

"You've got to be if you live on a boat."

Brandes followed Wismer out the door. They took Brandes's rented car. The airport parking lot had a respectable number of

104

cars in it, most of them owned by diners and not flyers. Still, as they walked into the lobby, a small craft landed. Three passengers got off. Brandes didn't know them, and all three passed quickly into and then through the tiny terminal. Outside, Brandes knew, there would be soldiers dutifully marking down the arrivals.

The plane almost immediately began to taxi again, turned into the wind, and in a few moments rose from the runway and was on its way to its next stop.

"No one got on the plane," Wismer said. "No one left."

"So what?"

"Oh, I don't know. Just thought I'd say something, I guess."

The restaurant was much as Brandes remembered it; he found that to be more comforting than he'd expected.

"See?" Wismer said, as if reading his thoughts. "Life goes on fairly normally." Wismer's uncanny knack for getting inside his head could become worrisome. The men let a middle-aged hostess lead them to a table that overlooked the runway, though Brandes doubted there would be much to see out there.

"May I get you a cocktail?" a waitress asked.

Brandes didn't even hesitate. He wondered briefly if Wismer would wear a disapproving look, but the older man didn't and in fact ordered almost at the same time.

"Manhattan up," Brandes said.

"Dewar's and soda."

Brandes opened his menu. Most of the appetizers were seafood—not a favorite of his. He decided on French onion soup and a beef kabob with chunks of filet mignon on a bed of wild rice. Wismer selected chicken francaise after escargot.

"Bread?" she asked. "It's all home baked. Pumpernickel, rye, and coconut muffins."

Brandes and Wismer both chose pumpernickel, and she carefully removed slices with the tongs and set them down onto their plates.

"When you're ready, gentlemen," she said, "please feel free to visit the salad bar."

Brandes almost had forgotten that. The airport restaurant's salad bar was one of its prime attractions. Never in the city had he ever encountered one like it.

He tore off a small piece of the warm bread, spread it with butter, and began eating. He was very hungry.

"Salad?" Brandes asked.

Wismer nodded, and both men got up. If anything, the salad bar had improved. There was a good assortment of hot and cold meats, cheeses, shrimp, and crabmeat in addition to lettuce and other vegetables.

Brandes created a substantial plate for himself, allowing room for the house special he remembered best. It was, after all, the airport restaurant's crock of famous homemade baked beans that always had made the salad bar outstanding.

From the outset of the meal it was apparent that Wismer's intent was to not talk about the current problem. Instead, he began to reminisce.

"Remember when you blew up my sink?"

Brandes grinned. "Which time?"

Both men laughed.

They had finished their entrees when Wismer looked over Brandes's shoulder. One of the few things Brandes did not like about the restaurant was that there were two entrances, and here he'd chosen to face the busier doorway. He studied Wismer's face, but he didn't seem alarmed.

"Well, looks like we'll be able to get a little medical update," he said. "And offhand I'd say that this crisis has done at least one good thing for our local physician." He chuckled.

Brandes turned, and he thought he would lose his dinner.

Not any stretch of his imagination could have prepared him for what he saw. His eyes briefly noted Shortell—*very* briefly. After that they stayed fixed, totally immobile, staring at the strikingly attractive blond woman with him.

Wismer must have felt Brandes stiffen almost immediately. "What is it, Alex?"

"Let's get out of here, Gerry. Now."

"Can't. Jonathan's spotted us. Hope he introduces us."

Just what I need, Brandes thought.

Cynthia had not yet seen him. He was certain of that. His own stare had broken when Wismer had spoken, and he'd turned quickly away. The wrenching in his guts would not stop.

*Damn!*

The situation had been complicated enough. Peter dead. People in his hometown dying. Someone trying to kill him. Allenberg pressing the right buttons. *I don't need this.*

Then Shortell and Cynthia were at the table. It took all Brandes's willpower to look up, and when he did meet Cynthia's friendly gaze, he saw that it continued to be friendly only because it was fixed there by simple shock. Trauma. Undoubtedly very much like that he felt.

"Hello," Shortell said. "I'd like you to meet Dr. Cynthia Ellis. This is Gerry Wismer and this is Dr. Alex Brandes."

Wismer rose. Brandes tried to.

"A very great pleasure," Wismer said, and his eyes immediately and fleetingly flicked toward Brandes.

"Dr. Ellis and I have met," was all he could stammer. *A pretty trivial comment*, he thought. *We've met. Boy, have we met!*

Cynthia didn't look as though she was enjoying the situation any more than he.

"Have you worked together before?"

"On occasion," she said. Her voice had not changed. Nothing about her had, he thought.

"I guess problems like we've got here could be an old home week for people in your jobs," Shortell mused. He apparently, Brandes thought, had not picked up on the tension, not as Wismer had. "I see you're about done"—he gestured to the table—"but maybe we can join you for a drink before we have dinner."

Brandes didn't know what to say; Cynthia wasn't having any luck either. Wismer stepped in. *Thank you, professor.*

"I think we'd better get along," he said. "Alex has had one hell of a day. I do look forward to seeing you again," he said to Cynthia and winked. "You're definitely the best addition that Lyle's had in a long time."

Cynthia smiled weakly, said nothing. Brandes rose fully and nodded to both of them. Perhaps his eyes rested on her a moment longer than would have been normal—he didn't know—but he did get the feeling then that Shortell had begun to recognize that something he didn't understand was happening.

"I'll probably see you tomorrow," Brandes told Shortell.

The other doctor nodded, and Wismer and Brandes left, Brandes scooping up the check from the table. He wanted to find his waitress and pay quickly. Wismer understood.

The drive back to Wismer's house was silent.

Wismer unlocked the back door and both entered. Brandes didn't even feel an urge to check the house. He really didn't care at that moment if there were people inside waiting for him, waiting to kill him.

*After five years*, he thought, *Cynthia!*

Wismer did not even wait. He went to the bar, poured two generous portions of Remy, and handed one to Brandes. Both sat, silent for several minutes.

"Will this complicate things, Alex?" Wismer finally asked.

"No," he said.

"I take it you knew her. Isn't that a clever way to ask such a thing? I can't think of anything original. But I'd like to help if I can."

Brandes knew that was true. Wismer's was not idle curiosity. He really only wanted to know what the schedule of the private bomb ticking in Alex Brandes was because he really did want to help.

And *that* helped.

"We lived together for about a year," he said and sipped. "Nearly a year. I loved her."

"You still love her."

"Yes. No. But it's different. I have no regrets, Gerry. What did not develop between us simply could not develop between us. I guess I feel sadness as much as love, sad that things couldn't have been different."

"Bonding," Wismer said.

"What?"

"Bonding. It's different than falling in love. People should talk about *fallings* in love, plural. We've got the capacity to do that quite a few times. And it's real love.

"Bonding's different. It might even quite literally be chemical. One day you are someplace and a woman is in the same place and you look at her and something inside you just . . . attaches itself. I don't know how to word it."

"You're doing pretty well."

"It's like geese," his teacher said. Brandes looked at him with an eyebrow raised, the rim of his glass cutting the brow line as he raised it.

"You know, there are a few hours after they hatch," Wismer continued, "when geese are very vulnerable. The first thing they see they think they are. Fortunately that's usually another goose. Pity the poor baby that sees a human first."

"Sounds like a good way to make a neurotic goose."

Wismer nodded. "It is. People differ only in a few respects. That's my theory, anyway. For one thing, it can happen to us any time, and that's why I think there may be a physical, chemical thing involved. For another, subsequent experience can *show* us that the relationship can never be. We may even be able to accept that. But we can't, no matter how hard we try, get rid of the gut feeling. The bonding. Am I close?"

"Yes, Gerry. You are. Maybe you're closer than I ever was. The only thing is . . ." he hesitated.

Wismer didn't. "You aren't totally convinced that there's no hope at all. You always, somewhere inside you, think it might be possible. Right?"

"Yeah." Brandes's voice was rough but low. "Yeah. I guess that's it. What do I do about it?"

"You don't want a hell of a lot." Wismer grinned at him; Brandes had to smile back. "Maybe tell me about it."

Brandes thought about that. He'd not wanted—ever—to discuss Cynthia with anyone. But with Wismer it was different, the time was different. And Cynthia would be a factor in what happened in Lyle in the days to come: Her presence could, if he let it, cripple his own efforts to isolate Peter's Pet.

*Should I already call it that?*

*I guess some part of me knew that all along. Don't jump to conclusions . . . yet.*

His thoughts whirred, and he suspected that she felt something similar. If so, the Centers for Disease Control might be about to lose the effectiveness of a very competent epidemiologist named Cynthia Joy Ellis.

His goblet-shaped crystal glass held enough for a healthy swallow, and it still would have some left over. He wouldn't have to get up for a refill.

"We met shortly after three A.M. on a Tuesday in a bar in midtown Manhattan," Brandes began. He laughed sans humor. "Nothing like a little accuracy now and then in one's recollections." Wismer said nothing.

Brandes more or less rambled on from there. Wismer didn't interrupt. Brandes told him about the first night he'd seen her and how he didn't see her again for nearly three months.

"Somehow she always was in the back of my mind. And I'd only seen her for *five* minutes and even then didn't even say hello! Bonding, you say. I guess I believe you." He'd next seen her in the bar on St. Patrick's Day. Cynthia had worn a brilliant green dress that set off her hair and her blue eyes and would have launched anybody's thousand ships.

Brandes, certainly a man of the world by then, a world traveler—an occasional *secret agent*—had followed her at a distance like a shy puppy as she walked Fifth Avenue and watched the parade. Even as he told Wismer the story, he had to grin, remembering the way he'd behaved. Finally, he spoke to

110

her. After that, it had been easy, ridiculously easy. Almost as though it had been preplanned by a third party.

One night of riding the Staten Island ferry, a first kiss. Struggling to find a parking spot, settling for one six blocks from her apartment, and walking back as the sun rose. Making love to her in the morning, sleeping next to her the rest of the day. Seeing her that night. Having her sublet her apartment and move in with him within a month.

Avalanche. Events had come like bouncy, energy-bloated boulders bounding down a steep slope. Nothing could stop them; nothing got in their way. He loved her, and she loved him.

At that point, Brandes felt he did deserve a refill. He gestured. Without a word Wismer took the bottle from the bar, walked to the sofa, and poured. Then he sat.

Then, Brandes told him, it all ended as incredibly swiftly as it had begun.

"We were in bed one night," he said, and suddenly didn't feel drunk anymore. "She said that the lease on her apartment was going to expire the next day. I told her that was no problem. She was subletting it—it didn't cost us anything. I told her to renew the lease and keep her tenant.

"She refused. She said she wanted to let the lease expire. God, Gerry, all I could see was a lone door closing, leaving me trapped. If she had no place to go . . . and if we had problems later on . . . and I wanted to get rid of her—well, how *could* I kick her out when she had no place to go?

"I could see that coming, Gerry. It was a trap. I knew it, and she knew it. I told her to renew the lease the next day or pack and leave. It was as simple as that. She left. If only she hadn't pushed, Gerry . . ."

"Maybe you'd have found something else." Those were the first words Wismer had spoken since Brandes began. "But I don't know that. I'm sorry it didn't work out for you."

Brandes nodded. "I never could get her out of my head," he said. "Still can't. But that's the damnedest part of it. I really don't think anything between us ever *could* work. I just feel sad that it

111

couldn't. Working with her isn't going to help. This bonding thing may be deeper than even you think. I don't need reminders—not any *more* reminders. Shit, Gerry, I still *live* with her.

"The 'Cynthia Joy' became 'CJ.' Then I abbreviated *that*. 'CJ' became 'siege.' The *Siege*."

# TWELVE

AFTER A SHOWER IN THE APARTMENT HE MAIN-
tained in Manhattan, Allenberg was back within a few blocks of
where he had traced "the message." Or *half a message*.

He ordered a shot of Jameson's and a tap beer.

"You look terrible, Adrian," Mike the bartender said.

"Thank you."

"Oh, you've looked worse. For that matter, lots of people—
some of them old friends of yours—look worse. That still doesn't
make you look any less terrible."

"Your barside manner is impeccable."

"Practiced."

Allenberg took a long draft of the beer.

The Lion's Head could be a haven. His visits were not nearly
as frequent as they had been.

Before he had been recruited by the agency (*that* had not been
an easy job for them), he had worked as a newsman in New York
and, like many newsmen, had made either the Lion's Head or
Costello's—or both—unofficial residences.

Perhaps it had been stories of his earlier career—he had been
*young* then—that had influenced his daughter and induced her

to become a reporter. *Maybe that won't happen to Jason. Then . . . there's worse.*

The long drink he'd taken from the beer mug had lowered the level of beer inside just enough. He took the shot glass, suspended it over the mug, and let go. He hadn't lost his touch, he thought. He hadn't made a drink like that in years; the Lyle situation must be getting to him.

He drank from the mug; the combined taste of beer and Irish whiskey was good. The bitterness of the beer had been dulled; the flavor had not been lost. Of course, he reminded himself, the real trick with this drink was finishing it. He hoped he hadn't lost his touch for shaking the last sips from the glass without dislodging the shot glass. Mistakes were painful to front teeth.

None of his old friends were in the bar. He had hoped some might be. He successfully finished his drink (the small glass had stayed at the mug's bottom) and went to the wall telephone.

"Yes?"

"Allenberg."

"That didn't take you long."

"What? What do you mean?"

"I mean," Kracke said, "that I couldn't have beeped you more than ten seconds ago."

Allenberg's beeper had not sounded; then he remembered. One of the problems with the Lion's Head was that some signals didn't penetrate it. Of course, *some* of the reporters liked it for just that reason, but editors were just as sharp as their reporters. Almost all the papers and stations had switched to services with more favorably located transmitters. Allenberg grinned; the agency hadn't caught up with the press.

"Whatever," he said. "Why were you trying to reach me?"

'You had a call. The guy said he wanted to talk to you about Lyle."

"The demands?"

"Not from this guy. At least he didn't make any when he called. He just wanted to talk."

"Who else could know of Lyle?"

114

"I don't know. I wish he *had* made demands. I'd feel more comfortable. The thought of someone *else* involved is not exactly soothing to my nerves."

"No. What was his name? Did he tell you where I could reach him?"

"He said you'd know. His name was Fitch."

"Are you there?" It was Kracke. "Do you know this guy?"

"I know him, Jim. I'll be in touch with you. Let me know if anybody calls in with demands or if anything new happens in Lyle. I want you to keep track of Brandes, too."

"About this Fitch guy . . ."

"I can't tell you anything about him, Jim."

He hung up the telephone, walked to the bar, and ordered the makings of another drink. If only things were simple; from points of view based on limited knowledge, things always were, yes. *The White House is getting involved. Fitch works there. But Fitch also is . . .* He never could explain that to Kracke. And if not to Kracke, why was he thinking what he was thinking?

He did not want to call Fitch, but that wasn't all he was thinking about. He had done unorthodox things before, of course. Things considered unorthodox even in *his* business. He couldn't believe the thoughts that were racing through his mind.

He considered an article he recently had read. It had been published in *ETC.*, the Journal of the International Society for General Semantics. Allenberg had been a student of the subject for years—hell, he credited that with much of his success in his profession.

The article was called "Imaging." Written by some Midwestern college professor, it had to do with the division of the brain into right and left hemispheres. The left, it seemed, thought in words; the right in images, pictures. It "thought" just as well; sometimes it might even come up with answers the other hemisphere didn't. But it couldn't *tell* anyone, except in pictures. The article was about what people could do to tap the other thinking half of their brains, and make use of those images.

Well, my left hemisphere is thinking of acting on a picture I

115

just saw in my head. I hope it's my right brain talking. But more than that. My right brain can be just as wrong as the left—you don't need words to be wrong. Still, it's providing one *hell* of an answer.

I think, Allenberg mused, that my left brain never would have thought of this because it couldn't bear the implications if it were put into words.

Of course, much depended on Fitch. *Fitch can help.*

He decided he couldn't call him from the public phone at the Lion's Head. Allenberg paid Mike for his drinks and left. Instead of going into another bar or into a restaurant, Allenberg decided to use one of the street telephones at the foot of Sheridan Square.

Fitch *had* to have a good reason for calling Allenberg's office. Such was not simply "out of the ordinary" in the dealings of Uisce Beatha directors. It was—as far as he knew—totally unheard of.

"This is Adrian Allenberg," he said when the telephone was answered. "I am calling Mr. Fitch."

There was some humming sound, not much. He knew the machinery of Uisce Beatha again was analyzing his voice. He also knew that when he was connected to Fitch—if the other man could be reached through the computer—he would not be in the Park Avenue office.

Allenberg would know where he was only if Fitch wanted him to.

"Hold on, please," a pleasant voice said. There was a chiming sound for a few seconds, and then a voice. Fitch.

"This is Allenberg."

"I've got to talk to you."

"You are."

"I think we should meet. I mean the telephone is hardly . . ."

"*You* are complaining about breaches of procedure? For shit sake, you called my *office!* And you told them it was about Lyle!"

"Yes. Well, I had to get your attention. I had to get to you."

"And now you have gotten to me. In more ways than one. So don't bitch to me about a telephone, for Christ's sake."

"No," Fitch said, and Allenberg could have sworn there was a giggling in his voice. "No, I guess it doesn't matter. I'm sure you'll agree that it doesn't matter when I tell you what I know."

"Look. Whether you trust public phones or not, one thing I can tell you about them is that they run on coins, and I don't have an unlimited supply. For God's sake, Fitch, what the hell is going on?"

"You have to stop the investigation in Lyle."

"*What?*"

"Oh, I don't want you to. The board doesn't. Nothing like that. *They* want you to."

"Who is 'they'?" he asked quietly.

"I don't know. But *I* got a phone call. A man told me to call you off. He said you'd already gotten a demonstration of just how easy it would be to spread the disease."

My God, Allenberg thought. This could not be happening. Uisce Beatha had been compromised. *Uisce Beatha.*

Whoever the hell had commissioned Peter Brandes to create that disease, whoever had let it escape, whoever had left him a half-filled half-of-an-hourglass in a Village apartment built on top of an underground river—whoever that was *might* know about the agency but *they also knew about Uisce Beatha, and there was no way for them to know about Uisce Beatha.* Allenberg had made "internal preparations" for many conceivable crises. This, he thought, was not one of them.

"Have you," he asked Fitch, as easily as he could, "fully understood what this means?"

"Yes. At least . . . well," Fitch stumbled, "I've tried. I think I have."

"I think I know how you feel. Have you told any of the other members?"

"No. I thought I should talk to you first. You are the one actually involved in Lyle. Of course, the others will have to be informed of . . . the other aspects of this . . . situation."

"They will," Allenberg agreed.

"I don't know when . . ." He was drifting, Allenberg thought. "Have you gotten anywhere in Lyle?"

Allenberg considered.

"I am sufficiently established in Lyle."

"That's a hell of a vague way to put it."

"That's more than you should get."

"I meant about the disease, anyway. That's what they seemed to be interested in. Have you gotten anywhere with the disease?"

"What exactly did they say to you?"

"Can't you," he was shouting, "for Christ's sake simply answer that fucking question?"

"No." Allenberg was amazed and—quite pleased—at how reasonable his own voice sounded.

"They said to not continue investigating it. They said you could contain it but that's all."

"You mean they honestly suggested that I cut off a community and let everyone in it die? Cut it off so thoroughly and maybe violently that there is no way the thing can escape?"

"I don't know, Adrian. I don't know."

"Did they give you an or else?"

"They said you already had that."

"That's it. No other demands. No money. No political prisoners released. No amnesty. No nothing. Just no playing with their bug. That only makes sense, you know, if they're getting something here we don't even see. I mean, there has to be a reason they don't want us poking around, and there has to be something they stand to gain."

"Well," Fitch said, "they did say something else that made even less sense."

"Terrific. And while I'm commenting," he said testily, "let me say that I don't want everything they said in dribbles, Fitch. I want to know all of it, and all of it at once."

"Yeah. I know. This other thing. It's very strange. They said that in six months they don't care if we find out about the disease. Six months."

118

"Oh, they'll let us look around then. After a few thousand people die." He snorted derisively. "And I'm supposed to buy this . . ."

"You mean you're *not?*"

Allenberg, for a second, was not quite sure of what he'd heard. "What do you mean?" he asked Fitch.

"I mean, you're going ahead with it anyway? Don't you see? If they let this thing loose everywhere—if that's as easy to do as they claim—we're talking about *millions.*"

"You think we should scratch Lyle for the sake of the greater good?" He knew Uisce Beatha members often made "mathematical" decisions, but he couldn't picture even such "long-vision" types accepting what Fitch was suggesting.

"Put that way, Adrian, I can hop on as high and mighty a horse as anyone else and say, 'of course we can't do that.' From down here, when my feet are on the ground and I'm five-five naked, I think we have to do what they demand."

Allenberg didn't answer at once. There was too much happening, too fast. "Well," he said finally, "maybe I am as likely to jump on a high horse as anyone else. But maybe I also stand a little taller naked."

He hung up the phone.

"Anything more recent?" Allenberg wasted no time at all on introductions or explanations. He wanted information from Kracke, but more than that, he wished he could bring Kracke up to date—*completely* up to date.

Of course, he knew that was impossible.

"I'd have beeped you," Kracke said. "Did you talk to that guy?"

"Yes. Anything from Lyle?"

"No. You want me to get word up there or something?"

"Yes," Allenberg said. "We all should be up to date. Get a message to Brandes. Have him call me directly."

"Who was this other guy, Adrian? Fitch? He can't be one of them. I mean, he wouldn't identify himself, would he?"

"No, Jim. He's just in a position to know some things, that's

119

all." He hesitated, then said, "He passed along a message from them, though. They want Brandes to stop."

"Do you want me to go up there?"

"No, I don't think so. Not yet. There aren't any reports out of there that should make me worry, are there?"

"No. Brandes may be still worried about shadows—but everything I hear tells me it's quiet."

"Good. But be ready to go anyway. Just in case."

"There are things here I don't know about, aren't there, Adrian?"

"What else is new?" Allenberg pressed down on the telephone cradle's lever, waited, lifted his finger. He deposited more coins and got an operator. He'd have to put this one on his credit card, he thought. Even as he asked for the number, he wasn't sure he was doing the right thing.

Well, he thought, right hemisphere, here's hoping you're not a crazy half a brain. He played with that thought. It was something the Midwestern professor hadn't said anything about. Could a person have a sane half and a crazy half? He wished he hadn't thought of it either.

"Hello?" His daughter answered.

"It's the grandfather of your favorite son."

"Hi, Dad. I didn't think we'd be hearing from you for a while. Everything all right in the city?"

"No. No, it's not." He stopped. Sighed. "I have some favors to ask."

"Pressing your family into service again?"

"'Fraid so. I like it less than ever this time."

There was a moment's silence at the other end. "You really sound worried, Dad. This *is* different, isn't it?"

"More than you can believe, child. More than you can believe."

"What do you want us to do?"

"Well, I want my juvenile delinquent grandson to unmend his criminal ways and use his new Sanyo computer, for one thing. I've got some names I'd like to get him to work on."

"Dad!" She didn't object to her son's complicity; he knew she wouldn't. "You have *far* greater resources than a teenage hacker."

"Just so," he said. "At the moment I don't, however, feel I can use them."

"This is getting into our gray area, Dad."

He sighed. He was afraid it would come to this. He and his daughter had an agreement—not tacit, not in writing. Verbal, but a hell of a lot closer to "in writing," he thought. She had her career. She was proud of her ability. She was willing to work with him and keep quiet. Usually. But the "gray area." That was different. There would come a point someday, she'd told him, when what he dangled before her was too much of a story. He would have to let her pursue it. She wouldn't ask *him* for special treatment or information. She'd just "notified" him that if she felt ethically bound to chase a story she would, and to hell with national security. He'd always had to accept her help with that understanding.

"Yes, I guess it is," he said. "When you know more you might decide not to follow up anyway. At least I hope you won't. But I understand our deal."

"Okay. What?"

"Right now I just want you and my grandson to snoop around on the names I give you."

"Fire away," she said.

He sighed and gave her the names.

# THIRTEEN

DINNER HAD BEEN TASTELESS. CYNTHIA HAD FELT two steps removed from the airport restaurant and from Shortell. He had tried to keep a conversation going at first, but soon it had become apparent to him that something indeed had happened when Cynthia and Brandes had seen each other. Shortell simply was disappointed, not hurt. He was a very reasonable man, even a somewhat fatalistic one, about such things. He had been very attracted to the young woman epidemiologist—any man would have been, he thought. But if there were other things at work here, he was no worse off than before.

Except, of course, for dinner. Shortell's very difficult-to-suppress humor in the face of adversity (how strained *that* had been these past days, he thought) had stepped in between the salad bar and Cynthia's stuffed sole.

"Okay," he'd said to her. "I'm not the only terrific-looking doctor around here. I'll accept that, Dr. Ellis, though it pains me deeply." She looked at him and smiled. "I'll not even pry. In fact, I don't want to know. What I do demand," he sounded serious—his face betrayed that, "is what I paid for. Your company at dinner."

She'd smiled, slowly at first, then more openly, with a shrug and a surrender.

"Sorry," she said. "It's an old—"

"Uh!" He'd held up a hand. "I was serious when I said I didn't want to know. Tell me instead about your middle-class childhood in the suburbs of Chicago. While you're at it, tell me about the unmarried twin sister you've got whom you've always secretly hated because *you* thought she was prettier."

Cynthia laughed. The rest of the dinner had been pleasant, more pleasant than if Shortell had been a different type of man. She liked him. But she couldn't forget Brandes.

Shortell had taken her back to the Tower and invited her for a goodnight drink. She was somewhat surprised she'd agreed, but Shortell's company, she realized, was helping hold old pain distant.

"What are you and your team going to do next?" he'd asked, sitting at a table in the near-empty lounge and placing down two Grand Marniers.

"Very much what we have been doing," she answered. The disease, too, was a subject that kept memory muted.

"Abel and Kathy—I don't know if you've met them—will be backtracking where everyone with the illness was, looking for something common or at least some links between the victims.

"I'll continue supervising the lab work, but that's pretty much over for a while. At least the first hectic phase. We'll check on the incubations, but at this stage the bug is pretty much in control of the time factor. If Kathy and Abel find anything interesting, we might send for reinforcements—specialists."

"I have met both of them," Shortell said. "They were already at the hospital talking to the patients. How much more specialized can you get?"

Cynthia laughed. "You should meet Tony Braccio. Tony looks like an auto mechanic even in his lab coat. In fact, when he wears it, he looks like one of the white-coated mechanics who worked in 'car clinics' that were big in the early 1970's.

"The thing about Tony is that you wouldn't be far off. He's a hell of a doctor, but you should see him with a wrench." She paused, enjoying Shortell's quizzical look. "Whenever we suspect something like an air-conditioning system is the common denominator in a disease's spread, we call Tony.

"No mechanic could take the medical precautions he does—and no other doctor I know could rip apart a couple of tons of machinery. *That's* specialization."

Shortell agreed.

"And that's not all."

He waited.

"He can put the damned things back together again, and I swear I remember once that the manager of a hotel thanked him for fixing it."

Both laughed

They finished their drinks; Cynthia realized that she was tired. Shortell, too, had been showing the signs of long hours spent seemingly fruitlessly.

"Thanks for the dinner," she said.

"Thank you for your company," he answered, and she thought she should be saying that.

Instead she asked, "Tell me, how did you know?"

"Huh? Know what?" They were at the front door, Shortell already stepping through.

"About my twin sister?"

"There *is* a twin sister?"

"There is. And that's not all. She *is* prettier than I am."

"Things are looking up." He grinned broadly.

"Sorry about that," she laughed. "She's not an unmarried twin sister."

"Damn."

They said goodnight again, and Cynthia watched him walk down the Tower's front steps. He was an attractive man, and she liked his company. What the hell was it, she wondered, about Brandes?

Cynthia walked slowly toward the stairs. Her room was in the middle of the center floor; she'd gotten one with a bathroom, and she was pleased about that. No one else was in the lobby. Perhaps

Johnny didn't expect any more guests: more likely he had no room for more.

She stopped at the registration desk as she knew she would. Alex was registered in 1A, and it took her a moment to place it because none of the upstairs rooms had letters. Then she remembered the annex. There was, of course, the very rational part of her that said, "Don't do this." As before, where Alex Brandes was concerned, she ignored it. She did not for a moment doubt that, as before, she would regret her decision.

Cynthia left the Tower through its side door, stepping down on a driveway that only was used by the hotel's owners. She edged around a large, dark-colored car—the driveway was narrow—and walked toward the rear of the property.

There was a very small yard, barely enough room for the umbrella-covered table and chairs and the Weber charcoal grill that stood there alone. The annex was only a few steps away; she walked around the side to find the entrance to the apartment.

Cynthia hesitated, looking at the tin 1A screwed to the door. Then she knocked. There was no answer, but the knocking jarred something loose that she hadn't seen. It had been tucked under the edge of the A and in the dim light had blended in with the wood.

The paper fluttered to the ground.

*My excuse*, she thought, disliked herself, criticized herself, and then repeated to herself, *my excuse*. He would see through it immediately, of course; not even give it a moment's consideration. But it still made her feel better to say that she'd come because he'd gotten a message and it might be important.

She thought of reading it, but it was sealed in a tiny envelope bearing the Tower's logo, and she didn't want to disturb it.

She heard no footsteps in the room. She knocked louder, and when there still was nothing, part of her felt relieved. But where could he have gone? There was little to do in Lyle at the best of times. Probably out drinking with that other man, she thought.

It was a pleasant night, and she decided that she would wait. The part of her that had felt relieved just sighed and accepted the inevitable.

She would not wait there, she thought. *No, I'm not going to let him find me camped on his doorstep.*

She walked to the driveway and along it to the front of the hotel. She climbed the steps to the porch. The double row of old-fashioned rocking chairs had looked inviting since she'd arrived in Lyle, though she had not before anticipated having time to use one of them. Cynthia relaxed, rocked gently. The envelope was in her lap.

Really, what was it about Brandes?

He had told her the story of the first time he'd seen her and how he'd never been able to forget her. She didn't recall that first encounter. She did, though, remember the St. Patrick's Day parade. After that, she had not forgotten him.

And why couldn't it have worked?

She *knew* that it couldn't, but always there was that lingering hope. It *had* worked, she thought. Until the night he'd told her to pack in the morning.

She'd not been entirely surprised. Brandes, she felt, had been acting strangely. She had wanted them simply to commit themselves to what they both knew: that they loved each other and could share their lives. Somehow he had seen that as a trap, although she'd never intended it that way, at least not consciously.

His mother had been alive then; Cynthia and Anne Marie had become very good friends. It almost seemed at times that Alex was not necessary for their friendship. She knew that the breakup with Alex had hurt her all the more because it meant losing contact with Anne Marie.

And yes, she thought, his mother had warned her often enough. "Don't push, Cynthia. Like most people, he doesn't like being pushed. But he carries it to extremes. Push and you'll have him going full steam in another direction. Wait. Someday he'll come home after a good day and say, 'Hey, why don't we get married?' I guarantee it"—she had smiled—"almost."

Perhaps Cynthia hadn't heeded that advice well enough, and to that extent, the end had been partially her fault. But he had

126

seen traps where there were none, and there was nothing she could do about that.

The nagging problem was, Why the hell didn't he just fade away? She'd certainly had other affairs—she knew *he* had. Why not the gentle passing into "history?" She didn't know.

She wondered if he also felt something like that. In a way she hoped so. But then again, she didn't really want him to suffer.

One Jeep with two soldiers passed. Otherwise, she seemed to have the night to herself. There were at first occasional sounds of others moving about their rooms, readying for bed. Then that stopped. Even nature's night sounds faded.

Cynthia slept.


"This just in, sir." Lieutenant Knotts placed a folded message on Colonel Lawrence's desk.

The light was not good. Lawrence's "office" was in what had been the informal dining room of the old house. He adjusted the Tensor lamp he'd earlier ordered from his aide. The message was only a few lines long.

> *Situational change is hereby ordered,* the message read. *You are to immediately terminate maneuvers. Your proximity to a potentially serious situation is considered fortuitous.*
>
> *An unknown illness has been discovered in a community near your location. You are ordered:*
>
> A: *To inform your men they are no longer on a routine exercise.*
>
> B: *To institute procedures for the segregation of the remains of those who are victims of this illness.*
>
> C: *To locate a site suitable for the eventual cremation of those remains.*
>
> D: *To take the above instructions into consideration in the discretionary briefing of your command.*

What an incredible load of horseshit, Lawrence thought. Still, he never expected any better; he never, in seventeen years, had received any better. His command's presence in the area was to be explained as "fortuitous."

This message meant he was limited still in what he could tell his own officers and men. It was a good precaution, he knew—frightened soldiers were as much, if not more of a problem as frightened civilians.

He could tell them there was a disease in Lyle, nothing more. The lack of an immediate quarantine might reassure them, but he strongly suspected his next orders would at least prepare for one if not directly order it.

The authority for the message was "very high echelon." He sighed and called in Lieutenant Knotts.

He would carefully prepare his own men, keeping them calm by telling them that their primary duty was to keep other people calm. *Classic tactic*, he thought. Then, when and if the time came for more "visible" intervention, his officers and men would have to take only one short mental step instead of the large leap that might render them as much a menace as scared townspeople.

Lawrence had two duties and knew it. One was to help in the control and, if necessary, containment of a particularly nasty bug.

Another was to keep his superiors looking productive, in charge and definitely—God, yes, above all—not responsible.

*What the hell*, he thought. *Occupational hazard.*


"She's not getting better, Emil," Doro said. She placed a fresh, cold cloth on her daughter Nancy's head.

"I know."

"She's getting worse. We have to take her to the hospital."

Jenner said nothing.

"Why? Emil, *why?* It's not like you. You're an educated man. You had me go to *two* doctors when I even thought I had blood in a bowel movement. I just don't understand, Emil. Why haven't we taken her?"

"We will, Doro. Tomorrow we will. I . . . I just hoped she

would get better. I've heard of too many people lately going into the hospital and too few coming out, I guess. And then there's the army . . ."

"Oh, Emil. They're here playing with satellites or something."

"Maybe. It's just that things don't feel right. But I guess we haven't got much choice anymore."

"She *is* getting worse, Emil."

And that was true. Nancy's temperature had spiked at 103. It had quickly dropped back to 101, but Jenner was not ignorant of the significance of the sudden rise. Finally, it had risen and remained at 103. Was Nancy dying?

*Dear God, should I take her tonight?* he asked himself, his fists clenched; he was crying.

By all he "knew" about medicine he should get her to Lyle–Mount Saint Sydney as soon as possible.

But something was . . . *wrong* at the hospital. Something was *wrong* with the disease, *wrong* with Lyle.

He should bundle her up now, put her into the Volvo, drive to the hospital. Maybe Shortell could be found. He knew and liked the young doctor. Maybe she would be better off. Maybe people were on the mend in the hospital.

*Maybe* . . . but the *feeling* would not go away.

It is a choice of fears, he thought. *I choose taking her to the hospital although I'm becoming afraid of what may be happening to my friends and neighbors there. I choose waiting even though I'm afraid waiting may make her worse.*

*I can't choose.* Never before had Jenner felt so immobile, so ineffectual. He hated the feeling inside himself; he hated himself for having the feeling.

"Tomorrow, Doro. If the fever doesn't break, we'll take her tomorrow."


Mr. Bertoli died.

# FOURTEEN

JASON WAS TIRED; HE HAD TO BE, SARAH THOUGHT. His eyes, however, were bright and alert. He enjoyed working with his computer, and all the more so when his acts of questionable legality were commissioned by his grandfather.

Some family, she thought. But she would not have had it otherwise. She trusted her father. She trusted her son. She knew Adrian Allenberg trusted both of them.

From her point of view—and from her father's, she knew—it was important that Jason observe a strict code of conduct. It was just that the code didn't necessarily encompass some of the more typical concepts of right and wrong.

Jason was not being taught to be a hypocrite. Once, when his teachers—PTA meetings, Sarah thought, should be like the ideal of the jury system, a meeting of peers—demanded that he memorize the lines on the base of the Statue of Liberty entreating every other country in the world to let their poor people come to the United States, she had pointed out that *memorizing* it didn't seem such a bad idea—as long as one kept in mind the growing sentiment against new immigrants.

Neither she nor her father wanted him to grow up with a fragile picture of the world, one that would be destined to be smashed when he was older. So Jason's education in morals and ethics had been eminently pragmatic.

"How's it going?" she asked him. It was near dawn; Jason's chatter on the underground hacker bulletin boards had followed the sun. She guessed, correctly as it turned out, that by then he would be completing his sweep of Hawaii.

"I've got a lot of stuff," he said. "Nothing too interesting about those men grandfather wanted. None of them have been arrested in this country, anyway."

That certainly was not surprising. If any of them *had* been arrested, Allenberg would have been stunned into immobility.

Allenberg had given Sarah the names of the Uisce Beatha board members who had been present when he had brought Lyle to the organization's attention. Fitch *might* have been contacted by someone because Fitch had a position—a visible position—in the United States administration. What Allenberg could *not* chance was that Fitch had been called because of his Uisce Beatha connection.

That, for Allenberg—and for the organization as a whole— would be nothing short of disastrous, nothing less than terrifying.

He had, therefore, needed a "minor" superficial check. Using Jason was just—*unorthodox* was hardly the word, he had thought. But he *couldn't* use government resources for the task. Then, too, Uisce Beatha's information-gathering net was spread wide, and very little got through it. The directors would have known within hours had he tried even subtly to use his own machines.

No one, he guessed, would find out that a teenage computer hacker was at it. He would accumulate enough information on totally unrelated subjects so that what he gathered on the directors would go unnoticed anyway.

Allenberg had not revealed the existence of Uisce Beatha to Sarah or Jason, however. He did not intend to. His family had no need to know about that vast mechanism; ignorance was even beneficial. And to Allenberg, family mattered very, very much.

Their knowing about Uisce Beatha someday might be necessary; that day had not come.

He had had, however, to tell Sarah about Lyle. He knew he had to give her something or else she would demurely smile and refuse to help him. He also knew better than to lie to her; in fact, it had not even come to mind.

Sarah looked at her son and was pleased by what she saw. "So, what *did* you get?"

"Not much."

"What have you got?"

"What I got cost me a lot. I had to give out access codes to some very nice accounts in trade."

"You'll find others," she said and grinned. "Besides, this is work."

"Oh, I'm not complaining. I *got* some good codes, too. I had to in order to get into machines with information on these guys. Mostly it's about their bank accounts and investments.

"That South American guy, Ryan—you sure he's South American?—deals a lot in coffee futures, but I guess that's to be expected." He chuckled but stopped immediately when his mother cocked her head to the right and raised her eyebrows slightly. "In case you're interested, he's selling right now."

"Fitch seems to like metals. He's bought everything from copper to palladium and silver. There's something interesting there, though."

"What's that?"

"Well, you remember when grandfather was explaining investments to me?"

She remembered. It had been several years earlier. Jason had managed to save one hundred dollars from his allowance and wanted to invest it. "I don't even care if I lose it," he'd explained. "I mean, I *care*, but I figure when you're dealing with a hundred bucks, a safe bank account giving me five percent means a whole five bucks a year.

"I figure with what I got it's smarter to take a chance on a big one."

She'd said nothing. He'd ceased to surprise her quite some time before.

"Yes," she said. "I remember."

"Put options. Options to sell. That's what he's buying. It's like he expects gold to drop when it ain't. Either he knows something nobody else does or he sure likes to hedge."

"You can discuss investment philosophy with him sometime. I'm sure grandfather will arrange it. There's nothing illegal about what he's doing, anyway."

"No."

"Anybody else?"

"Yeah. The Englishman, Albert."

"What about him?"

"He's broke."

Sarah said nothing. She couldn't know for certain, but she doubted her grandfather's list would contain someone who was "broke." She tagged the information in her mind, intending to tell him later that day.

Her own work also had involved trades. She'd called in some overdue favors from friends in other bureaus. Unlike Jason's investigating, though, she didn't expect hers to bear immediate results.

*Hell of a situation*, she thought. *My kid gets faster results than two networks and a wire service.*

Jason got up, stretched, and yawned.

"You want to get some sleep?" she asked.

"Yeah," he said. "Got one thing to do first, though."

"Breakfast?"

"No. Not hungry. I've got to check my bank book."

"Now? What for?"

He looked surprised. "Why, I've got to figure out this gold thing, of course."

"Oh."

"What are you going to do?"

"I'll leave a message for you to give your grandfather if he calls. You also give him what you've found out."

"Where will you be?"

"I'm taking a trip."

"Where?"

"New Hampshire," she said.

# FIFTEEN

THE SUN HAD NOT YET LIFTED MORNING MOIS-
ture from the car, but it was not the fogged windows that held
Brandes's attention. He stared disgustedly at the flat tire on the
left front wheel. Brandes looked around him, allowing the
freshness, coolness, and promised beauty of the New England
day to offset his feeling of frustration.

"Want another cup of coffee first?" Wismer shouted from the
kitchen door.

"No. I'd better do it and get it over with."

Brandes removed the jack and the spare from the trunk and
placed them at the front of the car. The ground was relatively
level, but Brandes did not like unnecessary risks.

He walked across Wismer's back lawn, dew seeping into his
shoes—welcome, refreshing. He opened the door to Wismer's
utility shed—a corrugated aluminum hut—and looked inside.
The morning sun illuminated the shed's interior for him.

He found chocks for the car's wheels. He picked those up,
walked back to the car, kicked them firmly under the rear tires,
and set about fixing the flat.

He had no idea how he'd gotten the flat. After removing the

tire, he examined its surface as best he could, but he found no tell-tale nail or shard of glass to explain what had happened.

Probably a slow valve leak, he thought. He hoisted the flat into the trunk. He would leave it at Andy's Amoco station in town and reclaim it in the late afternoon.

Wismer had offered him the use of his car, but Brandes had declined. He would have to have his own fixed sometime, he'd reasoned, and he certainly had enough on his mind without thoughts of a flat-to-be-fixed in addition.

He thought of the complications of the last few days, and he did not like his situation.

Each day the disease claimed new victims. The army was performing a balancing act that would not last more than another day or two at most.

*And Cynthia is here.*

He looked at his watch. Already it was nearly eight o'clock. Hell, he thought, I've got to wash up anyway.

"I'll take the coffee," he yelled toward the kitchen door.

When he entered and walked to the sink, Wismer already was heating the remaining morning coffee in the microwave oven.

"What are you going to do today?" he asked Brandes.

"The lab. Maybe check in with my bosses." He hesitated. "Maybe see my father."

"That may be unavoidable."

"Yes, I know. Peter confided in him a lot. He may have said something to him that he didn't write down in his lab notes. Gerry, I'd like to ask you a question."

"Of course." Brandes sensed that Wismer became more alert at that moment.

"It's about my father. I haven't heard of him getting involved in this at all. I mean, Colonel Lawrence didn't mention him. My own people didn't. It seems that someone should have gotten him into this—or that *he* should have gotten *himself* into it."

Wismer said nothing for several moments. He got up, reached for the still half-full coffee pot, and poured.

"CDC people tried to talk to him, Alex. He just wouldn't

cooperate. He wasn't nasty about it or anything—at least that's what I gathered. He didn't become *really* uncooperative about it until Lawrence tried to get him to come in and talk to him. He told the colonel to go to hell."

"I imagine the colonel loved that."

"Right. But keep in mind the colonel's orders as they are right now. Or what they *probably* are. You said he can't even tell his *own men* that there *is* a real threat. How could he force your father to do anything? He just had to live with it. I'm not sure," he said and paused, "that that will continue indefinitely."

"What do you mean?" Brandes asked. His tone revealed his discomfort.

"Well," Wismer continued, "if the situation gets worse—and I think it will—the colonel will get the authority to tear your father's house apart on the off chance that Peter may have left some clue there. It's possible, and it's one of the reasons I'd hoped you would decide to go see your father.

"I don't think your father needs the United States Army rampaging through his dead son's private papers. You, on the other hand . . ."

"Might not upset him as much. Maybe you're right about that—but just *maybe*."

Brandes purposely made a loud clinking noise as he set down his cup; Wismer noticed. "You seem to know a hell of a lot, Gerry. I mean, I didn't know about Lawrence's orders until I got here, and even then I had to piece things together from a lieutenant's comments." He looked squarely at Wismer. "How did *you* know, Gerry?"

Wismer didn't even miss a beat. He looked surprised. "Alex," he said, "you've been looking too long for too many vipers in your bosom. *You told me.*"

Brandes was startled for an instant and thought back to the conversation they'd had the previous night. He'd talked about Cynthia, of course. He remembered telling Wismer something about Lawrence.

*Damn. I can't remember what.*

He might very well have told Wismer. *I'm losing this, losing any grip I may have had . . .* He *felt* it. A goodly number of Manhattans the previous night had made their contribution, he thought.

"Sorry, Gerry. Just a little tense."

"A little tense? You've got every right to be. This situation simply *will* not continue as it has." He rose, took his empty coffee cup to the sink, and turned on the faucet. "The whole damned thing is too volatile. The army's position is based on a fabric of lies that can't possibly be maintained with the CDC running around and more and more people getting sick.

"Hell, Alex, I don't even know if I'm talking about *minutes* instead of hours. While we slept something horrible could have happened."

"Oh, so I'm to take the blame for accepting a second cup of coffee?" Brandes wanted to lighten the atmosphere.

"No," Wismer laughed. "I'll take that one. But I'll justify it; you needed it. In fact, it might be a good lesson for you. Take it from an older man and your former teacher . . ." He puffed himself up, looking preposterously self-important and just as funny as he intended to look.

"The slow minutes you spend to do the job well—and that means taking care of yourself—make up for all the fast minutes you waste if you *don't* take care of yourself."

He paused, then said, "That might even mean dealing with Cynthia."

"Let's hope it doesn't come to that," Brandes said and stood. He most definitely didn't want to have to think about dealing with Cynthia—and with himself—during the present crisis.

"Dealing with my father will be tough enough. Might even not be possible." He looked directly at Wismer. "Gerry, I really think the man might hate me. I mean you see TV shows about love that looks like hate and that sort of shit, but I mean my father just might really honest-to-God hate me."

"Tell you what," Wismer said, suddenly looking more cheerful. "I'll get an errand done for you, and you'll be able to get a head start on your work."

"Just how will you do that, teacher?"

Wismer cocked his head to one side as he considered his answer. "Sometimes your brother talked to me, too, Alex. Remember, he was one of my students also."

"The better-behaved one."

"Most definitely, the better-behaved one. But we talked about lots of things. Nothing having to do with any part of his work that could have led up to *this* mess, but we talked. He also used to leave a lot of stuff lying around here.

"Why don't you look at that stuff, have another cup of coffee, and I'll get Andy to work on your flat right away?"

"You have Peter's notebooks here?" Brandes asked. He realized when he spoke that the words were harsh, sharp, measured. But he did not regret that. If Wismer had been hiding something . . .

"No! It's nothing like that. It . . . has to do more with you and your family. Some snapshots and some personal notes."

"Gerry, I'm not here to review the reunion of a family that never existed. You of *all* people know that! What the hell are you talking about?"

"Quite a calculated decision, Alex."

Wismer was sharp in his own tone. "You, I believe, will have to talk with your father about all this. It is in *my* best interest that you be best prepared psychologically. After all, I live here, too. If you're my best hope, I damned well want you doing your best. Besides, Andy knows me. I'll get the tire done quicker."

Wismer picked up Brandes's car keys and left through the kitchen door.

"The stuff is in the secretary," he heard Wismer shout back. "Top drawer left."

With that, he was gone. Brandes heard Wismer start the car and then slowly drive down to the road to town. The house suddenly was very quiet, very empty. He finished the last of his coffee and went into the living room. The secretary was dark walnut and highly polished.

He *knew* nothing of this would be of value in finding answers to the disease. Somehow—somehow, and he wasn't certain just how because it had happened so quickly—Wismer had usurped control of Brandes's schedule and had just left him behind in the old house.

Without difficulty he found the papers and some slides that he had to hold up to the window light to see. Some made him smile. He looked at his watch.

He had about a half hour or so to read the few scribbled notes, to look at the pictures, and to decide for himself whether all of it was a waste of time.

It seemed a good guess that it was.

# SIXTEEN

WISMER HAD SAID HE COULDN'T EVEN REMEMBER from where he'd gotten some of the slides and snapshots.

Peter had not visited Wismer often, never had been anything like a friend, but from time to time he had tried to maintain his relationship with his ex-teacher, showing him slides of vacations and such.

He had left at Wismer's house only one complete package of pictures, taken on a trip to New York several weeks before his death. All the slides and scribbles were, to Wismer, no more than something to keep Brandes busy, and that gave Wismer time— time for something he believed he must do.

He had to talk to Alex's father before Alex did.

Too much might depend on the two men, father and son, at least *trying* to get along—Wismer had to try to lay some groundwork.

Although he had known him for years, Wismer did not consider Brandes's father a friend. He thought, though, that he could convince him that working with Alex was necessary.

*A rift at this point cannot be allowed.*

That final comment, the look in Brandes's eyes—he really believed his father might hate him.

*What if it's true?*

Peter Brandes, Sr., had been a very good diagnostician. At one time he'd shown *very* impressive promise as a surgeon. Then he had suffered a nephrotic kidney ailment that had taken, shredded, destroyed the man's career—at least, that was the way Brandes had seen things. He'd lost one kidney and no longer felt he could chance complicated operations with his low endurance.

So he had concentrated on his diagnostic genius, but Wismer knew it never had been enough; it could not make him whole, heal him. Brandes, Sr., as years passed, had begun to drink more and more heavily.

There was something else Wismer knew. He thought about it as little as possible as he drove. It was unpleasant—and, at that time, possibly dangerous. Neither Peter nor Alex ever had learned that their father's drinking had driven their mother to abusing her husband's pharmaceutical company-supplied drug samples. Wismer had seen her at low periods, watching her progress from Valium to—he suspected—intravenous narcotics.

Remembering those days, those events, and hearing Alex's comment about his father's hatred had spurred his sudden decision to talk to Brandes's father, with whom Alex just might have to cooperate if a town full of people was not to die. *They must be able to work together. A town full of people might depend on them. A town, for a beginning.*

As Wismer had grown older, his world had tended to become "tighter," he thought. *Once I would have thought of the world first. Now one town at a time is very, very sufficient.*

Wismer looked over the pastures as the car sped past them. Occasionally he caught a glimpse of a cow lying down in a pasture or of a horse standing and grazing.

The sun by then had begun to burn off the dawn fog. As he drove, he could see the slow progress of the mist as it rose from pasture to pasture, to melt into the sky. Now he remembered an occasion from his own childhood. *Perhaps,* he thought, *my mind is telling me something.*

*Remember the past. The present is slightly too rocky, undigestible.*

141

His family had moved to New England after his father had decided to "retire" at thirty-eight years old. His father had been a truck driver who dreamed of saving enough money to spend on what some might consider to be incongruous luxuries.

"If I were rich," he'd say, "I'd go to Berlitz for their intense course—you know, the one the government buys—in Russian. And then Hebrew, Arabic." His father had been a rare dreamer, Wismer knew. His dreams somewhat had come true.

Hard as it was even for Wismer in later years to believe, his father had taken a loan one year, invested in platinum—and had made a fortune overnight.

Well, he thought, if not a *fortune*, at least enough for a comfortable home for his family in the foothills of the Massachusetts Berkshires, for Wismer to go to school (his father's real dream)—and for Russian.

His mother had never been out of a city. He still could see her the first time *she'd* spotted a cow lying in a meadow. It had been midafternoon. The cow was relaxing, its head moving slowly as it gazed dispassionately across the horizon.

"I don't believe it," she'd said. "What a job. What a way we get our milk. These things can be lazy and they're *still* working."

Wismer, even though only fourteen then, had grinned.

Cows, he noticed, hadn't changed.

Wismer turned onto the road that led most directly from his home to town. He had to go through Lyle to reach the Brandes's estate. He could stop at Andy's and leave the tire on the way. Andy surely would be up—for him, Wismer laughed to himself, half the day already would have passed.

Much at eye level still was shrouded. He saw the lights first. Flashing blue.

They stretched across the road. The practice roadblock for the hypothetical quarantine. He slowed, stopped.

"Good morning, sir," a soldier said. He was young—weren't they all?! Soldiers *had* to be young. *You have to get them before they start thinking.*

"Good morning. Problem?"

"No, sir. I'm sure this'll be cleared up soon." Wismer noticed he was fidgeting, looking around as he spoke. "It's just that we have to get the names of people who are going further into Lyle. *Part of our exercise.*"

"My name's Wismer. I'm a retired teacher."

*Further* into Lyle, the young soldier had said. And *names?* What the hell business of the army was it that they have names? They were making him wait while they checked out his name; there was that, too.

*Something* new had developed overnight. Of that he was certain. Still, except for a little nervousness, the soldier had seemed all right.

He could just make out the faint outline of the soldier about twenty feet away. He was talking to someone else. The fog had not cleared enough for a good look, although the day promised to be clear and sun filled.

"Soldier!" he shouted out his window. The young man returned.

"It'll be a few minutes, sir."

"It's not that. Why don't I just take the detour?"

"Detour?"

"Yes," he said impatiently, gesturing to the narrow cut leading up a hill and the same back road Brandes had taken the previous day.

"We haven't let . . . I mean . . . I don't know. I've got to check."

There was a hurried conference between the soldier and another man, presumably dressed as a soldier although Wismer couldn't quite tell. A third man was called in, and finally the young one who initially had stopped Wismer returned.

"The lieutenant says there *is* a detour, sir. I've never had this duty before.

"He said that our orders today don't say we can give people a choice, really, but he says it's been standard all the time we've been doing this. You know the way?" He lowered his head; Wismer guessed he suddenly felt foolish. Was he, a newcomer to the area, about to question the locals about local geography?

143

"Yes, son, I know the way."

"It's pretty foggy. That road looks tricky. Maybe you should just wait . . ."

"Been doing this in my sleep for thirty years," Wismer said. Not quite, he thought, but he had to get the tire fixed and he most certainly had to get to see Brandes's father.

And now, he knew, he had to get back to Brandes and tell him the army had become a little more restrictive. He would like to know why—and he was dead certain Brandes would like to know why.

He turned and began mounting the hill.

Wismer had driven the road too many times to just remember. He sensed rather than saw its curves and large sudden drops.

The trip would be pleasant in clear daylight. He loved this area. He certainly had had his share of adventure in the world and had seen things and met people he'd never thought he would. When all that was done, though, he had returned to Lyle. His father had retired at thirty-eight! He liked sometimes to think that he had retired at twenty-six. That was how old he had been when he had started teaching. He'd enjoyed teaching very much.

The light brightened, the glare making the road even more difficult to maneuver. The brightly illuminated mist created a virtual blank white wall. He slowed.

Ahead of him he heard another engine. He knew the hill had steadily led him upward. Soon, he knew, he would be completely above the dew. He would emerge onto a clear road the way a jet seems suddenly to flick into reality when it soars through a cloud's top.

The engine sound was louder, but it didn't seem to be that of a car. It certainly didn't seem to be coming toward him; he would have heard more variations in the sound as the car or truck crested rises and descended into hollows.

Wismer moved the car to the right, nonetheless. If someone not totally familiar with the road was coming, he would need all the room he could get. Just ahead, just after a particularly severe curve, was Emil Jenner's latest project.

144

Well, Wismer thought, not Emil Jenner's as if Emil had ownership. Jenner had been hired by a New York City couple to build on a lot on the hill.

Wismer had met the couple; he liked them. They seemed to have come to Lyle with a willingness to relax while not giving up the electric charge only proximity to the city afforded.

Proximity, Wismer thought, could be very relative indeed. He was three-hundred-plus miles from New York, but it still was close enough to *reach* if there was a will.

The sound grew louder, more because of Wismer's motion than any oncoming vehicle. Then Wismer relaxed.

He suddenly felt foolish. It was the construction equipment.

The couple had wanted their house to be somewhat modern but had not wanted to offend their neighbors, whose houses were more than a century old and looked it. Their plans required some deep digging, Wismer remembered. What he heard was the heavy equipment warming up for a day's work.

He did not pick up speed immediately. The mist seemed to move, to swirl.

Breakthrough came unexpectedly and swiftly. Wismer pulled down the driver's visor with a jerk and angled it to cover the morning sun; suddenly revealed and shining very brightly.

He almost was at the curve, and he could hear the construction equipment's engine very clearly. He made the turn, and there it was, perhaps a hundred yards farther up the road. It was a backhoe, and as always, it reminded him of a single-pincered crab painted yellow and embossed with Jenner's company's name.

He couldn't see anyone in it, and for all he knew there might not be. *The driver simply might be warming the monster's engine*, he thought.

With the road ahead now clear, he felt it safe to increase his speed. He eased pressure onto the accelerator.

The back hoe lurched.

Not only did the vehicle move toward the road but the bucket at the end of the hydraulically controlled arm also seemed suddenly to have come alive.

145

It turned toward him.

Wismer did not change the pressure on the accelerator nor move his hands on the steering wheel. He froze.

The damned thing was coming toward him; the end of the arm was being extended like a hand waiting to be shaken.

Wismer turned his head quickly to the left. The drop was not sheer, but if he tried to accelerate to go around, he might go over the edge.

*Not a sheer drop,* he thought. *But not pleasant either.* The car would roll a good hundred feet before the trees had any chance of stopping it.

Finally he acted, moving his hand and leaning on the horn.

That was useless, he realized. The thunderous growl of the back hoe's engine almost prevented *him* from hearing the horn.

The entire incident happened both in slow motion and so rapidly he couldn't follow it.

The blade of the bucket dropped as the machine neared the car; it slid under the car's frame. There was a sliding, knocking, and then grinding sound as the car's own motion tore it over the edge of the blade. Wismer was thrown forward by the sudden braking, and then to one side.

The heavy machine's engine roared steadily, in a monotone. It seemed to wobble left and then right as it inexorably pushed at Wismer's car.

The car, screeching and protesting against sideward motion, finally reached the side of the road—and tipped.

The sun swirled in the windshield.

As the car continued to roll downhill, Wismer saw clearly the point where he crossed the fog line.

He was a jet descending back into a cloud.

Then there just was fog.


More than an hour and a half had passed, and Brandes welcomed the ringing of the telephone. He long ago had placed the pictures of and by Peter back into the manila envelope Wismer had given him.

He'd spent the rest of his time almost cursing his former teacher. *Damn! I mean*, he thought, *he knows the situation. He knows the time factors, the importance of passing minutes.* He had seemed, in fact, to be more cognizant of that than Brandes himself.

"Alex?"

He hesitated, not recognizing the voice on the telephone. "Yes?" No one was supposed to know he was there, he thought.

Then again, who the hell worth anything in his job could he really have fooled just by leaving his suitcase in the Tower?

He felt a little foolish about all that.

"This is Jonathan Shortell."

"Oh. Sorry. I'm getting my bearings this morning. Still am, rather. I intended to get over there after the lab, but Gerry. . . . Well, I had a flat—"

Shortell cut him off. "Alex. This is about Gerry. He had an accident."

Brandes numbed.

He almost literally could feel the downward progress of blood from his face, his shoulders, his hands. At that point in his life, Alex Brandes did not believe in accidents.

"What happened?"

"Some construction equipment got loose, knocked his car off the road. It rolled a few times. We had to use the hydraulic claws to get him . . ."

*It was my car*, Brandes thought.

"Damn it, Jonathan. How the hell *is* he?"

"Sorry, Alex. He's fine. I guess my bedside and family manner is a little out of phase these days. He's . . . Well, maybe not fine exactly, but he'll be all right if he gets some rest."

"Thank God. Has he said anything?"

"He never shuts up."

"What?" Alex almost held his breath. *What do I expect him to say?*

"He said he was sorry about the car. He said he's even more sorry about the flat. That doesn't make a hell of a lot of sense to me, but that's what he said."

"Nothing else?"

"He said you should use his car. There's a bread box on the top of the refrigerator. The keys are in it. Oh, he also said you might want to check with our local military leader."

"Did he say why?"

"He said to tell you the situation seems to have changed. He said you'll understand."

*Understand? Sure. Certainly.*

Brandes didn't have the slightest idea what he was supposed to understand and wanted to tell Shortell that.

"Can I see him?"

"I don't think you'll have much choice, Alex. He does need some rest. I'm not sure about a concussion yet. But I don't think he's intending to rest here. I think he plans to go home."

"Well, stop him, Jonathan. A man who just rolled over in a car and may have a concussion shouldn't be allowed to leave the hospital!"

There was a momentary pause on the telephone. "Alex. It might, after all, be best for his health to get him out of here. I mean, I'm not fond of this job at the moment myself. Not only that—I really could use the bed space."

*Welcome to the real world . . .*

"You want me to pick him up?"

"He says there isn't any time. He says your time is too valuable. I'll tell you what, Alex. I think I can get him to stay here for another few hours—if I promise to take a lunch break and drive him home. Unless something else develops that lets you or someone get him. And I don't think—well, that's beside the point. Okay? How's that?"

"That sounds fine. He's really all right, Jonathan? And that's all he said?"

"He's really okay, Alex. And he didn't say anything else, not even about the accident. We got more about that from the construction worker who called the police."

"What? You mean the guy who hit him called the cops?" *Do hit men report their crimes?*

"As best we can tell, the machine was idling and slipped into gear while the operator was getting some chains or something. Why? What else?"

"Nothing. Just take care of him."

"Right."

They disconnected. Brandes went back into the kitchen, saw there was at least another cup of coffee left, and began to pour.

Wismer might have had an accident, but it was in the car Brandes had been driving. After all, the *Charon* had been in the place only his boat was supposed to have been.

Since he'd arrived, he thought, he'd seen a lot of strangers but none who'd come up to him quietly and identified themselves as being from Kracke or Allenberg. For two men who little more than a day ago had been absolutely distraught about dangers facing him, they certainly didn't seem to have a lot of presence in Lyle, he thought.

*It's only because I can't see them*, Brandes told himself.

*Horseshit.*

Allenberg had some explaining to do. Very little was making sense, and Brandes was learning—a little to his surprise—that he basically was an orderly man.

He took the keys from the bread box and left. He had no key to lock the door after him or to get back in, and there was no guarantee even Wismer would have one after rolling around a few times in a car.

Wismer's car was older than the one he'd had, but he liked the 1976 Olds immediately; Wismer had had a tape deck installed, and Brandes liked his selections. He put Jane Olivor to work.

He exceeded the speed limit, passing the point where Wismer had been stopped and diverted by the roadblock.

Lyle, a community built around farms and basically by farmers, usually kept farmers' hours. Everyone should have been up and about. The streets hardly were bustling. They were not empty, but there was no *life* to them—no life in the people who walked them.

He stopped at the Tower, parked, and walked to his room in the hotel annex.

Brandes thought of Cynthia as he passed the porch, wondering if she still was in her room. He wondered if she had thought of him the previous night as much as he had of her.

Cynthia was a subject that had to be avoided.

He continued on to his room, opened it, and entered. Everything was as he had left it, as far as he could tell—but then, a search would have been made by a professional. Brandes did not expect the slightest sign of disorder.

He had taken a change of clothes with him the day before and had showered and changed at Wismer's. He wondered, though, if he should do something to make it appear he had stayed in the room.

Run the shower a while to get the tub wet? Toss himself around a few times in the bed? All this just in case his room hadn't yet been searched, but probably *would* be?

He didn't think it worth the effort . . . He had very little experience and doubted he could fool a trained agent.

"Good morning," Cynthia said.

For moments they just looked at each other. Brandes looked around the lab, then found himself able to reply. "It was a hell of a surprise," he said.

"Both ways. I thought you'd abandoned the human race."

"Yeah." *Nothing more to say about that.* "Well, my brother might have been involved in this one."

"Might have been? You know he was."

The old easily stirred feelings of antagonism toward Cynthia began. He loved her (*or was "bonded" to her?*); there certainly was no sense in denying it, especially to himself—but they somehow always grated on each other.

If it only could be otherwise! He wondered if she felt the same way.

"I don't know diddley," he said, maintaining control.

"Alex, this disease is like nothing anyone's ever seen. That means there's a damned good chance we've never seen it because it never existed before. If it never existed before, it was created, and—"

"I'll go over his notes."

"Of course. How's the boat? You did move onto a boat, didn't you?"

"The boat's fine. She's comfortable. I didn't know you'd heard about it."

"Somewhere. I heard about it somewhere. What got you off it? Peter?"

"Partly." His irritation already was increasing. What the hell could be so frustrating about a woman you . . . whatever?

She could have commented on the weather, and he would have been ruffled. *Defense? Probably. Defense is something most people are very good at even if they're not good at much else.*

"Then there are some people trying to shoot my ass off."

"Is that a good story, or is that a *real* real?"

Odd how little things came back so easily. They had always played a game. One would tell the other of some experience, embellished—or a downright lie. Either it would be accepted, or the other person could ask, "Is that for real?"

There were two options at that point. The storyteller could admit "slight exaggeration" or just stonewall it and say "of course."

The final test then was asking, "Is that a *real* real?"

No lies were permitted in answer to that question.

The game had been fun; the stories had been entertaining. Ultimately either lies were accepted because they made the story better or they were called and truth was affirmed. He'd never played the game with anyone else.

"That is a *real* real," he answered, and he regretted saying it. She looked concerned. He did not want Cynthia concerned about him.

"What's going on then, Alex?" She coughed as she said his name and took several seconds to catch her breath. "Swallowed wrong," she apologized.

"You smoke too much. There are people who are interested in this . . . problem," he said.

They walked as they talked. They had reached the main airlock, and Cynthia began cycling them through.

"I don't like that, Alex. It . . . scares me. I'm used to dealing with disease, yes. But . . . what do you know, Alex? About the disease?"

He stepped into the small chamber of the lock with her after they both took isolation gowns from a closet. Inside were two waste containers. One was lined with a transparent red plastic bag, the other white.

When they left, their lab coats would be put into the white bin. Any other trash went into the red. When the bins were emptied, both would be double-bagged in additional red plastic.

The trash would be incinerated. The red-white combination containing the lab coats went to the lab's laundry. There the white bag was dumped into hot water and disinfectant. It was made of a special plastic; it dissolved. As little contact as possible with potential contaminants was a most fundamental principle.

"Nothing, CJ." He bit his tongue, but she seemed not to have noticed. "You're right, of course. The thing probably was made here. They called me in just to look around and to try to think like Peter. At least I think that's why I'm here.

"Oh, I guess I'm supposed to do something medical if the opportunity arises." He chuckled, low. "But what I really am here for is . . . something like, uh, the caulking around a storm window. You are the ones—the CDC—who *are* the storm windows, the real protection. I'm an afterthought; I'm here so no one can say all bases weren't covered."

"Someone's taking you seriously, if they're trying to kill you."

"Someone is," he agreed. "There was an accident this morning. A friend of mine, Gerry Wismer . . ."

"I remember, from last night . . ."

"He was in my car this morning. Something happened; I don't know what. But, I don't know, CJ," he said, and this time the familiar term was easier to say, "maybe I'm just being my normal paranoid self. But I wonder about things like that."

"Probably why you're still alive," she remarked.

The sound of the compressor drowned them out for a moment as it dropped the pressure to that of the inside lab. The door opened, and they both stepped inside.

There were a half-dozen lab-coated technicians moving about. The atmosphere was not hurried. It was intense. Brandes recognized the difference and appreciated its significance. He felt intensity without recklessness was a hallmark of professionalism.

To the left was a long counter covered with racks holding eggs. It was there, he knew, that the team pinned its hopes on isolating an organism, although they also worked with some of the lab animals Peter had used—or, at least, was presumed to have used.

"Do you want to meet everybody?" Cynthia asked.

"Not on your life."

She laughed, a short laugh. "I expected that. You'll probably want to see Peter's office—that's outside, though, at the end of the hall—and his private lab. We call it his 'game room.' We picked that up from the regular technicians. It's over there."

She gestured. Across the room was another airlock door. It was closed.

"Is someone working in there?"

"I don't know," she said. "We generally keep the door closed anyway, maybe partly because Peter trusted only Linda with that combination. It's a shame she doesn't know anything useful about Peter's work. Apparently he didn't trust *anyone* that much. She's been a sweetheart, though.

"We have two people assigned to the room, and they go in and out once Linda's opened it . . ." She hesitated and then grinned. Whatever was behind her steady gaze, he thought, he preferred it remained unspoken.

*There are things to be avoided if the work is to be done.*

"I think there was something between them," she said, bringing that much into the open.

Then she sobered and a pain seemed to appear in her features. "Maybe keeping that number to herself is some way of hanging on to him. Be nice to her, okay?"

Brandes nodded.

"Still," she said, "until we know what he had in there we generally keep it closed, if not locked. The lab workers tell me that's what your brother did, anyway. Whenever he was in the

153

lab—either here or in the 'game room'—he kept the door closed."

"Did he keep any notes in there?"

"Yes. We haven't moved them. We're not moving anything out of here—and especially not out of *there*—until we have a better handle."

"Anyone make any sense of them?"

"Sure. No problem at all. They're not in any kind of code or anything. Plain language all the way." She snorted; he remembered the sound.

"Problem is, they don't tell us anything either. Maybe they'll tell *you* something."

"That," he said, "is what everyone is hoping for. Peter and I were not that close, though. Not really. I don't know if my being here is of any use at all."

"Oh, you're wrong there," she said, and for a moment he thought she was about to make a personal comment. Part of him begged her not to, another hoped for one.

"I'm glad you're sure."

"Not me, Alex." He relaxed for a moment. "If you were a shoo-in for failure—why, no one would be trying to kill you, would they?"

He wished she would stop pointing that out.

They walked on into the lab.

"Do you want to go right into the game room?"

"I think so. If I'm to be of any use it has to be soon. I want to read what's there and then go to his office."

"And if nothing then?"

He hesitated. "Then I'll see my father."

Cynthia was intimately aware of the relationship he had with his father. He was grateful for her tact in saying nothing.

"Is there a telephone in here?" he asked. "I'd like to check in with my hotel every now and—"

"*Oh!*"

He looked startled.

"I have this for you," she said. "I, uh. This is not that easy to explain, but I found this message for you . . ." She took the folded paper from her pocket.

He tried hard to control himself; later, at least, that's what he told himself. But the inevitable happened. *Something* about her *had* to annoy him. He didn't like it—not about her. About himself. As in the past, whenever he blew up at her, he later looked at the situation, rationally blamed her—and emotionally despised himself.

"What the hell do you do?" He almost shouted. Even so, his voice was loud enough for several technicians to turn toward them.

"Well, I thought I'd run into you when you came home last night. I was up late. I didn't want you to miss it. I mean, if you didn't check for messages . . ." *Like hell am I going to admit I got it from the door of his room!*

"Never mind." He took it and read Allenberg's note.

> *"We've had new developments; we feel you should be alerted."*

Alerted.
Alert.
Allenberg or Kracke would not have left more than that with a desk clerk.

He looked at Cynthia. She definitely seemed to have swallowed wrong this time, he thought. He had to wait until she stopped coughing and caught her breath. By then much of the fire that would have been in his voice was gone.

"I've got to go," he said coldly.

"The notes?"

"I'll be back in an hour or two. I want to see Gerry, and there's a phone call I've got to make. A few maybe."

He turned, left her—how often had he done it just that way?—and cycled himself out through the airlock.

\* \* \*

Allenberg felt the pressure his hand was exerting on his telephone receiver as—useless as it might be—the only *force* he could exert.

"Please call Mr, Kracke, Irene," he spoke into his intercom, flicking down its switch with his other hand. Gradually, gently, controlling himself as best he could, he replaced the receiver.

"Yes, sir."

It only would be moments before his secretary managed to find Kracke. Only two things ever would explain that man's not being available: his death or his decision not to be available. At a time of crisis, Allenberg knew, Kracke would not deliberately become inaccessible. And the former was . . . unlikely.

While he waited, Allenberg thought about the Lyle situation perhaps more deeply than he had before.

It had become personal.

As much as he cared for—and he did—Brandes, and as much as he needed the man, his problems were nothing.

Not compared to his daughter's decision to go to Lyle.

*Damn.*

The curse was directed more toward himself than anyone or anything else. He had dangled an irresistible carrot before Sarah, and she had reached for it.

But *now*, with Wismer out of action.

He was glad, at least, that his grandson had not gone to Lyle with his mother. But then, he should give her more credit than that. Hotheaded, singleminded, yes. She was all that and much, much more. But she never would have risked her son that way.

Besides, Allenberg smiled, and it was the first he'd managed since he'd learned about Sarah's trip, his grandson was far too occupied with trying to corner the precious-metals markets. God help the precious-metals markets, he thought, smiling more expansively, if still briefly.

"Yes?"

It was Kracke. "Jim," Allenberg said, "our main source of information in Lyle—on the nonmedical aspects—has had an accident. To me it seems to be just that. Ideas?"

"About whether it was an accident?"

"Please, Jim. You know damned well what I mean." He was getting irritable with Kracke—a bad idea, he thought. It was counterproductive: Kracke was imperturbable, and it would be wasted energy. "Is Brandes in any danger? And if he is, from whom? I may have to some extent wanted him there for bait, but I damn well did *not* want the bait nibbled. This is the last thing I need, Jim. Having him *think* he was in danger was one thing and was necessary. To have him actually *be* in danger opens more doors than I care to look through."

"It certainly does," Kracke agreed. "We've got no reason to think—Wait a minute, Adrian. We have been told to let go of the investigation. Perhaps whoever told us that isn't waiting for cooperation."

"I thought of that, too, Jim. I still think it's unlikely. Brandes isn't on to anything. At least not as far as we know."

Allenberg paused. Kracke said nothing. Allenberg's silence meant that he was coming to a decision, and Kracke had worked with him long enough to recognize such a moment when it came.

"Jim," Allenberg said, "get up there quickly. In person. Don't approach Brandes immediately, but don't go to any extremes to hide yourself either. He'll eventually know you're there anyhow."

"Fine. What else? There a *what else* sound in your voice."

"Sarah's gone there, Jim. Try to watch out for her, too."

"Certainly, Adrian," Kracke replied after a pause—a short pause, but it was there. "Certainly."

# SEVENTEEN

THE SOLDIERS HAD SEEMED AS SURPRISED AS JENNER.

They suddenly—to them—had been given orders that they were to function in the "real" world. Some had taken those orders with sneers, with disdain, with—when their reactions could not so simply be dismissed—disbelief.

Trained to fight, to do pushups, to follow orders—all of it had seemed a game. But now, it was as if Park Place and Boardwalk were real places on which real people walked, lived their lives. Died. The young soldiers were nervous, worried. They had never expected it to be . . . . real.

Emil Jenner had a cold "I-knew-it" feeling as he pulled up to the army barricade. He felt contempt for himself.

"What's the trouble, soldier?"

"Well, sir . . ." The young soldier's voice reflected his own unease. "We're supposed to stop all traffic entering or leaving Lyle, sir."

"I heard about the exercise. How long this time?"

*Let it still be an exercise.*

There was a desperate look in the younger man's eyes; it mirrored the feeling in Jenner's stomach.

"We, uh, were ordered, sir, not to take down the barricade until further orders. Maybe someone just got something confused. Those orders might come through at any time." He didn't look hopeful.

"Who gave those orders?"

"Colonel Lawrence, sir. He's in command."

"How do I talk to him?"

"You can't get to his headquarters. I mean, it's beyond the roadblock. And"—he hesitated—"we have orders not to let civilians use the communications equipment."

"Sounds like a pretty complete misunderstanding, doesn't it, soldier?"

"Sir. I'm sorry, sir." He straightened, tried to look military. "I'll have to ask you to turn around, sir."

Jenner gave a passing thought to ignoring him and trying to run the barricade, but all the men were armed.

*Would they use the weapons?*

He wondered what kind of "misunderstanding" covered the use of force against civilians trying to pass the roadblock. He couldn't find out, not with Doro and Nancy in the car.

"What's happening, Emil?" His wife's voice cracked as he began to turn and drive home.

"I'm not sure, Doro."

"I'm frightened."

He wanted to comfort her; more than that, he wanted to ease his own feelings of guilt for not having gotten Nancy out of the town sooner.

He did not know *how* he had "known."

But he had.

He felt ill, truly physically ill, as he thought of what his hesitation might have cost. It might have cost Nancy. Without her, Doro would collapse. He wished to tell her everything was going to be all right. He couldn't. He looked down at his huddled daughter. He could not see much more of her face than her eyes, and they were closed. A soft, brown comforter had been wrapped around her, as neither Emil nor Dorothy really knew when to keep her warm or when to try to cool her. She seemed to be asleep, pressed between them. Her condition had continued to worsen. He and Doro had *talked* about bringing her to the hospital in Lyle and had *agreed* they would rather get her to a city, he thought.

There had been those disturbing rumors. In the past day he had learned of the death of two friends in the hospital—Sarah Harlson, for one—and three other acquaintances.

He and others had been reassured when the CDC team had arrived that their presence didn't mean an outbreak of anything serious. Serious epidemics were the ones that made the news, the team told him and other interested Lyle residents. Most often, they'd said and laughed, they were chasing German measles.

The explanation had satisfied most people; to some degree it had satisfied Jenner. But not completely, he thought; something always had bothered him.

*And now I've waited until it was too late.* If anything happened to Nancy he never would forgive himself. *Why* hadn't he listened to that warning voice inside him? *Why?*

"Emil, what are we going to do? Her fever . . . it gets higher every time it goes up. Emil, I'm *scared*." Not half, he wanted to say, as much as I am. *And it's my fault.* "Should we take her to the Lyle hospital now?"

"No," he said. "I'll take her to Harbor View in the city."

"But *how*?" Her voice almost screeched. He couldn't tell her to get hold of herself. Not when it was his fault.

"I'll get her there," he said. "I'll get her there after it gets dark."

"He's fine," Shortell said.

Brandes had not realized his appearance made it appear he needed so much reassurance. He breathed deeply, willing calmness.

"Can I see him?"

"If he finds out you were here and *didn't* see him, I'll pay hell."

160

Shortell led the way along a corridor on the hospital's second floor.

"Anything new?" Shortell asked.

"No. I did get to the lab, but I had to leave. There are some things . . .".

"Yeah," Shortell said, breaking his stride. "She *is*—"

"Not her!" Brandes said and instantly regretted it. Had there been any doubt in Shortell's mind about a connection between Brandes and Cynthia, Brandes then had eliminated it. He smiled at the other doctor. "She is good-looking, isn't she?"

Shortell grinned. "Definitely that," he agreed.

Brandes told himself that at some future time he would tell Shortell the whole story.

Since he and she had moved apart he often wondered if she had found someone else, had married, and had had children. Part of him honestly wished that she had. He did want her to be happy. There always would be, he knew, a part of him that wanted what had been between them to continue.

Could Shortell be the answer? An irrational wave of jealousy swept over him.

Shortell opened the door to Wismer's room. Brandes was glad it was a private room.

"Hello, Alex. Didn't get your flat fixed."

His former teacher was sitting up, watching television.

"You've got it rough here."

"Don't let my nonchalance fool you. As soon as that . . . gentleman"—he gestured toward Shortell—"signs some papers, I'm getting the hell out of here. Too many sick people here."

Brandes could see Wismer almost immediately regretted saying that. The standard hospital joke had definitely lost its humor, considering present circumstances.

"What happened?"

"Big tractor or something. Back hoe. It pushed me off the road."

Brandes hesitated. He wanted to ask, of course, if the incident had been an accident, but he wasn't quite sure how to approach the subject. Besides, he thought, with Shortell in the room, too—Allenberg wouldn't like it. Just then, though, Shortell made his excuses and left. He had work elsewhere, much work.

"Sit down, Alex," Wismer said. "You were going to say?"

Brandes was nonplused. "What?"

Wismer started chuckling, graduating to a resonant laugh. "Sorry, Alex," he said. "It's just that, well, I can see the question in your head, and I can see you trying to figure out—"

"Enough!" Brandes realized he really was upset. He knew the response was silly. So he was easily read. So what?

*Hell of a secret agent.*

Wismer became quite still. "It might have been an accident," he said.

It was out. But why the hell should *Wismer* have suspected anything *but* an accident?

"There are some things . . ." Brandes began, but Wismer held up his hand, still covered by a bedsheet.

"I'll save you time and trouble, Alex. All out in the open. All at once. Yes, I'm familiar with your agency career and what happened in it. I'm sure I would have liked Hoeckle, too. I doubt Allenberg had anything to do with that, by the way."

Brandes was transfixed; numbed.

Wismer continued. "You've been wondering if Adrian forgot you. You couldn't find anyone here from the agency. Yes, Alex. Don't bother asking. I'm in contact with Allenberg—or at least I was."

"I can't believe this," Brandes said. "This is one hell of a coincidence."

"Don't be an asshole, Alex." Wismer stopped himself, sniffed. *Damn the smell of hospitals.* "Sorry, Alex, I know that's not how your 'old teacher' is supposed to address you. But it's true, so the hell with it. *There is no coincidence.*"

"It all is."

"Is it? Not at all, Alex. That's the thing about coincidence.

162

There are lots of sides to any issue and two ends to any animal—wait, that's not getting me where I want to go.

"To you it seems coincidence that you—you, who went off to join the government—should come back to your hometown and find one of your old teachers coincidentally working for the government. Right?"

"More or less."

"Children—when will they ever learn! Alex, when did you get interested in taking your medical inclination and putting it to work for the government?"

"I'm not sure. I thought about . . . things like that while I was still here in Lyle. One time I wanted to be an FBI agent, I remember. I did a career-day project on it." He smiled to himself, remembering, slightly embarrassed by the ingenuous character of the queries he had sent to FBI offices.

"Yep. So you thought about it while you were in school."

"Yes."

"And in school you had teachers. And I was one of them."

When understanding came, it came in a rush. No coincidence *was* involved at all.

Wismer had been the major influence that had led him to *join* the agency. He'd been recruited, and he'd never known it.

He thought of Hoeckle, of three years on the *Siege*, of sleepless nights—lonely nights at sea. Nights when Deneb and Riga might have been there to comfort him; nothing else. He wondered if he should hate Wismer as he had come to hate what role he himself had played in the agency. It was not easy; it was not possible. Crosscurrents of emotions rippled through him—mental, physical.

"See what I mean about coincidence?"

Brandes only could nod. What else in his life—literally, *in* his life—didn't he realize? The thought was unpleasant.

"Sometimes," Wismer continued, "something looks like a coincidence when you look at it from the end. When you look at it from the beginning, instead of coincidence you see something that's almost inevitable."

"I'm going to track down Shortell," Brandes said. "Is he part of this, too?" He could hear the irritability in his own voice; he couldn't eliminate it even though part of him felt it irrational. No one had forced him into anything—guided him, yes. No one had forced him.

"You mean the agency? No, he's not. Neither is Cynthia, in case you're interested."

Brandes realized he *was* indeed interested in that and also realized he'd not even considered the possibility. Still, it was better that Wismer had thought to add that.

*Values. The absolutes. Hate this, like that. Fight for this, die for that. Kill for that. Absolutes; the most transient of convictions.*

Brandes went to the nurses' station and asked for Shortell. The nurse looked at him for a second, as if to say, "Can't anyone leave him alone for a while?" But she had Shortell paged, and within a few minutes, the doctor called back. She gave the phone to Brandes.

"Jonathan, this is Alex. When do you think Wismer will be out?"

"Normally, I'd keep him here for another day," he said. "We need the room, though, Alex. And . . ." He hesitated.

"Maybe you'd better come here and talk in person."

There was some hesitation, but only moments passed between the time Shortell agreed and then appeared.

"About getting Gerry out . . ." Shortell picked up where he'd left off.

"Yeah. How bad is *it* now, Jonathan?"

"Some of the epidemiologists have changed hats. There's a limited amount they can do while they're trying to culture the thing, so they have come here to help. I need it."

"That bad? Maybe I . . ."

"Not on your life, Alex. I don't know all about what you're doing here, but I'm pretty sure it's to help *stop* the damned thing. I'd be a lot more comfortable knowing you're working at that.

"Besides, there's not much really that doctors or nurses are able to do for these people."

"How many cases now?" Brandes held his breath.

"Well, Alex, all the cases I told you about—the ones at the very beginning—are gone now. All of them. None to a recovery either. We have a hundred thirty-eight. You might say there's a regular turnover."

Brandes caught his breath. *My God, there had been developments in a day and a half.* He could hardly believe the astronomical rise.

"Christ, Jonathan, I had no idea. What are you telling people?"

"We really haven't had much of a panic problem yet, Alex. The only reason, of course, is that this is all happening so fast. It's only a matter of time before everyday conversation in the grocery store starts a hell of a situation in Lyle. And not *much* time at that.

"We might actually have a day or two, but not a hell of a lot longer. I hope you get some work done quickly, Alex. I really don't know *what* the government procedure is for something like this. Do they drop an A-bomb on us and sterilize the place?" The humor was lame, died unnoticed.

"Too expensive," Brandes said, and although he knew that idea was ludicrous he found himself wondering just *what did* the government do? For that matter, had anything this fast and lethal ever hit the country before? There had been the great epidemic of 1918—but some people recovered from that flu.

"What then, Alex? You've got something of an inside track. I'm sure of that." His voice had a nervous edge, an entirely understandable nervous edge.

"First," Brandes said, "those soldiers go to work for real. A quarantine. Then if the populace gets stirred up—or worse yet, organized—martial law and a dusk curfew. Then steps to stop transmission." His voice was flat, dry. He looked directly into Shortell's eyes, ignoring what he saw there and knew to be the product of his words. The truth had to be spoken. Shortell *should* be one of the first to know. He would be one of those most relied upon when the time came . . .

165

"How the hell are they going to do that, Alex? We can't do that."

"No, Jonathan. You don't understand. I mean halting transmission by sterilization. No A-bomb, Jonathan, but fire. Definitely fire. Even then," he said steadily, quietly, "we can't be sure fire would be effective against this thing. But we very well may have to try it."

"My God, do you think it's going to come to that?"

"Truth?" He didn't wait for a reply. "I think there's a damned good chance it's already come to that. If Lawrence has got the figures you just gave me—and I'd sure as hell bet he had them first—there's a damned fine chance he's already altered the character of his little 'exercise' out there and brought it a step closer to all-out quarantine. It's gotten out of hand, Jonathan."

"Yeah." Shortell's voice was weak. "Guess it has."

"Jonathan, the reason I paged you was to ask if I could use your office to make a phone call."

"Sure. The office is on the fifth floor. Turn left, end of the corridor. You mean they're still letting us talk to the outside?"

He'd meant it as a joke—at least partly. Brandes looked into his eyes deeply, saw the man needed reassurance that he *had* made a joke. Brandes could not give it to him.

"So far," Brandes replied. "But that won't last long without clearances."

"Shit." Shortell admitted to himself he was more afraid than ever. There were new things to fear. Not only the disease—disastrous as that might prove. Now there was the army and the people of Lyle themselves. His chest constricted with the fear he suddenly felt; his stomach churned.

Brandes went to the fifth floor and walked to Shortell's office.

He called Allenberg. The line was pulse-dialed, so he had to wait for the connection. While he waited he listened for any sound other than the computer-generated tones. He heard none, and he wondered when that would change.

Lawrence undoubtedly had everything planned out. Brandes

had seen some signal corps insignias; the colonel would know where every connection entered and left Lyle.

Brandes wondered what plans there were for the press. There was no way at all that a quarantine could be kept secret for more than a day, if that. Every network and local station and every newspaper and wire service within five hundred miles would converge on Lyle's perimeter.

That was Lawrence's problem.

"Yes?" It was Allenberg.

"Brandes."

"Thank God. Where the hell have you been? I left a message for you last night."

"Why didn't you call Wismer's house directly?"

There was a pause, then Allenberg said, "You know about that, then. Well, it never really was our intention to keep you in the dark about Gerry, anyway."

"Sure."

"I don't give a shit if you believe me, Alex. There's too much going on. Let's get to business."

"Okay," Brandes sighed. Allenberg was right. *I may hate the agency, my involvement in it, even at times Allenberg. But shit: It hurts when he's right.*

"Lawrence has sprung the quarantine, of course." Of course! *Hell*, Brandes thought, *I may not be the last person to find things out, but I'm way down on the list. And*, he added ruefully, *a good amount of the fault for that is mine.*

"And there have been demands."

"What do you mean, *demands?*"

Allenberg recounted everything from the hourglass in Greenwich Village to the call from Fitch.

"Who the hell is Fitch?"

"No one who really matters, except as a go-between."

"Great." *Demands.* Demands that he stop trying to find out what was going on.

"Adrian, why should that be such a shock to *you?* Shit, you got me here because you knew someone was trying to kill me to stop me from looking into this. What's so surprising about demands now? What the hell is going on?"

Allenberg was at a momentary loss for words, but only momentary. He couldn't tell Brandes all that had been a setup! The last thing he needed was to have Brandes quit, even if he couldn't get out of Lyle. Brandes was stubborn enough to quit and sit and watch, petulant enough to pout. Sometimes Allenberg was very disturbed by what he considered some of Brandes's childish propensities.

"It's just the first time anyone's *admitted* your importance," he said.

"Well, they were busy saying it in other ways this morning," he said.

"How?"

"You know damn well. Wismer's in the hospital. He had an accident while driving my car. Only we know better, don't we?"

Allenberg was ready to reassure Brandes. After all, *he* knew there wasn't really anyone trying to kill the scientist . . .

The *Charon* had been a legitimate accident upon which he'd capitalized. When that proved insufficient, there had been the Fire Island "stabbing." But never was there any real threat. *Never.* He felt uneasy.

*What if he's right?*

"Kracke will be up there soon," he said.

"You mean that up until now my bodyguard has been an old man who spent his last twenty years as a schoolteacher? Are you shitting me?"

"He's very capable," Allenberg said, wanting very much to change the subject. Then he had it. "One thing more I'd like you to do, Alex."

Brandes was aware of the new direction in the conversation, but he knew the futility of continuing to complain. He didn't want Allenberg accusing him of whining, even if he had every right.

"What?"

"I'd like you to meet my daughter."

This certainly *was* a different direction. Brandes didn't respond at first.

"You're trying to set me up on a blind date with your daughter while people are trying to kill me and there's a disease rampaging."

"Don't be an ass! I'm not fixing you up." Not a bad thought, though, Allenberg mused. It might serve Brandes right. He actually found some humor in that. "My daughter's coming up there to try to help." He couldn't bring himself to admit that she'd gone without telling him.

"Are you totally crazy, Adrian? You're letting your daughter into this mess?"

"We have a unique family, Alex. Maybe you'll understand when you meet her. She'll be arriving at the airport about four-thirty this afternoon. I'd really appreciate it if you could pick her up and take her into town, maybe stay with her until Kracke gets there."

"So he can take over the babysitting?"

Allenberg laughed loudly. "Hardly. She knows Kracke and may be able to help him. Of course, if you two get along, she might be an asset to you, too. Have you gotten into Peter's notes yet?"

"No. There have been . . . delays. I'm going to go back to the lab for them."

There was a slight hesitation and Allenberg said, "You know, of course, that there's no question now, Alex. The demands, the hourglass. Peter created this disease on purpose. You know that, don't you?"

"Yes, Adrian. I know that. My father never will accept that, but I know it."

"About your father . . ."

"I'll handle that if I have to. I may find something in the notes." Allenberg chose not to pursue it. "Just what does your daughter—what's her name?"

"Sarah."

"What does Sarah do for the agency?"

"She's not actually *with* the agency."

"Well?"

"Well, this is very awkward."

"Out with it!"

"She's a television reporter."

"Holy shit, Adrian. You *are* out of your goddamn mind!"

"It's not like it sounds, Alex. Just suspend judgment, will you? I think you'll like her. Really."

"Oh, sure, Adrian. Sure. I suppose you'd rather have her here so you can muzzle the news, huh?"

"Oh, boy. Are you in for a treat. Meet her, have dinner. Then call me back and repeat that."

"Goodbye, Adrian."

"Goodbye. Good luck, Alex. I'm afraid all hell's about to break loose in that town. Be careful."

"Yeah." He hung up and considered.

Bizarre.

The man definitely was bizarre. He looked at his watch. Already it nearly was four o'clock. He didn't have time to stop back at the lab. He would have to go to the airport first, pick up . . . Sarah. And then go to the lab.

But he *had* to get to those notes. Perhaps more so now that Allenberg had received the Greenwich Village warning.

# EIGHTEEN

THE SMALL BEECH LANDED GENTLY. BRANDES watched it through the airport restaurant's picture window. When he'd arrived at 4:15, he'd learned there had been a half-hour delay, so he had decided to get a drink and a snack.

He did not look forward to this new development. He could see little to be gained by Allenberg's daughter's involvement—especially since she was a newsperson.

What a life Allenberg must lead! he thought and laughed to himself. *Serves the old bastard right to have a child who constantly keeps sniffing at his heels.* If, he mused, that's what she did. She might, despite what Allenberg had said and despite his laugh, be little more than a tool of her father.

Events swiftly were piling on top of each other, and none of the changes was for the better. He only could hope that Sarah's introduction into the scene was not a development that would make things worse.

That "things" were getting worse was increasingly apparent. He had stopped at Andy's for gas. Andy was truly elderly and somehow timeless. He was grizzled and bent, but Brandes never could remember him looking any different.

"Tell me what's happenin', Alex. I need to know."

"You know about the disease, Andy."

"Yeah. I also know the army's been sniffin' around here for days, and finally this morning stopped sniffin' and put on the bite."

"They quarantined Lyle, Andy."

"Figured that. What else? I didn't get to this age by being careless. I wanna know so I can duck."

Brandes had to grin. "It could be worse, Andy. The Centers for Disease Control—"

"Ain't that much of a hick, Alex. I know what the CDC is. And I know they're here."

"Then what do you want to know, Andy? You seem to have everything now."

"Nope. I wanna *know*, Alex. I want you to tell me how bad it is, Alex. I know you; I know I'll think about your opinion."

"They're making progress at the lab, Andy . . ."

"Alex." Andy's voice was soft, but it managed to cut Brandes short. "Alex," he repeated and bent even more so he could look directly into Brandes's eyes, "I'm too old a cat to be fucked by a kitten."

Brandes blinked.

"There are more than sixty dead people. At least I think so. There's about a hundred forty more sick. Nobody gets up, do they?"

"No."

"It's what I thought. Thank you, Alex. I'm not, by the by, goin' to call everybody with those numbers. Me, Alex, I just wanna know. I don't panic too easy." He paused, staring again. "But, Alex, I know the people around here. Those numbers are bound to get out soon, only when they do they'll be bigger.

"Folks are goin' to notice they're losing neighbors real soon. What I'm tryin' to say, Alex, is, you be careful. Some of these people may decide they don't like scientists and doctors anymore.

"They might not," he said heavily, "look on Peter's brother too fondly."

172

Brandes's insides churned. He'd never thought of that aspect! He had listened nearly hypnotized by Andy. He couldn't remember the man ever having said so much at one time. Andy, he thought, is very definitely serious.

"Thank you, Andy. Really. Thanks."

"Take care."

Brandes had been happy that the plane was late. He certainly needed a drink after that meeting with Andy.

The plane was moving closer to the terminal when an army Jeep appeared on the runway and stopped about a hundred yards ahead of it. A soldier jumped out and waved the pilot to a stop. He walked to the nose of the plane, but they exchanged only a few words. Brandes almost could guess its content.

The door opened, and one woman stepped down. She was several hundred yards from the terminal; Brandes could not see her clearly. She carried only one piece of luggage. Brandes considered that a point in her favor.

Immediately the door closed, the plane turned, and within seconds again was airborne. There was no doubt in Brandes's mind.

He'd seen *the last plane out*.

The soldier took the woman's case and helped her into the Jeep. Brandes was impressed. He wondered if he was seeing the results of Allenberg's influence or Sarah's.

He finished his drink and left the bar. The Jeep had passed from sight, hidden by the building. He waited only a few seconds, and Sarah entered.

Brandes simply stared for several seconds. The woman was undeniably beautiful. Her eyes, though, were what really caught his attention. They were a translucent green; he idly thought about television—could it pick up that color? He doubted it.

"Miss Allenberg?" He ventured.

She smiled. "Close enough. Sarah." She kept his gaze riveted, and Brandes realized she had no idea who he was. He was not thinking very clearly.

"Uh, sorry. I'm Alex Brandes. I—"

173

"Alex! I'm glad I met you right away. My father told me something about you, of course. How is he?"

*She doesn't know?*

"It's pretty obvious you talked to him more recently than I, Alex," as if reading his mind. "I mean you *are* here." Brandes thought the opposite *obvious* but decided not to say so.

"He's fine. Sarah, I'm not too certain why he let you . . ." Her laughter was like a chime, and he realized he'd said the wrong thing. "Well, I'm not sure *I* think it's a good idea."

"Alex," she said patiently, "that's not a point I'll argue. I wouldn't ever anyway, but if you were watching my plane you'd know it doesn't much matter now. I'm here for the duration."

"For a story?"

"That, too," she agreed cryptically.

Brandes noticed that she was holding her suitcase again; the soldier had not come in. Presumably he'd gotten back in his Jeep and returned to picket duty or whatever.

"I'll take that," he said and put out his hand. He braced himself, but it never came. She nodded her thanks, and he took the luggage. He'd thought he had *something* about her figured out, some part of her classified. In his experience, many women with the self-confidence and poise Sarah had also were touchy when men opened doors for them.

Sarah was not one of those, he realized. Sarah, he thought, might very well *be* a category.

"I'd like to stop at the lab and at the army headquarters," Brandes said. "Time is becoming crucial in Lyle. For Lyle."

"I know. But I really did come here to help. I'm sure my father expressed at least a little confidence in me." She tilted her head to one side. Brandes liked the hint of the girlish in the woman.

"He did more than hint. He practically told me I'd be obsolete once you got here."

She laughed. "I like gallant lies," she said. "My point is this. If I'm going to be of any use, the time I spend here has to be quality time. It only can be if I know *everything* you know. So, I'll buy you a drink—and you spill it all out. All right?"

174

All right?

Sure, it was all right. What the hell. A minute ago he'd been ready to fly down the country roads partly because of the talk he'd had with Andy, because time was indeed a vanishing commodity.

Now, he thought, it makes more sense to have a drink with this woman and to talk to her.

He wondered what kind of relationship a man would have with this woman. What would she be like when it wasn't business? He wasn't sure he wanted to find out. And he wasn't sure he didn't.

Brandes held the door for her—again no complaint—and they sat at a table. She ordered a Manhattan, up. He ordered a vodka martini.

And then he told her everything.

Brandes rounded a curve in the road and was surprised.

"It was here," he said to Sarah. "When I left Lawrence's the last time, I was stopped by a squad of men here."

There was no sign of the soldiers or trucks that had made up the barricade.

"Not surprising, really," she said. "Things have gotten worse since then, right?" He nodded. "Our colonel—whatever else I may decide he is—isn't a complete fool. He increased the size of the quarantined area when it became apparent the problem had grown.

"Continue on this road a half mile *beyond* his headquarters, and I'll owe you a Manhattan, up, if you don't run into a roadblock and some very determined—and frightened, by the way—soldiers."

Brandes nodded again. "No bet," he said. "I have the feeling that there are some traits in your family that definitely are hereditary. I'm not sure I'll ever make a bet with you."

"I do bluff."

"Often?"

"Of course not," she said and turned the most bland and innocent face toward him he'd ever seen. He laughed; she also laughed.

"Charming house," she said when they reached the command post.

"Army only takes over the best."

A corporal sat at a folding table on the porch. Brandes looked for Lieutenant Knotts. He wasn't there.

"Yes?" the corporal inquired.

"I'm Dr. Brandes."

"I remember. But . . ."

"Sarah . . . Allenberg," she said.

The corporal soon returned and led them to the colonel.

"You know, Doctor? You understand that what I've done is entirely within my discretionary powers?"

"Yes. I understand you've begun your quarantine." He felt as though he were fencing. Nothing Lawrence had said should have made him feel that way, he thought, but still he did.

"Yes. We've expanded the quarantined area somewhat, too."

"I noticed," Brandes said.

"Look," Lawrence had all appearances of a tolerant man being perhaps pressed too far, "I am very busy right now. There are all sorts of things to work out . . ." Brandes could guess. "And I thought you belonged in a laboratory or something. Sorry to be that blunt, but we all have our jobs during this."

Lawrence effectively, for himself at least, had resolved the question that had been at least partially left open on their previous meeting. Brandes had no authority over the actions of the military. He was a snooper; he possibly was even useful; he was nothing more.

Brandes had not really ever thought he did have power over Lawrence; the agency's assigning him to the situation, however, had—as such things always do—left open many possibilities. Before, the colonel had not wanted to take chances. Brandes realized that whatever orders Lawrence had received overnight had come from an echelon more powerful than Allenberg.

"And who are you?" the colonel asked, looking not only at Sarah but making certain he did not miss a total evaluation of her figure—which was, Brandes reflected, somewhat overweight but still well worth evaluating.

"She's . . ." Brandes began, but Sarah finished.

"I'm Sarah Allenberg," she said. "I'm a reporter."

If all hell could break loose silently and unobtrusively, Brandes thought, it certainly did so at that moment. He could not even conceive of what must be happening in Lawrence's mind.

The silence, long enough to be uncomfortable, was testimony to the potency of the bomb Sarah Allenberg had just dropped on the officer.

The last thing—possibly, Brandes thought, quite *literally* the *last* thing—he had expected to have to deal with this soon was the press.

"There's a press blackout, of course," the colonel recovered. Nice, even, "everybody-knows-that" tone. Hell, Brandes was certain that blackout had just been declared.

"Temporary, I'm sure," Sarah said in a tone even more reasonable. Brandes's admiration for Allenberg's daughter was rising fast. "Until I can file, I'll just gather what information I can so I'm ready. You've told us about the quarantine, Colonel. Are there any exceptions? Medical personnel with samples? That sort of thing?"

In one fast attack, Brandes thought, she had turned a blackout into an interview.

"I'm not prepared to say very much right now, Miss Allenberg. I'll, of course, cooperate with you when it's possible. But please understand that this is a developing situation. I won't have much time to keep . . . the press . . . up to date on a moment-to-moment basis."

"Of course not!" She sounded almost shocked, and the reaction seemed to shock Lawrence. "Just tell me who your press officer is."

"No one's been detailed, of course—yet. I think I'll brief Lieutenant Knotts. Perhaps he can help."

"Thank you, Colonel." She smiled. "There is one thing I'm sure you can answer now, and I really think that since Alex and I will be moving around so much, we should know. Are the troops ordered to shoot to kill?"

Lawrence's face began to twist; he controlled it.

"Yes," he said. "They are. If someone tries to break the quarantine."

"We've got to move along, Colonel. I just wanted to stay in touch with you and, of course, to introduce you to Miss Allenberg."

"Thank you, Doctor. Very thoughtful." They turned to go when Lawrence said mildly, "One more thing." Brandes instinctively disliked the tone; it portended a message he knew he would like less. "There is a field just east of here, just inside our quarantine perimeter. Do you know the Haddon place, Doctor?"

Brandes did. Once it had been a working farm. It had been bought by a New York accountant who wanted a retreat with a lot of land and privacy—and of course, rumor had it, a tax shelter. The farm no longer produced. Dan Haddon let his neighbors use what grew to feed their livestock, though, and the community as a whole had accepted Haddon and his family.

"Mr. Haddon is vacationing in Europe," Lawrence said. "We have invoked emergency powers to make use of a small portion of his property."

"What for?" Brandes asked. He might be being lured into the question, but what the hell? He needed the answer; let Lawrence play games.

"We have ordered cremation for those who succumb to the disease."

Brandes whistled softly. "Colonel," he said, "there's a good possibility this town is going to react very unpleasantly to what's already happened. I'm certain they are going to be very opposed to having their relatives cremated in a farm field."

"I suppose they will, Doctor." His voice was hard, his eyes harder still. "But this bug isn't getting out of here. I'm going to stop it." How effectively, Brandes thought, the colonel managed to forget the medical personnel. "And just so you know *all* of it," Lawrence said, "we intend to exhume those who have already been buried and to cremate those."

"That's going to be difficult, Colonel, isn't it?" Sarah asked.

178

"Some of the bodies, I'm sure, went out of Lyle for burial already—before you instituted the quarantine."

A wicked smile cracked on Lawrence's face. "We considered early on that this might be necessary," he said. "A rash of wildcat strikes in some cemeteries has delayed a lot of burials. We can 'recall,' as it were, all but three of the corpses, and we're working on exhumation orders for those."

"Convenient strikes," Brandes observed.

"For us, very."

Brandes wondered just how fundamentally the United States government could intervene in and manipulate the lives of its citizens. Or was that too-exaggerated cynicism? He hoped so.

They left Lawrence and didn't speak until they were back in the car.

"What do you think of Napoleon?" he asked Sarah.

"I like him," she said, and Brandes's head swiveled quickly to stare at her. "Oh, I don't mean as a person. He plays at too many silly little skirmishes with people. But he's the kind of officer needed for this job, I'd say. And if he was the one behind that plan to keep those bodies available, I say he was one damned clever man."

Sarah Allenberg, Brandes reflected, was impressed by the damnedest things.

"I think we should stop by the lab," he said. "I have to get Peter's papers and start sifting through them. It seems like I've been here a week instead of two days. I don't dare take any more time for groundwork."

"No," she agreed. "You don't. I would like to stop at the hospital for five minutes, though. Is it out of our way?"

"I can make a loop, that's no problem. But you're not going to learn much in five minutes."

"Oh, this isn't for work," she said. "I want to visit Uncle Gerry."

Uncle Gerry, he thought. Of course. What else?

# NINETEEN

THE TREES, THE MEADOWS, AND AN INLET FROM A
river that would at another time have been pleasant scenery
turned into a blur as Brandes sped away from the hospital. New
tension caused him to grind his teeth. Brandes tried to blank his
mind—or at least to suspend his emotions—for just a moment.

Sarah's word had been good. She'd spent only about five
minutes with Wismer. Brandes had waited in the car. He felt an
urgent need to get the rest of Peter's notes from the laboratory,
even though he believed his search through them for information
about the disease would be fruitless.

He had not anticipated what would happen in Wismer's room
while he tapped his fingers to "Jellico Cat" playing on his tape
deck, waiting for Sarah Allenberg's return.

She definitely was someone worthy of her treacherous old
man, he thought. She had a degree of self-sufficiency he had
rarely seen before—in anyone, male or female.

She'd told him the most recent news so matter-of-factly: "Can I
take my suitcases home after we go to the lab?" she'd asked when
she had returned.

"I thought you might want to check in first," he'd said. "I

doubt there's much happening at the lab that would interest you at the moment."

"Oh, I don't know about that. Besides, I'm not *checking in* at the hotel. Uncle Gerry offered me a room at his house."

Brandes had inwardly groaned. He had a roommate, of sorts.

He slowed, realizing how fast he was driving, and the beauty of New Hampshire's scenery again could be appreciated. He concentrated on that, trying not to think about Sarah living in the same house. There must be a damned good reason, he thought. Gerry probably had been injured because *Brandes* was in the house. Would he have to worry about protecting Allenberg's daughter?

But Brandes could *talk* to Gerry. Despite Sarah's apparent capabilities, Brandes was not sure he could speak as freely with her present.

Don't try to fool yourself, he thought. *You know damned well that you just wouldn't feel comfortable sounding unsure of yourself in front of her.* There was something about her that made him not want to sound incapable or uncertain in her presence.

Brandes drove. The Futures laboratory, measured by time spent along New Hampshire roads, was about equidistant from the hospital and from Wismer's house.

The house now was inside the circle of Lawrence's quarantine.

His own concerns about Colonel Lawrence and his authority, Brandes knew, simply were an outgrowth of his mistrust of and distaste for any kind of governmental authority.

He said nothing. They neared the lab.

The Futures building was set back on a natural shelf in the mountain that rose above it. Years before the lab had been built, a road had been cut to the plateau. At one time there had been a house there; Brandes did not know what had happened to it.

No one had bothered to continue the road the rest of the way to the top of the mountain. It was very steep; there would have been little point, unless the state had put a park at the summit.

There were hiking trails there. Brandes had climbed them as a child and had become familiar with them. He and Peter and their father occasionally had gone on hiking trips on the face of the mountain.

Peter had been fascinated with a notch cut by nature halfway up the mountain's side. Their father had told them it probably had been cut by glacier activity. It was a perfect haven for hikers wanting to rest. It was much larger than a football field, covered with grass that never had been cut. A meadow on a mountainside.

Peter never had forgotten the meadow and had thought of it when the time came for him to build his laboratory. Some blasting, the improvement of the road to that point—and Peter had the ideal spot for the building in which he would make history. There was no doubt of that in Brandes's mind—Peter had intended to make history.

Wismer's car dipped over the final rise and into the Future's parking lot. It was nearly full. He drove around to the rear of the lot and found a spot in the shade of a large tank. He looked at it for a second, wondering if it had been there on his last visit, and decided that it had not.

New Hampshire winters could be cruel, though, he thought. Considering what fuel trucks would have to do to get to the plateau when the steep road was slicked with ice, it would have made sense for Peter to have installed reserve fuel capacity.

They left the car. The guard at the building's entrance waved him through, glancing only briefly at Sarah.

Brandes went directly to the laboratory area. He wanted the books kept in Peter's inner lab, not only those from Peter's office. He cycled through the first door of the first airlock and helped Sarah into a lab coat, explaining to her that it would go into one of the plastic bags when they left.

The inner door swung open with a hiss.

"Yes?" a pert, curly-haired brunette greeted them. She looked at Brandes's face and at Sarah and then she turned crisply back to him, her eyebrows rising. "Oh!" she exclaimed. "Dr. Brandes?"

"Yes," he said, a little taken aback, first by her energetic recognition and then by the rather somber look into which her face fell.

"I'm Linda Denard," she said.

"I'm pleased to meet you," he said. He was not certain if he had met her before and should know her.

"I guess you don't know me," she said. "Peter talked often about you though. I guess he never mentioned me."

A hopeful look was in her eyes. Brandes, though, couldn't lie. "I don't think so," he said. "My brother and I haven't really been in close—well, we *hadn't* been in close contact—for the last few years." He'd done what he could, he thought.

"That's all right," Linda said and turned toward Sarah. Brandes introduced her quickly. Linda nodded.

"I think you may know a few other people here," Linda said. "I know you know Cynthia, uh, Dr.—"

"Yes, I know her."

"She's over there," Linda said and pointed. Cynthia was sitting, her shoulders slumped. The search for their disease was tiring her, Brandes thought. A normally hidden part of him wanted to say to the rest of him, "Well, we'll have to do something about that . . ." He fought that urge. "She said you were in before but had to leave in a hurry," Linda continued.

"I had to make some calls. What's going on here?"

"Well, there's a hope, a possibility—not big, you understand—that we're on to isolating the antibody." She delivered the final part of her statement with a great deal of pleasure. Brandes hardly could blame her. It was the first good news they'd had since the CDC team had arrived.

Whether it would do much good for the victims—or future victims—remained to be seen. From an antibody an identification of the organism might follow and eventually a means of prevention devised. But the questions would remain: How difficult would it be to produce it? And how *much* could be produced? And then there was the possibility that the organism itself might change from generation to generation, mutating, modifying, making it impossible for scientists to keep the inoculations up to date and effective.

"That's very good news, isn't it?" Sarah asked.

"Very," Linda agreed. "Of course, there's a lot of work to do, even if we really are on it. Even then, the people who already have the thing . . ." she shrugged.

"Yes. I understand."

"I've come," Brandes said, "to pick up the notebooks Peter left."

"Yes," Linda said, and again he could sense a sadness in her. "I'll show you his other lab. 'The tank,' *he* called it."

"Speaking of tanks," he said, "isn't that one outside something new?"

"Oh," she said, and gave a small laugh. "That's 'the goose!'" She grinned at his quizzical look. "Peter always called it 'the goose.' When I asked him why, he told me to take a good look at what it did to the architecture of the rear of the building. He had a very good sense of humor," she said. Again the melancholy.

"What's in it?" Brandes asked.

"Peter only would tell me it contains water. He seemed to always be getting water trucked in. He really didn't tell me a lot—not about his work."

"You were close in other ways?" Brandes asked as she led them across the larger lab's floor, between tables with retorts and analytical equipment, incubating eggs, tired-looking technicians.

"Yes," she answered. "I always wanted to meet you. I know you and Peter hadn't been that close recently, but he did think an awful lot about you—and of you."

Brandes felt himself flush. He tried to examine just what he had thought of Peter. He pushed the question away. He wanted to be able to reach out to Linda to comfort her. He had the feeling that she felt greater pain at Peter's death than he himself.

They were approaching Cynthia. Brandes did not want to face her again after their hostile meeting that day. They always fought when they didn't want to. The "bonding," to use Wismer's word, remained beneath the surface of any encounter.

Cynthia was on her feet as they neared, and obviously angry. Cynthia was gesturing pointedly at a piece of equipment and talking to a man who seemed very much out of place. He wore a lab coat, but his shoulders were hunched—not from a poor posture but from a surplus of muscle.

"Just move the damned thing," he heard her say. The man grinned, apparently immune to her ire, and turned away toward the equipment she'd indicated.

"That's Rachek," Linda said, catching Brandes's look. "He moves things and such. He isn't a biologist or chemist. Not one of us." She looked at Brandes as if she expected a response. He couldn't think of one.

"You look tired," Brandes said to Cynthia. He realized as he said it that, from the other side of the room, he hadn't been aware of just *how* tired she looked. Cynthia was indeed haggard and lined; her eyes, while not bloodshot, somehow should have been, he thought.

"Tired. Yeah." She smiled and, Brandes thought, did a credible job of it. "You know what happened since . . . since you left only a few hours ago?"

"The antibody?"

"Maybe," she said and brightened. "We haven't stopped working since we saw a glimmer of a chance we had the damned thing. No one has. I'm not the only tired person in this room." She gestured, and Brandes automatically followed her movement. The others were either bent over instruments, had their gaze virtually glued to instruments, or were in their nonrushed-hasty way setting up necessary equipment for their next experiments. The CDC, he thought, certainly was getting its money's worth from its people. "And this is? . . ." Cynthia tilted her head to her, left, looking at Sarah and questioning Brandes.

"This is Sarah Allenberg. She's a reporter."

Cynthia's eyes opened wider, the fatigue that had been allowing them to droop disappearing. "Reporter."

"Yes," Sarah said and offered her hand. Cynthia took it. "I don't think he does people justice sometimes, though." She smiled. She meant Brandes. Cynthia smiled. Brandes tried to understand.

"He can be difficult," Cynthia replied.

"I'm also here helping my father. He's with the government, Cynthia"—how easily she slipped onto a first-name basis!—"and sometimes the instincts a reporter develops can be a lot of use in a lot of different situations."

"No doubt," Cynthia said, nodding agreement. "I knew a reporter once who got a job as a 'general troubleshooter' with a big corporation. I don't think they called him that . . ." Brandes realized the two women were walking away from him.

"May I cut in?" a voice said, and Brandes saw Linda still standing next to him.

He smiled at her. "Can you show me where Peter kept his things? The things in his lab here?"

"Sure," she said. "Peter showed me some of the things. He was working on a lot of different things, you know."

"What kinds of things?"

"*That*," she said emphatically, "is where I can't help you. He was more secretive than any of you . . ." Brandes immediately realized that she considered him a sort of "government agent"— well, he thought, wasn't he?—and that Peter had told her that.

He tried again. "You mean lots of ways of approaching some project or lots of projects?"

"Well, I really can't be sure of anything," she said. "I did know that he was very happy when . . . just before . . . he died. He must have come across something important. Not much of his notes make much sense, though. He usually was very organized, too."

"Yes," Brandes agreed.

"But *you* never were," she said as she led him through the second-cycle airlock and into Peter's private laboratory area. He glanced a question.

"He told me a lot about you, Alex. Can I . . . ?"

"Yes . . ."

"He told me a lot. Mostly about when you were children. He even told me about the 'three-day rule.'" She smiled.

Brandes laughed openly, loudly. "Christ," he said, "I haven't talked about that in years. But it was the 'five-day-rule' as I remember it."

186

"No." Linda shook her head with emphasis. "I know he said it was three."

"Hardly matters," Brandes said, still smiling. "Peter was always a little more methodical and careful than I was. It was his idea."

"Seems like a good one."

The "three-day"—or "five-day"—"rule" had been an invention of Peter's when they had been in their early teens. Peter had very seriously pronounced it as a rule of health and hygiene—and with good cause, Brandes reflected.

Peter had gotten very ill on a cream cheese and grape jelly sandwich he'd found in the refrigerator. Alex had told Peter he had made the sandwich only the previous day. In fact, he had made it more than a week before. No one had noticed it.

So Peter had gotten ill—violently ill.

When Peter had finished retching and questioning his brother, he announced in imperious tones the "five-day rule."

Anything perishable that was left in the refrigerator for five days and hadn't been eaten was gone. Declared wolf's head. Outlaw. Garbage. It *went*. No excuses.

It had been a good rule, Brandes thought. Also, it had been one that had been enforced throughout the years. He felt a sudden pang of regret, of loss, for Peter, one of the few since he'd learned his brother had died. He realized that after all the years and experiences that had separated them, that silly damn rule had to some extent kept them together because even on the *Siege* he observed it. If anything was in the refrigerator and not the freezer for five days—overboard it went. He knew Peter would have approved of *that*.

"Did you keep it like a good boy?" Linda asked, extending an arm into the private lab, ushering Brandes in. "The three-day rule?"

"Well, like I said, I remember it as five-day, but now that you mention it, yes, I did keep it like a good boy. I guess Peter told you how it came about, and after seeing him that sick, I guess it scared me. To tell you the truth, I've been following the five-day rule ever since then."

187

"Strange," she said.

"What?"

"Oh, the things we focus on, I guess. He made a great deal of telling me about that part of his boyhood just before he died. He even told me that when I met you—*finally*—I'd have to ask you about that rule and let you take all the blame."

"Yeah, well, I accept that blame. Where," he asked, "are the notebooks?"

She looked at him blankly for a few seconds. "Oh," she said. "Sorry. I was still thinking about the three-day rule and its corollary."

"What corollary?" he asked. He tried to remember, failed. It bothered him. It was as if something from his childhood suddenly was lacking. He didn't remember a corollary, and he didn't want to lose the tenuous feeling of connection with his dead brother that suddenly had developed in that short conversation with Peter's lover.

"I don't know," she said. Her expression was blank; she looked a little nervous, as if she'd strayed too far into a private family territory. "He just said that when I saw you I'd have to ask you about the three-day rule and its corollary. That's all."

Alex paused, then regained his perspective.

"Damned if I know," he said, sighing deeply. It disturbed him that he *didn't* know. *There are more important things to worry about*, he thought.

The notebooks were a disaster.

If the one he had seen was bad, he thought, these made it appear a model of neatness and organization.

Just a glance through them showed him that molecular structures and lunch and dinner dates were nearly inextricably interwoven. It would take more than just a few hours to make any sense at all of the books, he thought. *And even then I've no guarantee that they have anything to do with the disease.*

*Shit, Peter*, he thought. *For a guy who was neat and orderly enough to come up with the goddamn five-day rule, how the hell could you keep your lab notes the way I keep my checkbook?*

"Are they all there?" Linda asked.

"I don't know, Linda. He didn't keep them in very good order. I'll just have to work it all out, that's all." He hoped he sounded much more confident than he felt.

They left the lab and Brandes found Sarah speaking to Cynthia. Both women seemed to be enjoying their meeting, and Brandes felt pleased about that.

"Thank you, Linda," he said. "I'll get these back to the lab as soon as possible."

"Your time . . ." She shrugged. There was an impish look her face could achieve; he could understand how Peter had been attracted to her. "Do you need a ride?"

"No, I have a car. Why?"

"Oh, just that I heard about the accident."

*News had traveled fast.*

"I have a friend's car. I'm out back in the lot, behind the lab."

"Oh," she said, smiling, "under 'the goose.'"

"Yes," he agreed. "Under the goose."

"Ready?" Sarah asked, rising from her chair.

"Yes. I may have to come back to read the others, the ones in the office. I don't know."

"Or other ones he might have left."

"Yes," he said. "Other ones he might have left." A visit to his father seemed unavoidable, he thought.

"Drive through the town," Sarah said once they had left the lab.

"What?"

"You're taking a different road. This one will skirt the town. Don't you think we should take a look at the town? Lawrence has just put a padlock on these people's doors, for Christ's sake. We have to see how they're taking it."

"I'm not here as a social worker," he said. "And I'm not here as a reporter."

"You're human, aren't you?"

"Damned right I am. That's *human*. Spelled *h-u-m-a-n* and it's not spelled *g-h-o-u-l*. What would I gain if I saw the whole damned town in the streets ripping each other to pieces? Would that help me try to figure Peter out?"

"No," she said. "You're right."

Her sudden agreement was almost as perplexing and irritating as if she had argued. He drove toward Wismer's house. Hope for an antibody. At least it was a beginning. And, he told himself, it's likely to be a hell of a lot more of a beginning than I'm likely to come up with from notebooks cross-referenced with hieroglyphics.

Night in New Hampshire was unlike night barely three hundred or so miles away.

Lieutenant Teddy Knotts doubted he ever could get enough of it. He looked into the sky, identifying what constellations he could. Most he knew almost entirely from star guides he had read or from trips to the Hayden Planetarium in New York City.

There were nights at home when some stars were visible: Ursa Major and with it Polaris and the tip of Ursa Minor. The rest of Ursa Minor seemed to be covered by the nearly perpetual haze caused by "light pollution."

But that never dampened his interest or enthusiasm in watching the sky. As he often had, he thought of what life might be like on a planet circling another star; it was a great disappointment of Lieutenant Knotts's life that he realized he never would see any of those planets. He fantasized—as he always did—that one day he would learn enough to prove Einstein wrong.

After all, he thought, how could a contact with another planet be maintained if every time a traveler returned home—whichever planet that might be—"home" was a few hundred or a few thousand years "different?"

The mangling of time at near-light speed just couldn't be unavoidable, he'd told himself. *There has to be a way.* The thought made him grin. *As a scientist, I'm a damned good romantic.*

He had been very honest with Dr. Brandes when he'd admired

the scenery around Lyle. He'd been honest when he had expressed a sighing, soulful desire to someday have a farm like the one that was now the army's command post.

Lieutenant Knotts dropped his eyes from what he'd hoped had been Mizar—what's wrong with wanting good eyesight? he thought—and looked at the blazing light on the ground a few hundred yards away.

He watched the cremation pile with a fascination as great as he'd felt when he'd looked upward. It was a dozen persons—who burned so brightly that the stars beyond the flames were blotted out.

"Lieutenant," a silhouette called, walking rapidly toward him. The man was perspiring heavily. The heat nearer the pile of bodies and burning gasoline was intense. Knotts could feel it on his face as he watched the pyre and still feel the relative cool of the night air on his back.

"Yes?"

"Sir"—he recognized the man now, Corporal Lucan—"I think that's it for this load."

*Load.* Yeah, Knotts thought. *Think of it as a "load." Do anything to make it easier.*

"Very well, Corporal. Secure everything. Call in the next watch and let your men retire for the night." The corporal didn't move.

"Yes," Lucan said, after a second.

"Lucan, what's the matter?"

The corporal looked ashamed. "I'm sorry sir. It's just . . . shit, you *gotta* know—they're people."

"I know, Lucan. Believe me. The colonel knows. We all know. But they're not people, Lucan. They're *dead* people." He moved so the flames could illuminate Lucan's face and saw that he hadn't really reached the man. "Lucan," he said, "didn't you go with your squad yesterday into town for something or other?"

"Yes, sir. It was just a showup."

A "showup," Knotts knew, was the colonel's idea. It was a quick drive through Lyle in army trucks, carrying army personnel. Nothing more. Knotts understood the colonel's purpose, and he hoped it was enough. He wasn't at all sure himself that if he were a civilian and a citizen of the town he would be able to sit still, watch soldiers and doctors come and go—and hear of friends dying. *There will be a cure. I have to believe that, or I'll look as pale as Lucan.*

"You saw people then, Lucan," he continued. "They are alive and healthy." He didn't wait for an answer. "If we're to keep them that way, one of the things we've got to do is just what we're doing now. You do know that, don't you? You understand that?"

"Yes. Yes, sir. Just ain't easy, that's all. Some of the men—oh, don't get me wrong, they know that's true, too, what you said— but they're not taking it so well, anyway. I've got Kalco standing by the Jeeps so he don't hear them anymore." Knotts looked at his corporal.

"Hear them?"

"Just the noises of the fire, sir." Lucan looked embarrassed. "The crackling and stuff." He hesitated. "Just that. But it's enough."

"Anybody else getting jumpy like this, Corporal?" Knotts asked.

"No, sir. Just Kalco."

"Good. And you did the right thing sending him to the Jeeps. Keeping him away from the rest of the men. I don't want him worrying out loud."

"Yes, sir."

"Go ahead. Secure your detail, notify the watch. Get some sleep."

The corporal saluted and jogged off toward the flames. Knotts looked after him apprehensively. He thought about the living people of the town.

He just couldn't help putting himself in their position. Using those people as an example for Lucan only had brought that to the surface of his own mind.

Noises from a fire they will be able to deal with, he thought. But what about living people?

What if they decide to fight, decide to run?

Knotts again tried to find Mizar.

Emil Jenner slowly walked from his daughter's bedroom into the living room.

His wife faced away from the doorway; she had not yet looked at him.

How to tell her? he wondered. He walked straight ahead, put his hands on her shoulders from behind, and massaged her neck. She began to cry.

"Oh, God!" she screamed. "Already?" She swung herself on the couch, looking at him. Jenner never had before in his life felt so helpless, so vulnerable—and so guilty. *If only I'd taken her for help earlier.* That thought never would leave him.

"Yeah, Doro. I don't know what to say. I feel . . ." His large frame suddenly shook spasmodically.

He cried. Doro felt his pain, moved to his side, guided him down to the couch. She cradled his head. She tried to hold back her own tears, determined to convince her husband he was not at fault for Nancy's death.

*Do I believe it? Mightn't Nancy be alive if she'd been taken to the hospital?*

*Hadn't she urged that?*

*God! Please,* she thought. *Don't let me think such things now. If there were mistakes we both made them, Emil no more than I.* She continued to rock gently, holding his head; Emil Jenner continued to cry. In Nancy's bedroom the child lay motionless, a waxen image—no!—an image of health. Except that she did not breathe.

"You couldn't have done anything sooner, Emil. No one could have. It hasn't been dark that long."

She felt relief mixed with her grief and felt guilt because of it. But her feelings were normal, she told herself. She hadn't wanted Emil to run the barricades, carrying Nancy across fields or whatever, trying to keep out of sight of the soldiers. God, that would have been more terrifying still. And she might well have lost both of them.

193

The sharp outlines of the soldiers' rifles were vivid in her memory. *No! I could not have survived the loss of both of them.* She cried to herself, continued to hold Emil's head.

"She looks very peaceful, Doro. Like the fever left her at last. It's hard . . ." He gurgled. She rocked.

"Yes. I know. I have to see her."

"No."

"Yes." She was firm. She felt his head move, a nod. She released him, and her husband stood. The stains on his cheeks were marked. His eyes were swollen and were distant, nearly empty.

Dorothy Jenner got up and walked with her husband to the bedroom and saw that what he'd said was true. The girl did not look . . . dead. She looked asleep, no more. Her face was calm, her eyes closed—thank God for that!—and her arms were placed at her sides.

"She looks . . ." she began.

"She isn't," Jenner cut her off abruptly.

"No," she said. "She isn't."

Jenner moved to the bed, began putting his arms under Nancy's body, supporting her at the neck and knees.

"What are you doing?" his wife asked, confused, somewhat alarmed.

"Have you looked over that way?" He motioned with his chin. "The light." She knew what he meant. The bodies of victims of the disease were being cremated.

Even if Nancy had died from something else—but there wasn't any reason to think that she had—the army would take her, swing her up. Up. Into gasoline-fed flames.

*No!*

But then what? She looked at her husband, knowing he'd pictured the same thing and knowing that he had some sort of an answer.

"But what?" she asked.

"The culvert," he said. "For the time being. Then . . . then we'll think of something. When this is all over."

She knew the culvert. It ran under a very shaky footbridge. The term *bridge* hardly applied; the wooden structure covered no more than a few yards. Beneath it ran a stream. Although larger in the spring, it ran through their property year-round. She knew that the ground there, alongside the stream, was soft. She knew what Emil, her husband, intended. She nodded.

Nancy could rest there until the disease had been conquered. They would wait until they could bury their dead properly. They would not give Nancy to the army. Not to the fire.

Dorothy Jenner knew then that she never again would allow her husband to think with guilt of his refusal to take their daughter to the hospital.

Had they taken Nancy there, had she died there, she would be on her way to those flames just over beyond the trees, just past the boundaries of their land.

Nancy would be buried on their land.

She loved her husband, clung to him.

Jenner didn't say a word, but she felt he understood and was thankful for her support. He lifted Nancy. Dorothy held one arm until they were at the front door of the house. Then she let him go. There was an unspoken sense of what was and was not proper or expected there. She would see Nancy into her final resting place when that could be arranged. But for now it was Emil's job. She gently closed the door behind her husband and her daughter and sat down and began to cry in great, heaving sobs.

Outside, Emil Jenner took a large, deep breath, thinking how Nancy never again would do that. He looked up at the sky, aware of the glimmer of light still cast into the night by the fires of the cremation piles some distance away—but not far enough. He looked up and began walking to the culvert, his feet occasionally sinking into soft ground, his eyes occasionally picking out stars; he didn't know that he could see from where he was the stars that Lieutenant Knotts could not.

# TWENTY

"VEAL ROLLATINI," JASON SAID, LOWERING HIS menu, "and you'll have the veal parmesan?" Allenberg smiled and nodded.

Jason grinned. He enjoyed taking his grandfather to dinner. He was proud of his ability to properly perform as a host. He had been taught well, he knew, and he loved his grandfather and his mother for that.

People expected certain forms of behavior. They would judge him, respond to him, on the basis of his actions. Allenberg often had said that Jason already had learned what takes many people their first three decades.

"You don't have to like the way the real world works," his grandfather had said. "But it don't matter worth a shit what you think. Not if you want to pull the strings rather than dangle from them."

His grandfather—and his mother—had been right, Jason had decided. Once you knew you were in a game—and once you knew what the rules were—you could control a lot. Especially with people who still didn't realize they were playing.

"Glass of wine?" he asked Allenberg.

"We'll see."

When their waitress, Patti, arrived, Jason gave their order. No cucumbers on either salad. Blue cheese for both. Pasta as a side dish, not the potatoes. And a bottle of Ruffino Classica.

Patti nodded, wrote the order.

"Fill me in, Jason," Allenberg said and sipped water. He tore a small piece of bread from a loaf and buttered it. "What's new, if anything?"

"Not a lot," he said. "School was the same . . ."

"Girls the same?"

"No." Jason knew he was on the verge of blushing—he couldn't help it. "The girls are different. Oh, I mean, most of them are the same girls as last year—that's not what I mean—I mean they are *different*."

"But then, so are you." Allenberg smiled, chewing carefully the piece of buttered bread. While Jason had grown up in many ways faster than most, nature reserved some areas to herself, he thought.

"I remember when you told me that someday I'd actually *like* girls. It was Halloween—oh, I don't remember. A long time ago. There was a girl in a ghost outfit. I kept . . . teasing her."

Allenberg grinned broadly.

"First off," he said and moved back slightly as Patti put their salads before them, "you weren't just teasing her. You kept accidentally dropping eggs, if you'll remember. Eggs aside, that was the first time you were showing an interest in girls. I hope your technique has improved."

"Don Juan."

"Don't break your arm patting yourself on the back. Eat your salad."

Allenberg was intensely proud of his grandson. Never, though, did he forget: Jason still was young, a boy. As much as he had learned and as talented as he was, he still had that much more to learn. Allenberg subscribed to a theory that adulthood never is reached: It is something to which one aspires.

Jason grimaced.

"What's the matter?" Allenberg asked.

"Cucumbers," Jason said. "They put them on the salad."

"Where?" He looked at Jason's plate.

"The waitress must have seen them and remembered. She took them off. But the *taste.*"

"What do you want to do?"

Jason considered. He made a small motion toward Patti, and she came to their table.

"I'm sorry," he said. "Someone in the kitchen must have made a mistake. There were cucumbers in this and the taste still . . ."

"No problem." Patti took the salad. She asked Allenberg about his, and he admitted the cucumber taste also was in his salad and that he didn't like it. She took his also.

"Got to give her a good tip," Jason mumbled. Allenberg's eyebrows rose.

"Why? You had to send it back."

"She tried to help us, grandfather. She took them off. She made a mistake and now she tried to correct it." Jason patiently lectured his grandfather—adults could be *dense!* Allenberg smiled.

A few minutes later, Patti returned with fresh salads.

"Tell me about your computers," Allenberg said. That was a subject that never failed to bring out the child in Jason, and Allenberg could understand that very well. He himself loved gadgets.

"I'd like a new one," Jason said. "I'll buy it," he added quickly.

"What's wrong with the one you have?"

"It works fine. It's a shame it never caught on, actually. But the company discontinued it, and that means I won't be able to upgrade it. At least not very easily. I want graphics," Jason said, still munching and just about through his salad.

"Why?"

"Animation for one thing. Also, I've got a business idea." Allenberg looked at him and waited. He did not have to suppress a smile. He always took children very seriously. A bruised elbow was serious if they thought it was serious. So were early loves. So were early business ideas.

"What?"

Jason hesitated. "I'd rather show you," Jason said. "Just in case it doesn't work out." Allenberg nodded, finished his own salad. "I think I'll buy an Amiga," he finished. Allenberg asked no questions: computers were not his strong point. If an Amiga currently was the best for graphics, he was sure Jason would know it.

And if graphics was what he needed for his "business idea," then that was Jason's business also.

"How you going to buy it? I doubt your mother's giving you a few hundred a week in allowance."

"Investments," Jason said sagely. At this Allenberg did grin: because of a memory.

When Jason was five years old, he couldn't—as far as anyone knew—read. When he and Sarah had taken him to a restaurant, though, Jason had always wanted a menu. No one understood that for quite some time. One day Allenberg asked if he knew what was *on* the menu. Jason calmly had replied, "Sixty-seven fifty."

Puzzled grandfather. Puzzled mother.

"If you buy *everything*," Jason patiently had explained, "it costs sixty-seven fifty."

Now Allenberg asked, "What are you going to invest in?"

"Not gold. I thought about that, but that's out. Remember those guys we peeked at?" Very well, Allenberg thought. "These must be pretty smart people, right? I mean, really up there?" Allenberg nodded. "Then if Mr. Fitch is selling gold, I'm not going to buy it."

"Sounds like a good way to look at it."

"I'm buying platinum."

"Why?"

"Catalytic converters, for one thing. Also there's enough gold already mined and aboveground to last industry forty years. *Forty years!* That's . . . *forever!*"

Allenberg glanced at him. "Well, close enough, I guess. In a sense it's a lot closer to forever when you reach my age."

199

Jason thought about that and nodded. "Whatever happened to those guys?" Jason asked.

"Nothing yet. No reason anything should actually. Just covering all bases, I guess."

"What do you do next?" The boy's eyes were clear and clearly riveted on his grandfather's. He was interested in the workings of his grandfather's world—very much so, Allenberg knew.

*And I've made him and his mother part of it*, Allenberg thought.

Allenberg thought briefly about his belief that such involvement and the knowledge it gave them would benefit them. Was it an excuse because he needed and trusted them? He dismissed that. People, he felt, have a vast capacity for believing the worst of themselves. He did need his family, did trust them—and he also did believe that Jason would learn more from the real world than he ever would from Dungeons and Dragons.

"Well?" Jason asked. "Next? Sometimes you get a little lost it seems." Allenberg smiled.

"Guess I try to do something to get their attention." Actually, Allenberg thought, that will be a delicate matter indeed. Directors of Uisce Beatha could not be handled other than delicately.

"You mean shake the trees and see if you get any apples?"

"That's as good a way of putting it as any."

He desperately hoped he was an alarmist. Agents and agencies could overstep their bounds, and there would be some scandal. Congress would investigate. *The New York Times* would howl. *The New York Post* would give cautious applause and probably be the most realistic and accurate of the bunch. The scandal would, however, pass. *That* type of scandal would pass.

*But Uisce Beatha . . .*

Uisce Beatha never would become involved in a "scandal" in popular media but that was not reassuring—the whole damned organization and quite possibly a large part of the world could go "up" with it, and no one would know. People would see the effects of the blast but never hear the explosion.

He looked up and smiled as Patti delivered their entrees.

Sarah mixed drinks and placed one next to Brandes without a sound. He looked up from Peter's notebooks and smiled.

"Thanks."

"You think you'll get any answers out of those?"

"I don't know, Sarah. My brother may have been more organized than I am, but his organization was just that—*his*. He's got as much doodling in the margins as notes on the lines." He held open a book and showed her.

"You should see some of my old notebooks," she said. "I once decided that I'd give them over in court if I ever was ordered to. I'd go to jail to protect a source, but there'd be no sense in it if they asked for my notes. Nobody could read them."

"The judge could order you to decipher them."

"I can't read them myself after a time."

"I don't believe that."

She smiled devilishly. "I—pardon the way this sounds—don't care what you believe. I care what the judge believes." She flashed her wicked-looking smile again.

"I'm sure Peter could read these a lot better than I. Oh, I *understand* a lot of it. I recognize some symbols, words. I know some of the things he was working with. But actually trying to figure out *what* he did and what *results* he got: That's difficult."

He sipped his drink. It was a good martini.

"Good?" She asked.

"Perfect."

"Thought you might want a drier one. Lots of people do."

"All that just-stand-the-vermouth-bottle-near-the-glass stuff? No. Martinis have vermouth."

She nodded, sipped her own. "You have any idea what Peter was working on?"

"Not exactly. I know it had to do with genetic engineering, but he could have been trying to develop a cancer cure or a soybean that would grow in Antarctica."

"Can that be done?"

"The cancer cure probably has a much better shot. How much do you know about genetics and genetic engineering?"

"Some. I know all cells contain the genes that tell them what to do. I know the genes are all strung together on chromosomes. Genetic engineering is taking apart the chromosomes and rearranging them, right? And the more chromosomes, the more complicated the organism."

"Right except for the last. Unless you'd consider a potato to be more complicated than a person."

"Really?" She raised her eyebrows.

"Really. Of course, the potato just *might* be a higher form of life. Some people I know . . ."

She laughed.

"And you could also make things that kill people, right?" When she asked that, her laughter abruptly stopped.

"Yes. I just think it unlike Peter to have set out to make something like that. You don't have to *try* to make something that will kill people. Lots of the things that we make have properties we didn't plan for. That's why all the precautions at the lab."

"This might sound silly in view of what's happened, but doesn't that mean the research should generally be safe? That lab is pretty well put together, or at least it looked that way to me."

Brandes sighed. "Yeah," he said. "It should be safe enough. There are a few problems, though. For one thing, if I had just a few thousand bucks I could sit in my basement and hack up genes. I've always had nightmares about some high-school kid with a moderately rich daddy doing it for a science fair project."

"Dynamite."

"Damned close to it. Then there's what happens when they do check out as harmless. Maybe they're harmless in a lab, but released into the environment? Hard to tell. It was only in 1985 that we first did that—at least, officially. Somebody altered a bacteria that lives on strawberry leaves. It replaces the ones already there and gives the strawberry plant another ten degrees before it frosts over and dies. Could save millions in strawberries."

"What's wrong with that?" He looked at her, took another drink. She was, he thought, either truly interested or a very good actress.

"Maybe nothing. We don't know yet. Maybe anything. Maybe those bacteria will produce a chemical that'll scare off insects that pollinate strawberries, for all I know. I'm not a botanist. Maybe there's something we don't know about strawberries that makes it *imperative* for them to freeze every so many years to trigger fertility. So we get five incredible years—and then that's the end of strawberries. Maybe birds will like them better. Just maybe anything."

"Scary."

"Damned right it's scary. If we get away with playing with a system nature's developed over millions of years, we could very well make this world a garden. A paradise. That's the promise of genetic engineering. And maybe we can do it. After all, nature did it by trial and error, and we're doing it by at least having an *idea* of what we're creating. Or trying to create.

"Problem is, *what if we mess up?* Do we *undo* some millions of years of the success that trial and error has brought? The rewards are tremendous—maybe immortality, if you're crazy enough to think that's a good thing at this time. The risks are equally great."

"What I don't like about that, Alex, is that someone I don't even know—lots of people I don't know—are deciding to take that risk for me." She looked very thoughtful.

He nodded. He couldn't agree with her more.

Without asking, she got up and took his glass and walked to Wismer's bar.

"And the answer to what Peter was trying to do—and what he actually did—might be in there." She pointed toward the notebook as she set down the fresh drink.

"I hope. As you pointed out, I have to figure out what he wanted to do, and then I have to try to figure out what he really did. And how he did it. And once I know, there's no guarantee it will be of any use at all in stopping the damned thing. The CDC people stand a better chance of that, I think. I can throw around As and Gs till I get old and my boat sinks and still not be of much help."

"Uh? . . ."

"Oh. Shorthand for some pieces of genes."

"What are they? Tell me."

He'd come to realize that she indeed was interested but he didn't expect her to be *that* interested. He wanted to ask her if she really wanted him to go on, took one look at her face, decided to go on.

Remarkable woman, he thought. He wondered what had happened to her husbands, why she didn't still have one. Another time and in different circumstances—hell, he thought, *any* man would be interested.

"Proteins," he said, "are the building blocks of life. That is, they are the 'substance' of things. Enzymes, the chemicals that *do* things, like digest food and control body sugar, are proteins. The proteins are made of units of amino acids.

"These are the most godawful long chains of things you can imagine, Sarah. Sometimes there are thousands of amino acids in a protein chain. And every damned one of those amino acids has to be in the right place."

"That much I remember," she said and nodded.

"Well," he continued, "if the proteins are the building blocks, then the DNA is the blueprint. It's a nucleic acid, and it's got basically four things in it: adenine, guanine, thymine, cytosine. Long strands of combinations of that stuff make up the DNA and the genes. The order they come in is the pattern.

"In a cell another nucleic acid, RNA—which is almost the same but different," he paused; she let the simplication slip by, "picks up the DNA pattern and moves the pattern to where its instructions tell the cell how to make specific proteins. With me?"

"I think so. What were we fooling with here?"

"Well, don't let the terms throw you. The whole thing is pretty simple, at least on a high level. You take a chemical called a restriction enzyme and it cleaves the DNA apart just like a diamond cutter along a stone's fault. You maybe use a virus as a vehicle to squirt some DNA pieces into the cell; you add some glue, lipase, and cement the parts together. And it's, 'Well, hello there!' You've got a DNA chain that didn't exist before.

"You squirt some of *that* in a bacteria and let the cell take its directions for protein production from the new blueprint."

"And what if the protein it makes isn't what you want?"

"Actually, we're getting better at it. Usually it is."

"And what if it isn't?" she insisted.

"Well, there's a technical term for that. It's called a *wholeshit-loadoftrouble.*"

"Terrific."

"And," he said smiling, "don't forget what might happen if we *do* get what we want and expect."

"The strawberries?"

"The strawberries."

"The Strawberry That Ate Manhattan," she said and grinned.

"Not that drastic, I'd think," he said and smiled back. "But then nature doesn't need a drastic change for her to rearrange everything else."

"Like . . ." she paused, closed her eyes. "Let me use my imagination. A strawberry that wouldn't any longer attract one particular kind of bug, so those bugs die out, and those bugs are needed as food for certain kinds of birds that eat other certain kinds of bugs that destroy corn and . . ."

"You got the idea. Probably not that simple, but run with it. The corn isn't around to feed us or the animals we feed corn to. And they die. Carry it to any extreme you like. It isn't *likely* that *any* of that would happen—not likely at all. Really. But it's a risk we do take for the sake of getting more strawberries.

"The question is an old one. Is the benefit worth the risk?"

"I think I'm scared."

"I think you're smart."

# TWENTY-ONE

SARAH WAS A VERY GOOD COOK, BRANDES DE-cided. The damnedest part of it was he couldn't figure out exactly what she'd cooked. She didn't seem about to enlighten him and just had said, "A little bit of this, a little bit of that."

He noticed that she had settled into Wismer's house easily, very easily. He had commented on that obliquely, and she had answered obliquely.

"Lots of practice," she'd said. Whether that meant practice staying with Uncle Gerry or with settling into strange environments he was left to figure out for himself.

"Do you like it?" she asked.

"Yes."

"Little of this and that always works," she said with authority.

He was sure there was beef in it, but he couldn't call the dish a stew, exactly. It was more like stroganoff with a spicy under-current.

Dinner was relaxed and pleasant; Brandes was glad he had resisted his impulse to take her to the airport restaurant. It had been a very long time, he thought, since a woman had cooked dinner for him in a homelike atmosphere.

"Why don't you like my father?" she asked. The question came with no preparation; he *felt* his body and mind pause before answering.

"It's not that I don't like him, Sarah," he at last answered. "I don't like working for him."

"Why?"

"He didn't give you a briefing before he sent you here? And for that matter, the fact that he did send you here is enough to make me not want to work for him."

Of all things, she laughed.

"What the hell is so funny about that?" He began to wonder just how many men would be able to handle a woman like her.

"Just that for a scientist you're pretty good at claiming 'facts' that aren't facts. He didn't send me. I came. No doubt he was a little upset."

"Well, how did you know enough to come? Nose for news?"

"No. He told us about what was happening here and asked us to do a little work on some things. Mostly he meant making telephone calls from home. The personal visit was my idea."

"And who is us?"

"Jason, my son."

"Your *son*? He gets not only his daughter but his grandson involved in things like this and you ask me why I don't like working for him? He'll use anyone, that's why. I'm sorry, but Adrian Allenberg has got to be the coldest and most heartless bastard I ever met or even heard of."

"Wrong." She was not flustered. "It's got more to do with his philosophy of raising children than anything else, I guess."

"Some philosophy. I can't wait." Holding back his temper was becoming more difficult.

"Look, Alex. Look at history. Not just American history, *all* of history—at least at all we know of it. Our technology and such we can pass along to our children so it looks like one generation can push the next a bit further. But things don't really work that way. We treat our children as children, and that would be fine except for our definition of *children*.

"We start them *all over again*, and, of course, a lot of that *is* necessary because many things can be explained but never really learned until they are experienced. But not everything, Alex. You can't *tell* a kid about the real world and get him used to it.

"For my father, and for me, the parent's role is to best provide our children with tools needed to survive and prosper.

"You don't teach a kid to be macho; you teach him when he can win and when he'd better duck. Most people ask their kids to trust them, to believe what they tell them. What's one of the first things most parents teach them? Santa Claus. You think it has no effect on a kid to find out his mother and father lied? If they lied about that, *then how much of the other stuff is true?*"

Sarah had done much thinking about all this, Brandes realized. She sounded convinced without sounding dogmatic; he found he agreed in principle with much of what she said. But, to agree with all of it? . . . Would that mean really agreeing with Allenberg?

"Yeah, well, a lot of people would argue there's something special in the fantasy we allow our kids."

"Yes," she said, serious—and he could see just *how* serious. "There's something special and very deadly." She paused. "Shit, Alex, what other animal does it? Do you think a grizzly bear mother would teach her cubs about the Big Dipper dropping salmon to eat? That 'fantasy is good' argument is made by *adults*, Alex. Worse than that, it's made *for* adults. It's continued, probably, by adults trying to justify what their parents did to them and what they did to their own kids."

There was something to that, he thought. But espionage? He asked as much.

"He's never asked Jason or me to do anything remotely dangerous. When I was grown and decided to do something dangerous, like come here, it was my decision. Like I told you: He's probably very upset. But he wouldn't have stopped me if he could have.

"And when Jason's grown, he'll know what honor and trust mean, and he'll know how much of it he can expect in other people. And how much he can't. If he decides then to do something dangerous, I won't stop him either."

She paused again for breath and added with a smile, "Of course, I'll be very upset."

Brandes said nothing for several moments. Even then his first movement was to take a drink of wine and a mouthful of her creative cooking.

"This might be personal. I mean, I know it's personal, but it might be too personal. Do you have a husband who agrees with you on all this?"

"If," she grinned crookedly, "I had a husband who agreed with me on this I might—just might, no guarantees—still have a husband."

"Scared them off, huh? I can believe it."

"Scare you off?"

He blushed. She laughed.

"I'll be able to work with you," he said a little weakly.

"Coffee?"

"Yes."

"So why don't you want to work with my father?" she asked, clearing dishes and moving toward the kitchen. He followed her in, and although she seemed intent on making coffee, he did not doubt that he had her full attention as he told her of the story of Hoeckle, starting from the hotel and hair dryer incident.

She finished the coffee, served it, and listened at the same time. She asked no questions, offered no comments. He tasted the coffee and liked it, although in coffee making, he thought, he had her beat.

"And you think that after you filed your report—no, because of your report—my father had Hoeckle killed?"

"Yes."

She said nothing for a moment and then said, "Could be."

The phone rang before he could reply, and he was glad of that; he was not sure at all how to reply.

"Yes?"

"Alex? Jonathan."

209

"Yes, Jonathan. Something new? I was just finishing din—"

"Cynthia has it, Alex."

Brandes's stomach clenched convulsively, spasmodically. Sarah must have noticed and immediately took the telephone. Brandes let her. She spoke a while to Shortell and hung up.

"Tell me about her, Alex," she said gently.

"Do you still love her?" she asked as they pulled into the parking lot of the Lyle–Mount Saint Sydney Hospital. The warm glow of the home-cooked dinner and her company, the stimulation of talking to her about her father and her son—all gone.

"I'm not sure," he said. "Gerry calls what I've got 'bonding.'" He paused. "What *I've got*—like it's a disease. Christ, *she's* got a disease. All I've got is a lot of mixed-up emotions that my ex-teacher points out might be due to a million-year-old instinct."

"I'm not sure of the bonding, Alex. I don't think I have any experience with things like that. But with people I have. I have a lot of experience with people."

"So what do you think?" he asked, trying to smile; she saw that.

"Don't do that, Alex," she said. "You're not in the mood for smiling. Don't do it out of consideration for me. I don't know Cynthia very well; I just met her. But I think I would like her sometimes I make my mind up about things like that very fast. And I'm very sorry this happened."

"She's like that, too," he said.

"Like?"

"She makes up her mind about people almost immediately. Oh, she's always been able to change her opinion if she's been wrong; she just seldom is wrong. I think it's a talent . . ."

Sarah let him ramble a moment.

"As far as what I think, Alex . . ." She paused. "It has to do with my definition of love," she continued.

It took him a few seconds to remember what they'd been talking about; Sarah deftly had let him run, deftly she was bringing him back. "To me, you've got to point at something and give it a name. It doesn't come with one. I'm not saying this too well."

He parked the car; neither of them moved to get out.

"Which came first, Alex, the chicken or the egg?" she suddenly asked. It caught him off guard; also, it momentarily caught his attention, maneuvering its direction away from thoughts of Cynthia.

"What the hell does an unanswerable question like that have to do with a definition of love? Of whether I love her?"

"Because it's not unanswerable. I know the answer. I've known it since I was twelve and heard the question for the first time. I couldn't believe people would waste so much time arguing over something so obvious.

"It's the wrong question, Alex. The real question is when did the first person use the word—or *a* word—for egg and point at one. When did he do it for *chicken?* And if you want to be really playful and ask, 'Well, then, what word was used first?' I'd tell you it was the first time someone uttered a sound that a modern English speaker understood as *chicken* or *egg*."

"And *love?*" Sarah, he decided, was a complexity of a woman.

"Love is a feeling, Alex. You feel many emotions evoked by many things. When the day comes that you meet someone and feel a feeling you can point at inside yourself and use the word *love* to describe it, then *that's* love.

"You've got to do the pointing, Alex. And it's not a one-second thing. It takes a lot of thought, and it's hard. But it's the only way I know to answer that question."

"I think," he said after a pause, "I like that."

They left the car and entered the hospital.

"She's on the next floor," Shortell said. He had been at the door waiting, but if someone had asked him to be honest, he would have had to admit he was there just to take his own mind off Cynthia. The momentary flash of competitive jealousy he'd felt when he first learned of Alex now seemed embarrassing.

"What condition is she in, Jonathan?" Brandes asked. Sarah

211

had already repeated what Shortell had told her on the telephone, but mightn't there be something new?

"She's pretty far gone already, Alex. She must have been exposed a day or two ago. She says she just attributed everything to overwork. Until tonight. She collapsed at the lab, and the ambulance brought her here."

*Damn!* Brandes cursed himself. "I should have known it, Jonathan. I think back now, and I can see her—*see* her—in my mind. She was sick."

"And the difference?" Sarah asked. She could see where he was going, and guilt served no one when undeserved.

"There wouldn't have been any," Shortell cut in. "The course of the disease is . . . too well set. No difference. I'm sorry, Alex. I'm *very* sorry."

*Him, too,* Sarah thought. They went to Cynthia's room.

The room flickered with the light of the television, which hung from a bracket on a wall. The only other light was a dim nightlight above the bed.

The colors are wrong, Brandes thought. All wrong. He remembered having thought that at other times and in other hospitals. Why, he wondered, did hospitals use lights that made even healthy people look sick? But of course he knew it was not only the light.

Cynthia was dying.

He pointed inside himself, or tried to, and still, much to his discomfort, could not tell what word to use.

Shortell walked to the bed and flicked the light switch twice, brightening the room.

"Hello, Alex," she said. Her voice was a whispering breeze through leafless trees. "Hello, Sarah."

"Hello, Cynthia," Sarah said, her own voice gentle.

"We think we've definitely found a viral antibody, Alex," Cynthia said and smiled.

That was good news indeed, and it slid from his awareness as soon as she said it.

212

"Is that important?" Sarah asked.

"Yes. Oh, yes." She brightened.

*I should be doing this*, Brandes thought.

"A viral antibody is something that is made by the host," Cynthia explained. Everyone, Brandes knew, not the least Cynthia, needed not to think about Cynthia. "It's not the virus itself. Just shows that a virus has been there. A signature."

"That sound like it must be good news," Sarah said. "I guess you could use some, huh?"

Sarah's instincts were right, Brandes knew. Acceptance had to come to Cynthia eventually; this was a good way.

"How are you feeling, Cynthia?" he asked. "Pain?"

"My hands," she said. "Not bad yet though."

There, it was out. Yet, the inevitable had been recognized without being spoken.

"I'll visit again," Sarah said suddenly, and took Shortell by the arm and led him out. It was done so quickly and smoothly that neither man at first understood what was happening.

"Alex," Cynthia said.

"If it tires you to talk . . ." he said. She interrupted.

"Shut up, Alex. If I get tired talking now, I'll get a hell of a lot more tired if I try to say the same thing tomorrow." He nodded. "All I want to say is that I love you—*Sssh*. Not the way a woman would love the man she could spend her whole life with. Just kind of a differentiated love." She smiled at the term. "I'm sorry that things never worked out."

He thought about what she said. He thought hard, reached hard, poked mind fingers into mind crevices.

"I love you, too, Cynthia."

She smiled. He stooped to kiss her, but she looked alarmed and held up a hand. "This is not a trip you take someone you love along on, Alex."

He smiled and squeezed her hand. Gradually his grip relaxed. He could say nothing else. "Go to work, Alex," she said.

Leaving at all seemed *wrong*. Not leaving, perhaps, more

cruel. *God, the emptiness, the loss. I do love her. Sarah was right.*
He nodded. He turned to go.

"Could I see Sarah a moment, please?" Cynthia asked.

He was faintly surprised but nodded, left, and sent Sarah in to
see her. He and Shortell said nothing. In a few minutes Sarah
had returned.

"Gerry can go home with you if you like," Shortell said.
Brandes registered surprise again. "He's fine." That, at least, was
good news. They followed Shortell in silence to the lobby where
Wismer waited.

Wismer watched Brandes closely after they returned to his house.
He had been prepared to be worried about him, remembering the
conversation they had had about Cynthia, knowing Brandes's
feelings. What he saw, though, both encouraged and in some
small admittedly sentimental way saddened him.

Brandes was taking Cynthia's illness—her death sentence, for
that matter—very well. He'd accomplished it by allowing himself
to become hardened. *Experience*, Wismer thought, *is for man
the fire that tempers whatever steel he possesses.* That they would
have need for such temper, such hardness, Wismer considered
axiomatic.

Later he would look back at the moment and remember the
words to the tune that then was a mental Muzak. From the
*Fantastiks*, it concerned a boy and a girl who thought they'd
reached a comfortable plateau in growing, only to be told that
they still had to be "burned a bit and burnished by the sun."

"One for me," Wismer said when he saw Brandes walking
toward the bar.

"You all right? No concussion?"

"Lots of water on this old brain. Good cushioning effect. I'll
have Wild Turkey, rocks."

Brandes did not even nod acknowledgment but just began to
mix the drinks.

*He's past that for now*, Wismer thought. *No need for nodding,*

214

*for the minutiae of social graces. It will pass, but I hope not too*
*soon. We may need it, the edge.*

Wismer took his drink, sipped. Brandes and Sarah sat. Wismer saw one of Peter's notebooks on the table in front of the sofa. He reached for it.

"Not much help there, Gerry."

"Not much help anywhere right now, Alex. Maybe the antibody . . . but I'd still like to look." He picked up the book.

"I haven't given up on Peter's notes, Gerry. I want you to understand that. I want you to know that I'm going to go through all of them—*all* of them, Gerry."

"I never doubted that, Alex. Or," he managed a shadow grin, "at least I don't doubt it." He settled back, flipped open the book, and immediately could see why any man might have thought the material useless.

He understood a considerable amount of it—how much would have surprised Brandes—but understood it only so far as the construction of individual experiments was concerned. Whatever the long-range thrust of Peter's research was, it could remain hidden in the pages of the spiral-bound book. The fact that it *was* spiral-bound was unsettling in itself, Wismer thought. Pages could be torn from such books and not be missed.

*Brandes might not have thought of that.*

He considered and looked at the cover. Next to the manufacturer's logo was the notation that the book contained 150 sheets. He started at the beginning, counting.

He glanced only superficially at the pages as he flicked through them, tallying. Doodles were everywhere—that was part of Peter's style. One pattern, though, was repeated over and over again. He never would have noticed that except for his flipping through so quickly.

No pages were missing; Wismer closed the book and remembered Peter. The doodling brought back a mental picture of the young scientist, made him a person once again. That he had *been* was easy to forget under the circumstances. They all were riding the crest of a *tsunami*, the wave barely noticeable at sea that builds to a wall of water near the shore—that kills.

Wismer remembered talking to both Peter and Alex when they were young. *Peter's father*, Wismer thought, *didn't make him want to be a doctor.* "Ben Casey" *had*.

The show had begun with a solemn voice narrating as the symbols for "Man, Woman, Birth, Death . . . Infinity" appeared on the television screen.

Peter had watched the show regularly, Wismer remembered. It was not uncommon for Peter's questions in class one day a week to be about a particular disease. Then, years later, Peter repeatedly had doodled the symbols in the margins of his notebook. He seemed, Wismer thought, to have jumbled them up a bit. But then, he thought as he replaced the notebook on the table and returned to his drink, "Ben Casey" was a long time ago.

# TWENTY-TWO

ON THE PREVIOUS DAY, ON THE DAY ON WHICH Cynthia had been diagnosed, had someone asked a Lyle resident—chosen at random—what he thought of Frank Selden, that person probably would have hesitated a second and then answered, "He pays his bills on time."

Frank Selden neither was widely liked nor disliked. He owned a 120-plus-acre farm near the southernmost boundary of Lyle, and he left it rarely.

Business brought Selden into town. Only business. He arranged sales of harvests; he bought supplies, usually a month's worth at a time. Selden, somewhat sullen and dark, in a dull workman's shirt, had come into town only days earlier; so no one had expected to see him at least for another month. And in Frank Selden's case, out of sight literally was out of mind.

Until the day after Cynthia had been diagnosed.

Even then, had circumstances been different, had some of the more sociable residents of Lyle not *seen him*, the swarthy Frank Selden might not have come to mind for quite a long time.

The quarantine woven around Lyle had not been in effect long enough for the full gravity of the matter to become part of Lyle's consciousness. Every few hours, it seemed, one or more families drove to a roadblock. Someone would, with properly indignant outrage, demand to be allowed to pass. The soldiers would refuse. The people would grumble but turn around—for those who had tried to leave Lyle, for those who had *insisted*, the weight of the situation indeed became manifest. Stern looks even from young eyes, coupled with the authoritative *slap-click* of an M-16 bolt, made their point.

Most who had attempted to leave neither were sick themselves nor did they have with them anyone who was. Many simply wanted to be able to come and go as they pleased. There were some who very singlemindedly wanted to flee the invisible death lashing Lyle.

Frank Selden, though, had been sick.

His fever already spiking 103 at times, Selden had been stopped by Specialist Timothy Minish as he'd tried to leave, to visit his own doctor who lived nearly twenty miles away in Bantam.

Minish was nineteen years old; the M-16 held across his chest was not enough to give him a great deal of confidence. He just *felt* foolish giving orders to people twice his age. He knew he had the authority. He simply felt shy and uncomfortable.

He knew that for the most part, the people took things tolerably well and left behind nothing more than an echo of abuse lingering in the morning air. But still he was uncomfortable.

Frank Selden had not simply turned back. His bluster, his pointing finger, once actually touching Minish's chest, caused the young soldier to stutter. He'd been about to call two other men on duty, but before he could, Selden had jammed his Toyota truck into reverse.

He'd screeched to a stop about ten yards from Minish, thrown his transmission into drive, cut left. Minish had stared uncomprehendingly for several seconds as Selden's truck tilted against the dirt embankment and slid clear of the roadblock's Jeep.

There had been no time for thought. Nineteen Minish may have been, but because of that, the edge given him by his recent training was sharp. With a shout to the other two soldiers, Minish had spun; and all three had emptied their magazines into the rear of Selden's truck, striking the fuel tank, creating a ball of fire to rival the just-breaking sun.

Minish stood transfixed, not aware of the movement behind him.

Twenty yards from the roadblock, Elliot Wescott pushed his fourteen-year-old daughter, Liz, to the floor of the family station wagon.

Gently he slid his car into drive, took his foot off the brake, and allowed the engine's idling speed to turn the car in a wide circle to the left.

He accelerated as achingly slowly as possible, and only when he turned a curve did he give full throttle as he drove back into Lyle.

Wescott was a prudent man. He'd no idea what those soldiers might have done if they'd turned and seen there were two eyewitnesses to Selden's death. He did not want himself and Liz to be the only ones who knew what had happened on Bell Pike.

Wescott decided that, though his fears might be groundless, there wasn't one damned good reason for ignoring them. He was going to make sure *everyone* in Lyle knew. *Spread it around,* he thought. *Spread it around fast, get rid of it.*

Colonel Lawrence learned of Selden before word reached Lyle, but Lawrence knew the news would travel; it would not stay confined for long.

"Lieutenant," he said. His voice was neutral.

"Sir."

"They couldn't have shot out the tires?"

"No, sir," Knotts answered. To himself he thought: *With their experience, they were lucky to remember how to fire, let alone aim.*

"Call Dr. Brandes," Lawrence said. "Tell him what happened. Tell him I want a town meeting or something of the sort—whatever the hell they call it here. I want it quick. This evening, this afternoon—I don't want them to have time to think. I want to tell them before they tell me."

"Yes, sir."

"Get Specialist Camber."

"Yes, sir."

"No, I don't mean call him here." He shook his head. "Tell Camber I want all phone lines cut in and out of Lyle. With two exceptions. You tell me Brandes isn't at the hotel but at his old teacher's house?"

"Yes, sir."

"Brandes's calls go through. For now. So do CDC calls to and from the laboratory."

"Yes, sir." Knotts stiffened, ready to salute and leave.

"That's not all, Lieutenant. Calls to and from the lab and to that house go through, but they go through a post Camber will set up. I want to have a record of who calls on those lines. And a tape."

Knotts was dismissed; Lawrence watched, still apparently impassive. No one knew better than Lawrence just how much of his calmness was the product of officer training and years of experience. *Reality is where it gets you,* he thought. Occasionally he wished he only had been "fit" for combat positions, but he was far too good at being the citizen-soldier—or, more precisely, the politician-soldier. Lyle certainly seemed destined to strain the limits of his capabilities in either role.

"The human interest side of your story is sure going to pick up steam," Brandes said and hung up Wismer's telephone. "That was the army." He looked at Sarah.

With most people, he would have played by entrenched social rules that would have kept him silent, waiting for the expected, "So something happened? What?"

With Sarah it was not that easy; he realized it never would be, not with her. She simply expected him to say something useful.

*I might get to like that,* he thought. *But right now some stupid old conventions might be welcome, too.*

220

"Somebody's been shot," he said. "A guy named Selden, a farmer. He tried to run the roadblock on Bell Pike just about dawn. Army shot him."

"I knew him," Wismer said. He sat just around the corner of the kitchen table from Sarah. Brandes stood near the white wall phone. "I didn't know him well. No one did, really. He was sick?"

"I don't know. Lawrence said his men told him Selden just acted crazy. He might have been sick, delirious. Shortell told me that one of his patients was asking for political asylum because he was being chased by gray Jell-O sent by the FBI. It's not hard to get a person delirious, and a little chemical change or a temperature rise can put anybody in a nut ward if the doctors don't know what they're looking at."

"For all I know," Wismer said, looking at his coffee, "Selden could have been nuts anyway. In twenty years I don't know if I ran into him more than a few dozen times. And if I did, I don't remember."

"Whatever," Sarah said, and, of course, she was right.

"Somebody else, guy named Wescott, saw the whole thing. Thought he was next. Came into town looking for anybody who'd listen.

"So now Lawrence's got Jeeps going all through the town announcing a public meeting in the hospital auditorium later today."

"And you're invited," Sarah said and nodded, adding nothing more.

"Sure am," he said and sat near his own coffee. "Command performance."

"Watch him, Alex," Sarah said. "He's not only out to protect his own ass. He's out to save other people's asses. Someone who cares about nothing but himself isn't that hard to handle, to figure out. Somebody who's cradling his own rump and still keeping an eye out for those other people—that's a dangerous person. And I doubt you're one of the people Lawrence is going to want to protect."

"Not likely."

"Worse than that," Wismer said. "Don't forget, Alex. It was Peter—*your* brother—who probably dropped this thing on these people. You might be a native here, too, but that might actually be turned against you."

First Andy, now Wismer—Alex knew they were right. It made sense that Lyle would vent its frustration, its hatred, on a known target. After all, he and Peter weren't outsiders who had taken advantage of them. They were "of the people"—and as such, betrayers.

"I'll do my best."

"I'll be there, Alex."

"Thanks," Brandes said. He'd be happy for the company.

"Let's start to go through the notebooks again," Sarah said. "Maybe you'll find something that might help. Check with the lab, too. Maybe that antibody paid off."

Brandes nodded, picked up his coffee, and walked toward the living room. Peter's books still were stacked on the table in the room's center.

"I'll check on Cynthia," Sarah said. Brandes nodded, grateful.

Several times before, Brandes had seen similar assemblies. He had worked one summer on a small county newspaper.

He knew what a no-win situation looked like. Masses of irate people congregated, not to get answers to their questions or solutions to their problems, but to vent anger at whoever presided over the meeting.

There were automatic good guys and bad guys.

Anyone on a raised platform in front of the room was a bad guy.

Anyone in the audience was one of the oppressed, ignored, and righteous minority.

The worst part of it, Brandes thought, was that quite often the impressions of the people were justified. He had seen politicians he *knew* to be corrupt—hell, they'd even offered him ten or

222

twenty bucks for "good reporting"—standing like martyrs in front of their constituents, pleading for understanding.

Also, he had seen the reverse. There had been times when the public outcry was no more than a collective gnashing of teeth against a whole world of wrongs; those on the platform merely happened to be convenient targets.

The crowd in Lyle was something between those extremes. They had been entering the hospital's auditorium for forty-five minutes by the time he, Sarah, and Wismer had arrived.

"Here's where I get off," Sarah said and grinned.

"Can't take the heat?"

"Heat is all the press gets," she said. Remembering that one summer he'd worked as a reporter, he knew what she meant: Reporters only knew they'd done a good job when opposing forces hated them equally.

"No one belongs up there," he answered. He left her near the first row of brown metal folding chairs and stepped up to the platform.

*They're not throwing anything yet*, he thought.

*Good sign?*

Never had his life on the *Siege* seemed so distant.

People still were finding seats, and he looked down into the faces of those who already had established themselves. Their faces were not friendly.

He made no move to say anything, to start the meeting.

*He* hadn't called it. It was Lawrence's show, Lawrence's curtain.

Brandes took one of the chairs that had been piled against the wall. He sat, looked around, and was very glad to see Wismer leaving Sarah and walking up to join him.

"You're a celebrity," he said.

"Yeah. Thanks."

"Not that bad, Alex. Not all that good," Wismer said, "but not *that* bad."

Brandes was about to ask where the army representatives were when they arrived. His immediate feeling was relief; he was not the primary target. The throng at the back of the room rose and yelled, overshadowing the crowd noise that before had been dominant.

Lawrence had arrived.

"Now *he*," Wismer said, "might have trouble."

"The son of a bitch deserves it."

"Needless to say, you won't announce that, will you, Alex?"

"And let one part of the federal government be fed to the sharks by another? Me? Never. Not that it's not done every day, but, hell, this is public."

"Yeah, it's public. It's also *your* public—people who knew you when you were a little Alex." He held his hand palm down about three feet off the floor, and Brandes had to smile.

The crowd reluctantly moved aside as Lawrence made his way into the room. Two soldiers and Lieutenant Knotts were with him, but he was several steps in front, eschewing whatever protection his men supposedly might offer.

"At least they're not armed," Wismer said, noticing that at the same time Brandes did.

"It would not have been a good idea, would it?"

"No."

"The man is a pro."

"That is the least reassuring thing you've said."

Lawrence stepped up the platform on the opposite side. One of his men unfolded a chair, and he sat.

The soldiers left the platform and took up positions at its foot. Lawrence looked around, saw Brandes, and locked eyes with him. He didn't smile, but after a few seconds he nodded briefly.

*Son of a bitch*, Brandes thought.

It was Johnny Avery who mounted the dais last and stepped up to the auditorium's microphone, going through the almost inevitable feedback adjustment ritual.

"Please quiet down," he said. Brandes could see that he was very nervous. Avery always had been somewhat nervous, he thought. He probably worried each day about making some self-imposed deadline for changing of the Tower Hotel's linen.

His voice had little effect. The people did begin to move less, to lower their voices, but Brandes doubted it had much to do with Avery's request.

"Let's get to it," someone shouted. Brandes could not see who, was not sure after all the years that had passed that he would recognize the speaker if he could see him. "Frank Selden's dead. Got shot. Got blown to hell, for Christ's sake. What the hell has anybody to say about *that?*"

Avery jittered. He looked about, saw Brandes. He was about to speak when Brandes shook his head and nodded to the other side of the platform. *Hell with that, Johnny,* he thought. *I'm not fielding them for Lawrence because it's easier for you to talk to me.*

Lawrence didn't wait for Avery. He rose and stepped to the microphone. Several angry voices shouted at him; he said nothing.

When they were at last quiet, he swept the audience slowly, left to right, his eyes moving only as his head moved. Brandes thought he resembled a closed circuit camera covering a bank lobby; it was eerie to watch, and apparently, it was more eerie for those on whom Lawrence's eyes rested briefly. The audience was very still. Lawrence, Wismer thought, was very much a man in charge.

*At least,* Wismer thought, *he looks like he's in charge.* No one in the auditorium, which had been designed to seat about 350 people and then held more than 400, could be impervious to the projection of Lawrence's military bearing.

"I'm breathing the air in this room," Lawrence began. He paused. "It's the same air you are breathing. It's the same air Frank Selden breathed. It's the same air my men are breathing.

"Ladies and gentlemen," he said, then paused.

"George C. Scott, move over," Brandes whispered to Wismer.

The colonel continued: "We are all—that's *all*—in the grip of a tragedy and an emergency.

"Tragedies, emergencies, these are things that test our idea of 'community.' They also are the things that make a community.

"My men and I were in this area on maneuvers when this

situation developed, as you know. We received our orders directly from Washington." He leaned forward. *The human touch*, Brandes thought. "We were ordered to help you, not hurt you. We were not the people who loosed this terrible disease on your community."

Brandes stiffened, felt he could punch the bastard—felt Lawrence's punch in his own midsection.

"That's all in the past, too, though. Doctors have come from around the country to help, too. But you have to help us, and you have to stick together, to be a community, to do that."

"He's certainly good," Wismer said. Brandes saw, to his surprise and annoyance, a look of genuine admiration on his former teacher's face.

There was some shuffling in the audience, but no one spoke. In a matter of minutes, Lawrence had gotten to people who had wanted to tear out his throat. Yes, Brandes had to admit, Lawrence was good.

"If you were living in a neighboring town," Lawrence said, "you wouldn't look very kindly on a person from Lyle bringing a disease with him to your home.

"Was Frank Selden a member of this community?" he asked, and both Brandes and Wismer knew the colonel had done his homework on the town's relationship to Frank Selden; Lawrence, however, seemed not about to let that be obvious. "Perhaps to many of you, his friends, he was. I don't know. But was he a member of the community when he chose to say, 'To hell with the rest of the world, I'm taking care of myself?'"

Lawrence might have gotten away with it.

The grumbling violence and anger of the town had not dissipated, though; it had been soothed, but the sore still was there.

"My Nancy . . . " A cracking voice shouted from the middle of the room. Lawrence looked quickly at the man, surprised. Brandes recognized Emil Jenner.

Jenner caught himself just short of announcing Nancy's death, but could not force himself to silence.

226

"No, Colonel," he spat the word. "I'm not asking for us to be special people, better than the people in Bantam or anywhere else. But," he swung around, his arms loosely following as he spoke to the audience and shouted, "we're no *less* important than they are either!"

There was a roar of agreement.

"No one said you were," Lawrence had to shout himself to be heard. "No one said that. But would it do any good to spread this thing beyond Lyle?"

"Why *is* it in Lyle?" another voice demanded, a woman's.

"Yeah," Jenner picked that up, stopped, and then his face brightened as one having an epiphany. "Your maneuvers were awfully convenient, weren't they, Colonel? I mean, here you were, with just enough men to shut off a small New England town, and you happened to be here just when some goddamn disease that kills everybody it touches happened to break out. Some coincidence, no, Colonel?"

Brandes did not like the way this was moving. He nudged Wismer, turned, looked at him. Wismer had seen three steps ahead of Brandes; he looked stricken.

"Well, what if not a coincidence . . ."

*Wrong!* Brandes thought.

"*What?* Shit, Colonel, we're farmers, but damn you if you take that as having to do with our IQs. We all know what you people did in Utah. How many sheep did you kill out there, Colonel? Were you testing some sort of shit like that here, Colonel? Was Lyle"—his voice rose to a hysterical screech—"just big enough for a good test and not big enough to matter a fuck to the Pentagon? Is that it, Colonel?"

The entire auditorium was in an instant uproar.

"Christ, Alex," Wismer said, "this meeting better end soon."

"If it doesn't, they're going to pull his heart out."

"Are *you* out of your mind, Alex?"

Brandes looked at Wismer numbly. The teacher rolled his eyes and had to shout to be heard. "Who the hell do you think they're going to come for, Alex? Lawrence with his machine guns? Or you, the brother of their Frankenstein, the guy who *made* 'the invisible death' for Lawrence and his cronies?"

Brandes felt cold. The thought that people he'd grown up with might turn like that on him was chilling, surreal. He looked at Lawrence, hoping the colonel would say something. For the first time since the meeting started, Lawrence smiled as he looked at Brandes.

*Son of a bitch!*

But Lawrence did take control, and when he did, Brandes knew it was not to help him or the other doctors. The colonel had to maintain order. *Wouldn't look good*, Brandes thought. *Few hundred civilians shot to keep the peace.*

Lawrence took the simple way out. He reached under the chest-high podium and twisted the volume control on the public-address system, sending feedback screeching across the auditorium. The sound made most of the people stop speaking suddenly and put their hands over their ears.

"Ladies and gentlemen," he said, as he turned the amplifier down again. There was a deprecating tone to his words, Brandes thought. "My appeal to you as Americans has not seemed to have much effect. I'm sorry. I really think you should be sorry, too. But that's an aside now.

"Here's the situation. I am in command of an army unit that has been ordered to quarantine this town. I can tell you that this crap about testing biological weapons on a New England town is so absurd even *you* won't believe it tomorrow when you calm down and think about it."

He managed to sound disgusted-with-children, disappointed-with-comrades, and man-in-charge in one tone, Brandes thought. He found himself sharing Wismer's admiration even more.

"We will follow our orders. These orders, whether you choose to believe it or not, are in your own best interests. And in the best interests of all your neighbors.

"*No one will pass that perimeter.* We *told* you our orders were to close this town, using whatever level of force necessary. Frank Selden didn't believe that.

"I suggest you learn from him."

A profound stillness covered the audience. Lawrence turned, looking for comments. He began to say something when a man near the rear exit stood.

"And the phones, Colonel? You afraid we're going to spread germs on the telephone wires? If there ain't something damned funny going on around here, why the hell did you cut the telephone lines?"

Lawrence looked at the man blankly for a second and then held up his hand, gesturing for patience. He walked to Lieutenant Knotts and whispered to him a few seconds, bending his ear next to Knotts's mouth. He nodded and returned to the podium.

"Sir, I don't know anything about your telephones. This is news to me. Lieutenant Knotts said he'll have his men look into it—most of our troops are signal corps, you may have noticed. In the meantime"—he gestured expansively—"if any of you have urgent messages that have to get to loved ones, please give them to my men—any of my men. They will be taken to my headquarters, and the entire communications capability of this unit will try to deal with your problem.

"Now understand, please. We can't take chit-chat calls, and any business calls will just have to wait. We haven't got the capacity to handle all that. But until we can restore your normal service or get it restored for you, we're available to handle your emergency traffic."

There was a general rumbling of approval.

"What's wrong with the phones?" Brandes asked Wismer. The older man smiled.

"With ours, nothing. I suspect it will stay that way, too. I just wouldn't say anything on them that I wouldn't want the colonel to hear."

"Oh," Brandes said, understanding.

"And now, to fill you in on the medical aspects of this," Lawrence said—Brandes cringed—"I'd like to let Dr. Alex

Brandes say a few words. You all know him, and you all knew his brother, Dr. Peter Brandes. I'll ask you not to take up too much of his time, however. He's here to help solve this problem, and every minute we take him from that job might be a critical minute."

He stepped down. There was no applause, but there were no catcalls either. Brandes rose on decidedly unsteady feet. He was glad that Wismer rose and walked to the podium with him, then stood a few steps behind.

They knew him all right, he thought. And Lawrence damned well had made certain they remembered his relationship to Peter.

"John, Emil," he said, thinking if Lawrence had wanted to underline his contact with the people he might as well use it. "All of you. Most of you know me. More importantly, you knew Peter. I'm not really given to defending the military too much"— *Soak it, Colonel*, he thought—"but in this case the colonel has made some good points. This isn't a test of a biological warfare weapon," he said and wished he could be as certain as he sounded. "Whatever happened here—and there is certainly a chance that Futures' work was involved—was not intended to hurt people.

"*I* know that Peter never would have intentionally made anything that would harm anyone. Don't forget, too"—he paused—"my family is a victim of this, too. Peter is dead. My brother is dead.

"The colonel also was right about something else. Whatever happened here, this isn't the time even to begin thinking about blaming anyone—not even the army. We've got a problem. *We have got a problem*. And it's that problem we'd better deal with. Colonel Lawrence is dealing with it as he's been ordered to.

"I know you aren't fond of feeling trapped here. Neither am I. Something in our New England heritage, I guess," he said and noted that some of the people smiled.

"Well, we have to draw on something else New Englanders are known for. That's strength.

"The CDC people have come here voluntarily from all parts of the country—they're not natives. Colonel Lawrence's men aren't natives either. But they're here. Like the colonel said, 'We're all breathing the same air.' These people have put their lives in danger to help us and to help stop the spread of this disease.

"The methods—as in Frank Selden's case—might seem hard to accept," he said. He paused, leaning. *I can do the homey touch, too,* he thought. "Any one of you would be as determined and would take the same actions if you'd been given the responsibility."

"Just tell us, Alex," Avery said, "what the medical situation is." Brandes had to look to his right when Avery spoke. He still was on the dais, but he'd been silent so long Brandes had just about forgotten him.

"You all know Gerry Wismer," Brandes said. "Most of you know him as a teacher hereabouts. He's also a damned fine scientist."

*And what else?* he wondered.

"He and I are going over Peter's notebooks word by word to try to find any clue—if that's where there is one.

"The CDC people and the Futures technicians are working around the clock trying to find the cause of the disease. And"— he paused, straightening—"they've found a viral antibody that may point them in the right direction. This thing could be a virus; finding the antibody is like finding a virus's footprints. It doesn't tell you everything, but it can give you some important clues.

"We *will* find an answer to this thing."

"What's this antibody?" someone asked. Brandes could not see who. "Is it a vaccine?"

"No. It's not a cure, either. But it eventually could lead to a vaccine. I don't want to raise anybody's hopes too high—but I want to raise them to a point that you know there *is* hope. All I'm asking you now is to hold together. To honor the quarantine. To help us if we need it—and we need your help, if it's only support for those CDC doctors."

He paused again. Still there was some isolated whispering,

some head movements like isolated patches of grain waving windless, but he felt the worst was over.

"John"—he turned his head as he said it—"Dennis, Judy, Elliot—all of you, all of us—let's get to work. Please."

He stood straight, nodded toward Avery, and walked off the platform, Wismer with him. They walked to where Sarah sat.

No applause, but no abuse. *Maybe that makes me and Lawrence even.*

The meeting was over.

# TWENTY-THREE

ROCK OF A MAN.

*Rock*, he thought. *Brittle, cracking, crumbling rock.* Love was not an emotion that came easily to Brandes ever. It never had come easily or automatically when he thought of his father; he doubted if it ever had occurred to his father at all. Perhaps for Peter it had been different. But Peter Brandes, Sr., did not love at all. Not his children, certainly not his wife.

Brandes had no doubt of that.

All of that, of course, he thought, meant that the small but cumulative doses of expertly applied torment he'd just endured had been for nothing. Nothing at all.

Brandes bent his head over the wheel of the car and rested his forehead on his arm. If tears were in order, he thought, then he was somehow "out of phase."

He felt nothing but a reinforcement of the emptiness his father generally engendered.

Peter had left no notes in the house, he'd been told.

"Had he wanted you to get a message," his father had said, "do you think he would have left it with me? You must be desperate, Alex."

He'd stood and just looked at the now-aging man. Slate gray hair, the face—yes, stone and, yes, crumbling. Stone soul, yes, a slate gray soul. Brandes hoped it was guilt but doubted it. Guilt was not an emotion for a god whose creations had failed, not even of a god self-ordained. Such felt anger only.

God, the hatred.

He started the car. He wanted to just *be* back at Wismer's house. His former teacher, he remembered more vividly than ever the earlier years, those during which Wismer had been more than a teacher and, if less than father—well, how the hell could he tell? He had nothing against which to measure the man and what they meant to each other. Wismer was more than father, too. He was, perhaps, what fathers should become. As sons age, good fathers become brothers, he thought.

No notebooks. He'd made the necessary trip. He'd suffered what he'd known he would suffer. He had not been rewarded for his efforts.

There was and always there would be, he knew, a persistent question: Did his father have any of Peter's notes and was he simply being his father in denying them while his last son and an entire town died during the final spasms of his own aging pride?

God, the hatred.

"Take Peter's car," his father had said and grinned a grimace. "Then you'll not leave empty-handed." And in panic and in pique Brandes had done just that. *Damn the man*, he thought.

Why his brother had left *him* a car he didn't know, but to get away from the house and his father—*Fall of the House of Usher*, move over—he'd taken the car; he'd arrange to have the other towed.

It seemed surreal that any man could announce a gift of a $32,000 car as a means of inflicting exquisitely refined torture and pain. Brandes, Sr., had managed that—and could, no doubt, manage much worse.

Sarah. He wanted to see her, too. The woman had a strength he never before thought he'd find in another woman, a woman other than Cynthia. And Cynthia. He wanted to be with her, too.

Then he did cry.

Cynthia was dying. *Soon*, he thought.

*Soon she will join the others on Lawrence's pyres.*

Gravel of the main driveway crunched beneath the wheels of the Mercedes 280-D as Brandes hurled it away from his father's estate. It was a somewhat unusual auto. Peter had bought it in Europe. Few 1983 Mercedes cars had standard shifts. Peter always had favored them, though; and the silvery car had four speeds floor mounted and a powerful eight-cylinder diesel.

More, he thought, from desperation than any real hope, he had searched the trunk and glove compartment. Aside from a jack and spare, the only thing he'd found was one slightly worn-looking collection of Shakespeare's plays—*Peter and his Shakespeare*, he had smiled—but no notebooks.

Brandes had not the slightest idea of what he would do with the car when he returned to the *Siege*.

How far away *that* seemed!

He flung himself and the car away, away from Peter, both Peters. The grounds of the estate were set well away from the remainder of the town and were in the only sector through which a major highway ran. Still within the boundaries of the municipality though, the estate was within the army's lines. The short stretch of divided highway that cut the corner of Lyle diagonally was open, but there was little traffic. There were only three exits in that eight- to ten-mile section between the points at which the soldiers had set up their roadblocks.

Brandes very much hoped the townspeople had taken Lawrence seriously.

*They damned well should after Selden, but who really could tell?*

People were odd. Frightened people more so. *And*, Brandes thought as he swept a wide curve, *they must be scared.*

*I'm scared.*

He entered the divided highway; he would exit just before the roadblock. Wismer's house was only a half-mile farther on.

A loud roaring interrupted his thought. It sounded distant, but he checked the rear-view mirror. He saw nothing. Whatever made the sound—a continuous, distant roar now—was making a hell of a lot of noise, he thought.

Either the local police or, more likely, a passing army patrol should make short work of a car without a muffler: the cops probably to relieve tension, the army out of concern it might be part of some diversion created by someone trying to penetrate its lines. As he drove on, the sound got louder.

Peripheral vision caught a flash of light in the driver's side mirror. Brandes turned to the other mirror again. The source of the noise rapidly was gaining on him. Then he saw lights.

It could not be a car, either. He saw the distance between the headlights change; he had to pull his own car back from the road's shoulder, so absorbed had he become in the view to his rear.

When one light swerved drastically away from the other, the answer was obvious. Motorcycles. Chopped bikes. *What the hell are chopped bikes doing here?* he wondered. *What are they doing in Lyle?*

He wondered if the riders could have come around the roadblocks somehow. He hadn't thought about Lawrence taking precautions against dirt bikes and ATVs, but he doubted the colonel had overlooked the possibility. If they were from out of town, he could not imagine why they would want to get into Lyle.

*Of course,* he thought, chastising himself. *The outside world doesn't really know.* To kids on the outside, the roadblocks were a challenge. *Poor bastards. They can't know what they'd blundered into.*

The bikes were large and powerful. The amber points of the running lights on either side of each bike's headlamp easily were visible. The right-hand light on each dipped as the cycles followed the contour of the road. Brandes had slowed instinctively because of his familiarity with the road; it was curved more severely than it looked.

The bikers, though, apparently lacked his knowledge. One

looked as though he would not make it; Brandes saw a shower of sparks where a footpeg caught pavement.

*Dumb.*

Brandes looked straight ahead. The road was a dark stretch of asphalt marked by the flashing of broken white lines picked out by his own headlights. He flicked on his high beams; no other cars were in sight. A slight drizzle began, and he switched the wipers to "intermittent."

Brandes again glanced into the mirror although the constant noise of the cyclists was sufficient to tell him they still were there. One seemed to have dropped back slightly from the other; a good precaution in the light rain.

*Enemy territory formation*, he thought. He grinned. Since childhood he'd liked to create fantasies about the things and events around him when he was doing something basically monotonous—like driving a dark road that virtually was deserted.

Brandes once had had a motorcycle, and he knew why those behind him avoided the road's center. Of course, it was not to avoid land mines; he smiled, turned on the tape player, and hummed to Neil Diamond.

Years of traffic had deposited a patina of grease and oil on the lane's center; in a sprinkling rain, it easily could mean a messy accident if a bike rider hit that nearly invisible strip at the wrong angle and speed.

One rider increased his speed. Brandes felt a tingle of apprehension. For the first time since he'd left his father's house, he remembered some of the *present* facts of his life.

He realized he'd been caught up in the past. There were people who did not want him to make progress with his investigation.

Two motorcycles and Brandes. Alone on a dark road. Suddenly the situation seemed sinister. He turned up "Beautiful Noise" on the player and tried to calm himself. *Hell, if they wanted me that badly, a sniper could have solved the problem.*

Or could it?

Everything in its own time. Maybe his potential killers had

other goals than simply eliminating him. Perhaps something had made it—inconvenient—to have him shot.

He had his answer—the one that most immediately counted—within seconds.

Brandes pressed his foot harder against the accelerator, but the lead biker had been determined. He growled up to the trunk, the light filling Brandes's car, causing him to squint. Then the cycle moved slightly left, accelerated again, was even with him.

Undefined tension yielded to sober fear.

Brandes turned his head to the left. A fairing covered the handlebars of the powerful machine; the cyclist's white helmet contrasted sharply with the black motorcycle and was highlighted by strips of reddish-orange reflective tape.

The cyclist turned in Brandes's direction; a knot formed in the scientist's stomach. There no longer was any sense in denying what he'd known somewhere inside himself since he'd first seen the bikers begin to close the gap between themselves and his car.

Brandes could feel the man's eyes on him although he could see no face; the rider was wearing the dark-tinted shield usually reserved for daytime—and unnecessary anyway because of the fairing.

The biker gave Brandes the finger and signaled him to pull over.

*Sure,* Brandes thought. *Good luck.*

Whatever the possibilities—Brandes didn't care if they were some outer part of Lawrence's patrols—the last thing he intended to do was to pull over to the road shoulder.

He would not be victim to that madness. He thought of the meeting. He remembered the hostility.

*Are they the villagers come for their Frankenstein?* he wondered. *Or are they from Allenberg's world?* It hardly mattered, he decided.

He accelerated, momentarily pulling ahead of the motorcycle.

The noise was deafening, yet the thundering roar grew louder still and deeper as the bike again matched his speed after coming alongside. Sixty-five miles an hour. He could, of course, go much faster—but so could they.

He had one thing on his side, he thought. The entire length of the road was not more than ten miles between roadblocks. He was fairly certain of that. If he could keep away from them for just minutes, Lawrence's soldiers would be in sight.

The cyclist, apparently, knew that, too. He leaned right, his fairing scratching the side of the car.

Instinctively Brandes pulled to the right to avoid collision, and his radials broke free, riding a millimeter of water as he slid toward the shoulder and the blurred wall of trees. He clutched, downshifted into third, and pressed harder on the gas. The engine whined out the sudden increase in rpms. The tires bit through the water to grab again at the paving. Bitter herbs in his mouth—fear, he knew. He was alone.

He was alone.

The other bike approached, passed quickly—Brandes guessed the size of the machines to be at least a thousand ccs—and took up a position directly in front of him. It slowed, and he was forced to drop his own speed.

They intended to stop him, but he had only a few miles—and a few minutes—to the safety of the army's lines. A flash of irony: He'd not thought he ever would look on Lawrence or his men as representing safety.

He bit his lip, realized that he'd bitten it too hard in his concentration. There was a slight coppery-salty taste in his mouth. The motorcycle continued to slow, and he was forced to brake harder. Brandes felt the tug of the shoulder strap against his left arm, the buckle tucked into the flesh of his abdomen; a gripping spasm seized his midsection.

Breathe.

Deep.

Calm.

He cast about in his mind for something to do; desperation galvanized him.

Let the bastards get themselves killed.

If they were allied with whoever had rammed the *Charon*, whoever Kracke had knifed on the Fire Island path—then let them die. And if he was to be a part of it, then he might as well enjoy it. An overwhelming hatred of them and of everything that had taken him from the *Siege* and his carefree life struck him. He wanted to hurt someone.

He wanted to hurt *them*.

He wanted to kill.

Brandes knew himself well enough, though. He knew he couldn't sustain such an urge for long. *Too civilized for that*, he thought.

*But I can hold it long enough, you bastards. Just long enough.*

He was down to thirty miles an hour when he floored the accelerator and shot directly toward the bike in front of him. By then the other had crept forward also, apparently also intending to cut in front of him.

Brandes intended to smash ahead, to break their barricade—to *hurt them* if he could. A collision at any speed of two motorcycles and a Mercedes, he smiled morbidly, would have to leave the car the victor.

One biker turned and lifted his hand. There was a flash of orange, and then the windshield on the passenger side flowered with cracks.

Brandes sat stunned, his eyes wide. He felt terror. There was no doubt left: These were not bike-gang members out for a mark. These were professional killers and he was the target.

*And Allenberg, where the hell are you?*

*Shit*, he thought, *Tomas could have protected me better if I'd stayed on Fire Island.*

Brandes hit his brakes hard, trying to increase the distance between his car and the bikers. Ramming them suddenly seemed out of the question. The several-ton advantage he had come close to gloating over as he'd bored down on them had evaporated— the closer he got to them, the shorter the range for their pistols.

The motorcycles also were slowing after having momentarily

dashed ahead in response to his aggressive, albeit short-lived, attempt at crashing through.

Brandes downshifted to second and let the clutch out fast, yanking hard left on the steering wheel as he did so. The engine whined as it was braked by compression; and again the tires skidded up into the water layer, and the car moved down the highway somewhat sideward.

The unexpected move caught the bikers by surprise. They were a hundred yards ahead as he pushed against the gas, harder than necessary to floor the pedal. He aimed directly at the grassy center divider. The wheels caught as the sideward motion slowed and—if only the oilpan and the transmission cleared . . .

They did.

With a loud thump and an upward leap that banged Brandes's head against the roof, the car skimmed along the grass.

Then he was in the northbound lane, headed back toward his father's house. He felt a sudden exultation, then realized he had no reason to feel exultant. He hardly was safe. He was going in the wrong direction.

But they had to give up. He looked in his rearview mirror and knew that crossing the divider would take them too long. He could leave the highway and take a longer way around. He was certain then that they were strangers to the area, an area in which he'd grown up. Once on the less-traveled roads, they would not even find him.

*Perhaps that's why I feel good.*

The exit was three miles ahead.

Brandes wondered if he'd damaged the car, hoped again that he hadn't ripped into the oilpan or the transmission. Once off the highway and on to the secondary roads, he still would have only ten or twelve miles to cover.

Anger developed as his desire to destroy/survive diminished. Anger at the cyclists and at Allenberg, anger at his father, at Peter. Anger at all that stood between him and a glass of something with Tomas. Anger at himself for not being angry enough.

*I've got thinking to do when this is over. When this is really over.*

He calmed, downshifted, braked, and turned on to the ramp. And he could not believe what he saw.

Two headlights, the distance between them changing as they approached, glared into his windshield.

Impossible.

But there was hardly time to dispute it. His calmness evaporated as if it never existed. The cyclists' sheer determination stunned him, awed him.

Terrified him.

Brandes thought quickly and realized as he listened to the guttural roar of the engines that they must have taken the construction road near the highway. He severely had underestimated their ability to handle their motorcycles.

Reflexively, his foot slammed hard on the brakes; and when the wheels skidded, he jammed the gears into reverse, let out the clutch, and pressed fully on the accelerator. The car shuddered and groaned in protest, and the gears were gnashing teeth—but the car shot backward.

He only could hope the road still was deserted.

Again his conscious, rational mind—what he considered to be so—was shocked and somewhat repelled at what his animal mind did as it took over control of his body. He felt and knew that, this time, the primitive in him would not give way easily, would not retreat, would fight and either kill or die.

The car still floored and still in reverse, Brandes for a second time jarred the expensive machine over the ten-foot-wide divider. There, surprising them again, he rammed to a stop and then jammed through all forward gears in an attempt to gain an unbeatable lead.

There were two flashes behind him, striking his eyes from the side mirror. His rear window popped and cracked, then came the sound of a shot. The blast of the second could be heard, but the bullet apparently had missed the car.

Just as he no longer questioned his own determination, he no longer doubted that the bikers behind him were just as determined.

His only hope lay in speed and an accumulated lead. He was afraid.

*But the fear feels good.*

The speedometer crept slowly as the car neared ninety, passed it, went on. Bare miles to go, less than a minute to a mile.

The car trembled at 100; Brandes looked into his rear-view mirror, grinning.

Then he realized his situation was hopeless.

The overpowered cycles could outrun the Mercedes on any short straightaway in just seconds. There was no doubt about it. He was fascinated by the ever-larger-looming lights coming at him from the rear in his headlong rush down the dark road at more than 105 miles an hour.

They *would* kill him.

They would win.

Brandes suddenly found himself wanting the terror, fighting to keep it, to grip it, to let it grasp him.

They passed him with ease, but he had come to expect that. He wondered what their features were like beneath those tinted shields.

One of the cyclists fumbled with something; Brandes could not see what. The biker twisted his body and threw. Brandes had no chance to react.

A plastic bag split on impact with the Mercedes hood, and the world whirled at a slower rate as gobbets of oil flew up to the windshield. He flicked on the wipers, but the thick splashes could not be cleaned away so easily.

They had won. Maybe. He knew he would have to stop.

He slowed quickly—he hoped more quickly than they expected—and knew by the rough jolt he received through the car's frame that he was on the road's shoulder.

If he could get out fast enough. Get the trunk open. A tire iron.

Anything. Anything to at least try to fight back.

243

Or perhaps his sudden stop would put them far enough ahead to allow him to flee into the woods, and perhaps flight was the better option.

*They* were armed with more than tire irons.

Brandes flung open the car door.

"Stop there, man," a deep voice called—it was much, much too near. Brandes froze and turned to look at the one who had spoken. He held a stubby automatic in his right hand; Brandes couldn't make out anything more about the gun, and it might not matter. Still, he felt that anything he learned might help him. *Just keep thinking that. Thoughts like that imply there is a course of action. They imply a future.*

"You," the man said and stopped four paces away, "have been quite a problem." The other cyclist, also armed, was only steps behind. Brandes felt his thin hope sag, but it did not die completely.

He felt cold, alone, and surprisingly unafraid. Not calm. Just suddenly chilled as if the night air itself had been honed to an edge and had a place within him.

He might die, but he would not kneel down and allow the pistol to be placed behind his ear. No. They wouldn't have it that easy.

Seemingly from nowhere and seemingly somehow to have all the time in the world to do so, Brandes remembered a passage from a Norman Mailer book. The main character had recounted a feeling that had overwhelmed him on a battlefield. It had allowed him to do things he never would have thought of trying. Mailer's character had called it a feeling of "grace," and Brandes had never totally understood it.

He realized he understood as he looked at the still-helmeted cyclists.

The man walked closer.

*That is a mistake,* Brandes thought. *I know it is, but I don't know how to exploit it.*

The gun lashed out, struck him across the side of his head; he fell to gravelly clay, rolled, and got up quickly, surprising the

244

man. He did not intend to attack the biker—he only was determined to carry out his decision not to die on the ground.

The roll, though, twisted his feet and legs; and as his knees snapped back open, his insteps accidentally hooked around the other man's legs.

The cyclist fell hard; the automatic roared into the air. Without thinking, Brandes kicked the gun hand, and the weapon flew away.

He knew he had no chance of getting the other biker, but the startling development had stunned all three of them.

*Victory might well belong to the first to recover.*

Brandes ran toward the trees, fell purposely, rolled down the steep incline of the roadbed and into the brush.

He looked up, a red haze still misting his eyes from the impact of the gun near his temple. He wiped blood that ran into his eyes. A scintillating gray still floated across his vision, but it was diminishing. He rose, hunched, aimed himself at the thicker trees only yards away.

And his head exploded as the second cyclist smashed the butt of his gun into Brandes's skull.

He felt himself being dragged back up to the shoulder.

*Well, what the hell. I tried. I really tried,* he thought, and that thought gave him a soaring sense of satisfaction as if what had to come next no longer mattered, as if he indeed had won.

Brandes twisted his head; it rocked with pain, and his vision twirled for a few seconds before settling on the biker he had tripped: Black leather. White helmet. Nearly black face shield. A robot. A science-fiction monster. A killer. A Darth Vader . . .

He almost giggled, and instead doubled and retched with sudden nausea.

"Couldn't let it go, could you?" one of the bikers asked.

Brandes looked up; he'd never considered that they would say anything more to him.

"What the hell do you care? Nobody's getting anywhere anyhow."

"Maybe not, not yet. But it's only a matter of time. Your

brother wouldn't have made it that hard for you to figure out. How far have you gotten?"

Brandes looked up again, this time nonplused. He said honestly, "I really don't know what the hell you're talking about . . ."

A boot crashed into his ribs; he thought he heard the crack of bone. "Peter didn't leave anything!" He tried to make it a shout; his voice was more an agony-rich whisper.

"Shit he didn't."

Brandes tried to think. Considering what the man had said at least diverted his mind from the pain filling his side.

Peter had known. *He had known*.

And he'd left something. So all this wasn't a waste of time. He laughed, coughed. To find that out on the pitch-black, deserted highway with two gunmen standing over him certainly *made* it a waste of time.

"Son of a bitch," one of them said. "The fucker doesn't know."

"What . . ." Brandes began; again he was kicked.

"Shut up, Doctor. I hate to hear dead men talk. It gets on my nerves even to think about it."

The other cyclist was silent and began to walk toward the bikes.

*He doesn't want to watch*, Brandes thought.

*Too late, Peter. Too fucking late. I hope you had good reason for making things difficult.*

Then, as he looked into the dark face shield and the barrel of the rising automatic—*Good, it will be a head shot*—the scene again changed to slow motion. It was a scene he later would have great difficulty explaining to anyone.

He saw the man's eyes.

His nose. His mouth.

And all of that clearly was impossible since he was wearing the shield.

But he wasn't wearing the shield. The dark plastic had gone, vanished.

White fiberglass on the left side of the helmet suddenly turned red and exploded into shards of plastic mixed with blood and brains.

Brandes's eyes widened as did the biker's. The small entrance hole of the bullet was black under the man's left eye. The gun dropped; the large man slipped dead to the ground, his torn head only inches from Brandes's face.

Brandes's stomach turned; he ignored the pain in his side and rolled over and got to his knees.

The other cyclist was more than ten yards away—and stood frozen in place for several seconds before frantically jumping on a cycle and thumbing the starter. Again the roaring noise rushed to fill the unnatural, vacuumlike stillness that had surrounded the tableau.

Then the monster bike was gone; Brandes watched the red taillight dwindle away, wobbling and waving. He heard the biker shifting through all five gears as fast as possible.

And Brandes still had no idea what had happened.

He stood, doubled over, got to the Mercedes, and leaned over the fender. He looked back at the corpse, only then realizing that even in the instant the face shield had shattered that he knew the man.

It was Rachek, the sullen laborer he had met at the lab.

He vomited.

Then there was another sound; involuntarily he crouched down. It was a car engine, though, and it covered the dwindling noise of the retreating motorcycle.

Brandes looked toward the new sound. He edged in front of the Mercedes, still instinctively trying to protect himself.

Headlights illuminated the shoulder as the car rolled onto it and slowly approached him. Brandes stood in numb confusion as it came closer. The headlights blinked out, but the persistence of their brilliance prevented him from seeing through the windshield and identifying the driver.

The door opened and a voice called out, "Looks like I've got a full-time job, Alex."

A voice he knew. Kracke.

Brandes let himself relax and immediately found himself slipping. He had to grab at the fender of the Mercedes to stay upright. Kracke saw that and ran to grab Brandes's shoulders, holding him up.

"All over, Alex."

Brandes looked at the gory corpse only yards away on the ground. He looked down and saw that his own clothes were sprayed with the man's blood. He felt awe and shock and nausea—and he felt alive.

"For now, Jim," he said. "It's all over for now. Only for now."

Kracke nodded wordlessly and led him to his car. His own mind feverishly tried to assimilate what he'd seen since his arrival, since he'd followed Brandes more out of boredom than any great sense of urgency.

He remembered how he and Allenberg had seized on the *Charon* incident to convince Brandes he was a target—and, when that hadn't been sufficient, actually had staged an "attack" and a "spoil" for him.

*The* Charon *wasn't an accident*, Kracke thought. *We were blind, smug. Stupid. God, it's amazing the man still is alive.*

# TWENTY-FOUR

DOROTHY JENNER ASKED HER HUSBAND, "ARE they really doing anything? Emil, are they getting *anywhere* with this thing?"

"Does it matter?"

Emil sat small, sucked in upon himself, in a chair near the fireplace. He'd said little since he had taken Nancy to the culvert, had done less. The only exception was his appearance at the town meeting, and his wife had hoped from his vehement outburst there that some sort of life again was present in her husband.

Emil was everything now. She needed him. She felt isolated, left out, lonely—more lonely than ever before in her life—and it was made all more poignant by the fact that he sat not three steps away from her.

Yet he never crossed those few feet of hardwood floor. He never came to her, put his arms around her, told her that *he* at least still was with her. And, God, did she need that.

"Alex Brandes seemed sincere," she said.

"Yes."

She got up and moved across the room to the sofa, which faced the television. She turned it on; he said nothing. Before, he always had either watched with her or had smiled his leave-it-off smile.

He did nothing as she switched the channels and chose the late news.

She did not at first realize that the newscaster was speaking of Lyle. Emil heard it and turned his head. It was the first time since the town's nightmare had begun that they had known for a fact that anyone "outside" even knew about the epidemic.

"It couldn't be kept secret forever," he said. "I'm surprised they managed a few days like this. The quarantine and all. Their goddamn quarantine." His face seemed to close again; what life remained within the man withdrew again inside him.

"State health authorities," the newscaster said, "have announced that a quarantine has been placed around Lyle. There are reports that the disease is believed virtually isolated in the community and that, in fact, it was created there in a genetic engineering laboratory named Futures, Inc.

"No representatives of the laboratory have spoken to the press; indeed, it has not been possible for reporters to speak to anyone in Lyle because of difficulty with the telephone lines.

"Phone company officials said they are investigating the disruption in service and have predicted that links with Lyle will be reestablished shortly.

"Meanwhile, army troops under the command of Colonel Mitchell Lawrence have been providing emergency communications for the town. Lawrence was interviewed earlier this afternoon by radio telephone . . ."

"Everything possible is being done," a taped voice said, and the station flashed a still photo of Lawrence. "I'm sure public health officials can give you more details on the medical aspects, but I do know that doctors from the Centers for Disease Control have been in Lyle for several days and have been working around the clock.

"No one is minimizing the danger of this disease. We are doing everything we can to find ways not only of containing it but treating it and ultimately completely preventing it. We do need the help of the people of Lyle—and I have to say that, so far, they have been remarkable in their ability to deal with this situation and in their cooperation with those of us who have to enforce the quarantine."

"Son of a bitch," Jenner said, his voice very soft, very low. Doro heard him but knew that he never intended that she hear him. It was not that he didn't want her to hear. It was much worse, to her, than that.

It was that he didn't care if she did hear, did not care if she didn't. He had stopped caring somewhere in the fields, where the culvert was, where Nancy was.

Doro went into the kitchen.

"Emil. Hot chocolate?"

She did not expect an answer, except perhaps a grunt, and was inordinately pleased when he said, "Yes." Still there wasn't any life in his speech, but she thought it had to be a good sign that at last he would speak at all, answer her at all, and recognize that *she*, too, had lost her daughter and was suffering.

She put Saran wrap over the large measuring cup of milk and set it into the microwave. She adjusted the power control to a half-power cycle and set the time for a minute and a half. She spent the time trying to think of something, of *anything*, she might call out to the living room that would cause her husband to make some sort of response.

*He died, too,* she thought. *And it's not fair, because I didn't, and I'm being left alone.*

The oven's long beep sounded, and Doro took the cup and placed it on the kitchen table.

When would they uncover Nancy? When would they bury her? *God,* she thought, *if this trouble lasts too long, what kind of condition will my daughter's body be in when Emil goes to the culvert?* She hadn't thought of that before; and as she did, her stomach churned, bile rose to her throat—bile, sharp and acrid.

She poured a small amount of the warmed milk into mugs, and then she added sugar and Krön cocoa. It was a luxury item that Emil always had argued really was a necessity. She made a

251

paste of the mixture and then gradually added the remainder of the milk to the mugs. She rinsed out the measuring cup and spoon and picked up the chocolate.

Emil had not moved.

That she noticed as soon as she shouldered through the kitchen door. Neither had he touched their television. Doro wondered what must be going on in a mind that outwardly quiet, that immune to outside prodding and pushing and noises and loud-voiced television hawkers. What was happening in Emil's mind? What torments? Perhaps potentially worse, what was *not* happening? Was his mind a blank, a premature oblivion, a consignment to unscheduled flat black?

And all that while the heart beats on?

The heart is supposed to stop before then.

She let the door close behind her.

"Chocolate," she tried, reflexively, to sound at least somewhat cheerful.

"Thank you," he said. Emil took the mug and drank a large swallow. He had been sitting forward, elbows on his knees. After swallowing he sighed, sat back.

"Emil," she began.

"No. Don't, Doro. I've got a good idea of what you want to say. Just let *me* say that I'm sorry about all this." Suddenly he seemed animated—moreover, intense in his animation. "I'm sorry about being somewhere else while you've had to stay here and cope with the whole damn thing. I'm sorry I blew up at that meeting—no, I take that back. About that I'm damned sure not sorry at all. The bastards.

"What the hell gave them the right? Why here, Doro? To make something like that in a town, with people. With *children*. Why, who gave them that right? God, I just wish I could find out who I wanted to hit! I guess it's that more than anything, honey. I have to hit somebody, and I can't find a target. It's not Alex, and if it was Peter, he's sure paid long ago. It's not the army, much as I hate them for not letting us take Nancy through.

"I just don't know. And"—he stopped—"I think what I've

been doing is in a sense hitting you because I can't find them. Whoever the hell *them* is."

It was the most Emil had said in some time. Dorothy didn't care about the contents as much as the fact that he said something.

"Emil," she said, "there aren't any words. I know, if that helps. I understand."

"I know you do. Drink up."

He made an attempt at a grin and took another mouthful of chocolate. "Good stuff," he said. He always said that. She nodded and raised her own mug to her lips, but she was interrupted by a knock on the front door. No, not a knock, more of a bang.

That sound was followed by the twisting of the doorknob and the sound of someone pushing.

"What's that?" she asked.

Emil already was on his feet, though. He walked quietly to the room's side, near their fireplace, and reached into a drawer where he kept several guns. Emil did not hunt; he liked guns. She saw him pick an automatic from the drawer, check its clip, and pull the slide back once. He edged toward the door.

He motioned her to stay where she was, to make no sound. Doro looked more closely then and saw the doorknob turning. Whoever was trying to get in wasn't putting much effort into the attempt, but neither was he making a very good attempt at being unobtrusive.

Suddenly the sounds stopped.

Emil stopped.

He turned and moved back toward Dorothy.

"Listen," he said. "I think I know who it is. I don't want to have to use this, and if it's who I think I sure as hell don't want to be holding it when I open the door. Can you handle it? Do you remember?"

Doro nodded, took the weapon.

It was a Beretta, .25 caliber. Emil had shown her several times how to use each of the three pistols they owned. She always had admired that in him; Emil did not like to be unprepared for anything. In another few years, he probably would have shown Nancy how to use them.

There was a scuffling sound on the wood of the porch.

"What?" she whispered.

"The goddamn army," he said.

"But why?"

"After the way I blew up at that meeting? And after we were stopped trying to leave town? They know, Doro. Somehow they know we had a sick girl, and I messed it up. I'm sorry, Doro."

"You only said her name once, Emil, and you stopped yourself. They can't know," she said, her lack of conviction breaking her voice.

"*They* know. I *feel* it. And they've come to get her."

"What are we going to do?"

"First I want to find out why they just didn't come in. I think they're looking through the other windows on this floor. Probably trying to find Nancy."

"You mean they want her? Her . . ." She had trouble still with the word. ". . . Her *body?*"

"Yes. She's not going onto that fire of theirs, Doro. I swear it."

There was fire in his eyes, she saw. It worried her. Emil had blamed himself for so much. He had assumed the burden of guilt for Nancy's death totally, feeling that he had waited too long to try to get her to another town's hospital. He hadn't been aggressive enough at the roadblock. He hadn't—oh, she was sure *his* list went on.

She didn't hold him responsible for any of it, but that was not the matter in question. He believed he was responsible. Maybe a psychiatrist would say he was trying to generate guilt feelings or something, but that didn't matter either.

All that mattered now was what he intended to do.

She remembered Selden.

*God*, she thought, *don't let them kill him, too. Please. I need him. Oh, God, I need him.*

Emil Jenner moved to the kitchen quietly and slid to one side the half-length calico curtain over the sink. He let it go, returned.

"No Jeep out there," he said. "They must have parked away from the house." He paused, turned, and looked at her. "I thought about it, Doro. Give me the gun back. It's not going to matter what they see. What matters is what I've got.

"They're not getting Nancy. Promise."

Jenner doubted he ever would forgive himself for that emotional moment at the town meeting.

*I sent her to the fires.*

Dorothy realized she still held her mug in her left hand; it rested on her lap. She put it down, raised the gun that she loosely held in her right hand. She looked at it and then lifted it, offering it to Emil. She prayed he would do nothing "foolish," but in her mind then she knew she was not certain exactly what that word meant. Everything had changed, was changing.

There was another sound; Emil took the gun. He moved very quietly to the door. Dorothy was transfixed, her vision set on the door but aware very much in her peripheral vision of Emil standing just to one side, the side on which the hinges were mounted.

There was a knock, a low, soft knock. Emil straightened.

It was a strange knock for a soldier. No one with a *rifle* would knock that way, he thought.

He reached toward the knob, his arm kept low, beneath the level of the inset window.

He twisted the knob; she heard the mechanism *click!* release. The door slowly opened.

The cup of chocolate dropped from Dorothy's hand as though the nerves suddenly had gone dead. She felt her neck trembling, knew that the tip of her chin was vibrating up and down in the grasp of shock too difficult to assimilate because the impossible never can be. And it was, of course, impossible.

*It's impossible*, she thought, but her head continued to move, her body to shiver. Emil had not moved, had not yet seen.

Covered with damp, already moldering leaves, Nancy stood in the doorway, her face streaked. Her clothes were filthy, her eyes bright and bewildered.

"Mommy," she said.

Emil stiffened when he heard the voice; Dorothy collapsed. The Krön chocolate spread over the hardwood floor, staining it.

Flames rose into the sky. They were not high, not particularly impressive. The fire was enough to do its job, no more. Lawrence looked out of the window of his headquarters. From there he could not actually see the flames, but he could see the glow cast against the night sky.

He stood next to his desk, his eyes still fixed on the sky.

*They'll owe me when this is over*, he thought.

He picked up his telephone, punched a single button.

"Lieutenant Knotts."

"Lieutenant. This is Colonel Lawrence."

"Yes, sir."

*Christ, give me regular troops on something like this. Not these. I can hear the man snap to attention. Cowboy stuff, comic book stuff.*

He sighed.

"Lieutenant Knotts. I believe we should start the next phase immediately. I've read the latest reports, and we seem to be pretty much caught up with the most recent victims."

"We are, sir. There are a few still, but we've, uh, disposed of most of them."

*Disposed.* Well, why the hell not? Knotts needed some word, certainly.

"Yes. Well, we have quite a few to go. Not as many, but still a sizable number. Keep in mind I don't want some big fucking bonfire out there. I don't care if you've got to do them one at a time.

The disease isn't going to spread with a delay of a day or two, but this town could wrap itself around our ears if it suddenly sees hundred-foot-high flames out at Haddon's place."

"I understand, sir."

Lawrence's orders had been explicit; Knotts was somewhat annoyed that the colonel thought he had to repeat them. Getting rid of the infected corpses was vital—but even more so was not unduly exciting the raw emotions of Lyle's residents. Knotts had seen them at the town meeting. His men were armed now, yes, but still he would not want them to have to face those townspeople fueled by more adrenaline and less caution than simple army orders could give his own men.

"We can start on the others," Lawrence said. "Begin exhumations with the most recent."

"Sir?"

"Yes?"

"Well, the others have been there longer. I mean, well, doesn't it make sense to get them out of the ground first?"

"Might seem so at first, Lieutenant. Think about it. The ones most recently buried are more likely to have the disease organism still active.

"The others—well, if they're going to infect something, they've either done it already or they're not going to. At least it's less likely. Make sense?"

"Yes, sir. It makes sense. I'm sorry. I . . ."

"Lieutenant." Lawrence had to handle his men carefully, perhaps his officers more so. They were not seasoned troops; they were being called upon for the first time to do something *real*, he thought. "Don't apologize.

"None of us has had an assignment like this before. *None* of us." *Stress that*, he thought. "It's going to take some getting used to. So far the men are doing their jobs very well. If we continue to keep ourselves under control, the men will continue to do well."

"Thank you, sir. I'll order the first details to begin exhumations as soon as we put together the list chronologically."

"Very well," Lawrence said. He hung up the phone and looked back out the window.

Something was going on that he did not know. He had known that for the last few days. It was something not in Lyle, of course. It was in Washington—or at Langley. *God forbid, not at Langley.*

But his men were in the right place at the right time. *Fortuitous.* Horseshit, fortuitous.

And his most recent orders were not signed with any name he recognized; in fact, they were not signed at all. They ended with identification codes that, when decoded, said simply that they were "acceptable" or "not acceptable."

All his had been signed with "acceptable" codes, and he had acted accordingly. He knew there were men both in the military and in Congress—and one or two more closely identified with the White House—who counted on him to make an unpalatable situation at least explainable publicly, while doing everything he legitimately could do to contain the most deadly disease he ever had heard of.

But the wheels within wheels in the state and defense departments undoubtedly were spinning, each with its own momentum, each with its own direction, and without question each with its own reason for doing exactly what it was doing—and the hell with those who got in the way of those wheels.

Brandes still might, but Lawrence considered the scientist pretty much defused. He had behaved well enough at the town meeting, but he could have done better, Lawrence thought.

His initial orders had been simply military in nature. Be in position to impose a quarantine. Later adjustments to those orders were less obvious in origin. Lawrence could tell, just by the wording, the tone. Not many men might be able to detect that, but he could. His career was as political as it was military; he could recognize the touch of a politician when he saw it.

Cooperate with Brandes completely.

He smiled as he remembered that one. He'd played that very well, he thought. Brandes didn't know of the message; Lawrence at once and quite well had read Brandes that first day they had met.

Brandes understood his own position even less well than Lawrence understood just why Brandes was there.

Lawrence just hadn't been able to resist trying to establish superiority over the doctor.

Goddamn doctor. *Doctor!* They make us well *after* they give us fucking diseases; and when they run out, they create some new ones. Lawrence had little use for most doctors, most scientists.

Brandes hadn't exactly folded, but he'd told Lawrence what he wanted to know and what he had expected. He could push Brandes because whoever was running Brandes hadn't given their ferret the slightest idea of just how much power he had and from where he could draw reserves if he needed them.

*Tough.*

The flames rose, dipped, flickered, faded. Twenty years earlier he had seen such a sky. It knew beauty, those flames, those colors. It was man's answer to nature's aurora borealis, its light rising from below whatever obscured the horizon; in Lyle that was trees. When created by men, though, the source must not be considered if the lovely, comforting thought of beauty was to be maintained. Man did not create such beauty by creation; he did it by destruction.

*Conflagration* was such an expressive word, he thought. Many words in many languages had a flavor for him, an effect on the tongue.

He continued to watch the oranges—there were many, the number infinite, the reality a continuum of the spectrum—and thought about that. He was mesmerized. He knew it; he didn't care.

Such envelopment in beauty could be a relaxation from true feeling, true thought.

*Gemutlichkeit*, he thought. A good example. It was a totally untranslatable word. Lawrence's German was mediocre; still, he had learned to *feel* that word. *A family gathers on a cold, snowy, still evening around a pleasantly, reassuringly warm fireplace, arms around each other's shoulders. No word is spoken. Each feels something . . . a belonging, a contentment.*

It could not be translated, but Lawrence felt he knew the word's meaning.

*Conflagration* was like that. He could feel the meaning, taste the word.

And he did not like it when he thought of it while looking at the cremation pyres. The association had too much of a taste of something out of control, of destruction without purpose. And this had purpose. Just as had the fires and flame-lit skies of years ago when a jungle burned, when villages burned, when he was a captain.

He shook his head violently from side to side, tearing his eyes from the view from his headquarters.

Lawrence sat down, wondered just whose irons were in that fire, wondered if he was going to be called upon to pull them out.

He also wondered just what he could expect in return after he'd done that. He'd been a colonel long enough. For a brief moment he remembered again other man-lit night skies; colonel long enough, he thought. More was needed; more was what he would get.


Trilby had been head nurse at Lyle–Mount Saint Sydney for nearly a decade, but no one would have believed that on first meeting her.

She didn't look old enough.

Tall, thin, brunet, she'd had her share of being chased by staff doctors. Sometimes she regretted that her professionalism actually caused her to *miss* passes that were thrown at her during working hours.

Most of those, however, had been made years before—before she had taken charge of the night nursing staff at the hospital. No one really challenged Trilby. The nurses certainly didn't, some doctors might have liked to have had the courage, and occasionally the administration toyed with the idea.

Even her *patients* behaved.

Trilby didn't mind working with Dr. Shortell at any time, though. She recognized the worth of a man, and she saw a competence and compassion in the young doctor that had earned her respect.

In any event, the current crisis required her total attention. It also pointed out to an annoyed and much-embarrassed adminis-

260

ration that she was shockingly accurate in her conclusion that the size of the nursing staff was inadequate at the best of times and tragically, if not criminally, deficient in case of disaster.

"Code blue," a voice announced from a speaker in the ceiling. The voice was not loud. At night the volume of the public address system was turned down.

Trilby waited, listening. There wouldn't be much she could do, she knew. *Blue* had only recently been introduced into the hospital's lexicon. It did not mean a cardiac arrest. There would be no crash cart racing down the corridor. It meant that someone else had slipped into the final phase of the Futures Illness.

What a horrible impromptu name, she'd thought. At least it hadn't been widely used; at least it had not *yet* been widely used.

"Code blue. Three-fifteen."

The room number caught Trilby's attention. So many patients had come and gone it was amazing she could keep any sort of track at all. But 315 was familiar.

The CDC doctor had been shuffled to that room only that afternoon. That was it.

Trilby had seen Dr. Shortell's face when he had looked in on the woman. She had felt sorry for him. He obviously had more than a professional attachment or at least had had hopes of something more with the pale but still undeniably beautiful doctor.

It had had to happen, of course.

It happened to all of the disease's victims, and the next step was equally inevitable. The code-blue coma phase always ended the same way. Trilby really did feel bad for Dr. Shortell; the man deserved someone like that woman. She wished there was something she could do, but she knew better.

When Cynthia was moved from Room 315, it would not be to another bed in another room. When that time came—as Trilby knew it must—she would be moved, at least temporarily, to the morgue.

# TWENTY-FIVE

"WHAT WOULD YOU RATHER HAVE?" BEN DORFMAN asked. He looked across the table at Jimmy Rhodes, another epidemiologist. Traffic in the CDC cafeteria at that time of night—more the morning of the next day—was light. Only three other tables were occupied, and Rhodes was the only other person who worked in the same department. Dorfman didn't even know some of the other late-night workers; he suspected some might be bachelor-degree holders qualified for such exciting jobs as washing test tubes. He, he believed, was far beyond that; on paper he certainly was.

In practice also, he might be considered more advanced, more talented. Dorfman was neither popular nor shunned; his abilities were recognized.

He would have more than that.

Dorfman was a very ambitious man—perhaps a drive that could, in a scientist, lead more easily to misery than to recognition. Like anyone else, scientists, of course, had egos; wanted to get ahead. *Nothing wrong with that*, Dorfman often had said.

While nothing might intrinsically be wrong with that ambition, it nevertheless was true that when a scientist—as opposed to an industrialist—"slit throats" to climb upward, the result was more likely to be the letting of real blood. Those arguments Dorfman thought specious.

Whether climbing upward meant being nominated for a Nobel Prize or getting an invitation to speak at the International Rubber Conference in Tokyo, egos inevitably were present and a factor.

*And there's nothing wrong with that. Nothing at all.*

Most scientists, though, in Dorfman's view, tended to have their ambitions more suitably clothed, subdued, than people in private industry. What was "unseemly" might be eschewed, but what was beneficial to one's career—well, there *were* ways to make such things noticed by higher authorities.

"Shit, Ben," Rhodes said, "I've heard that one a half-dozen times in two weeks, and this is the first time I've heard it from you."

"Then maybe mine's different."

"At this hour it's worth the risk. 'What would you rather have? Eternal bliss or a ham sandwich, right?' "

"Right."

"Okay, a ham sandwich."

"Yeah, but why?"

Rhodes expelled a sigh. "I hope I get this wrong," he said. "There's nothing better than eternal bliss. That's premise Number One. Number Two is that a ham sandwich is better than nothing. Ergo, the sandwich is the answer. Well?"

Dorfman shrugged. "Sorry," he said, "that's the way I heard it, too; and the girl who told it to me swore that her answer was at least a little different." He chafed that his answer was *not* different.

"Well, it wasn't. Eat your ham sandwich and be happy you're doing better than eternal bliss."

"It's not a ham sandwich."

"I'm too tired to be a picky bastard with you tonight, Ben. If you're trying to provoke me so you can get your own adrenaline

263

going and use it for a few more hours' work, you're looking in the wrong place. Tonight, at this hour, I think you could insult my mother—and I love my mother."

"Just trying for conversation," Dorfman said, smiled, and bit into something called a "tuna pita pocket."

*Rhodes can be such a wise-ass bastard.*

"I've got all the stimulus I need. Just trying for conversation."

"Then talk to me about Cuba, for Christ's sake. Ask me what poison we could use to bump off Castro. You know, give me something challenging, useful."

Dorfman stopped chewing, looked at Rhodes. He began to laugh around a mouthful of tuna.

"You know," he said, swallowing, his chin dipping and rising again as his throat rippled, "I may even have an answer to that."

"How to bump off Castro?"

"Why the hell not?"

"Shit, Dorfman, you've been up too long. This thing in New England is getting loose in your lab. Only it's eating your brain."

"That Lyle bug is going to win some prizes for me, Rhodes."

"I have a brother who was nominated for a Pulitzer once. I was impressed as hell. Then he laughed and told me it didn't mean a damned thing. He worked for a middle-sized paper that would pick somebody every year and assign him to read *all* the paper's stories for that year. Then the guy would just pick a few and submit them for all sorts of awards. My brother couldn't even find out what story he'd written that was up for the Pulitzer. The guy who picked them had forgotten. That's what prizes mean to me. Enjoy your trip to Stockholm, Dorfman." Rhodes giggled, laughed more openly, picked up a notebook from the cafeteria table, and left.

Dorfman was not in the least subdued by Rhodes's cynicism. *You'd love it if you won one, wouldn't you, asshole?*

He was about to announce to his superiors—*Shit*, how he hated to call them that!—that he had developed something that stood a damn good chance of being a cure for Lyle's disease.

Lyle's disease.

*Lyle's disease.*

He thought about that, continuing to munch on his sandwich. The thing didn't have a name yet. Maybe that would stick. After all, there wasn't a hope in hell of getting the thing named after *him*, and the next best thing would be to be the person who coined whatever name was going to be affixed to the thing.

Like Legionnaire's Disease.

Better to have a hand in naming it than not, he thought. Maybe the cure would be named for him.

The Salk Vaccine.

The Dorfman Vaccine.

Except that his was not strictly a vaccine. There was a possibility of using it in an attempt at preventative immunization, but basically it would attack existing active viruses—much more of a treatment than a preventative. It had the side-effect, though, of stimulating antibody production in an uninfected organism.

The *mechanism* of the thing was what was different.

That was it!

The *Dorfman Mechanism.*

It wasn't really new. Oh, it was new to established medicine, but not to Dorfman. He had been working on recombinant DNA ever since he had gotten out of Rutgers University.

Not all of his research was approved—but then it had not been voted against, either. He'd done it the smart way. He'd not bothered to tell anyone what he was doing.

Dorfman always had enjoyed working in laboratories, although he didn't always enjoy telling people what had started his interest.

Simply, it was the glassware.

He had been about ten when he'd first seen a laboratory.

That one was located in a General Foods factory that made, among other things, Jello. His mother had worked there in quality control. Every few hours she would go from machine to machine, taking samples. Then she would make Jello. She tested it. Sugar content, density. Things he didn't understand at that time.

265

He had been very impressed by his mother's power, her authority. She hadn't meant that to be so, but one day he had asked her what happened when she found something was wrong with some of the Jello.

"We dump it," she'd answer.

"The package?"

She'd laughed.

"We dump the *whole thing*. The whole batch. Sometimes tons of it are in a machine. I find something wrong, tell them to dump it, and it goes right out the chute into the Hudson River. *Whoosh!*"

He'd had visions of tons of Jello hitting the rather oily water of the Hudson—and turning the river into some sort of enormous but inedible dessert.

His real legacy from that job of his mother's, however, had sprung from the one time she had taken him with her to work and had shown him her small cubbyhole of a laboratory.

The glassware had fascinated him. The shapes, the elegance of retorts, the functionality of beakers, the ground glass fittings. He never could explain to himself and—God forbid!—he never had tried to explain to anyone else what it was about all that glassware that made him want to work in a laboratory someday.

His interests had, of course, developed far beyond thoughts of testing instant puddings. Biology fascinated him. It had been a plus that the pursuit of his interest in it could be coupled with an opportunity to work in a laboratory—complete with glassware.

Dorfman had gone to Rutgers because he lived in New Jersey at the time, and Rutgers was the only school he could afford to attend.

His choice of major was lucky; although Rutgers was a state university and not considered in the same league as a Harvard or a Columbia, one department there was respected throughout the academic community—biology. So, Dorfman had prospered because of his family's lack of prosperity.

He had made the most of it, he felt. He was the youngest researcher at the CDC. Once he had wanted to be a field operative, an epidemiologist who actually worked "out there." That goal had dissipated when he had learned that "out there" more often than not meant a small city whose seventh-graders were suddenly and disproportionately afflicted with German measles.

Lyle's disease, though, that was different.

He would not have given up the thought of field work if he always could be assigned to projects like Lyle's disease. Lives in the balance, a population to be saved.

An award to be won?

Too late for the field work now, he thought. His place had been established in the laboratory. The glassware no longer had the glamour with which childhood had endowed it, but he did not regret that his career had rooted itself in the lab. There was great opportunity there for someone willing to work, to seize advantages.

There was much greater opportunity than there was in the field. And, for someone who *also* did not give much attention to the rigidity of superiors, for someone who was unafraid—the opportunities were unlimited.

Quietly, he had utilized the lab's facilities for his own work. But much of that work had had to be done outside of the CDC lab, of course. Too much of it would have been obvious. Almost all of the preparatory work had to be done with John Masta-filippo, a chemist he'd met in college and who had been a friend for nearly a decade.

John owned his own company, with its own laboratory, geared to research in ceramics. At first Dorfman had not been convinced of the future in that field, but John was very persuasive. Ceramics were the "synthetics" of the next decade.

A company like John's would be the next Xerox or Polaroid.

"Get in at the bottom, now," John had advised; and Dorfman had done that, putting all his savings—and his last two years' tax refunds—into the company. He received shares and more. He received permission to use the laboratory in the evenings. John was no fool, Dorfman often had thought. Ceramics might be part of the future, but they only were part. Genetic engineering was right up there, too. And if Dorfman made some really significant advance in John's lab—well, investment could work in several directions.

The CDC labs had been vital, of course. John's lab simply could not provide all that Dorfman needed. He could, however, prepare materials for analysis in that private lab—sometimes that took weeks—and then a half hour's work with CDC electrophoresis equipment was all that was needed.

Lyle's disease could not have timed itself more perfectly for Dorfman. It provided a perfect opportunity to find out if his work of the last thirty-four months was worth anything at all.

And it *was!* Dorfman rose from the cafeteria table, thinking about the technique, about how well it *did* work. Thinking about what recognition waited just days or weeks away.

*Invest in me, Jack!*

Dorfman thought of all this and became excited anew. He had to see Heathcliff. He went to his lab on the floor above.

Heathcliff was a pig. Literally.

Well, Heathcliff, was a *baby* pig. He provided a wonderful subject for the tests Dorfman had performed. People might not like to admit it, but in some ways pigs were anatomically closer to humans than were apes. That, Dorfman had once argued (and had been silenced—the bastards), might have annoyed Darwin.

Dorfman admired Peter Brandes, although he never had met him. Both men had pressed ahead into a new area, one that *truly* would or could revolutionize life.

*Forget the Industrial Revolution, forget Titusville's oil, forget the assembly line and steamboat. The genetic, the biological revolution would cast those previous into its own deep shadow. And he and Brandes were part of it.*

Heathcliff was well. Dorfman had known he would be well, just *known* it.

Yet, Heathcliff had been injected with blood fractions from the first batches to arrive in Atlanta from Lyle.

Part of it was luck, serendipity, Dorfman admitted. His own

research had been ready, Lyle's disease had developed—and then, of course, Heathcliff had been available.

Dorfman bent, pushed a finger through the mesh of the piglet's cage. Used to such treatment, Heathcliff bounded over and placed his chin over Dorfman's finger, enjoying his scratch even if he had no itch. *Pigs*, Dorfman thought, *are very like people, indeed.*

The lab door opened, Allison walked in, and Dorfman thought the timing could not have been better. He had intended to make a few notes and then call her to tell her of his achievement.

"Dr. Lasser, I'm glad you dropped by."

"I thought it about time. We haven't seen much of you lately." Which, of course, wasn't true. What she meant was that she and the other directors had not had any reports from him on his work on the Lyle problem.

"I've been busy," he said.

*Damn it, why the hell do I also seem to be apologizing to people? To those who are supposed to be my superiors? None really is, in a sense that matters.*

"And?"

Well, that was a question he could answer. "I found something that works."

Her eyebrows rose markedly, then dropped. "A serum? A vaccine? Already?"

*Damn her tone. Damn her condescension.* Still, this moment had to be carefully handled, his use of the lab made to appear an inconsequential off-the-cuff line he had pursued in his spare time.

"Not in the traditional sense," he said, and she smiled. "I've built a virus."

Her smile died. "What the fuck do you mean?" He winced; Dorfman did not like hearing obscenities from women. But he knew that she was listening, all right. She was poised to lash out at him if he wasn't careful.

"I work, not for pay"—thank God he'd thought to add that!—

"in another lab a friend lets me use. I developed a technique. It works on the Lyle thing."

Lasser's face remained unreadable. "Let me get this right, Dorfman." No "Doctor!" "You have been working in another lab and have worked with recombination."

"Yes."

"And the lab?"

"Great care. Always."

*Why the hell was he apologizing?*

"Too late to do anything about that," she said, half to herself. "What exactly did you do or do you claim to have done?"

*Claim to! Up yours, too, Doctor!*

"I succeeded in creating a virus that neutralizes viruses."

"Explain," she said. Her face was chiseled stone.

"I haven't had time to test it extensively," he said, feeling more confident, "but it works with Lyle. Normally a disease virus injects its genetic material into a healthy cell and 'orders' that cell to change its programing, to drop everything else and make more viruses or maybe even to make a few protein changes. Mine invades the same cells."

"This is your idea of a cure? Infect the person twice?"

"You could look at it as an infection, I guess. Mine doesn't kill the host, though."

"It? . . ."

"It changes the damaged cell's programing again. The cell will reproduce the disease virus still, but the new virus makes changes in the instruction set. After the disease virus has been replicated and the cell wall broken, the new organisms invade other cells— just as before. But *my* virus has changed their coding. They *can't* order the *next* healthy cell to make any more viruses!"

It was out, spelled out. He felt a great relief and a surge of pride.

"You mean that *your*"—somehow when she said it, it didn't sound the same—"virus makes the disease virus . . ."

"Sterile, yes. The disease only can proceed so far, once the new virus has been introduced."

Allison Lasser stood quietly for several moments. Then she nodded her head.

"If this checks out, Doctor"—*Victory!*—"you may have made one hell of a breakthrough." She nodded again and turned to leave.

Dorfman said nothing; her sudden attitude change and decision to leave surprised him. He knew she was impressed, but somehow he had expected more.

*What the hell,* he thought, walking back to Heathcliff's cage. *I did it, and she knows I did it. Let her be in the corner for a change.*

*Stupid shit,* she thought.

Dorfman had to go, and even that wouldn't be enough. The crazy bastard was playing with recombinant DNA in some *basement* somewhere. Dr. Allison Lasser knew very, very well how affordable and easily purchased equipment for such research had become. She had considered, once, writing a memo urging that health legislators consider regulations and laws regarding the sale of the equipment.

She couldn't take the chance that the asshole's idiotic research *hadn't* produced results, though. She would have to get a supply of it, order it tested.

She would have to ship some of it to Lyle. It would take years before the FDA allowed its use generally, she knew. But she, not the CDC, of course, could try it out quietly on a few people in Lyle who were sure as hell headed for the fire, anyway. It had been done before.

If the stuff worked, she realized, Dorfman probably would get at least a Nobel nomination. *God,* she thought as she walked more hastily down the corridor to her own office, *if that pitiful bastard has made a virus that interrupts the reproduction instructions in all other viruses, he even deserves the prize.*

*Even if he is an ass.*

She still wanted very extensive proof, she thought. She considered again how best to get a small supply of Dorfman's concoction to Lyle for no-code testing, and she decided to

271

contact Brandes. She knew *of* Brandes. She knew he was not part of CDC, of course.

And that was precisely what she wanted.

Let *him* pick someone who didn't have a chance anyway. Let *him* give the serum. He was with some secret part of the government. (She thought that outright, hysterically laughable—even how much alcohol and how many sponges her lab used were something or other secret. The government was a manufacturer in a way. Its product was paper, and on it all was printed *secret* or *top secret*, or God knows what—maybe because there weren't any people who really did know.)

Let Brandes and his people take the blame if the serum killed rather than cured. She thought of the logistics and immediately began cursing her own actions.

Dorfman had *made a virus!*

She was shocked with her own recognition of just what she'd been thinking about.

*God, where has my mind been? That pompous ass has made a virus while working for us!*

She quickly covered the final few steps to her office and picked up her telephone. She called security. Dorfman's lab had to be put off limits, isolated. The goddamn fool's other lab had to be isolated. The people in Lyle might be able to try Dorfman's virus, but she would issue strict orders to Brandes about how it was to be used. Selected patients would have to be moved to the Futures lab itself. Only under conditions of stringent isolation could the stuff be tested.

*What if Dorfman's given us something worse than what we had?*

Even the possibility caused her to shiver.

Whatever he had come up with, one thing was clear to her, although she could not yet see just how she could do what must be done. If he'd succeeded, politics might be involved.

Still—potential prizewinner or not, Dorfman was an asshole, and Dorfman had to go.

# TWENTY-SIX

"JESUS!" WISMER SAID WHEN BRANDES AND KRACKE entered. "What the hell happened to you?"

"A short story that could have been shorter," Kracke said.

Wismer and Kracke fleetingly exchanged glances Brandes could not understand. Sarah had been standing near the door to Wismer's living room; she held a brandy glass in her hand. She said nothing.

"Tell me," Wismer said. It sounded like an order; Brandes was glad Kracke did not appear to take offense.

"I have to make a call first. Some of this just has to be handled by local cops, and they can find the mess out there on their own. We can't get anyone in here to clean up with the army sitting around. At least not easily. But I want to start the wheels moving in the background." Kracke went to the telephone.

He very much wanted to know who Rachek was, had been.

Kracke fully expected one of Lawrence's officers to monitor his call. He and Allenberg, however, over the years had developed a not only obscure but—some said—intuitive form of communication. Lawrence would be guessing for days. If Kracke could reach Allenberg.

Sarah had gone into the next room but never had been out of hearing range. No one seemed to mind that or even consider it. She returned. Kracke finished his call and, in much plainer language, told the story very briefly.

Sarah had another glass in her hand when she returned. She said nothing; she walked to Brandes and handed it to him. He looked at her, nodded thanks. All of them walked, glasses in hand and Brandes still with lingering shock in his eyes, into the living room to sit, to hear it *all*. Brandes, though, couldn't help admiring the calmness with which Sarah had taken the initial few words of the story and the way she'd gone to get him a brandy.

Kracke spoke.

"After your accident," he nodded toward Wismer, "Adrian Allenberg felt I should come here. We felt that there was sufficient reason then to think someone wanted Alex stopped."

"*Then?*" Brandes asked, at once angry with himself for interrupting but even more angry with Kracke and Allenberg. "For God's sake, you had to kill someone on Fire Island to keep me alive. It takes Rachek and a blown-away motorcycle helmet to convince you people?"

Kracke truly was imperturbable. His eyes locked Brandes's. He said, "We did not then have any—*any*—reason to think you would be in danger *here*, in Lyle."

What the hell are you people? Damn, you can wipe out somebody like Hoeckle because of no more than a flimsy report, and then you see an attack—*see* it, for Christ's sake—and you don't think there's a danger? Do any of you know what the hell you're doing?" Brandes drank, generously; it was good brandy. It burned; it felt good.

"Yes," Kracke said. "We know what we're doing. What is important now is that there is—someone *really* is—trying to kill you. Things have changed, Alex. Whoever wants you wants you enough to send people *here*."

"They wanted to kill me enough to send people after me more than a dozen miles at sea on a foggy night!"

Kracke for the first time seemed momentarily uncomfortable;

that soon passed. "Yes, Alex," he said. "We know that now, don't we?"

"And what is there that's so important about *here?* What makes Lyle different from Fire Island? From the Atlantic? *What?*"

"The origin of the disease, for one thing. *Your* disease, by heredity, your . . ."

"*Cut that shit!* I inherit nothing." Thoughts of his father. *No,* he thought, *I inherit nothing. Nothing.*

"A poor choice of words," Kracke responded. "I did not mean the sins of someone passed on, anything like that."

"Then what?"

"I meant that you did inherit something, Alex. Something. Some information. Your brother told you something, left you something."

Brandes said nothing; he stared at Kracke. "You couldn't know that, could you?"

Kracke looked puzzled; Brandes continued: "You were a hundred yards away—more. He said it. Rachek said it. He told me that, that Peter had left something. You didn't, couldn't know, but you *do* know. *How?*"

"You think that's hard to figure out? Why the hell do you think they tried to *kill* you so many times?"

*Careful,* Kracke thought. *Careful. He's not stupid.*

Brandes sighed, knowing Kracke had a point yet still not entirely satisfied.

*Something feels wrong. Just . . . wrong . . .*

He sank into a living room chair, still holding his drink and realizing that he had taken only one large mouthful from it. He put it aside and thought: *First time I've passed up a drink I can remember.*

Wismer smiled.

"Peter left nothing," Brandes went on. "Those notebooks are full of scribbles."

"Nothing?"

"Not so far."

"Maybe that's what they're afraid of. The 'not yet.' *Nothing so*

275

*far.* But it doesn't mean it's not there. And there's something else . . ." Kracke's voice changed.

"Yes?" That was Sarah.

"It means"—and then it was Wismer—"that they aren't fighting you, Alex. They'll kill you, yes. But they aren't fighting you. For some reason, they are fighting time."

"Explain," said Sarah, and Brandes could have kissed her.

"Look at Lyle, at this town. We have an army quarantine. We have people dying. We have people being cremated. *Burned without family consent, without any care for it.*

"How long can such a thing last? We've mentioned this in passing, but that's just the word we've missed: *passing*. This will be opened to the authorities, to the press. To the world. There *is* no way to prevent that."

"So?" It was Brandes.

"So, there is no *hope* of keeping this secret. That's not important. Whatever you may find in Peter's notes or in your memories of your brother is important far beyond the limits of Lyle."

"People are dying," Brandes said, his voice very soft. "You said that." Everyone in the room heard *Cynthia*, said nothing. "Can you really think of anything more far-reaching than Lyle's disease spreading beyond the town limits of Lyle? Can you?"

*God, this is a disease for which we haven't got a cure and so far only a few clues, some antibody.*

"It's a disease that mandates the *burning*. Can't all of you see that? If this gets out, there will be a hell of a lot more *burning*."

"You're right," Wismer said. "Still, there's more. Something that does not depend on secrecy about a disease—*that's* simply *impossible*. Something in which time is the only factor." He seemed to drift off, thinking quietly.

"Maybe it's not in the notes?" Sarah said suddenly.

"What?"

"Maybe not in the books. Maybe he did leave you something, something that was an answer. But not in the notebooks. I have to believe that those people who tried to kill you know something that you don't—that we don't. Peter *left* something."

At that moment a great tiredness settled suddenly onto Brandes. He was tired of the games, tired of being a counter on a board. He was tired of Kracke and of Allenberg and of Peter and of—all of it. All who had lied, who had manipulated, who had forced him into this situation.

He felt anger.

Cynthia would die because of this disease; they all might. Except maybe for the people who had convinced his brother to make it.

And *that* suddenly made sense. Peter would not have made this horror for himself. He would have made it—for the people who now most probably were those trying to kill Alex Brandes.

But why?

What had they asked his brother to make? Certainly not a biological warfare agent; Peter simply *would not have done that.* But something they prized so highly that they wanted the architect dead before the last stone was set in the pyramid.

Poor Peter. Poor unsuspecting Peter. And yet . . . he must have suspected something, felt uneasy about something. Assume Peter had left something behind. Take it as a given. Axiomatic. And take it also as given that whatever message he left was *for him.*

Then, however Peter had concealed it, couched it, Alex was the person who most likely could find and understand it. A sudden unsettling thought struck him as he concluded that line of reasoning.

*Son of a bitch. Allenberg, running on instinct, just may have been right in demanding my cooperation.*

More questions remained unanswered than answered. Perhaps more even than had been asked.

"And who are 'those people,' Mr. Kracke, Mr. Agent? You *must* know more than you're telling me? You had to *know* that I was a target for that boat, for that guy on Fire Island."

"Let's say I definitely had reason to believe one of those attacks would—or maybe I should say *might*—occur."

"Why?"

277

"Allenberg."

"Hell of an answer."

"Hell of a man, and that's truth. More than that I can't say. Sometimes I don't ask."

"Good soldier, huh?"

"Aren't you *goddamn* glad that I am?"

"I'm sorry," Brandes said after a moment. God, was he ever glad that Kracke was a good soldier! He remembered the roaring of the motorcycles, the fear, perspiration with a different taste and texture to it, the metal-taste of terror. Rachek. The guns, the kicking. Yes, he had reason to be glad Kracke was a good soldier, and he was sorry he'd made his comment. "It's been a rough night."

"From what you've told us, a lot rougher for others," Sarah said. Brandes looked across at her—seeing her, then seeing, somehow, Cynthia; and then again, somehow, Sarah.

"You take that particularly well."

"I do? I'm sorry. That was not the impression I meant to give. Really. Let's go to sleep, all of us." She turned toward Kracke: "Or *can* we sleep here?"

"Uh, well, I thought Alex should go to the room he'd taken at the Tower."

"No." It was the first time Wismer had spoken for quite some time. "There're other arrangements." Kracke raised an eyebrow.

"What arrangements?" Kracke asked.

"Andy has a building in back of his gas station." Kracke looked confused; Wismer explained, "Andy has a station in town. He's been here probably longer than the town has." He chuckled.

"Well, even if that's not so, he's been a friend for a long time. I trust him. He actually has a few buildings on his property. They're not easy to see from the road—the station backs up against a hill, and the buildings are up there. I think it's a good location, and Andy has agreed to let Alex and Sarah stay there."

"Wait a minute . . ." shouted Sarah. "No one's trying to kill *me*."

"That's why I suggested only Alex go to the Tower," Kracke said, looking at Wismer. The older man considered.

278

"You're right. Sarah can stay here."

Brandes could not remember if he'd ever seen Sarah look ewildered before: She did then. "Like I said, wait a minute. his time for other reasons, but wait a minute. Why so quick to ange your mind, Uncle Gerry?"

"No reason for you to be *with* the target if you're *not* a target," randes said. Everyone looked at him; he grinned as best he uld.

"Exactly," Kracke said.

"Ahh. Got it." She twirled her brandy glass in her fingers and niled herself.

Wismer nodded. "Pack up," he said to Brandes. "Andy doesn't ay awake much past midnight anymore; claims he's getting too d."

"I have to call in again. I have to reach Adrian," Kracke said. Vismer nodded that he understood, and Kracke walked to the lephone. Brandes rose, ready to go to his room to collect his ings. For Brandes, that meant a small case. When he returned, Vismer was at the foot of the stairs; Kracke was dialing.

"What about you?" Brandes asked Wismer. "And what about m?"

"Jim will do whatever he has to, Alex. I've been in this house a ong time, and I intend to stay here. There isn't anyone after e."

"But someone could get to you and find out where I am."

"Eventually they'll find you anyway, Alex. Hiding you in a wn quarantined by the army isn't hiding you for long. The ove is to give you time if you need it . . . time if *he* needs it." Ie gestured toward Kracke, who by then was talking to someone. And I don't intend to be a hero—if anyone comes here reatening—I'll just tell them what they want to know."

He sniffed, looking at once elderly priggish and amusing; both randes and Sarah smiled, first to themselves, then at each other. racke hung up the phone and walked toward them while randes still was on the fourth step.

"What?" Wismer asked him.

279

"I have to call back. He's not there yet. He's out, at a meeting.

"He'll get the message when he comes back. I'll stay down here for a while. You"—he nodded toward Brandes—"just go where you're going. Adrian must know about tonight," Kracke said. "He'll push on the Rachek thing, too. I'd like you to think about that, Alex."

"I just met the guy."

"I know. But run that part of the day over in your mind a few times. Think. Remember, he wasn't alone."

A shiver went up Brandes's back. *Christ, he'd forgotten the other biker.*

*That* was incredible.

"Yes," he said, "I know."

Kracke nodded, went back toward the sofa.

"I'll have him leave by the back door," Wismer said. "You," he said to Kracke, "get some sleep, too. Sofa's comfortable."

Kracke said he was certain it was.

"I'll see you tomorrow if I have to wait late. No one in the office seems to know exactly where Adrian is, only that he's meeting with a man named Ryan."

Brandes left. Kracke said, "Almost time to go." Sarah and Wismer looked puzzled. Kracke smiled, explained: "Allenberg *was* at a meeting. He'll call in a few minutes. Then I leave."

"To where?" Sarah asked.

"First to look at Andy's. Then to Alex's room at the Tower. You gave me *that* idea," he said to Wismer. "I'll tell Alex. He'll be able to reach me in an emergency, but I'm pretty sure they'll try his room before they find him at Andy's."

# TWENTY-SEVEN

ALLENBERG HAD HAD LITTLE TO SAY, BUT HE sounded amused. *Something certainly had lightened his day,* Kracke thought.

"Do you have good news?" he'd asked first, suppressing his own news about the attack. Moments for Allenberg to feel good were few; seconds would make no difference in Lyle at that point. *Let him be happy a few seconds longer.*

"Just about Jason," Allenberg said. His voice lost its humor, its softness. "I would imagine your calling me will not make me happy."

Couched in phrases Lawrence would find difficult to understand, but which made perfect sense to Allenberg, Kracke relayed his message about the attack.

"Clever, weren't we?" Adrian replied, his voice hardly a whisper. "We see bogeymen where we're sure they're not. We convince somebody they're there. We congratulate ourselves. And then the bogeymen are there, have been all along.

"Do you need assistance?" he had asked Kracke.

Kracke had considered. Alone he could provide only minimal protection for Brandes.

He would have liked to have said yes.

"No," Kracke had told Allenberg.

It would be too difficult to introduce new faces.

Even the CDC doctors, the short time that they had been there, psychologically had been accepted by Lyle's citizens as "belonging" there.

The complement of players on Lyle's stage was too well established. Kracke ruled out a "medical" cover for additional agents.

Not alarming the scientific team was important to Kracke—professionally. He had not yet ruled out the possibility of Brandes's enemies being secreted within the CDC contingent. Perhaps, he'd thought, he was not worried about alarming them as much as he was alerting them—or one or more of them, those who mattered.

He had considered. Backup was inadvisable.

Rachek had been employed at Futures. At least he had *been* at Futures. Kracke and Allenberg hardly could expect any cover to hold in the very group that already had produced at least one and possibly two assassins.

*One had gotten away.*

Kracke thought of that constantly: *One motorcycle had left that highway slaughterhouse.*

*He* could not forget that.

After the call, Kracke had made ready to leave the house and to change his "home"—that word used by such men in a way few others could fully understand—to a place closer to Brandes. And possibly closer to those hunting Brandes. When he quickly had scouted them, he had considered using another of Andy's outbuildings.

Several small, little-used buildings dotted Andy's irregularly shaped piece of land, and the old man probably could have made a good seasonal profit by renting them. Most were habitable, if "rustic," and comfortable, even if some seemed converted stalls.

Kracke liked his idea better. He drove slowly, carefully—roads would make him slightly more nervous than normal for a short while—into the center of the town and to the Tower.

He bypassed the desk and the lobby and walked in the shadows alongside the building until he reached the separate annex behind the main hotel. He had Brandes's key. He moved into the room.

The hotel was close to Brandes's new "home" with Andy. Also it would be the first place after Wismer's that an opponent would check and still be the *last* place an opponent would expect to find a man such as Kracke.

Kracke grinned when he thought of that possibility.

He turned off the room light and pulled a light blanket over himself. Even in summer and in rooms without any air conditioning, Kracke could not sleep without *something* covering him. Something, of course, that easily could be discarded.

No one had noticed Kracke enter Brandes's room in the Tower annex. He felt fairly certain of that. Still, before he had settled into his bed, he had taken precautions as routinely as others would brush their teeth. Small black plastic squares, an inch on each side, he had fastened with double-sided tape to the windows and to the door. Kracke carried those with him everywhere. Once the same concept had been marketed in mail-order catalogs as a means of finding lost keys. *Clap your hands, your key ring beeps!*

The key rings never had worked for Kracke, and he doubted they'd ever really satisfactorily worked for anyone. The mechanism, though, was useful for sensing vibration.

With some modifications, the same circuitry was in the small boxes he had deployed in his room.

Even as he'd taped them to the windows and to the door in such ritualistic fashion, he was conscious of them. Usually he was not, did not think of the key rings. He couldn't decide why he thought of that then.

He went to sleep wondering why he'd thought of those small black boxes, used for one purpose but designed for another.

He'd never really thought about them before.

Eventually, the throat dryness, the perspiration, had disappeared. Brandes's mind had allowed him to really accept what had happened to him on the highway that night. He slept.

283

# TWENTY-EIGHT

THE SILENCE, THE *STILLNESS*, THAT HAD SETTLED over Lyle was not the normal quiet, the silence born of peace, of a New England town. Clear morning skies did nothing to freshen the emotional, fear-charged quality of the air itself.

The deathly silence swiftly seeped into and through Wismer. He had parked his car near the Tower Hotel.

After Brandes had gone to Andy's accommodations, Wismer had spent some time going over Peter's notes—the same ones, time and time again.

If the answer was there, it was in pieces. Jigsaw pieces.

He held some.

Brandes probably held others.

*He hoped* all somehow would come together. *He hoped*.

Wismer closed the car door and cursed. It had snapped shut, but the lock hadn't fully engaged. He twisted his body and slammed his buttocks into the door, finally hearing the mechanism click—for no real reason he could think of, pleased with himself for having defeated the perversity of the car.

He walked across the street without looking. There was little traffic in the half-conquered, thoroughly frustrated, and totally terrified community.

Three other persons were in Lyle's general store when he entered. David stood behind the counter, obviously filling in for his brother for the morning. The second was Avery, from the Tower. The third was Emil Jenner.

Everyone in the store seemed happy.

Wismer stopped quickly after he entered, the jingling of the bell over the door just above his ear—feeling immediately that he'd gone far enough.

*Damn.*

*They've gone—gone irrational,* he thought. *It's the next step, maybe, the next logical after the screaming and the fear. Hysteria.*

"Good morning, Gerry!" Jenner said, walking over to him, clapping his arm just below the shoulder. Wismer couldn't reply. He tried to think of proper things to say in such situations. Lyle lay in sickness and stillness outside. Jenner had cried outrage at the town meeting.

*I'm not a psychiatrist,* he thought. *What do I say?*

"Good morning," he said.

"Yes," Jenner said, "it is."

All of them were staring at Wismer, at the puzzled and even frightened look on his face.

It was Jenner who burst out laughing, and the instant he did, Wismer felt his muscles tense; he prepared himself to leave quickly.

"Gerry," Jenner said, sobering somewhat, "I guess we all know what you're thinking, and I guess I can't blame you. Look out there"—he gestured toward the storefront, through the storefront—"and I guess no one's smiling. So, when something happens that *can* make us smile, we've got to hang on to it."

His face momentarily became serious. "We've got to forget the army's here and, and—and all of that. At least every once in a while. When we can." He grinned.

Wismer could understand that, but still he remained cautious. Jenner sensed it.

"It's Nancy, Gerry." Jenner burst out. "It's Nancy. *My daughter.* It's Nancy.

"*Nancy is alive and well!*"

Wismer did not, could not react.

Jenner continued. "Last night," he said, "she just was all right." Jenner hesitated. He had done so before, when telling the story to others he had met that morning. The news had been too good—too *wonderful*—not to share. But he couldn't tell them that he had buried his daughter and had thought her dead. He just couldn't do that.

"She was sick," he said. "At first . . . at first I thought she had . . . it. She didn't *have* the damned disease! That's my good news. Look, I'm sorry—but only a little bit. I know I'm supposed to be a . . ." He stiffened to wooden-Indian posture and tried not to smile, "staid and sober member of this community."

He relaxed from his posturing and smiled again. Even Wismer smiled, though not yet certain why. "It's just," Jenner said, "that my Nancy is all right. She didn't have it."

Jenner was *not* a frivolous or easily excitable person. Wismer knew that. Although Jenner might make fun of the portrayal he'd given, he *was* a staid and sober member of Lyle's community.

"Gerry," Jenner said, his face somewhat more composed but the happiness still apparent, "I know that there are people dying here. I know that I could get it, you could get it. I know that the army and the government are working on it—I know all of that stuff from the meeting. And I know that maybe I shouldn't be so happy.

"But I can't help it. Gerry, when Doro and I thought Nancy had this thing we were lost. *Lost.* There wasn't anything we could do or anything anyone around here could do. There wasn't anyone we could go to. Anyplace.

"*That's* really true. There is no place you can go around here without running into one of Lawrence's roadblocks. I know all of this. I know we're still in a helluva situation here. But don't blame me for being happy. *Nancy's all right!*"

Wismer couldn't blame him. But Jenner didn't know what *really* might have happened.

She'd had it all right.

The symptoms had become widely known. As he left the town meeting he'd heard people talking. They *knew* the symptoms. Jenner and Doro would not have missed them.

But Nancy's *recovery* had to be explained somehow.

Wismer's heart raced. *God, someone who's survived!*

Nancy Jenner just might make all of Peter's notebooks superfluous. Nancy Jenner might be a walking repository of agents needed to fight the Lyle disease.

"Emil," he said, "that's terrific. I'm very glad. You're sure Nancy's all right?"

"Never better. We cleaned her . . . Well, she was a little sick . . . and this morning, she ate like she hadn't ever eaten before in her life! She's fine! She's alive. Nancy's alive!"

"I couldn't have heard anything better this morning," Wismer said, and he meant it. "But, Emil, I don't really understand."

"None of that matters," Jenner said, more forcibly than he had to, Wismer thought. *He's holding something back. Is it important? As important as Nancy just might be?*

"I think you should let Dr. Shortell look her over. He really should see her."

"She's fine, I tell you."

"Emil, I don't know how much biology you need to know in your business. But there's a chance—just a chance, got that? —that Nancy might have had the disease."

Jenner's face turned ashen in a second. *How much biology do I know?* Wismer thought. *I never thought blood could drain from someone's face that fast.*

"You mean she still might—"

"No! That's not what I mean. If she's okay now, she probably will stay that way. But there's something a lot more important here. If she *did* have it and she's alive then she's the first person to recover from it . . . *ever.*"

Jenner was not ignorant. Wismer caught himself before his explanations became too simplistic. Jenner could and would understand.

"She might be the answer." It was a statement.

"Yes," Wismer said, and it was his turn to be pleased, to smile. "We may have the answer for all those other people." Wismer's excitement grew. A *survivor!* "Emil, you've got to get Nancy into the lab so they can run some blood tests on her."

Jenner looked thoughtful. "I know the importance of what you're saying, Gerry. It never occurred to me. But Nancy is my only daughter, and that lab *made* the fucking disease that is killing people around here. The disease that—if you're right—almost killed her, too, for that matter. She's not going to that lab, Gerry. I'm not taking any chance on losing her. Not again."

While that last meant nothing to Wismer, he certainly could understand Jenner's feelings.

"Emil, you know it has to be done."

"Yes," Jenner said. He nodded as he spoke, his voice now steady and even. "But she's not going there. Not to where they made this thing. And she's not going to the hospital where there are people dying of this thing."

"Emil . . ."

"No! Can't you understand? She's not going someplace where she can *get* it *again*—if she had it in the first place. *No!*"

"All right," Wismer said. He walked toward the counter of the store, his right hand raised to his chin, his face apparently thoughtful. "Dr. Shortell can go to Nancy. How's that? He can take blood samples, and we'll see where we go from there."

"No. Let Alex do it."

Wismer was surprised; his hand dropped to the counter in front of David. "Why?"

"I'm not sure, Gerry. Maybe it's because Dr. Shortell has been with too many of them—the dying ones, I mean. Maybe he carries it! Maybe because Alex's brother made the damned thing in the first place."

"Now that's not fair, you know that. Besides, if you feel that way, I'd think he'd be the *last* person you'd want touching her."

"Sure I know that," Jenner agreed. "It doesn't have to make *sense*, Gerry. It *feels* right. Maybe I want him to have a closeup look at Peter's handiwork, get his own hands in it. Somehow it seems to make sense that he wouldn't *dare* hurt Nancy. I can't explain it, Gerry. That's just what I feel."

Wismer stopped short of telling Jenner about Cynthia, about just how close a look Brandes already had.

"That's not logic I can argue with, Emil. I'll tell Alex."

His goal had to be to get samples from Nancy, not to defend Alex Brandes. "We'll do it anyway you like, Emil. I *know* Alex wants to end this thing. No matter *who's* to blame."

"Sorry," Emil said, and he didn't say anything more on that subject. He looked down for an instant, remembering placing Nancy in the culvert, covering her with leaves just starting to decay, still wet.

*I can't tell them I buried my daughter.* He considered what Wismer had said about Nancy being a potential avenue of hope for those fighting the disease. Jenner nodded.

"Like I said, I understand. Alex can do what he has to," he said. "Sorry, Gerry. Really."

Wismer thanked him, nodded, turned and walked toward the door.

"Hey, Gerry!" It was David, and it was the first time either he or Avery had spoken in several minutes. Wismer looked first at Avery; his face was drawn, and he'd been listening closely, but Wismer was not sure much of what had transpired actually meant anything to him.

Wismer thought Avery must be having his own hell of a time running a hotel full of transient CDC doctors.

"Yes?"

"What did you come in for?"

"Oh." Wismer had totally forgotten. "Sorry," he said. "I needed some twelve-gauge shells."

"Oh. Army bought us out." David grinned wickedly. "But what the hell, Gerry. Here . . . on the house." He reached under the counter and threw a small plastic bag to Wismer. It contained a dozen shells. "A good businessman always keeps a little backup stock for his regular customers."

"Thanks," Wismer said and left. He was grateful for the shells; he'd made his mind up to get them as soon as he'd heard Brandes's story about the motorcyclists.

But he also was nervous.

*How many "regular" customers does David have?*

*How many people in Lyle are armed?*


"I brought him here for breakfast," Kracke said, as Wismer walked into his house. Brandes and Sarah were seated at his kitchen table. Before them were empty plates, but Kracke apparently also had assumed the role of chef and was standing at the stove. He flinched slightly, his bacon spattering.

"I've got news," Wismer said. He felt very pleased with his morning. Brandes and Sarah looked up at him; neither looked very much awake.

Wismer told them about Nancy.

Brandes's face, of course, was the first to change, to light.

"Gerry, she could give us what we need."

"*If* she had it," Wismer cautioned. "Jenner still says that she didn't have it and that he was worried over something else needlessly. There's something else he's not telling me, but I don't think it matters. He has agreed to let you take blood samples from the girl."

"*Me?*"

"Yes." Wismer explained. "He's not willing to put her in contact with anyone too close to people who have the disease. It's a little odd—but maybe not so wrong—that the one place most people seem to want to avoid is the hospital."

"I think I can see their point," Kracke said, forking crisp bacon onto several layers of toweling. Sarah nodded.

"So, what do I do? Is he bringing her here?"

"No. I think you'll have to go out to their farm. Jonathan can get what you need from the hospital."

"Oh, shit."

"What?"

"Gerry, I'm a *doctor*, but I'm not a *doctor!* I mean I don't know how to take blood from someone, how to preserve it. I'm just not that kind of a doctor."

"Well," Wismer said, "you'll have to get Jonathan to go with you. I'm sure that with maybe an answer looking at us he won't complain about wasting his time. You'll have to explain to Jenner why you need Jonathan, though. He's sensible enough."

"Maybe Jonathan *will* consider it a waste of his time," Sarah said.

"Why?" Wismer's eyebrows twisted; it was a mannerism unique to the man and seldom shown.

"Time for *our* news," she said. She laughed openly, confusing Wismer even more. Kracke still transferred bacon from pan to paper, but by then even Brandes was smiling. Wismer couldn't take it. "What the hell are you talking about?" he asked, drawing out each word slowly.

"We had a call from CDC in Atlanta," Brandes said. *He's relishing this*, Wismer thought, *but I think I'm going to forgive him because I think I've got to like what he's going to tell me.* "They got a guy named Dorfman down there. He's discovered a serum, Gerry. A serum—or at least something like a serum."

Wismer's face went momentarily blank. "A serum?" he whispered. Then he again became controlled. "What do you mean *something like* a serum?"

"I'm not sure myself," Brandes admitted.

Kracke moved to the table and set down the bacon, returned to the stove, and began cracking eggs. He seemed to take little interest in what was happening and being said, but Wismer, for one, knew better than that. Men like Kracke never *showed* interest.

And they never were without it, either.

"Well?"

"A Dr. Lasser called. She said that this guy, Dorfman, created another virus; and that his virus interferes with other viruses. It's not a serum in a sense we know."

Wismer stopped smiling totally. Sarah and Brandes immediately saw his face change, his eyes change. By some sixth—or seventh—sense, Kracke knew and turned from his scrambling to look at the stone-faced former teacher of high school biology.

"Terrific," Wismer said. "Another invention let loose. Goddamn and fuck them all."

"Gerry," Brandes said, getting up, walking toward Wismer, "this may be an answer, a solution. Besides, it can't be dangerous in itself. The government—"

"Oh, can that, Alex. The government's got nothing to do with this." He snapped, nearing violence in his voice. There was a part of Wismer that could not tolerate naïveté, not in a crisis. "The FDA didn't give this Lasser or this Dorfman some sort of emergency authority after doing some sort of emergency testing. Act your age.

"Damn it, Alex, can't you *see?*

"They're going to use Lyle for a goddamn enormous fucking zoo full of guinea pigs, and they're going to *let loose* another manmade organism.

*"Can't you see that?"*

Brandes felt his jubilation drain, but he determined not to let go immediately of something that might help. The Lyle problem was much too severe for that.

"Well, Gerry," he said, "there's a chance it might help." *And then there's Cynthia.* . . . "And we've already got a quarantine in place. If they're going to try this thing . . ."

Even Kracke stopped moving momentarily and then broke the spell by cursing over his scrambled eggs turning brown.

"Something new for you, isn't it, Alex?" Wismer asked. He immediately regretted his sarcasm but found he couldn't control it. He pressed on, ever harder, all the time hating himself for what he was saying, all the time unable to stop, *unwilling to stop*.

"I remember you left the agency because of the death of one man. Now you're willing to risk letting loose—on purpose—something unknown just because the environment's already contained."

Brandes was shaken. "Shit, Gerry. Sorry. Desperation talking." He said no more, but he began to think deeply despite himself. There was much thinking for him to do. He was badly stung by Wismer's outburst; the pain did not make any of it less true.

*No, the problem is the truth of it doesn't make it less painful.*

Sarah stood. "Well, then what are you going to do? They're flying this stuff in here by helicopter after they've had time to produce enough of it. What are you going to *do*?"

Both Brandes and Wismer shook their heads. Kracke simply continued to cook.

"I'll tell you what you're going to do," Sarah said. She stood a tall five-feet-six, straight, radiating the feeling that *she* was the one with the strength, in control.

Wismer sort of grinned slightly; he'd seen Sarah come to a conclusion before when those around her couldn't or wouldn't.

*Her father would get a hell of a kick out of this*, he thought, fleetingly.

"You've got a disease here that is wiping out people by the numbers. You've got the army cooping up the next likely victims and burning the unlucky ones. You"—she pointed to Brandes; he flinched—"have a woman you love *dying* of this disease in the hospital. And," she softened, "you've got a dangerous tool that just might stop all this. Might help all those people. Might help Cynthia.

"It also might be a disease all by itself. But the area *is* quarantined, as Alex pointed out. He may not like what he said, but I do. It's as close to a closed environment as you'll ever get and still be working under real-life conditions. Are all you scientists suddenly scared of really seeing what you've made with taxpayers' money?" she sneered.

"Damn it! When you've got *almost* nothing to lose, you've got *almost* everything to gain." Her eyes were fire, and Brandes thought later, her nostrils really *did* flare.

Sarah looked around her, measuring, then turned and walked toward the door to the living room. "You," she said to Wismer, "can continue to doomsay all you like, but I'd advise you to keep studying Peter's stuff.

"You," she said to Brandes, "can see if that little girl can help and maybe make this Dorfman stuff unnecessary."

Wismer and Brandes exchanged looks.

Neither spoke.

She was not through.

"And *you*," she yelled at Kracke, who turned, a spatula in his hand. "You're not getting away with just standing there and cooking eggs. You know what my father'd say about that—but I don't need him here for this." Kracke's face was like Medusa-stoned flesh caught in a moment of shock.

"You cook all you want, but you keep them"—she gestured to Wismer and Brandes—"alive long enough to do something useful."

"Yes, *ma'am*," he said.

# TWENTY-NINE

ALLENBERG WAS TIRED, ANGRY—YET HE COULD not help feeling amusement mixed with a misplaced (perhaps) sense of pride.

And if he did feel even brief relief from tension, it in no way was derived from news from Lyle.

He knew of the Dorfman development, of course—and that offered some hope—but had not yet learned of Nancy Jenner's recovery.

The disease, its containment, its cure, its *origin*—all remained paramount concerns; and he was also worried about Sarah's and Brandes's safety. Still, Allenberg grinned as he thought, *But that grandson of mine . . .*

He looked at a framed picture of Jason on his desk. It had been taken the summer before. Tousle-haired, grinning, and squinting in the bright light, Jason stood with one arm around Emma, a neighbor's mare. It was one of Allenberg's favorite pictures of his grandson. Next to it was one of Sarah, running through the field outside the New Jersey house. She was twenty-five pounds lighter then, he thought. *And she will be again. She said so, didn't she?*

He took his eyes from the pictures reluctantly. Much lay ahead for Lyle, for Brandes; much lay ahead for his daughter. For himself.

For Allenberg, the organism was just a beginning.

He had to answer: Who caused it? Why?

He had thrown most of his staff's resources into trying to find out who possibly could *want* the disease not cured.

Yet someone didn't.

People *were* trying to kill Brandes.

His intercom buzzed, and he wasn't surprised when his secretary told him he had a call from Fitch. He had expected it—as he expected calls from every other member of the Uisce Beatha board at whom he'd had Jason "peek."

Jason, though, hadn't been satisfied with finding out about holdings in coffee futures, in some company called Musto Explorations, and in platinum.

He'd decided, apparently, to help out his aging grandfather some more and—as he would have put it—"to shake the trees a little," to go a step further.

Jason had entered the computers at a superficial level and had left instructions "from" each of those men to alter their portfolios.

But he hadn't actually been able to get into the accounts and make the changes. *Thank God there's some security*, Allenberg thought.

Still, the previous day, each man apparently had been called by his broker or account executive for confirmation of some rather startling transactions.

Allenberg didn't know what Jason had hoped to accomplish. Maybe he'd thought someone would fear gross improprieties had been discovered and that that someone would run to the Bahamas or someplace—alerting his grandfather.

That, of course, hadn't happened.

Instead Ryan, for one, had utilized either the enormous resources of Uisce Beatha or his own considerable connections, and when Jason had called back into the system, had traced him.

An adolescent in western New Jersey could cause one hell of a lot of trouble, Allenberg thought.

296

Ryan had taken the whole thing very well. He'd taken Allenberg out to Elaine's on Second Avenue for a drink and had been typically Carlos Ryan.

"Adrian," he'd said, "your department is recruiting them very young these days."

After he had explained, Allenberg had been embarrassed. Ryan did not ask how Jason had learned his name, but the fact that he had was something Ryan would not forget. Neither would any of the others.

Allenberg felt secure enough in his position on the board—he remembered some blunders a few of the others had made that dwarfed his own—but still he would be rebuked at the next meeting and would have to apologize to the assembly.

Meanwhile, he thought, it looked as though he was going to spend a day apologizing to them individually. He was certain that Fitch was calling for just the same reasons Ryan had. He would have to go through the entire thing again. And again. He sighed.

"Hello," he said into his telephone.

"Adrian, we have to talk."

"Yes. I know. I think I can explain the whole thing."

There was a harsh laugh from the other end. Fitch, Allenberg thought, was not going to make this any easier. "No, Adrian. You can't. I can. That's why we have to talk. We have to talk about Lyle, *and* we have to talk about the small matter of tampering with computers. Actually, we have to talk about *both*."

Allenberg was not certain he completely understood Fitch. "Have you gotten other demands that we quit looking into Lyle?" he asked.

"No, Adrian." Again, the laugh—a rough sound, hoarse. "Not exactly. Do you know New Jersey at all?"

"What?"

"New Jersey."

"What are you talking about?"

"We have to meet, Adrian. Today. This morning. *Now*."

"What's it all about? I can't just leave here. Where do you want me to go? Why?"

"The why of it you'll find out when you get there. I can't talk on the phone about this. Adrian, this is something very vital. I'm sure you'll agree with me when you've heard it." He didn't pause, didn't wait for Allenberg's response.

"Eleven o'clock in the stadium of Warinanco Park in Elizabeth, New Jersey, Adrian. I really think you should be there." He hung up the phone.

A *stadium* in Elizabeth, New Jersey? Allenberg replaced his own receiver carefully and slowly.

Something had happened, that much was certain; and equally certainly, it had not been caused solely by a young boy jostling computer codes. He got up, went to his coatrack, and put on his jacket. He left the office.

"Tell someone to meet me downstairs with a car," he told his secretary. It was early, but he liked to be early to meetings he didn't understand in places he never had been.

"You want someone with you?"

He thought for a moment. There was no reason he would need anyone but the driver. "No," he said finally. "But see if Bernie Kohl is available for driving." She nodded, began dialing. Bernie officially was a driver but only because a bullet had smashed his left shoulder. He had limited mobility in that arm. But his right arm, Allenberg knew, was good. Very good.

"You want to take the Holland or Lincoln tunnel, sir?" Bernie asked. "I can take either tunnel, but I think the Holland might be better."

"The Holland it is."

Soon they were inside one of the tunnel's twin tubes, and Allenberg watched the tiles slip by.

Traffic was not heavy.

"Where in Elizabeth, sir?"

"Warinanco Park. Know it?"

"I'm surprising myself, sir, but I do. I had a nephew who once lived in Linden. My sister's boy. We used to fly a glider in an open field there when I'd visit."

298

"Is that where I'm going? An open field? Is that 'the stadium'?"

"No, sir. The stadium is in another part of the park—it's a pretty big park and in surprisingly good shape. The general area's not been faring well in recent years. The stadium is just a cinder track. It's not far from the field, though. I mean, the park isn't *that* big."

"Well, it's the stadium we want, Bernie."

"Yes, sir." Bernie never questioned where his superiors had their meetings and why. His job depended on his lack of vocalized curiosity; and besides, he had none.

Allenberg put on lightly tinted sunglasses as they left the nearly two-mile-long tunnel. The morning sun was bright, but it was the haze that really hurt his eyes more. Bernie kept driving straight, and soon they were on the Pulaski Skyway, a double-humped bridge spanning a slice of Jersey City and then a section of what possibly was the world's largest garbage dump and almost certainly the world's longest-smoldering fire.

Allenberg once had heard that, deep in the ground, the embers had burned for more than thirty years. He doubted if anyone knew how to put the damned thing out even if anyone wanted to.

The dump also had the local reputation of being the last resting place of former Teamster boss Jimmy Hoffa. Allenberg had never believed that. He favored the fifty-five-gallon-drum-just-outside-of-Detroit theory.

Bernie drove by Newark Airport and kept to Route 1-9. After another few miles of nothing but twisting highway, bordered by the airport's North Terminal and some motels and car-rental agencies—and, for relief, a Budweiser brewery—they stopped at a traffic signal.

"Elizabeth, sir. I'm not sure my way of getting to the park from here is the most direct, but it's the only one I know for sure. May I ask what time you must be at the stadium?"

"Eleven."

Bernie checked his watch as the light changed to green. "No problem, sir. But"—he hesitated—"we'll only have ten minutes to spare."

"This is not that kind of meeting, Bernie."

The agent-driver opened his mouth to speak, paused, said only, "Yes, sir." Allenberg smiled. *Only ten minutes. Not much at that, but it was there.*

*Good*, thought Allenberg. He didn't mistrust Fitch, he realized, as much as he'd distrusted the man's tone on the telephone. There was an urgency coupled with the taste of menace, and that certainly could have nothing to do with Jason's activities.

*If there is new trouble*, he thought, *it's more than my grandson trying to "shake the trees."*

Elizabeth's streets were nondescript. He could not even say they were like those in a small city anywhere. As if with intention, that part of New Jersey to him always seemed to carry grayness to its ultimate shade of darkness and drabness.

Bernie turned several times and finally made a left that brought them into the park. It contrasted greatly with what he'd already seen of the area. Straight ahead a wide and open field, neatly cut, provided its few visitors with a break from the monotone on the outside—just *over there*, beyond the thin and insubstantial barrier of trees.

After a few hundred yards, Bernie turned right again. "This road goes around the whole park in a big circle," he explained. "On the other side there's a pond of sorts. The big field we used is on the other side of the trees straight ahead. We'll go about a quarter around the circle, sir, and you'll be at the stadium."

Allenberg smiled as he listened to Bernie's "tour guide" voice. Bernie, as a matter of course, was doing his best to supply his superior with a lay of the land. *Not that this situation requires that*, he thought.

The car drove slowly, not only because of the limit but because a young couple on a motorcycle in front of them was taking its time, enjoying the soft curves of the one-way road.

"In there, sir," Bernie said, and turned right. Allenberg could see, to his left, the stadium, sunk ten or twelve feet from the roadway. Bernie turned the car, facing the stadium, placed it in park, and asked Allenberg, "Do you wish me to keep it running, sir?"

"I don't think that will be necessary," Allenberg said. "This is a friendly meeting."

"I understand, sir. May I then keep it running for the ventilation?"

"Yes, Bernie. Of course."

Bernie got out and opened the door for Allenberg. Once out, he was able to see the field itself better. There were five people running around the track. All were dressed in shorts; three wore sweatbands on their foreheads.

Three sides of the track led to embankments that were topped either by parking lots or by low bushes. Only the far side was different. *Different!* Allenberg thought. *Damn thing looks like the Colosseum should look. Real ruins.*

Concrete, he guessed, benches stretched up the higher embankment on that side of the track. At the track's level there were several dark, small doorways. Gateways for the lions. *Who the hell designed this?* Allenberg wondered.

He also wondered if it ever was used. Perhaps, he thought, local high schools used it; young bones and bodies might sit on those bleachers. Parents would bring cushions.

He shielded his eyes. "There, sir?" Bernie asked tentatively and pointed toward one of the black openings in the featureless stone. Allenberg looked where Bernie pointed. Yes, there was a man in a suit. It had to be Fitch. *Damn him*, Allenberg thought. *Why the hell on the other side of the field?*

"Is there somewhere to park over there, Bernie?"

"No, sir. I could drive up on the other side and just pull over, though, keeping the engine running in case the county police tell me to move." Allenberg didn't like that idea. *Where had Fitch parked? Had his driver just dropped him off with instructions to return on a schedule?*

"No, Bernie. The slope here isn't bad. I'll go down and walk."

Bernie's eyes looked stricken. "Sir," he said, "I can be much closer over there. If I walk around with you I can't leave the car running . . ."

"Thought that was for ventilation, Bernie." Allenberg immediately softened. "Thanks for your concern, Bernie. I'll be all right. Just stay here with the car."

"You mean you don't even want me to walk there with you?" Bernie sounded incredulous; Allenberg noticed and grinned inwardly as Bernie dropped the "sir."

"Friendly contact."

"Sir, I almost never say, do . . ." He stumbled for words, his hands raised and then lowered, gesturing without content. ". . . anything like this. Sir. But I'm a *driver* now because of a *friendly* contact." His eyes beseeched.

Allenberg hadn't thought about Bernie's own past, how he had gotten his shoulder shattered. He remembered. It had not been in a dark alley of a mud-hut Middle Eastern village or a chill-swept dock in Russia. It had happened outside Henri Bendel's in midtown Manhattan, one of the city's most fashionable areas, one of the least threatening.

What was to have been a simple exchange of envelopes in Bernie's mind was more like Bernie suffering a fatal heart attack in his "colleague's."

Quick reactions had saved Bernie's life, forced a more overt action than ever intended—and had rendered his shoulder "materially" irreparable. No "repairs" had been possible for the other man.

Allenberg understood, and as he remembered the incident, he felt a chill. This *was* different, though. About Fitch he had no qualms; he might personally never be able to develop any deep affection for or friendship with the man, but he did trust him.

Always, though, the question remained: *What had put that flavor of menace and urgency into Fitch's voice? Was Fitch himself in danger? Was there someone deeper in the darkness of that roughcut doorway?*

"How fast do you do the hundred?"

"Sir?"

"If it looks like . . . anything . . . get your petunias over the middle of that track fast, Bernie. *And* leave the car running."

"Yes, sir." Bernie still did not look happy.

* * *

Fitch made no move to leave the shadowy shelter of the doorway as Allenberg crossed the grassy oval in the middle of the cinder track. It was a considerable walk, farther than he had anticipated. One of the runners managed to pass him twice before he reached the other side. He had second thoughts about leaving Bernie so far behind.

*Is there someone behind Fitch?*

*For that matter, who the hell are the runners?* He felt a shiver.

Allenberg stopped at the edge of the grass. Only the faintly marked lanes on the track separated him from where Fitch stood.

"I think I'm getting too old for this," he called out. "Why don't you do a little walking?" A shape moved from the shadows; Allenberg tensed.

But it was Fitch, and he was alone.

"Certainly, Adrian."

"Why here? What's this all about? At least Carlos had the good manners to take me out for a drink before he complained about my grandson."

"Yes," Fitch said. "Your grandson. Quite a remarkable boy."

"He thought he was helping," Allenberg said. "The exuberance of youth. He couldn't have done any real damage—not like I'll do to him when I get my hands on him."

Fitch shrugged. "Oh, what he did isn't important, Adrian. I thought it amusing, actually. What is important is that part about your getting your hands on him."

"What do you mean?"

"What I mean, Adrian, is that that won't be possible. Jason has been kidnapped."

# THIRTY

WISMER BROODED. HE WAS ALONE IN HIS TOO-large house, the others having left an hour earlier to meet Shortell and make arrangements for getting a sample of Nancy Jenner's blood.

Emil Jenner's manic peak had been passed; Wismer had called him as soon as he'd awakened, and Jenner had agreed to let Shortell visit his farm to take the sample—if Brandes went along. Kracke had gone, too.

Sarah had said she wished to see the bungalow behind Andy's station. He doubted she'd be there long, and he doubted even more that she would bother to check in with him before she went her way. She was like that. Like her father.

The actors all in place, he thought. All playing their roles. *Let's not leave out Lawrence. The young soldiers. The people who bought David's shotgun shells. All of them. Me, too.*

He wondered what Lawrence had thought of the attack on Brandes. He had not contacted Brandes, Wismer knew. Yet the retired teacher had no doubt at all that Lawrence's listening post had most certainly taken an interest in a motorcyclist assault on the scientist-agent near the focus of the entire situation.

The colonel also, of course, would know about the Dorfman development. He would know that a "serum" of some sort had been created. Also, he would know that there had been a delay in delivery of a sufficient quantity.

Even had he not intercepted the calls, Lawrence would have *had* to have been informed about that; he was not likely to take kindly to a helicopter dropping down within his quarantine boundaries without his authorization or knowledge.

Wismer wondered if the army knew about Nancy Jenner. Lawrence, he thought, would have to be very perceptive to glean anything from his own brief call to Emil.

Wismer sipped his third cup of coffee and debated whether to inform Lawrence about Nancy himself. He really didn't give a damn if the colonel was kept up to date, but it was possible that giving some hope to the colonel would relax him—just in case he was worried about what Lyle's citizens might do if there seemed to be no hope at all.

Peter's notebooks—all of them now, he hoped—lay on the table in front of him. He had read through them all. They'd told him much—and very little. Peter's organization might have made sense to Peter. He found it hard to credit the books to the orderly mind he once had taught in high school and had seen develop into that of a first-class researcher.

It was as if Peter had *tried* to make his records a jumble that only he could understand—or perhaps those close to him might *eventually* understand.

*I'm trying, Peter. I'm trying.*

He reached down and casually flipped open what he believed to be the last book in the sequence.

The standard symbols abounded. An adenine there, thymine there. Throw in a few guanines . . . even those were jumbled. There was nearly an infinite number of possible combinations of the four basic building blocks of the nucleic acids—and so nearly an infinite number of possible organisms with productive or destructive potentials.

*Or both?*

Even beneficial developments might be found to have effects in addition to those sought. Had Lyle fallen victim to such an organism? Or had the illness been *designed* to be deadly?

He could not believe that of Peter. He just couldn't.

But that it was Peter who had created whatever was decimating Lyle he did not, could not, doubt.

He skipped through the pages, pausing again for a mouthful of coffee and grimacing because it had cooled. He got up, took the cup into the kitchen, and placed it in his microwave oven. He punched in a minute and a half, and allowed images of nucleic linkages to pass his mind's eye as the digital counter ticked off seconds. Deftly, he roused himself when it had a second to go, and he opened the door to stop the machine. He hated the extended *beep* that sounded when the oven was allowed to turn itself off.

Wismer took his steaming coffee back into his living room and returned his attention to the notebook.

Something was in there.

He was sure of it.

The coffee now was too hot; he blew on it.

Every few pages, apparently randomly, Peter had scribbled his symbols that were his tribute to memories of "Ben Casey": man, woman, birth, death, infinity.

Except Peter had screwed *them* up, too.

Wismer looked for a pattern; could Peter's jotting somehow indicate pages that *mattered?* He began at the beginning, trying to find a pattern.

The coffee was still hot enough almost to scald—it was the temperature he liked. He sipped and looked. Nothing came to mind.

Suddenly something *did* come to mind, but it had nothing to do with the notebooks, at least not directly.

Wismer got up and walked to his desk on the other side of the room. He opened a side drawer and took out the packet of photographs he had shown Alex. If he was right . . . he flipped through them.

Most were just "touristy" shots of New York City. There was a series of pictures taken at the United Nations Plaza. There were a half-dozen taken from the vantage point of a high building; he guessed the Empire State Building. They were as inadequate in depicting such panoramas as such pictures must of necessity be.

Several were pictures of Linda, Peter's girlfriend and co-worker from the lab.

She appeared also in the one picture he'd sought. He *had* remembered correctly.

She's pretty, he thought. It was the picture that was odd. Linda stood just in front of a nondescript building wall. She was smiling. Wismer squinted and could make out a sign next to her identifying the building as housing the offices of Joseph Papp's New York Shakespeare Festival.

And on the wall next to her, so out of place that it looked like nothing more than graffiti, were chalked the distorted "Ben Casey" symbols.

*You're telling me something, even now, Peter. I know you are.*
*And I haven't the damnedest idea what it is.*

Brandes could not shake the inner chill he felt, and he suspected that he was not alone. He drove at a moderate speed over the narrow but well-paved road that led from Jenner's farm back into Lyle's center. Kracke and Shortell were as silent as he, and he was certain they felt something akin to his discomfort.

There had been something *wrong* with the Jenners, he thought.

The strangeness had not been pronounced in Nancy, the young survivor, but Brandes and Shortell could accept that she still was recovering from the illness.

Dorothy Jenner was oddest, Brandes thought. He braked at a curve, took the opportunity of going slower to snap a tape into the car's cassette player. It was a recording of a direct-disc of Lincoln Mayorga, and its expanded dynamic range rebounded in the car's confines.

307

"That's better," Kracke said suddenly.

"Yeah, none of us is the life of the party," Shortell added.

"So you both feel it?" Brandes asked.

"Shit, yes," Kracke said. "I just don't know what the hell I feel."

"A little like you just came out of the Twilight Zone?" Shortell asked and grinned.

"A little like I'm not quite out of it would be a better description."

"Did you see her eyes?" Brandes asked no one in particular.

"The mother?"

"Yeah."

"That's all I could look at. They were empty. The kid's were, too, but that I could understand. She looked like she still felt pretty weak."

"She didn't have a fever, though," Shortell said. He had convinced Emil Jenner to allow him at least a cursory examination of his daughter. She was fine, Shortell had anounced, except for slightly higher than normal respiration and pulse rates.

"I guess it just was a totally understandable fatigue. However her body fought off that damned disease, it must have fought one hell of a fight. That kind of thing takes a lot out of a person.

"But the mother . . ."

"Did you notice that Emil seemed to make an effort to stay between us and his wife?" Kracke asked. "It almost was as if he were more afraid for her than for the kid."

"Maybe we're just all spooked. I know we're all tired. Even if we all had a good night's sleep, we'd be tired."

"It's the stress," Shortell said. "That's all." He didn't sound convincing even to himself. Tension was fraying the fibers of the mind, he thought. The invisible mental ligaments tying together the bits and pieces into a pattern of sanity.

"Maybe this will be it," Shortell said as the tape ended and Brandes turned it over. He held up a small metal box. Inside were four vials, each holding three ccs of Nancy Jenner's blood. In that

308

blood, everyone prayed, was the reason a young girl had survived when others had not. In that precious life-fluid might lay the life-or-death difference for thousands.

"Maybe," Brandes said.

"Do you guys want to stop for lunch?" Kracke asked.

"I can't," Shortell said. "I want to drop two of these tubes off at the lab and arrange for shipment of the others to Atlanta. I'll have to get in touch with the army for that, I guess."

"You guess right," Brandes said. "But I think we can count on our colonel to grease the wheels in this case." He turned his head slightly, addressed Kracke. "How about we let Jonathan off in town where his car is and then you and I get some lunch. I'll buy."

"Consider it a business expense," Kracke said and chuckled. "You're on."

They reached Lyle in another ten minutes. No one commented on the emptiness of the streets.

Brandes pulled up to the Tower. Shortell said goodbye and left.

Brandes pulled the car away quickly. They could have eaten in the Tower's bar, but the oppressive stillness would have dampened what little spirits the eerie Jenner family had left them.

"We're going for a treat," he told Kracke. He headed for the airport.

Wismer cursed and paced his living-room floor. A half-hour earlier he had had a call from Allenberg that could be described as nothing other than cryptic in the extreme.

Allenberg's tension could be *felt*, but only through the way he spoke, not what he said.

A package would be arriving within the next several hours, he'd said. He told Wismer to have Kracke pick it up at Lawrence's headquarters. It would be sealed; Kracke was not to accept it if the seal had been broken.

Lawrence would be informed of that.

Allenberg had hung up without waiting for a response. Wismer readily understood that the package had to contain information Allenberg wanted to get to Brandes—or to all of them—without having Lawrence involved. That was why use of the telephone alone was out of the question.

Wismer continued his pacing.

*It can't take this long to get blood from a kid. Where the hell are they?*

Sarah had spent the morning wandering around Lyle, trying to absorb what she would need when it came time to air a story about the disaster. She'd borrowed a car from Andy; Brandes had taken the Mercedes his brother had "left" him.

She made perfunctory stops at David's store and at the Tower. She had briefly visited Futures Labs and had talked a short while with Linda Denard; she had learned nothing new.

For the last hour, she had sat in the dimly lit hospital room where Cynthia breathed raspingly in the coma from which she had virtually no chance of recovering.

*Except, perhaps, for Dorfman's discovery.*

But Sarah held out little hope for that. Even if the material worked, could they really hope it would have an effect on so far advanced a case as Cynthia's? Sarah doubted that very much.

She had sat there quietly; she felt an unusual kinship with the woman she'd barely known before disease had swept her away. She knew why, too—Brandes. Sarah was convinced that Brandes was a very lucky man to have the love of a woman like Cynthia.

She also thought to herself, as she considered Brandes, that had things worked out differently, Cynthia would have been a lucky woman to have Brandes. He had some things to learn, some things about himself to face, she thought. *But I like him.*

Lawrence made no attempt to hide his irritation.

"I want to know what it is," he said to Kracke.

Both men were seated in the commandeered headquarters, Lawrence behind his table-*cum*-desk. Kracke said nothing, only glanced at the one other man in the room.

Thomas Breen was about five years younger than Kracke, but already he had mastered the ability to keep his face completely passive, unexpressive, and—most importantly—unresponsive.

He sat, back straight, to one side of the desk. A briefcase rested on his lap. It was a somewhat unusual case, both the lid and body having handles that came together neatly when the case was closed. One side of a pair of handcuffs was laced through those handles; the other "bracelet" was fastened around Breen's left wrist.

"No," Kracke said. "That's not possible, Colonel."

"I'm the military commander in a military area."

"Almost correct. You are the *military* commander. But despite the imposition of a quarantine, there has been no declaration of martial law." Kracke shrugged.

"Actually, it wouldn't matter if there had been. The agency I represent would not in any case be subject to martial law."

"Oh, really?"

"Really."

Breen said nothing, did not move.

"You may," Kracke said, "call whomever you like. As long as it doesn't take more than five minutes. Whatever is in that case concerns me, my assignment here. I'm sure it's urgent."

Kracke saw no reason to add that Wismer had been steaming about their "luxury lunch hour" when he'd told them about Allenberg's call and had sent Kracke to Lawrence's headquarters. Kracke wanted to deliver whatever news it contained quickly.

"Your communications have not been interrupted; you know that. If it's that urgent, your superiors could have called you."

"Telephones are notoriously untrustworthy in my business."

Both men knew damned well what both meant. Lawrence was infuriated and knew that there wasn't a thing he could do. A phone call would be a waste of time.

"The delivery must be made here, of course," Lawrence said. "Mr. Breen can't cross the quarantine unless he wants to stay in Lyle—with you."

"Of course," Kracke said and understood perfectly. Lawrence had not had to say: "You're not getting out, you know. *That* I can stop." Actually, Kracke doubted *that*, but he wasn't about to say it.

Kracke nodded to Breen; the younger man dispassionately took a key from a vest pocket, opened the cuff around his wrist, and held it open. Kracke held out his hand, and the other agent snapped the lock shut. He handed Kracke the key and stood up.

"Thank you, Thomas," Kracke said. "My regards to everyone."

"I'll be sure to tell them, sir." They shook hands, and Breen turned and left without a glance at Lawrence, who snorted scorn as the athletic-looking agent closed the door behind him.

"You have your package," he said. "Lieutenant Knotts will escort you out."

"Thank you, Colonel." Kracke stood; he did shake hands with Lawrence. *What the hell. I've tweaked his nose enough for one day.*

Brandes and Wismer were waiting for him in Wismer's living room. Wismer was the more impatient, but both men were eager to see what could be so important that Allenberg had resorted to hand delivery.

And it had been hand delivery with a vengeance. Breen had flown from Newark to Bradley International in Connecticut and then had chartered a helicopter that had landed him in a meadow right next to Lawrence's headquarters.

Probably, Kracke had thought, flying had not been all that much faster than driving. But the method sure as hell must have impressed Lawrence.

Kracke opened the handcuffs, removing them from both his wrist and the case. He flicked the catches open and withdrew a manila envelope. It was the only item inside.

Brandes felt the urgency in his stomach as Kracke tore open the envelope. He reached for a gin and tonic he'd been up till then only nursing; he took a large mouthful.

Kracke read silently for several seconds, and his acquired unresponsive face lost its battle for composure.

"Oh, my God," he said. He didn't wait for them to question him. "Allenberg found out whose behind the mess," he said. "Allenberg's grandson, Jason, has been kidnapped . . ." His voice cracked. "Allenberg's trading himself for the kid. I think I'd better just read this."

Neither of the other men said a word. Both were dumbfounded. The extent of the disaster could not adequately be *felt*, let alone expressed.

*And Sarah*, Brandes thought. *My God, what about Sarah?*

Kracke sat; Wismer put a glass in his hand. He drank deeply, put the glass on the coffee table, and began:

Alex—all of you. I now know from where the Lyle disease came, and I know the reason for its existence. I do not know how to stop it. We may never know.

Sarah, please forgive me. I was wrong to involve you and Jason in this—I guess I've been wrong all along. No one with a job like mine should even have a family, let alone do what I have done.

Jason has been kidnapped by the people who tried to kill Alex. I have agreed to exchange myself for him; I've been assured he'll ride away from here healthy.

Of course, in general I wouldn't trust these people any more than I'd trust Mrs. Flannery's mean bastard bull, but I can't see what they've got to lose, so they'll probably keep their word.

Alex, you'll be glad to know that even though Peter did create the virus (yes, it is a virus, but that's only part of the picture), it never was intended to be a disease. Bacterial colonies altered by the viruses have a unique ability to "fix" precious metal. I'm not allowed to say more.

These people want time. We were wrong about them

wanting to stop you from discovering a cure. They don't give a shit if Lyle dies—they don't care any more if it lives. What they don't want is the nature of their organism known for several weeks. I've been told to order you to stop your research. You can guess the "or else."

Allenberg nodded in his chair.

"Want a pillow, Grandpa?" Jason asked. Allenberg looked up at the young, yet strong face of his grandson.

"No, that's all right. How's things?"

"They've got me making lemonade again. I don't mind; it keeps me busy."

Allenberg grinned. "We'll be all right, Jason. Where are they?"

"The Fitch guy is in the living room making phone calls. Two men are outside the house in front, two in the back. There aren't any more of them."

"How do you know?"

"I measure the lemonade." He gave a wicked smile.

"They may find us, Jason. I do mean that. Your mother's no dummy, and Kracke is very experienced."

"I read your note." He shrugged. "Maybe you're right."

Allenberg could have kissed the kid for the roundabout way he spoke.

*He'll get out of this. Sarah, I promise. Jason will live.*

*And even if we do, the real crisis will only have started.* Allenberg wished he did not have to think about that—but, obviously, he had no choice.

That Fitch, a member of Uisce Beatha, was behind the disease was bad enough.

What that *portended* was so enormous in its implications that Allenberg found it impossible to force comprehension of the total picture at any given moment.

Fitch had commissioned not a disease but a virus that was used as a carrier for modified genetic material. The virus "attacked"—

314

and altered—a colony of bacteria. They in turn had an incredible affinity for gold. Seawater filtered through large enough beds of the bacteria at sufficient rates would make the project very commercially feasible indeed, Fitch had assured him.

Allenberg remembered that, several years earlier, a genetic research company had come up with a similar process. The Brandes process, though, was hundreds of times more efficient, allowing the processing of vast quantities of seawater to extract the traces of gold in it.

In a few weeks, Fitch had said, the project could get under way; until then, any research into the virus or the bacteria was a threat. Afterward . . . it would not matter.

Had Fitch simply wanted to get rich, Allenberg would have fought but not hated nor feared him. But Fitch was *not* heading the project to get rich.

"Did you really believe we were alone?" Fitch had sneered. "Did you really think the one-worlders of Uisce Beatha were the be all and end all of power?" He'd laughed loudly, raucously.

Allenberg had been sickened by the terror he felt. Often thoughts of Uisce Beatha's extraordinary reach and influence had made him uneasy.

Now he knew a truth he wished he could simply forget: *My God, there is a corollary to Uisce Beatha.*

*Yes, if I get out of here the real crisis begins.*

"What do we do?" Brandes's voice was weak, cracked.

Kracke looked at him for several seconds before replying. "We change the way we're going about this, I'd say."

"Going about it? What do you mean? You read that thing. They'll kill Allenberg and the kid if we continue. You forget there was a biker who got away. Someone—at least some *one*—in this town is working for them. They'll know if we don't stop."

"Alex—" Kracke began, but Wismer cut him off.

"Jim, let me. Alex, we have to go on. It will make no

difference. These people have no intention of letting them go. Adrian knows that. He won't expect us to stop for a minute."

"But . . ."

"But, *shit*," Kracke said. "I said we'll go on—but I also said we'll do things a little differently."

"How?"

"Do you—*you*—have to be here for the Dorfman tests or the work on the kid's blood?"

"No. I'll probably just try to tear those notebooks apart again. Then, if any of those tests *do* come up with something, I'll see if the results ring any bells, jibe with something Peter wrote down."

"I thought so. And you?" He faced Wismer.

"I'm too old, Jim. Besides . . . I'm thinking." He obviously was. At Brandes's mention of the notebooks he glanced at them, and it seemed impossible for him to look away. Suddenly he walked to his desk and picked up the battered copy of Shakespeare Peter had left in the car. He leafed through it, ever more absorbed in his own thoughts.

"Too old for what?" Brandes asked, but Wismer didn't hear him.

"For what we have to do," Kracke said. "We're going to get the boss and his grandson. Then we're coming back here. You said yourself you really haven't anything to do immediately."

"*Nuts*—that's you. You're nuts. We don't know where they are, for starters. Then there's the minor matter of Colonel Lawrence's quarantine and the other matter of a spy for the kidnappers roving around. *Nuts.*"

Kracke sneered. "Quarantine, shit. I'll think of something. As for the spy, he or she has been ordered to report on whether or not you're still working on the disease—visiting the hospital or lab and such.

"As far as *where* they are, no problem. If you knew him better, you'd know he told us they were being held at his house in western New Jersey."

"Jesus," Brandes breathed. "You're serious. Why me?"

"Two reasons. For one thing you might be helpful. But there's another. Adrian ordered me to stay with you and protect you. If I can't stay here . . ." He raised his shoulders in an elaborate shrug.

"So," Sarah said. That was all. She sat very still on the edge of her bed in his bungalow behind Andy's station. Brandes sat in a chair near her.

"I'm sorry."

She looked at him, puzzled. "Why?"

"Why?" He stammered.

"I'm not being cute, Alex. I'm not in the mood for it. You had nothing to do with this; you have nothing to be sorry for."

"I guess I just needed something to say."

"Yes. That I understand. When is Jim planning to leave?"

His eyes widened in shock. He'd told her nothing of the plan to rescue Allenberg and Jason. "How the hell do you know?" he asked.

She smiled. "I know Jim."

Irrationally, he thought, he felt a pang of jealousy when she said that.

"It's the only course of action he *would* take. Technically, he's disobeying his orders in not doing everything he can to help Lyle, I guess. But he's been with my grandfather a long time, Alex. And he knows that those men have no intention at all of letting either my father or my son live."

"Everyone seems certain of that except me."

"Be certain, Alex. I imagine you're going, too."

"Yes."

"Thought so." She grinned crookedly. "Jim wouldn't disobey his orders to *that* extent."

*She sure as hell knows him.*

"That's what he said."

"So, when?"

"A few hours, I guess. He said he had to make some preparations, and he wants it to be dark." He paused.

"Sarah, we'll do our best. I think I've gotten to know you well

317

enough not to say anything stupid like, 'Don't worry, we'll get them.' But we *will* try. We'll get the bastards, Sarah."

"Get them?"

"Do you think Kracke plans on arresting them?"

"No, I'm sure he doesn't. But that doesn't bother you?"

Brandes hesitated. He tried to say something, lost his words in his feelings, remained silent.

"You've changed, Alex."

"Yes. I've changed." His voice was low but did not, to his surprise, lack a subtle strength he thought he'd never display. "I've changed."

"You say a few hours, Alex?"

"Yes."

"Then do me a favor, Alex. Would you?"

"Of course. If I can."

She smiled. "I'm sure you can.

"Please make love to me."

---

Dusk was forming, settling, a blanket over the already cheerless town. Darkness, Wismer thought, could add little more to the pall. He looked from the window back to the notebooks and the volume of Shakespeare on the coffee table.

His stomach was tight with doubt and with a fear greater than anything he'd ever felt before, greater than any he ever imagined he *could* feel.

He'd thought from the first that he was on the right track—and he still believed that to a large extent he was. He'd been very pleased with himself.

The dogeared Shakespeare. On impulse, after hearing the contents of Allenberg's note, he'd flipped through the book. He'd done so earlier, when Brandes had first brought it into the house. He'd known Peter well enough to know that Peter had thought like a scientist; he'd thought in "chains"—one piece of information carefully forged into the next, each link discrete and each necessary for the whole.

318

So, the book—and it fit. Peter had underlined the title of one of the plays. It was *The Merchant of Venice*.

Wismer had felt gut-right that Peter somehow had *known* or at least suspected that he would die before he could tell anyone about his discovery. He had not trusted the men with—or for— whom he worked. Whatever clues he left would have had to have been very vague, very oblique.

"Precious metal," Allenberg had said.

*The Merchant of Venice.*

What more mercenary a work could Peter have chosen?

And all that had been fine. Wismer had felt very self-satisfied; he'd poured himself a congratulatory Scotch and had sipped it, still idly flipping through the book and letting his thoughts run unguided.

And then he'd stumbled across a second marked play. His mind, so highly trained and experienced in seeing patterns others almost inevitably would miss, made a gigantic leap.

A terrifying leap.

The Scotch churned in his stomach as he watched the dusk. He thought again about that taste of night. He'd been wrong a few minutes earlier, he thought.

Lyle has, God help it, ever so much deeper to sink into despair, into darkness.

*God help us all.*


Corporal Dan Starociak wiped his sleeve across his forehead, smearing dirt, mixing it more thoroughly with the perspiration that poured from him. He was tired.

He jabbed down with the tip of his shovel and heard the clunk of metal against wood. It was a sound he had been hearing all day; the digging up of bodies had become that much of a routine.

"Frank, when are you going to give me a break?" he called up from the grave.

"Soon, digger. Soon." Corporal Frank Rutkowski rumbled laughter. He'd have to get to work, soon, Starociak thought.

*When I get the stiff uncovered, it'll take both of us to get it out of here and into the truck.*

Then they would drive across the field to the cremation site. There, as darkness crept in, the flames would be leaping high, and both men would perversely begin to look forward to the back-breaking work of digging up the next casket.

*Anything* was better than duty at the fire.

Starociak decided he could use a break. Lawrence had been pushing hard. Every man not on quarantine was working extra hours so that the cremation count would become current with the death rate.

*Shit duty.* Starociak reached into his breast pocket and took out a cigarette. He rested the handle of his shovel against the wall of dirt and leaned back against it himself.

*God, am I going to sleep tonight.*

He struck a match.

Rutkowski later would recall no scream, no sound other than the massive explosion that erupted from the grave, the pillar of fire that shot skyward, carrying with it nearly unidentifiable pieces of Corporal Starociak.

When he got the report, Lawrence paled and issued orders. Men were to take extra precautions. Townspeople who had spoken most vehemently at the town meeting were to be put under immediate surveillance.

If the "villagers" had begun to booby-trap the graves, he wanted not only to protect his men but to apprehend those responsible.

All perimeter personnel were alerted; extra ammunition was distributed. Lawrence awaited the Battle of Lyle.

# THIRTY-ONE

A FILM OF LOW CLOUDS HAD SLID OVER THE NIGHT sky, blocking starlight and diffusing the light of the moon to a uniform dullness.

What light there was washed over the dirt-streaked faces of Wismer and Kracke as they drove in silence along a road devoid even of night sounds.

The trees crowded the road, tall figures even darker than the surrounding night, bending over at the tops, promising a canopy of daytime green, nighttime threat.

Life and death.

Both men were absorbed in thought on just that subject. Kracke could not explain why, but his mind wandered back . . . It was three years now. *You expect to see a lot of things in this business*, he thought. *You do. Most you forget, the rest you try to forget . . .*

The airliner crash three years ago in Spain—it was one of those things, he thought, you try to forget.

He had learned that a bomb had been placed aboard the 747 liner—the "how" of that in itself was something he doubted he ever would forget. He had rushed to get word to Michelmore, his local control. He had been too late.

The jet had come into its final approach normally. Jets in flight were beautiful things to Kracke. In his convoluted world of shades of dimness, often things that seemed mundane to others were beautiful; they were sights to be held, held long enough for the tingling to touch the spine's base.

It was a small bomb, Kracke remembered. He had *been* there when it went off. There barely had been a puff of smoke from the belly of the airborne giant. But it was enough; the bomb had performed as intended.

The plane instantly dropped a matter of twenty-five feet—no more. Then it struck the supports for the flashing strobe lights meant to lead jets safely to the end of the runway.

Instead, that day they had assisted death.

Metal screeched across the flat grassland at the runway's end. One support, toppling, remained erect long enough to tear a gash the entire length of the jet's underside.

Hydraulic lines were split, torn. Controls instantly were made useless. Emptied in seconds of the hydraulic fluid that was blood to the plane, the lines themselves became no more useful than empty veins. The mere human strength of the crewmen, unaided by the vital amplification of power provided by the hydraulic system, could not as much as budge the jet's control surfaces.

The jet, almost majestically, rose on one side. The left wing touched the ground, at first seemingly delicately, and then had torn off and catapulted and cartwheeled across the meadow, bouncing and disintegrating.

For the first time Kracke realized he himself was close enough to be in danger. He ducked below the level of his car, not knowing where debris next would be scattered.

The Boeing continued to turn. In amazement, Kracke watched the other wing strike, shear off. The fuselage, upside down, dropped a final few feet to go the last few yards to the road that ran perpendicular to the runway.

The most horrendous sound he thought he would ever hear was the metal of the jet's body *scraping* on the pavement. It had seemed it never would end.

But it had.

Then it had been the silence that had struck him. It did not last long and, in fact, probably never really had existed but only seemed to in contrast to the grisly death screech of the mortally wounded aircraft.

Next had come the low sounds, the moaning sounds, the crying sounds, the sounds of pitiful weeping.

Rescue workers already were spraying foam over the remains of the fuselage when he'd stood to look over the vision of hell he would never forget.

A scene only a contemporary Dante could envision—and then possibly only under the influence of a hallucinogen—lay spread out before him.

Kracke had seen battles, battlegrounds. Even the carnage of those had not prepared him for wreckage strewn before him. *It was the mixture of the wreckage*, he'd thought once, trying to explain why he'd felt as he had.

There had been debris both organic and inorganic, both animate and inanimate—and then there had been the animate that soon would cross the line into death.

Suitcases, backs of seats, pieces of plastic and aluminum mingled with arms and legs, torsos.

One man had been perfectly lucid, sitting in his wheelchair; he'd had a hole in his forehead at least four inches across. Kracke had found it nearly impossible not to stare at the man's pulsing brain. Then, suddenly, the man had smiled at Kracke, his eyes had glazed over, and he had died.

So simply, so peacefully—so unforgettably gruesomely.

Kracke shook himself.

He could not get those images out of his mind as he and Wismer drove toward the army checkpoint on the road.

"They'll have to do something," Wismer said, clearing his throat. Kracke, pulling himself back from his memories, wondered at once what had been going on in *Wismer's* mind while they drove.

He knew that Wismer had not always been a teacher. His early twenties had been spent in work quite different. That much he knew. He had no idea what Wismer had seen and done—such things never were discussed, sometimes not even with oneself.

But he suspected the now-retired biology teacher could match the memory from which he'd just emerged. *Of course.*

Wismer turned a final curve, and the lights of the roadblock shone through the windshield, causing each man to raise an arm over his eyes. Wismer slowed and stopped about ten feet from the side of a Jeep that had been placed across the road.

Lieutenant Knotts had drawn late duty, but he had barely an hour left on his tour. The young soldier approached the car.

"Lieutenant," Wismer said through the window, "we have to talk to the colonel. It's vital."

The officer had seen Wismer before and recognized him. "Mr. Wismer, right? I'm afraid that's not going to be possible. We're not letting *anybody* through these checkpoints. Not day, not night. Sorry."

"This is urgent," Kracke called from the other side of the car. "Please at least call the colonel."

"At this hour?"

"At this hour," Kracke said and got out of the car. Wismer could feel Knotts tense, but Kracke only reached into his pocket for his identification. "Please examine this carefully, Lieutenant. *I* say it's urgent. *I* say, 'At this hour.'"

Lieutenant Knotts had walked carefully around the front of the car and had approached Kracke close enough to examine the proffered card. His eyebrows rose a fraction.

"Sir, uh," he stammered. "I . . . just wait a minute, okay? I'll call headquarters."

"Thank you," Kracke said and turned to Wismer. "He didn't look too surprised to see that we're not exactly scrubbed and dressed for church."

"No, but he noticed. I think he's curious—*that's* why he'll call Lawrence. Duty like this looks for an excuse to break routine; it encourages curiosity."

A few minutes passed and then Knotts's voice called out.

"Gentlemen, would you come to the phone, please? The colonel would like to talk to you."

Wismer and Kracke walked the few feet to the rear of the Jeep containing the communications equipment.

Wismer took the receiver from Knotts.

"Colonel, this is Gerry Wismer. Mr. Kracke and I have to talk to you. Immediately. It's a matter of the greatest importance."

"So talk to me." The colonel, Wismer thought, had been dozing when Knotts had called. He could well imagine the hours the commander had been putting in the last few days.

"Colonel, this is not something I think we should discuss on the telephone." He looked around him. Knotts—and now he saw there were two even younger soldiers near him—was out of earshot, but he had no idea what other ears might lay between his end of the line and Lawrence's.

"Let me put it this way, Mr. Wismer. Talk or go home."

Wismer sighed. "He wants to talk on the phone," he said to Kracke.

"Asshole. Well, go ahead. Security's his problem. Talk to him."

Wismer stared at Kracke for several seconds. Both men knew what had to be told to the colonel. But, as Kracke had said, Wismer thought, the asshole is responsible for his own security.

Wismer talked for several minutes. When he finished, there was a slight background humming on the line, noticeable because Lawrence had not replied. The teacher wondered if he was going to get an answer when the colonel said, "Get me Lieutenant Knotts, Mr. Wismer."

Wismer said nothing. It was the colonel's next logical move. He waved to Knotts, who came at once.

"He wants to talk to you." He handed over the phone.

"Lieutenant Knotts, sir," he said—and that was all he said for several moments as Wismer and Kracke watched his face gradually change character and color. They saw his eyes widen. Both of the other men easily could understand why. At least they *thought* so.

They were wrong.

"Yes, sir," he said finally, in a weak voice, and replaced the receiver in its cradle. He stood still for several minutes and then called to the other soldiers, "Thomas, Willetts. Come here."

They stood on either side of Knotts as he turned to face Wismer and Kracke.

"Thomas, Willetts. Arrest these men immediately."

Wismer's shock was complete. The sound of bolts being pulled on M-16s was loud in the night. He was frozen as he watched the muzzles begin to rise toward him and Kracke.

*The goddamn fucking colonel is crazy.* Then he realized what was happening. *Lawrence is just going to do* nothing. *My God, I thought I'd had horror enough tonight.*

What was happening was *unbelievable.* Nothing short of that. While Wismer stood rooted and watched the scene in slow motion, he caught another movement at the edge of his sight.

Kracke, in one fluid gymnastic motion that took all three inexperienced men totally by surprise, caught Knotts under his chin with the edge of his right hand, killing the lieutenant easily and quickly and pushing the body onto the top of one of the other men's rifles, forcing it down.

His foot swung at the other soldier's weapon, knocking it aside. Kracke leaped forward.

Wismer was spellbound. Never had they conceived of an unarmed man attacking three soldiers, two armed with automatic weapons.

They had no chance at all against Kracke's deadly proficiency.

Now Kracke ripped the weapon from the soldier he'd kicked and used it in a vertical butt stroke, taking the wide-eyed youngster under the chin and snapping his head back like a whip; the cracking sound was anticlimactic.

The remaining soldier still struggled to free himself and his weapon from the body of his commanding officer—everything else had happened so *fast.*

There was a glint in Kracke's right hand—and then it vanished, into the side of the boy's neck.

His shocked eyes lost luster; he fell, the agent allowing the knife to slide back out, dripping as the body sagged.

Kracke turned to Wismer, who still had not moved.

"I'm sorry, Gerry. I know they only were kids, but . . ."

For a moment, Wismer said nothing—just looked at the incredibly efficient killer who stood next to him. When he did speak, he said, "No, Jim. I'm sorry. I should have taken out one of them."

"Let's get back to the house. Brandes and Sarah should be there by now. We don't have much time, Gerry. You know that."

He paused; Wismer nodded. "And we've just increased the size of the opposition considerably. This"—he gestured to the carnage—"will be discovered pretty quickly after Lawrence starts wondering why we haven't been delivered."

"I know. It's going to be a long night, Jim."

"Maybe we can buy a little time, anyway," Kracke said. "Help me." He lifted Knotts by the shoulders; Wismer lifted the feet. They put the body, its eyes still wide in surprise but frosted over, dry, in the rear of the Jeep. They piled the others in on top of their officer.

As he'd hoisted Knotts, Kracke had taken keys from the lieutenant's pocket. He flicked through them, quickly finding one he wanted. He got into the Jeep and started it.

"Which side of the road, Gerry?"

"Go the way it's aimed. There's a pretty steep drop about thirty feet in, behind those trees." He gestured.

Kracke drove where Wismer had indicated, weaving carefully between the tree trunks.

Soon Wismer could not see him but only could hear the sporadic gunning of the engine as Krack negotiated dips and rises. Then there was silence; the engine noise had disappeared completely, and Wismer stood in silence, looking around him.

He felt dazed. The nightmare they had hoped to end by going to Lawrence only had deepened, and the road they had been forced to take most definitely was a one-way road.

They had to go on now—and fast.

There was no turning back.

*Death wins here*, he thought. *No matter where we start, what we do, death wins. We can hope only to hold down its score.*

Kracke walked silently from the undergrowth.

"I hope that Lawrence is going to be pretty busy on the phone for a while. I'll kill that son of a bitch someday, but I'd sure as hell hate to be in his shoes right now." Kracke paused, and added, "I will kill him, you know."

"I know."

"By the time he notices we're overdue, he's going to be pretty strung out. If he sends out a detail to look for us, maybe not finding the Jeep or the men will make them think we're on our way and they somehow missed us. These guys don't know this area very well yet. We may have bought a little time. Not much."

Kracke picked up the two rifles and handed one to Wismer. He pocketed the .45-caliber sidearm he'd taken from Lieutenant Knotts. He had his own pistol, Wismer knew. But Brandes—or Sarah, for that matter—might be able to use the additional firepower.

*God, I hope it does not come to that.*

They quickly walked back to the car; Wismer spun it on the road and began his race against time and at least two highly organized opponents.

He wondered if *they* knew about *each other*.

Brandes and Sarah were looking through a plastic bag Kracke had left for them in Wismer's house. They had not been there long; their lovemaking, intense, insistent at first, had eased into a tenderness.

Neither of them felt that what they had done was in the least out of place. They had done what seemed best to relieve the intolerable tension of an intolerable situation.

"I guess you should get into these things," Sarah said and lifted a pair of dark jeans from the bag. "I think they'll fit.

"I don't know where they are," she added, looking at him and speaking of Kracke and Wismer, "but I don't think they'll be too much longer, and you have a lot to do tonight."

"I wonder how Kracke intends to get through the quarantine," Brandes said.

"That," Sarah said, "is one of his specialities."

Brandes again felt a flicker of irrational jealousy when she spoke of Kracke with such familiarity.

*What the hell am I thinking? I sure as hell have no claim on her. I doubt that any man does.*

Brandes took more clothing from the bag. All of it was dark. Unsure of Brandes's sizes and eager to be gone, Kracke had gathered several sizes.

Despite how they had spent their afternoon, Brandes—with a little embarrassment—told Sarah he'd change in the next room.

Sarah grinned; he blushed at his silliness.

In another five minutes he was outfitted in dark blue. He wore black boots, dulled with a layer of shoe polish applied but not buffed off. Brandes wondered if Kracke would demand that they blacken their faces.

"Cute," Sarah said when he returned to the living room.

"Thanks."

They both were fidgeting and talking for lack of anything better to do. Whatever lay ahead for the next twenty-four hours was totally in the hands of James Kracke—and, Brandes suspected—to some extent, Gerry Wismer. His teacher. His old, gentle, softspoken teacher.

"They should be here any time," he said. He gestured to the note Wismer had left for them on the coffee table.

*Jim and I have some things to do, Alex. You put on the stuff Jim got. We'll be back as soon as we can. Eat something. That is not a suggestion. It's an order. While you're at it, make extra sandwiches for all of us.*

That had been the easiest part of the note for them to obey immediately. Both were famished when they'd arrived at the

329

house. They heated a can of Dinty Moore stew, which they split, and then each ate a roast beef sandwich. Now a half-dozen more sandwiches were wrapped and in a paper bag on the coffee table within immediate reach. They could move swiftly as soon as Wismer and Kracke returned.

Both turned expectantly at a sound outside the rear door. They started toward the kitchen, Brandes picking up the sandwiches. He chided himself: *I'm too tense, too taut. Maybe Kracke will have to change. We might be here another . . . long five minutes.* He ached to get started just to release some of the constantly increasing tightness in his chest.

The door opened; both Sarah and Brandes stared at the two men who entered.

Their hands were filthy, and their faces were streaked with grime. Brandes saw what looked like dried blood on Kracke's right wrist, but the big man moved his hand easily enough and didn't seem to be hurt.

Both wore dark clothing, Brandes saw. And that dark clothing somehow had acquired a none-too-thin layer of mud and particles of grass and twigs.

"What?" Brandes began, but Wismer held up an imperious hand.

"We have to move. Now," Kracke said. "Good; I see you remembered the sandwiches. Throw a couple of cans of soda in there, too. Sarah," he said, "you put on one of the other outfits. We're *all* going. Let's get our asses out of here—*now.*"

"What do you mean, *all going?*"

"How many goddamn meanings you get out of that?" Wismer seethed. "There is no time to explain. Sarah, get *dressed*. Alex, get the damned soda."

Sarah began to strip. Brandes did not move. "No matter what the hell happened to you out there," he said and gestured to their clothing, "we can't just all leave. How the hell will *four* of us get through?"

"My problem," Kracke said. Then he, too, raised his voice. "Alex, get your damned ass moving or so help me I'll kick the damned thing."

His words galvanized both Sarah and Brandes.

Wismer swiftly moved into his den area and opened the top left drawer of his desk. He took out his .25-caliber Beretta and an extra clip of eight shots. He slipped it into his pocket.

It all took only seconds.

The four of them started toward the back door when the telephone rang.

Everyone froze instantly; eight eyes saw nothing but the suddenly somehow ominous plastic device. None moved to answer it at first. Wismer and Kracke then exchanged glances.

"What do you think?" Kracke asked.

"Maybe Lawrence. Maybe. *We* obviously can't answer it."

"I don't suppose we . . . no, that wouldn't work. Alex might be able to buy us some time, though, if he just says that he hasn't seen us and sounds innocent when he says it. Lawrence may think we'll still have to come back here before we run—he'll have been right. But he might think he's still got time to beat us here."

"Might work."

"What the hell are you two talking about?" Brandes demanded.

"It's better you don't know—exactly—yet," Kracke said. "Just answer the telephone. It probably *is* Lawrence or one of his officers. Just sound natural, and if he asks about us, just tell him that you haven't seen us and we haven't called.

"Tell him you were supposed to meet us here and that you're waiting. Be pleasant enough—but just enough. Don't change whatever picture he's got of you. Understand?"

"Yeah. I think so." Brandes looked doubtful but then walked over to the table and reached out for the phone. He paused, then picked it up in mid-ring. Immediately his face relaxed as he turned to the others.

"It's okay," he said. "It's Jonathan."

He listened then, and his face seemed to turn to wax, then to stone.

"Oh, God," he sighed into the phone. "Oh, God."

He turned to the others again but looked directly at Sarah as he said, "Cynthia is dead." He began to cry, his hand still gripping the telephone even after having replaced it in its cradle.

Wismer gasped, and Kracke shot him a swift, stunned glance.

*This changes it all. We thought it could get no worse—and it's gotten worse. Oh my God, has it gotten worse!*

"Where is she?" Kracke asked loudly. Brandes didn't answer. Kracke strode forcefully to stand in front of him and grabbed his shoulders. "Damn it, Alex, *where is she?*"

"She's dead, Jim." Brandes's voice was abnormally soft, almost childlike.

Kracke could stand no more. *There wasn't time for any more.*

"Goddamn it, Alex. *Where the fuck is she? Where? Now? Where?*" He shook Brandes with each word, until finally some comprehension came back into Brandes's face.

"She's in an ambulance, of course. She's on her way to the . . . cremation . . . the . . . She's dead, Jim."

The sudden softness of Kracke's voice contrasted dramatically with his previous outburst: "No, Alex. That's just it. She *isn't* dead, Alex. Do you understand? Do you understand what I'm telling you? *Cynthia is not dead.*

"*None of them*"—he gestured widely—"*were dead.*"

# THIRTY-TWO

IN ONE SPOT—AND ONLY ONE—PAINT HAD BEGUN to peel from the woodwork around Wismer's kitchen door. Brandes had just noticed it.

*I could have stayed here for months, maybe years,* he thought. *Never would have noticed that. Getting sharp.*

Coherent thought fought. Lost. His mind simply could not yawn a vast morning yawn, one capable of encompassing a world, a new world by orders of magnitude more alien than that brought by mundane dawn.

He stared at the paint chip; it was on the doorframe's left side, next to a shelf that held some of Wismer's crystal—Orefors, Baccarat.

Crystal. *The word has a sharpness, but then* sharpness *has a sharpness, and I have onomatopoeia in the second degree . . .*

"Alex!" It was Sarah.

He looked at her, realizing that not all that much time had passed. *Thoughts* had passed. Very fast. Thoughts very far from where he was, from Lyle, Cynthia.

"Yes," he said. It was not just the news of Cynthia's death— and the immediate contradictory news from Kracke—that had numbed his mind for that fleeting (but never, he knew, to be forgotten) moment.

It was the recognition of the implications of Kracke's *last* words.

*None of them had been dead.*

Living people—*living people*—had been buried, had been burned. *My God, had been autopsied.* His stomach twisted in revulsion.

He didn't understand how any of it was possible. Wismer would explain that.

But he knew it to be true. He just *knew* it to be true.

*Oh, God, Peter. Why didn't you just kill them?*

He began to weep.

"Not now, Alex," Kracke said. "Gerry and I had a little time to take it all in, so I'm not pushing as hard as I should." He briefly remembered his own mental re-creation of the 747 bombing. "But I *do* have to push, Alex. We have to help these people, and the best way—the *only* way—to do that now is to help Adrian and Jason. And"—he hesitated—"we have to get out of here before Lawrence comes."

"We have to tell . . ."

"No," Kracke said. "Look, I'll explain it all as best I can in a few minutes. *But we have to get out of this house and away from here this minute!*"

Brandes nodded, vigorously. Yes, he thought. Have to move. *I have to get out of here.*

He and Sarah preceded Kracke and Wismer into the rear yard; Sarah knew that they had hung back to make some sort of last-minute plan. She very well understood how the news about Cynthia had made useless any plan they already might have had.

*Any plan Jim had to get Alex and himself out was useless even before then. Or I wouldn't be wearing these clothes.*

Kracke knew he would have to help Brandes save Cynthia from Lawrence's funeral pyres, Sarah thought. She was certain of that. Also, she knew that if he did not feel he *had* to help the woman, he would let her die in order to succeed in his assignment.

But Brandes would be of absolutely no use to him if they didn't at least try to rescue Cynthia. Worse, he might become a serious liability.

"We'll separate," Wismer announced when he and Kracke had caught up. "Sarah and I have a few things to do. Alex, you help Jim with Cynthia."

*Leave it vague, leave it simple,* he thought. "Take back roads whenever possible. Alex, Jim will explain to you about the army.

"*We have to stay away from them.*

"I know it doesn't sound like much time, but you'll only need a half-hour if you're going to succeed, Jim. Then we meet at Andy's.

"If Lawrence is beginning to miss us—or already knows we're running—a half-hour is about all the time we'll have before we *really* start running.

"Good luck."

He didn't wait. He and Sarah got into his car, still warm from its day- and night-long use. Brandes and Kracke got into the Mercedes.

"Jim, I'm . . . I feel like I'm waking up or something. I'm sorry if I've been a little . . . disjointed."

"You're coming out of it quicker than I thought you would," Kracke said as he released the clutch, taking the car out of Wismer's yard just ahead of the other car. "It's not an easy thing. It wasn't easy for Gerry or for me—and we've . . . seen a lot."

"What did you see tonight, Jim?" He twisted in the passenger seat, looking directly at Kracke's chiseled profile. "What is happening? *What did you see?*"

Kracke thought only for a few seconds, trying to determine a proper point to begin.

"Gerry figured out some of the things in your brother's notes," he said.

"It looks like Peter *expected* to have trouble with the people he was involved with. He left enough messages—Gerry will explain all that better than I can—but they were so scattered that it took somebody like Gerry to put it together.

335

"To be honest, Alex, I think Adrian and I made a mistake when we concluded you were the logical person to go through your brother's things. I think he considered you likely to figure everything out—eventually.

"But I think he really targeted his little cryptic notes at Gerry. He's got, uh, the kind of mind necessary for this sort of thing.

"Of course, it's a damned good thing for you we did bring you in. Peter's sponsors—Adrian's kidnappers—also figured you to be the focus. That's why they tried to kill you."

"You mean it was a good thing you brought me in so I could be the target, don't you? That way they'd leave Wismer alone."

He stopped only a second, but he was not brooding, Kracke thought. He seemed simply to be analyzing his situation, his importance.

"Of course, you didn't *plan* it that way. You *would* have—but you didn't. In any event, Wismer was kept safe. Have I got that about right?" Brandes's voice rang of innocence instead of "righteous"—and Kracke, the professional, would have thought—misplaced anger. Kracke was impressed.

"A good enough analysis," was all he said to Brandes.

"I really don't understand, Jim," Brandes said. "I mean about the rest of it."

"Neither do I, not everything. Adrian has held back on something, even from me, and I doubt I'll ever find out what that is.

"They hired your brother, probably promising him some new toy for his lab—I don't know. And Peter made a virus that changed a specific organism's genetic structure to give it an extraordinary affinity for trace metal in seawater.

"Gold, we think," Kracke continued. "Gerry thinks so. Got something to do with *The Merchant of Venice*. Only Peter was concerned with what *other* effects his bug might have—especially on living things.

"He found out he'd created something totally incredible.

"He'd created an organism that for a length of time could create simulated death."

"And he died before he could tell anybody," Brandes finished. "Do the people who killed him know what they've got?"

Kracke swung his head from side to side, double-clutched, shifted. "I don't know, Alex. I really doubt that it matters to them whether or not Lyle dies or just *looks* dead. All they want is a few weeks of using this thing with no interference. To get that they'll kill. Anyone generally. You, specifically."

"Except it was Gerry who figured it out."

"Gerry only figured out the disease part."

"Then they know about the illness," Brandes said with sudden authority. Kracke turned his head, stared for a second at the now grimly smiling scientist.

"Why do you say that?"

"Because they *know* that any cure for the disease will also be a weapon that could destroy their gold-gathering colonies."

Kracke thought about it. *Makes sense.*

"What about the army, Jim?"

Kracke did hesitate then and not only to find a point of beginning. He knew Brandes's record verbatim. How would he react to what Lawrence had done? To what *he* had done? He could see no alternative, though, to telling Brandes.

"Gerry and I," he began slowly, "went out to where the graves of the earliest victims are. Lawrence hasn't gotten around to them yet. Gerry needed proof for his interpretation of Peter's messages.

"That was part of the problem, by the way. Peter didn't leave *a* message. He left his hints in *triplicate*, for shit's sake. While we were trying to string them together end-to-end, he was dropping them in parallel."

"He would," Brandes said, and smiled. He thought fondly of Peter.

*He didn't make a weapon. Not on purpose.*

The car swung as Kracke rounded a curve.

"I need your help here, Alex. Where's the direct route the ambulance would take? I want to cross it as far from the cremation site as possible. And we haven't much time."

"Not hard," Brandes said. "Two hundred yards after the next

turn; it's a sharp one. There's a left. Take it. The road's bumpy but it takes a few miles off the run. Besides," he said, "I saw the ambulance the other day. Those guys aren't trying to get anywhere in a hurry."

Kracke grunted and downshifted as he approached the curve Brandes had indicated. He turned onto the smaller road, more like a path. It was pitted. It never had been paved.

"The army," Brandes reminded him.

"Yeah," Kracke said. "We—Gerry and I—opened a grave and—well, there was proof." He could not bring himself to describe the way he'd felt when Wismer had pried open the lid to reveal the still all-too-alive-looking corpse with bulging sightless eyes and outstretched hands on which rivulets of blood had flowed and dried as the "corpse" had revived and tried to fight his way back to the air and the light.

Brandes was silent. Kracke sensed something wrong, then Brandes asked quietly, "Was it Peter's grave?"

"No," Kracke said.

"Some of the people were embalmed, you know," Brandes rambled. "That was before the town knew it had an epidemic and had to get rid of the bodies quickly. Peter, though. They *knew* he died of some strange bug, so even though he was first, he wasn't embalmed. Did you know that, Jim?"

"No."

"That means he woke up buried."

"Don't think—"

"I won't. Really, I won't. I don't think I can."

"We went right away to an army checkpoint to get a message to Lawrence. Gerry got through on the phone and told him. Hell, Alex, we're talking a couple hundred people here. We had to get him to stop the cremations immediately."

"So he did. So what? Why was there a problem?"

Kracke snorted. The car bucked, as the undercarriage scraped over a larger than average rut in the road.

"He ordered Lieutenant Knotts to arrest me and Gerry."

"That doesn't . . ."

"It makes perfect sense. That bastard politician with chickens on his shoulders was thinking about his ass and the asses that can—and would—shit on him. Think about it, Alex. Wonderful press: U.S. ARMY INCINERATES HUNDREDS ALIVE. No damn way. He just ordered everything to continue as if nothing had happened."

"But everyone else in town . . . What? . . ."

"Alex, I don't know. He can't just kill all of them. He'll probably take that Dorfman serum coming in and claim it cured everyone."

"In the meanwhile, though, more people . . . We've got to tell Jonathan."

"Christ, Alex, *grow up.* You tell Shortell and you're signing *his* death warrant. Lawrence does not intend to have *anyone* who knows about this survive. His own men don't know."

"Knotts doesn't know?"

*Tough time coming.*

"Knotts is dead, Alex. So are two other soldiers. They tried to arrest us. I had no choice."

Brandes said nothing for a few minutes. Kracke took the opportunity to look more closely about. The road seemed better traveled now, smoother at least. He judged the main road linking the hospital to Lawrence's pyres to be about a quarter-mile away.

*Close enough.*

"I guess you didn't," Brandes said finally.

Kracke breathed his relief audibly. He also felt more comfortable about reaching into the back seat for the M-16s.

Brandes took the weapon from Kracke and carefully turned it in his hands, his face showing no emotion.

"I don't see any reason for killing those guys in the ambulance," he said finally. "I don't think I can do that."

"I've no intention of doing that," Kracke said. "We may have to shake them up a bit—looking at one of these things from the wrong end takes the idea of resistance out of any sane person. Don't worry. We won't hurt them."

Now Kracke turned off the car's headlights and slowly moved

ahead by the much dimmer yellow illumination of the parking lights. By the time he stopped, their eyes already had begun to adjust to the night.

"Follow close behind," Kracke said and silently moved off at the edge of the road. Brandes followed, not succeeding nearly as well in being quiet, his feet seeming to find all the dry twigs Kracke's somehow totally missed. Silence was not a major concern of the agent, however. They made fast progress, and by the time they could see the road they had grown completely accustomed to the dark.

"The road from the hospital twists a lot for the first few miles. If they had to take others with Cynthia, they probably were delayed some more minutes in leaving. Still, we have taken a bit of time getting here. I doubt we'll have more than five minutes to wait."

"Then what?"

"For you not much. I'm going about fifty feet up the road. You stay here. When I move out into the road and start waving this thing around, and the ambulance stops, it'll be just about below you." He pointed down the gentle ten-foot embankment. "You just walk up to the passenger side, aim the rifle in the air and loudly pull back the bolt. Has a wondrous effect."

"Sounds simple. What do we do with the attendants?"

"I'll show you." He smiled. "They won't be injured, Alex."

As he finished speaking they heard an engine just around the curve nearest them. A strange frown crossed Kracke's face, but he shrugged and moved swiftly to his predetermined position, blending eerily into the night and the woods.

Brandes waited alone and suddenly felt lonely.

Cynthia was down there. And he did love her. She was not dead—but soon would be, in a most horrible way, if he failed.

He felt a burst of hatred toward Lawrence. He hefted the M-16. *I could use this on him.*

The glare of a headlight bobbed around the curve before the vehicle.

Then Brandes saw it.

An army Jeep. Two soldiers.

*Christ. Now what?* He looked in Kracke's direction but could see nothing. *Lawrence couldn't have known.* He dismissed that thought. It was much more likely, he thought, that the commander simply was being a very professional and thorough soldier. He probably had assigned an armed guard to accompany all the ambulances after he had received Wismer's call from the checkpoint.

*But what do I do, Jim?* He did not know. He remained where he was, hoping that Kracke, when he made whatever move he now intended, would somehow make Brandes's expected role obvious.

The Jeep rumbled by, and about twenty-five feet behind it, the ambulance followed, its mint-blue lights flashing, lending strange, flicking light to the bordering trees and undergrowth.

Brandes hunched lower, afraid suddenly that the light just might sweep by his position.

An eruption of chattering gunfire broke the night, and Brandes could see the flashes from Kracke's rifle. The Jeep shuddered to a halt, and the soldiers reached for their weapons, but in a catlike bound, Kracke was alongside them. Brandes could see him clearly in the lights of the ambulance.

Kracke had shoved the muzzle of his weapon into the neck of the nearest soldier and must have ordered both to be very still.

They were.

Kracke had not underestimated the effect of the M-16's presence.

"Down here," Brandes heard Kracke call. "Go to the ambulance. Get the attendants out. I'll take care of things here." Brandes wondered just what that meant, but he really doubted Kracke—incredibly proficient killer as he might be—ever killed anyone when it was avoidable.

Brandes scurried down the slope and went to the ambulance's door. He loudly clicked the bolt as Kracke had instructed, but there was no need. The terror on the face of the white-clad attendant was very apparent, and Brandes suspected the driver

341

looked no better. When the man turned and looked at Brandes, his eyes widened further, and he stammered.

"Dr. . . . Dr. Brandes?" His confusion mixed with his terror.

"Yes. You're not going to be hurt. Just do what you're told. There are some things going on in Lyle that you don't know about. What we're doing is for everyone's good. Do you understand?"

The man nodded slowly, his fear gradually easing, ebbing from his features. "Sure, Doctor. Whatever you want. You, uh, won't need that thing."

"I know."

"Have them tie each other up," he heard Kracke yell. He thought about that. Maybe Kracke had a technique for that; he had a better idea.

"Get out," he said. "Both on this side." They did. "Get whatever IV Valium you've got from the back. What you don't see you can't talk about."

"Look, Doctor." The man hesitated and his head turned toward the road behind them. He seemed to weigh something in his mind. Then he said, "Dr. Brandes, I don't like this army shit. I don't know what's going on, but I've lived in Lyle a long time. I know you; I knew Peter. Look, there's another Jeep—or there was. It was about a quarter mile behind us. They must have heard those shots. I thought you should know."

Brandes stared at him.

"Quick," he said. "Back in. Drive the ambulance up to the first Jeep. *Fast.*" He grabbed the molding around the open door and hung on, only his feet and hands inside the ambulance. At that point, he knew, the attendant could have pushed him out. But he didn't. Brandes began to relax. Kracke would not have approved, he thought.

When Brandes got to Kracke he saw the two soldiers neatly trussed with their belts and the slings from their rifles.

"What the hell are you doing?" Kracke yelled.

"There's more. There's—"

Cracking, snapping gunfire sounded from behind him and to

342

one side. Brandes dropped flat, almost as fast as Kracke, and he heard slugs rat-tatting into the front fender of the ambulance and into the rear of the first Jeep. There was a grunt of pain from one of the bound soldiers. He'd been hit.

The red-orange muzzle flashes pinpointed the soldiers.

Without thinking—that, at least, was how he would remember it later—Brandes squeezed the trigger of his M-16 and held it down. A sheet of flame burst from his weapon and he swept it across the area from which he'd seen the first fire. He heard one piercing scream. Then Kracke's own firing joined his, and there was no return fire. Kracke got up and looked at Brandes.

"They were firing wildly," Brandes said as if explaining why he'd decided on wearing a red rather than yellow tie. "They might have hurt Cynthia." Kracke said nothing. Brandes was changing before his eyes; he wondered if it was that good. It was necessary, but was it fair?

Brandes turned to the attendants. "Get the Valium." One did. Brandes loaded syringes, and both men without complaint allowed themselves to be sent into a temporary semioblivion. Brandes took two more syringes to the Jeep. He needed only one. The other soldier was dead, the wild shot having struck him at the base of his skull.

"Now?" He quietly asked Kracke.

"Let's look."

They opened the rear of the ambulance. Four heavy-gauge, dark green plastic body bags lay in the ambulance. They hefted them out, what would have been a grisly task made much easier by the knowledge that they were not handling dead people.

One at a time they opened the bags. Cynthia was in the third. Brandes looked down at her. She was so pale, so beautiful. Kracke put a hand on his shoulder. "She'll be all right, Alex. Help me with the others."

"What?"

"We're going to dump them out there"—he gestured—"in the woods. With luck Lawrence will think we took all of them and won't search. Whenever the "disease" passes, they'll wake up. At least they'll have a chance. If we leave them here . . ." He didn't have to finish. Lawrence simply would have them taken to the cremation pile and the toll would climb.

They lugged the bags one at a time into the underbrush. They scattered leaves over them as best they could. Finally they were done.

"Now we get out of here, Alex. Let's get Cynthia to the car."

"What about the soldiers?"

"Hiding them, the Jeeps, the ambulance—we don't have the time, Alex. Besides, I think Lawrence knows enough by now to have started looking for us—all of us—very earnestly. We have to move, Alex. Speed can be vital."

With the apparently lifeless weight of the plastic bag dangling between them grotesquely, the two men, their rifles slung over their shoulders, occasionally were silhouetted by the still-pulsing blue emergency lights as they made their way up the embankment and back to the Mercedes.

# THIRTY-THREE

"GERRY," KRACKE SAID, HIS VOICE LOW BUT CARRY-
ing subtle severity, "I assume there is one goddamn good reason
for this."

All—Brandes, Sarah, Wismer, and Kracke—had gathered as
planned and according to Wismer's instructions in a poorly lit
large room in the rear of Andy's station. Kracke and Brandes had
not removed Cynthia from the car. Oil smells underlay the taste
of the air.

Kracke's eyes were fixed on Linda Denard.

Moving more into the light cast by one of the dangling naked
bulbs, Wismer faced Kracke. "The best, of course," Wismer
answered and smiled.

Kracke relented. From Wismer, that was, to Kracke, enough of
a reassurance. Even Wismer, though, recognized that it *barely*
was enough. *I will have to make the reasons stronger.*

Everyone, Brandes noticed, relaxed as though synchronized
with Kracke—particularly Linda Denard, since she obviously
was the source of the friction between the men.

While Brandes and Kracke had intercepted the ambulance and
had taken Cynthia, Sarah and Wismer had made two stops. One

was at the small boardinghouse where Linda Denard lived. The second was at Andy's.

The first, Wismer thought, I *know* was necessary. *I hope I never regret involving Andy.*

"We have to get into the lab one more time, Jim," Wismer said. "We have to see if Peter left *tangible* proof." His eyes sought Kracke's. They met them; they held. "We have to hope he left something," he said. Kracke nodded and looked away for a moment.

"We've got a body that will come back to life," Kracke said after the pause. "We've got the notes."

"No," Wismer shook his head. "We can't *prove* anything with the notes. And . . ." He hesitated. He had not yet seen Cynthia's body; even though he knew they had her, she—the whole situation for that matter—seemed unreal. "And," he continued, "we don't know when Cynthia will recover."

"We do!" Brandes blurted out. Everyone looked at him, surprised. "I *knew* when I saw Linda," he said and realized that that was little explanation for the others. Yet he *felt* very confident in his conclusion.

Still, his thoughts were disjointed; he *instinctively* knew he was right. He readied himself to explain and thought: *I'm explaining as much to myself as I am to them. Just to get it together. Just to have it make sense. Peter, why did you . . .*

All of them were looking at him.

"Peter," he began, "told Linda that, if she met me, she was to remind me of the three-day rule. It seemed silly then, when she first mentioned it."

He paused and looked around; naturally, only Linda was nodding.

"Uh, Alex," Kracke said and wobbled his head, not so much in encouragement as it was to say "get on with it, damn it."

"That rule and all"—Brandes shrugged slightly, unable to explain Peter so easily—"is too complicated to go into; it's something from my childhood. Mine and Peter's. Remember, Linda?"

"Yes. I remember very well. You told me it was the five-day rule. I told you Peter told me it was the three-day and said to tell you something about the corollary . . ." She looked perplexed.

"But what does that mean, Alex?" Linda pressed. "What's the big deal? One of you forgot how long you could keep a cream-cheese sandwich. You were kids."

"No," Brandes said. "Look, it's one of those you-had-to-be-there things. We never forgot the rule. *Never.*"

"I'm not following anyway," she said. "Keeping the damn sandwich according to your rules is only a time difference of . . ."

"That's *it*. The difference in time. The *corollary*. Don't forget that. Peter was telling us the whole story—at least the parts that matter to us right now. He *knew* I wouldn't forget our rule—and he knew that by screwing it up I'd listen closer to what he had to tell us . . ."

*God, Peter, I listened. I really did listen. But I listened so late. But you were so damned difficult. They were right. You told your story in—triplicate. Do you get the blame for this one, Peter, or do I?*

Brandes looked around him at still-blank faces. "We used to throw food out after it had been in the refrigerator for five days. It was a standing . . . routine . . . as we grew up," he patiently explained.

"When Peter told Linda about it, he changed it to *three days and mentioned the corollary.* Within three days of being pronounced dead they wake up. *Don't you see?*"

All displayed different . . . curious glances, yet . . .

Wismer was the first.

"Yes," he said. "Makes sense. I've been working on the mechanism of the thing in my head. This makes sense, fits in.

"Peter sure as hell picked a screwball way to tell us—but then none of his messages have been exactly light reading. Instead of the food going bad in five days—read *dead*—things do the opposite, the corollary, in three days." Wismer paused. "I don't

347

give a shit about respect for the dead. Someday, Peter, I'll get you back for this one."

Wismer thought of his own difficulty with the "Ben Casey" symbols. On the TV show, there were the symbols for man, woman, birth, death, and infinity. Peter's notes and the side of the Shakespeare Festival building, had read: *Man, Woman, Birth, Death, Birth.*

*Oh, yes, Peter. If there's a life after death, someday I'll get you for all this.*

"It might make sense to you," Kracke said, "and I hope it does. But all I care about is getting out of here." He paused, then asked outright the question that had been bothering him since he and Alex had joined with Sarah and Wismer—and Linda, as it turned out. "About *her*, Gerry?"

"You're right, Jim," Wismer said. He waved Brandes to silence.

They could discuss the disease later.

"Linda knows the combination to the inner lab," he explained to Kracke.

"Shit," Kracke said. He damned well knew what that meant. Linda Denard was blackmailing them.

*You want the combination, you take me with you.* Wismer did not have to explain further.

Kracke pictured Wismer and Sarah going to her boardinghouse and talking to her. Wismer would not have given away anything he had not *had* to, Kracke was very certain of that. If Wismer had felt it necessary to tell the woman about the disease, he had to have been convinced that she would not cooperate otherwise— and that she and access to the lab were vitally necessary.

Kracke had not expected that much "toughness" in the lab technician. He looked at her again, wondering.

*Still, she knows she's facing death. That can make most people tough.*

He respected Wismer; he would refrain from voicing any doubts. *But she was still yet another person . . .*

"You have some plan," Kracke said.

"Andy has helped—a lot," he said. "He's talking right now to his grandson—or great-grandson . . ."

"How?"

"Radio. Don't worry. It's CB and your best cryptographers wouldn't understand a damned word of it."

"Fine."

"His grandson will have a truck for us on the other side of the mountain behind the lab." He paused. "We have to get the proof from the lab, with Linda's help, and get over the mountain."

No one at that time said anything else. Neither did anyone move. The mostly vacant room, stone-walled and able to echo slight sounds, was tomb quiet.

"Not much to ask, Gerry," Kracke said.

When he finally smiled, everyone relaxed. But he added, "You do realize that the chances of pulling this off have progressively gotten slimmer and fast are approaching non-existent?"

"Tell me," Sarah suddenly asked, and Brandes realized Wismer must have filled her in on Lawrence and the army, "what are our chances if we stay *within the quarantine?*"

"That's simple," Kracke said. "They're simply nonexistent."

"Seems to settle it," Sarah said. Everyone seemed to agree.

Wismer went into the next room and returned several minutes later, smiling. "Andy wanted to drive us to the lab," he said. "He figured if our cars were found here, Lawrence wouldn't know where the hell we were . . ."

"We can't . . ." Brandes began. Wismer looked at him, surprised it was he who spoke up.

"No," Wismer said. "We can't. He can't be left here if Lawrence suspects him. But the old man's stubborn. He's following us. We drive halfway and leave the cars. He takes us in his truck to the lab and leaves us. Andy's promised he'll go home." He smiled again. "I'm pretty sure I believe him. From there on, we're on our own."

"This," Kracke said, "is going to be a hell of a long night."

Once on the way, with Kracke, Sarah, and Cynthia in the lead car, Wismer filled in Brandes as best he could about the disease. Linda sat in the rear seat, listening intently but saying nothing. Brandes began with a question.

"Just what have you figured out about Peter's work, Gerry?"

"Nothing I can prove," Wismer said. "I've got a theory. Peter created a virus for use as a vehicle. It carried a new genetic code to the cells of a bacterial colony and altered the bacteria, creating the organisms that separated out the gold.

"The virus, though, *also* would transmit altered nucleic acid to cells of living animals—higher animals. That was what he was working on.

"Somehow his virus suppresses vital functions to the point they become undetectable.

"The lowered metabolism needs damned little oxygen—and I'd guess that little bit was supplied by the organism itself.

"It somehow manages a low-energy separation of the body's water into hydrogen and oxygen. The hydrogen diffuses through the skin. I figured that out after talking to Lawrence from the checkpoint. He told me one of the graves 'blew up' and killed one of his men and that he suspected people were booby-trapping the graves.

"They're not, of course. The soldier somehow ignited the waste hydrogen and—poof."

"But the machinery we use," Linda said. "No brain waves— they're *dead*."

Wismer snorted. "Really? This may be something to give the organ transplant people sleepless nights. We can detect tiny currents today we couldn't thirty years ago. So thirty years ago someone could have been pronounced 'brain dead' and have his heart and liver and kidneys snatched—if we'd had the transplant technology then.

"But what happens thirty years *from now* when we can detect even tinier impulses? No, Linda, I don't think people are declared dead because they *have no* brain waves. They're declared dead because we *can't measure them.* Yet."

"That takes some thinking about," Brandes said.

"Yeah. But let's get back to our immediate situation. Which is very, very dangerous, I might emphasize, and we don't have a hell of a lot of time.

"The point is, Cynthia waking up in three days isn't a guarantee we'll have proof. We've got the army chasing us—we're dangerous and armed as far as those soldiers are concerned.

"It better not, but what if it took us three days to get where we're going? She'd be up and around—and no proof of anything. And if we're caught *before* she wakes up, they'll burn her because *to all our instruments she is dead*.

"We have to get something a lot more tangible, and if Peter left it, it's in the lab. And"—he gestured backward, toward Linda—"this young astute negotiator has the inner combination but isn't talking unless we take her."

Wismer wanted to stare at her sternly, reproachfully. He couldn't.

*Wouldn't I have done the same thing?*

In the lead car, Sarah and Kracke had just rounded a curve. Kracke looked into his rear-view mirror, making certain Brandes was keeping up. For about a quarter-mile after the turn, the road was relatively straight, and he also briefly saw the lights of Andy's truck.

*Plucky old man. Someday I owe him a drink.*

He and Sarah also had been discussing the twist in events that included Linda Denard in their already—for Kracke—outrageously large group.

Kracke clearly was very unhappy. He grunted. "I *understand*, I guess, blackmail of a sort. A happy thought, no.

"Sarah, I know damned well I could get through this quarantine alone. I'm ninty percent sure I could get through with Alex—that was the plan, anyway. But with all of you—and a *body*?" He shook his head.

"And then we take some kid's truck? Lawrence isn't going to just sit on his hands if we *do* break his lines. He'll use some story—hell, he can tell the *truth* about his soldiers getting shot—and get police help."

"That's why *we* have to be armed, Jim," Sarah said. "With answers and with what we need to back them up. Gerry's right about that."

"And," Kracke asked, "what if Alex's brother *didn't* leave anything in the lab?"

"We should be there soon," she answered.

Lawrence had slammed down the receiver of his telephone.

*A damned disease isn't enough. One that's manmade isn't enough. Now this.*

He had been on the telephone—on what he fervently hoped was a secure line—with his direct superior in the Pentagon.

The brigadier had not immediately been available; Lawrence had had to call to . . . . somewhere. It had been a "somewhere" other than his home, too, Lawrence knew.

The general had not liked that.

*Hell with him.*

Lawrence, of course, had *said* no such thing.

As quickly as possible after ordering Wismer and Kracke arrested, he had reached the brigadier, apologized however insincerely for the inconvenience, and had relayed the catastrophic news—and, practically holding his breath, informed his superior of his own field decision.

There had been a long pause. A very long—Lawrence thought—pause.

*He's weighing. He's looking over his shoulder. He's deciding just who's ass—along with his own, of course—will be chopped. If any have to be.*

There lay Lawrence's real hope. Perhaps none *had* to be. He had explained that he intended to make certain no one with knowledge of the disease's true characteristics be around to speak. It had been a drastic step.

But with Wismer and Kracke in custody, it had seemed possible. He would find out who else knew—Brandes, perhaps he woman reporter. Perhaps Shortell. If necessary, all could be handled.

And the burning would continue.

Wismer and Kracke had correctly guessed Lawrence's final plan. The Dorfman serum was due in soon. It would be administered. It would "work."

Lawrence didn't give a damn if he would be causing the victims to be injected with sterile water. The Dorfman serum would work—and the victims eventually would regain consciousness.

*Then* the cremations could stop. Then and only then. To do so sooner would be a personal and political disaster far outweighing the personal tragedy of Lyle, the colonel reasoned. He could not even allow himself to consider the ramifications if the public ever found out that the army had burned living people.

If the public ever found out *he* had burned living people.

At that point, he had not considered what would happen to him or his "bosses" if word ever got out that he knowingly continued to burn living people. Not at that point . . .

Lawrence tried to examine his own feelings. *I should feel guilty. I don't.*

He doubted if those above him ever felt guilty, either. They certainly had, in their time, ordered more men to their deaths than were involved here in Lyle.

*The circumstances were different.*

But a life was a life, he told himself. *People are like apples and oranges. You can't put one next to the other and come up with "two." One person is no more nor no less valuable than a thousand.*

What mattered in his work, Lawrence thought, was the outlook that held one was not *more* valuable than a thousand. Hell, if you can kill one, you can kill a hundred with no more guilt . . .

The brigadier had gotten back to him within a half-hour.

And had agreed with his solution.

Lawrence had taken gulps of air in relief. He wondered just

how far up the general had had to go with the problem and thought it likely that the decision tree had thinned considerably by the time final confirmation of his course of action had been made.

Lawrence would not at all be surprised, though, if it had reached into the White House.

*Someone is making some very major decisions. Not like them, really . . .*

It had, of course, been made clear to Lawrence that backing for his action was unofficial in that *he* was the sole man responsible for making certain that no one ever knew. Lawrence had felt quite confident that he could promise that.

And then Kracke and Wismer had escaped.

Lawrence had felt a lurching sensation in his guts when news of the checkpoint massacre had come in. For several seconds he had almost lost control of himself.

*I've never been closer to my own, my personal, disaster. Never.*

Lawrence had successfully resisted his urge to shout orders. As calmly as possible, he had called in his troops from the graves and cremation site and had redeployed them to the other checkpoints and to places he considered it likely Kracke or Wismer might have gone.

They had not been at Wismer's house, and his men had not been able to determine if they had gone there. Another patrol had gone to the hospital. Lawrence personally had called Shortell, just to "chat." The doctor had not seemed any more concerned than would be expected in a physician dealing with a deadly epidemic. He had not, Lawrence thankfully noted, sounded like someone who had just been informed he'd been pronouncing living people dead and had been dispatching them to a flaming field.

Still, Lawrence had kept some men stationed near the hospital.

What had bothered him in those early reports was that none of his men had seen Brandes or the reporter.

*If they also knew and had fled . . .*

That, he knew, only could compound his difficulties.

He had taken the precaution of giving ambulances an escort and of sending a patrol to the Futures lab. Several other men stayed just out of sight in the shadows across the deserted street from the Tower Hotel.

Everyone else doubled up on the perimeter. No one, Lawrence vowed, would get past his checkpoints.

Kracke worried him more than the others. He was too capable. *If they try anything, they will hide and try to send him through for help.*

He was quite confident that his men eventually would find anyone hiding within the quarantine's perimeter.

And then he had received news of the ambush of the ambulance. More of his men were dead. He allowed news of that to spread through his command—quickly. He would not at all mind having his men slightly trigger-happy when it came to Wismer and Kracke—and perhaps Brandes and Sarah Allenberg, if necessary.

"First Sergeant," he had said to his ranking noncom—the oldest member of his command and, since the discovery of the Jeep bearing Lieutenant Knotts's body, the closest he had to an officer he could trust.

"Yes, sir."

"I want a search of that area around the ambulance. I want to know what the hell happened to the bodies that were in it."

He could not imagine Kracke and—whoever—carrying off four bodies.

*But why else would they attack an ambulance?*

He had no certain answer, and uncertainty unsettled the colonel.

"Yes, sir. And if we find any?"

Lawrence managed a look of mild surprise. "Why, First Sergeant, those corpses could still be highly contagious.

"Burn them, of course."

\* \* \*

Kracke's attention was caught by the repeated blinking of high beams in his rear-view mirror.

"What is it?" Sarah asked.

"It looks like Andy signaling us. Maybe he sees something behind him. These roads twist so much we might not be able to see."

"If that's the case, though, he wouldn't want us to stop. I mean, if he sees soldiers behind us . . ."

"You're right. But he must want something."

Kracke slowed and then stopped on a narrow shoulder. Behind him he saw Brandes do the same. Wismer got out of the other car and waited while the truck lumbered up and stopped. He walked around to the driver's side and spoke at some length with Andy.

Finally, shaking his head, he walked to the car Kracke was driving.

"What is it, Gerry?"

"That old goat," Wismer began, his voice low and grumbling. "He says just ahead is the best place for us to leave the cars and move to the truck."

"We're not halfway there yet, Gerry. I don't like having him with us any longer than we have to. We can't take him with us . . ."

"*He* knows that, Jim. But he's also right. I hate to admit it, but there's a small clearing ahead. We can get the cars at least fifty feet off the road there. It really is the best place. Once we passed that last crossroad, we passed the last place we can turn before we get to the lab, anyway."

"All right." Kracke still was reluctant, but he also admired the old man's courage. Andy knew very well he could not hope to cross the mountain with them.

*And if he is associated with us and caught in the quarantine . . . Lawrence will allow no survivors.*

They continued another few hundred yards and saw that the old man had been right. Just beyond the next curve, the shoulder widened considerably on their left. Kracke and Brandes pulled the cars onto it and as far from the road as possible. When they

ot out, Kracke looked at them. He wasn't satisfied by any
means—a sharp patrol would spot the cars—but it was the best
they would find on the road. At any other point, even a half-
asleep soldier could not help but notice the vehicles.

Andy had pulled his truck to a point between the cars by then.
He didn't get out, just waited.

With Brandes's help, Kracke took Cynthia's body and gently
placed it in the rear of the open truck. He returned to the car and
took the rifles on his next trip.

For Linda and Wismer, it was the first time they'd seen the
dark green plastic of the body bag, black in the limited light
except when the men passed in front of the car and truck
headlights. Its very presence underlined the desperation of their
situation in a way nothing else possibly could have. Everyone was
silent as they also got into the back. Only Kracke took a front seat
next to Andy.

"Shotgun, eh?" the old man grinned.

Kracke smiled. "Damned sight better," Kracke said and hefted
the M-16. "Same general idea, though. Let's just hope I don't
need it."

"Son, only time you ever gotta hope never comes is a time you
need something like that and *don't* have one." He nodded his
head sagely. Kracke smiled in the darkness, and Andy's truck
regained the road.

They bounced along the road, no more than six miles from the
Futures lab at that point. Kracke and Wismer had planned to stop
the truck at least a quarter-mile from the lab and approach on
foot.

Carrying Cynthia would not make the walk easier, but Kracke
had pointed out that, since they were going to carry her over a
mountain anyway, a short walk on relatively level ground should
not be too great a hardship.

Lawrence was beginning to worry Kracke. The colonel had
had enough time to take some steps.

*What steps?*

He could guess some. He assumed Wismer's house had been

357

visited. Perhaps the hospital also. There was no doubt in his mind that the checkpoints and the foot patrols between them had been reinforced considerably by then.

The nagging question was, of course, whether Lawrence had stationed men at the lab. Kracke had not mentioned any of this to the others. If they simply could not get into the lab, he had decided, he would have to convince Wismer that further proof might be *desirable*—but *unobtainable*.

They then could skirt the Futures' area and continue on the precipitous slope that led up the mountain.

He hoped.

"Tango patrol to base," a voice crackled over the radio behind Lawrence's desk. He had been sitting there ever since Wismer had called from the checkpoint.

By then, Lawrence had received reports from several of his patrols, and he was feeling more uneasy as time passed.

Brandes and the woman were nowhere to be found. He only could assume that they had been contacted by Wismer and Kracke and now knew the truth about the disease.

That, of course, made it imperative they also die. And that, he thought, could complicate things for him very considerably. Killing men who had murdered his soldiers could easily enough be explained, but the woman . . . a *reporter* . . .

*Still, a way will be found. It has to be. Something will develop.*

That two more persons were likely to know of the disease's real character was upsetting in itself, though. He thought of the brigadier and dreaded more than anything having to report that the number of enemies with the damaging information probably had doubled.

Under no circumstances did he intend to tell the general *that* until all were dead. He most certainly had no intention of telling his superior of his *plans* to kill Allenberg's daughter. That would have to be a *fait accompli*.

*That old paper pusher'd shit his drawers if he knew beforehand.*

He turned to the radio.

"This is Colonel Lawrence," he said. He hated answering the amned thing himself, but he'd sent his radio operator out of his makeshift headquarters soon after he had received Wismer's ramatic call. It was far better to have to handle the telephone nd radio himself than even to allow the possibility that nowledge of what was happening spread to one of his own men. Had it, Lawrence would have had to have arranged for that man's eath, too. That, he thought, could be complicated—and his ituation was far too complicated already.

"Sir," the voice said. "This is Corporal Dennis. One of my nen spotted some cars alongside a road here. They're well back, ooks like they're supposed to be hidden."

Lawrence felt adrenaline surge. "How many cars?"

"Two, sir. One a Mercedes."

*Damn. Brandes—and probably the woman—know.*

"What road, Corporal?"

The junior noncom gave him map coordinates, and Lawrence ad to get up and walk to the wall to locate the position on the arge-scale chart pinned there.

He felt an excitement build.

"Corporal," he said, flicking the transmit button on the desk-mounted microphone, "from what direction did your patrol ome before you found the cars?"

"From the east, sir."

*Got them! Goddamn it, I've got them!*

They had to be between his patrol and the Futures lab. And hat road was the only way to and from the lab.

*What could they want there?*

Lawrence considered sending his patrol along the road, queezing his prey between it and the men he had stationed at the ab.

But the purpose of the enemy was unclear. That bothered awrence. He was too good a soldier to not want to understand is enemy's intentions.

*They should simply be running. They should have been at one of the checkpoints—or between them—by now. They aren't running . . .*

*And if what's in the lab is important enough for them to endanger their chances of escape, it's damned well important enough for me to find out what it is . . .*

"Corporal," he said.

"Yes, sir."

"I want you to stay right where you are. I want you to deploy your men in the undergrowth alongside that road. The men we're seeking now have, I believe, several more allies. We want them all.

"I do not, repeat do *not* want you to stop them as they reach you. I want a full report first on just how many of them pass you after they get back to their cars. Call me then and prepare to follow them at a safe distance—undetected.

"Remember this, corporal, those people have killed at least five of our men so far. I'll bring up another patrol from the other side. I want them in a crossfire. Under the circumstances, I don't want you men taking unnecessary chances. They took the weapons from the men they killed, Corporal. Do I make myself clear?"

"Yes, sir. Very, sir."

"Good."

Lawrence flicked a knob on his radio console and tuned to the frequency used by the patrol he'd sent to guard the lab.

"Corporal Fox, here, sir."

"Corporal," Lawrence said. "The people we are looking for are armed and very dangerous, and I have reason to believe they have reinforcements. Reports indicate they are heading for the lab."

"We'll be ready for them, sir."

"No, you won't, Corporal. You'll get your men the hell out of there and move west on the road leading from the lab.

"You will allow them to pass unmolested toward the lab and again allow them to pass when they leave the lab.

"Tango patrol will be waiting further down the road, and they will be joined by another unit. When the time comes, Corporal,

I'll tell you. When I do, remember that these people have killed at least five of our men. Understand?"

"Yes, sir!"

Lawrence sat back and grinned to himself. He had them. They would have to take the road back from the lab and retrieve their cars. Then, he thought, they intend to make a run for a checkpoint.

*They'll never get to one. And I'll have whatever was so important to them to make them risk going to the lab . . .*

# THIRTY-FOUR

ANDY'S TRUCK RATTLED AS IF EVERY BOLT AND rivet in its frame had worked itself loose. Kracke had—and he saw that Andy had noticed and had grinned—adjusted his side mirror so he could see traffic behind him.

So far, there was none.

Kracke hoped it remained that way. He shrugged off a tickling sensation. He maintained his frequent vigilance and checked the mirror while trying to convince himself that such *feelings* could just *be* feelings and nothing more. He kept looking into the mirror, but each time saw only rows of trees sweeping away from him, those lighted only by the taillights of Andy's truck.

In the rear of the truck rode the others, with Cynthia.

Kracke never would have given any of them his bottom-line estimate of their real chances. He certainly did not feel confident.

"You can't take me, can you?" Andy's throaty voice interrupted Kracke's thoughts; and Kracke thought, *Not now, Andy, not now.*

Instead of asking to join them, the old man laughed. "Don't worry so damned much," he said. "I wasn't asking for a ticket. I just asked a question."

"No," Kracke answered honestly, "we can't take you. Andy, I wish we could. But our chances . . ."

"Shut up, young man," Andy said, touched his brake, slid around a turn. He by then was only a mile or so from the lab. Kracke shut up.

Andy continued. "Like I said, I wasn't asking for a ticket. I had a point to make. I'm an old son of a bitch, and you just damned well admitted you can't get *me* out of here.

"I've been wondering about what you're going to do with the one that can't walk at all."

He jerked his thumb to the rear. Kracke knew what he meant.

Privately he had worried about the same thing.

The truck jumped, thumped. Andy—and Kracke—ignored it.

"Take this, Jim." Andy used his right arm to reach just behind the seat and lift a canvas bag over it and into Kracke's lap. Kracke did not open it but moved his hands over its longtime grease-soiled surface.

He did not know what was inside it; he could only guess. Andy obviously had more to say.

Kracke held an inordinate, possibly—but he did not think so—respect for those who had achieved old age, or at least an age older than he himself had.

"Just carry it, Jim," Andy said. Kracke was struck mostly by the old man's use suddenly of his first name. He felt as if he had been accepted.

*And, to be honest, I feel honored.*

The bag's contents could wait until later; he placed it on the floorboards between his legs.

Kracke did not want to stop too close to the lab; with the vibrating and clanking truck, he certainly wanted as much distance as he could get.

*Who might be there now?*

Kracke knew that the lab had a token security system, and most of that only simple electronics. It probably, he thought—and here he unwittingly agreed with the late Peter Brandes—drew less attention that way.

He reasoned that there might be some CDC people still working there. It was late, but Lyle's disease knew no clock, no measure of light and dark, sunrise, sunset. They, like the disease itself, might be working around the clock.

Brandes and Linda, at least, *belonged* there. Even if doctors and technicians were working into the night, there should be no suspicions.

But after they got out of the lab, the success of the entire plan, the escape—the survival—depended on him.

He knew that. Everyone else also knew it.

He doubted Sarah or Wismer—perhaps not even Alex Brandes—would blame him if it ended in failure. It was not that kind of dependency. Kracke simply was the *best* chance in a situation that offered very few chances.

"Andy," he said, "I think I would like you to stop about a hundred or so yards from here, if you know a convenient spot."

Even on the rutted road the truck had been making good progress, but still there would be a considerable trek to the lab.

"No problem," the old man answered. "It's a little more than that, but close enough. Good place to park."

Kracke shot him a sharp look.

"Good place to turn around, too, I hope?"

Andy grinned.

"I said I'd go home. I will. Yes, it's also a good place to turn around."

Kracke nodded and said nothing more while the old truck bounced on the road. Then, he thought, it was time to ask Andy the details of the arrangements he and Wismer had made. He had waited long enough.

He did not doubt Wismer's ability—nor, he decided—the old man's. But he *had* to know.

"What about your grandson?"

"Great-grandson," Andy corrected. "He'll be there. You just get that . . . group . . . over the top and he'll meet you on the other side. His truck's newer than mine. You'll like it." He chuckled. "Lot more comfortable."

"Andy," Kracke hesitated, "why—"

"Shut the hell up and get ready."

Andy didn't say anything for several seconds, then broke his own silence. "Look, Jim, there's some things gotta be done. You think I'm risking my life and my own kin. You're damn right, too. But I had a talk with that boy. And I don't need to talk to myself. Just take what help's offered. Don't ask any questions. Okay?"

The instrument lights from the dash were weak yet clearly outlined Andy's profile. The strong, straight nose focused attention. The low-level light, unable to illuminate the skin itself, failed to give any indication of Andy's age.

*I know his skin is wrinkled. But the profile says strength. Maybe when I'm that old . . .*

"I sure as shit hope if the Russians invade they try it through New England," Kracke said quietly. "They won't stand a goddamn chance."

He fell silent, and by then, they had reached the spot.

"All out," Andy said. He grinned his crooked grin. Kracke felt true affection for him.

The army patrol had had to move quickly after receiving Lawrence's orders. The soldiers had made their way, cautiously, about 150 feet from the sides of the road, paralleling it, and only had had to drop flat once—as Andy's truck passed.

An arm and hand signal, the familiar "follow me," and they moved again for another quarter mile and then took up positions.

They waited.

Andy turned off his lights and then the truck's engine as they reached the clearing. It was, Kracke saw, more of an indentation in the growth that bordered the road.

Kracke did not rule out the possibility that Lawrence already had dispatched soldiers to stand watch at the Futures lab. To announce their presence to soldiers . . . Kracke did not wish to consider all that that would mean.

Allenberg and Jason waited, and he must reach them. *That* lay ahead, seemingly immeasurably far ahead.

But Kracke used that goal as a personal focus. By being able to think of a goal so very far away, those closer—no matter how difficult they might be to attain—seemed less threatening.

He got out of the truck's cab and took the canvas bag with him. He walked around the front of the truck and stopped next to Andy.

Brandes and Sarah already had jumped to the ground. Wismer had hold of one end of the body bag. Brandes reached and grabbed the other and together they managed to lower Cynthia to the ground. Wismer then turned and helped Linda down.

The night around them was very quiet, apart from the expected "noises" of a New Hampshire night—simply the sounds of animals and insects. Kracke welcomed them not for their lulling peacefulness, but because their presence was at least some assurance that his party did not have the type of "company" it was avoiding. For him, the lack of natural sound was more to be feared than the hissing of a nearby snake.

"Time for you to go," Kracke said to Andy, who had not left the cab.

"I know."

"Thanks."

"Take this," the old man said and handed Kracke a walkie-talkie. "It's old, but it works."

Kracke took the radio. He did not think he would ever use it—that would mean talking either to Andy or to his great-grandson, and he certainly had no intention of doing *that*—but Andy's giving it to him also was confirmation for Kracke that the old man really did intend to turn around and go home. Kracke was pleased at that thought.

"Good luck, Jim. The best."

"Thank you, Andy."

There seemed much more he could have said: those things spoken best by not saying them at all. He turned and went to the others.

"Alex, take one end," he said and gestured to Cynthia.

*It's so hard to think of this as Cynthia.*

Although Kracke was much younger, and without question in better physical condition, Wismer did not wait for him to take the other end. He simply bent over and did so himself. Kracke's place was ahead, unencumbered.

Kracke, Brandes, and Wismer had rifles. Sarah carried a pistol. Linda alone was unarmed. In addition, Wismer and Kracke had sidearms. Kracke also carried the canvas bag Andy had given him.

Kracke motioned. Their long walk began.

Brandes and Wismer managed to carry the body bag without stopping. But the ground was level, and they knew the next leg of their journey would be much more difficult. Already, their arms and shoulders ached.

Both men occasionally transferred his end from one hand to the other and did so without stopping.

Kracke, about ten yards ahead, hissed and held up one arm. They were close enough to the lab so that its perimeter lights and parking lot lights easily silhouetted his hand.

Everyone stopped. Wismer and Brandes gladly lowered Cynthia to the ground.

"I'll have to go in," Wismer said. "With Linda, obviously. I think it would be a good idea to take Alex, too."

"That leaves the . . . three . . . of us," Kracke said. "Gerry, I'm not comfortable. Sarah and I can bring Cynthia around that clearing." He gestured toward the far side of the lab, the side nearest the beginning of the steeper slope of the mountain.

"It simply is fact that she and I could not take her much farther. You don't have much time. I'm not sold entirely on this anyway, Gerry. It's that I know you. I trust you enough to believe this is important. But there are other important things here, Gerry.

"The truth about what's going on here has to get out—or a best attempt has to be made.

367

"Adrian and Jason have to be retaken.

"If you don't find anything in five minutes, Gerry, I'm going over that hill."

Wismer hesitated and then said only, "Five minutes."

He nodded. He knew that if Kracke decided he had to move he would take Sarah. He also knew Kracke would leave Cynthia. Undoubtedly he would do his best to shroud her, to cover her with leaves, but there was no question that just he and Sarah could carry Cynthia over that mountain.

Wismer looked up. It was not much of a mountain, he thought. The Appalachians had been old and eroding when the Rockies were upward-thrusting newcomers, with dizzying heights and sharper, cleaner, younger edges. Still, for them, this was a mountain.

*Definition of a mountain: any damned hill big enough you aren't sure you can get over it.*

He turned to Brandes and Linda.

"Let's go," he said.

*Little chance. Little chance.*

All three passed into the lab without any difficulty at all. They belonged, Wismer reminded himself.

While all of them were well-versed in the procedure, the smock-donning in the first airlock took half a minute.

"Dr. Brandes, Linda," said a surprised technician. "Late."

"Yeah, Howie," Linda said. "Late, just like you."

"Then again," he said, "I guess you have to be here."

Neither Linda nor Brandes understood that exactly, but simply nodded.

"We're going into the other lab," Linda said.

"You're the only one who can," he said and grinned. "I don't ask too much. I keep more girlfriends that way. Once it even kept a wife for a while."

Linda laughed, and Brandes smiled. Wismer spent the time sweeping his eyes around the lab. There were four other white-coated persons working. From their postures and from glimpses he occasionally caught of their faces, they were working on established routines.

Brandes pulled on Linda's arm, and she broke away from the technician, who went back to his work. They walked across the room to the door to Peter's inner lab.

"I guess it doesn't matter if you watch," Linda said. "Once you're in, it doesn't matter if you know the combination or not. You'll have what you want, and I'll just have to trust you."

"We said we'd take you, Linda. We will. Besides, I'm not sure if going or staying is the more dangerous for you."

"I'll decide that," she said and almost pouted. Then she lifted her right hand and drew a series of semimusical tones from the touch pad on the wall. There was a click.

She pushed at the door, and immediately all were aware of the sound of a compressor starting up, working to maintain the lower inside pressure. All three stepped through.

"How many times have you opened the door?" Wismer asked.

"For the CDC, twice. A few other times, like when Alex first came to the lab. Not more than four or five times."

Wismer nodded and began a survey of the apparatus on the counters.

"Gerry," Brandes asked, "what the hell are we looking for?"

"Something Peter left. I *knew* Peter. Damn, Alex, in some ways I knew your brother better than you did." Brandes did not dispute that.

"All the books that were in here we already have gone through."

"Not a book, Alex. A folded-up sheet of paper stuck somewhere, maybe—but I hope not. Now just *look*."

Most bottles and vials carried standard labels identifying them as reagents or solvents. Brandes felt totally lost and knew Linda felt much the same.

Wismer looked at his watch, said nothing, and began to look through the contents of the wall-mounted cabinet above Peter's main workbench.

369

"These are things you'd expect here, Gerry," Brandes complained.

"Of course." Wismer paused and looked patiently—as patiently as he could—at Brandes. "But think, Alex. *Think*. Peter wasn't going to draw a skull-and-crossbones, for Christ's sake. Look for the bottle where he misspelled alcohol or something. Look for *something*."

As he spoke, his hands and eyes had continued their search along the shelf, his eyes darting from container to container. Only when he stopped talking to Brandes did one of the labels register in his mind.

*Got it. Damn it, I've got it. I know I've got it.*

"Let's get out of here," he said.

"What? . . ."

"Just go. Jim isn't going to wait much longer. He meant that. And I found what I want."

Linda and Brandes were disoriented by the sudden change in Wismer but followed him. They sealed the inner lab door; again compressors rumbled. Without speaking, they walked with him to the initial airlock, entered, and began removing their coats.

"Linda," Wismer said, "your friend Howie wasn't in the outer lab just now. He's probably out here. Go ahead and run interference, will you? Say all the goodnights and that crap. I think he's a little more interested in you than in us, but we can't let that slow us down."

Linda nodded and finished ridding herself of the lab clothing; Wismer was still working at it. She went on ahead. Brandes finished removing his own covering and helped Wismer.

They threw all the clothing into the "contaminated" bag.

"Alex," Wismer said, "put this in your pocket." He handed him a small glass container. Brandes was confused; his eyes showed it. "You're younger, Alex. Just put it away. It's what we need."

"How do you know?"

"Read the label," Wismer said.

Brandes lifted the bottle—he'd already had it halfway into his pocket. In it he could see a white powder—no, he thought, white crystals. One word had been written on the red-bordered paper label: *Juliet*.

"Did you find what you wanted?" Kracke asked as they rejoined him and Sarah at the far end of the lab's property.

"Enough for what I need to do, I hope," Wismer said.

Kracke grunted, said nothing more. He gestured toward Brandes and the plastic body bag. Brandes picked up one end. Kracke then said, "This isn't going to be easy. Sarah, you'll have to go ahead. Find the easiest path for us. Linda, stay just behind me and Alex. Gerry," he said and handed one of the M-16s to the older man, "you watch the rear. Let's do this."

The lab's lights diminished quickly as they moved. The first few hundred yards gradually sloped, but when Kracke and Brandes stopped to rest, to allow their burden to rest, they looked ahead and saw that the ground rose quickly ahead of them.

"What's it like up there?" Kracke asked.

"It's worse for a while. The state was going to make some sort of park at the top once, so it would have been possible to drive up eventually. It's been many years since I walked this."

They could hear Sarah returning; she had been only about ten or twenty yards ahead.

"There's no way around this steep part," she said and sagged onto a large boulder. Even unencumbered the climb had exhausted her. "After that, though, it gets level again. At least more level. I think I can see a place where somebody once started to grade it."

Brandes nodded. "That's where the project began and just about where it ended."

"Alex, take the front," Kracke said, and hitched his weapon higher on one shoulder and Andy's canvas bag on the other. He moved to the other end of the body bag. Brandes took hold, but soon had to ease Cynthia back down as he sought a handhold in the splintered rock ahead of him.

The next ten feet were very steeply inclined, as Sarah had said. Repeatedly, he had to lower Cynthia and find a handhold, reach with his free hand, lift the bag up a few precious inches.

Behind him Kracke did something similar.

Brandes had just stopped for the fifth or sixth time; he looked up. Halfway, he thought. After that short stretch, it should be easy. For a while.

*And after that?*

He stretched out his left hand again, ready to grab the plastic loop at the bag's end, when a crackling sound interrupted him. He stopped and looked about. Everyone froze in place, only their eyes wildly sweeping around them.

"Radio," Kracke said. "Damn."

"What radio?" That was Wismer.

"Andy gave it to me."

"Wonderful."

Kracke lifted it from the clip that had fastened it to his belt. He adjusted the volume, and the crackling subsided greatly.

"Jim," a voice came from the speaker. Kracke pressed the transmit button and said, "Yes?"

"No time to be fancy," Andy's voice crackled. "I just passed a Jeep off the side of the road. There's soldiers out here."

Brandes felt his stomach clench. Kracke's face grew rigid. If there were soldiers waiting, Lawrence knew their group had been to the lab. He knew they still were within the quarantine. And he expected them to return the way they had come, possibly to reclaim their cars.

But they were going the other way. Up, Kracke thought, was the only hope they now had. He looked at Brandes and at the climb ahead of them.

*How long will Lawrence wait?*

"Did anyone see how many people are with you?" he asked Andy. Maybe, he thought, Lawrence thinks we're in the back of the truck. Maybe he's setting a trap.

"They were off the road. I doubt they could see anything. I'm just going to keep moving."

"That's all you can do, my friend. That's all anybody can do. Thanks."

"Sure thing. I'll be fine."

*Like hell. If Lawrence really thinks you're involved with us . . .*

"Sir, Tango."

"Yes," Lawrence answered.

"A truck just went past us. We let it."

"Good," the colonel said.

Before the soldier could report that he'd seen only one person in the truck, Lawrence hastily had twisted the knob that changed the frequency of his radio.

"Corporal?" he asked, speaking to the other patrol, the one still farther down the road.

"Yes, sir?"

"They're coming toward you. The truck is between Tango and you. I don't want it to pass you."

"No, sir. I mean, it won't, sir," the corporal said without hesitation.

Kracke started to reclip the radio to his belt and with the other hand reached for his end of Cynthia's body bag. Not one moment could be wasted now, he thought.

Before he managed either, though, the radio crackled again. Andy's voice again claimed their attention, but with a new urgency.

"Jim! More of them."

Kracke froze. For seconds he only could picture the old man driving his truck along that dark road with squads of soldiers not only behind but in front of him.

"What's happening?" he hissed into the walkie-talkie.

"Jim, they're going to know you're not in this truck, that's for damn sure. This time they ain't hiding. This time . . ."

There was a repetitive sputtering sound and then silence.

373

Kracke slowly lowered the radio to his side, his hand hanging limply. Then he shook himself to rid his mind of the thought that suddenly was dominant.

*Lawrence . . . For Andy, Lawrence.*

"Alex," he said, more loudly than he'd intended. "Grab the bag. Bring Cynthia back down here."

"Sir," the corporal reported, "there was only an old man in the truck. No one else."

Lawrence said nothing for several moments, then rose and walked to the wall-mounted map.

*Not possible. Not possible. It's all uphill that way. Still . . .*

He picked up the radio microphone. He should have time, he thought, if they hadn't already made much progress.

*Just in case . . .*

He called the sergeant in charge of the road checkpoint best situated.

"Sir?"

"Sergeant. Leave two men at the checkpoint. Take the rest around the mountain. I want you on the other side."

"Yes, sir."

*They are between me and a mountain. If somehow they expect to get help on the other side—even if they can get over the damn thing—I'll be there, too.*

Lawrence felt confident.

It was one of the last things Kracke wanted to do—and the one old Andy apparently somehow had known he would have to do.

Brandes struggled with his end of the body bag, but finally everyone again was on level ground.

Kracke took a deep breath as he unslung the canvas bag from his shoulder.

"Hurry," he said. He looked at *all* of them; none could see that, all could feel it. "Into the woods."

Brandes, still not understanding, held on to his end of the

lastic bag and followed Kracke. By then Kracke had opened the anvas and had removed a shovel. It was folded. He twisted a nob, made it straight, retightened it. Then he used the shovel ke a spear and thrust it into the ground. He walked toward randes.

"Alex," he said, "we probably will not survive. I think you've nderstood that from the beginning. But we have to try. We may ave all along had very little chance—now, since Lawrence is losing in, with Cynthia we have no chance at all. We can't hide, un, and still carry Cynthia"—he pointed toward the mountain's rest—"up there. We have to bury her here and take our hances."

Brandes stood very still.

"No."

"We have to."

"She is alive, Kracke. She is *fucking alive!*"

"Yes," Kracke patiently tried to calm Brandes. "Our chance is er chance, Alex. If we make it, we can come back and get her. If ve don't do this, don't hide her the only way we can, she'll be remated with the rest. You *know* that."

"So we cover her—"

"No!" It was Wismer. "Shit, Alex, this is not a child's game ve're playing. This ain't the rehearsal. This is real life. Cynthia ery well may die here. You may, I may. There's a damn good hance all of us will. Listen to him." He gestured toward Kracke.

"Moments only, Alex. If I have to, I'll leave all of you here and un for it. Allenberg—and getting our information out—is more mportant than any of you, any of us. We can't carry her, Alex. Ve'll never make it. Lawrence will get us. And," he paused, "we an't just cover her. Not if you care for her."

"What?"

"She has to be *buried*, Alex. Buried. It's her only chance. They'll *search* around here. She can't be like the others we left. She has to be *buried*."

"But if she wakes . . ."

"It'll be our job to get back here before she does."

"No, no. You can't be serious. It would be like Peter. I haven't
thought about it, but Peter . . . He must have tried to claw his
way out of the ground. No, goddamn it. We can't leave her."

"Goodbye, Alex."

Sarah had spoken. Brandes swung around.

"Why did you say that?"

"Because I'm leaving. With Jim, if he'll let me. Maybe we'll
live and somehow get someone back here to save Cynthia."

"But you'll be dead. I . . . I am more sorry for that than I
can say."

"I don't . . ."

*Can't you see?* Take her; we all get caught. Toss leaves over
her and she gets found and cremated. Bury her and take our best
shot—not that that's much, anymore—and she has a chance.
We can come back before she wakes.

"Yes, if we fail, she dies a pretty horrible death."

Sarah seemed to be losing her temper.

"Goddamn it, Alex. Jim is right. This is the fucking grown-up
world. The choices aren't between three sour things and one
sweet one. *There are no sweet choices. Aren't.* As in, *don't exist.*"

Her chest was heaving. Sarah moved to a rock and sat.
Throughout the whole confrontation, which could not have
lasted more than three minutes, Linda Denard had been silent,
her eyes moving from person to person.

Brandes began to turn, to walk away, his head bowed,
thinking.

"No!" Kracke shouted. "No wandering off to meditate. Stop
being a fucking asshole infant." His voice was louder than he'd
intended.

Brandes did stop. *Is that what I'm being? Is that what I was
with Hoeckle? But this is Cynthia . . .*

His breath rasped, but he turned.

"If we get out of here," he said, looking at Kracke, "and if we
live, and if we come back, and if she's dead, I'll kill you. I know

can't do that . . . easily. But I'll find a way. Do you understand that? I'll kill you."

Kracke nodded. He wasted no time. He began to dig.

It took only a few minutes to bury Cynthia slightly more than three feet down. Kracke had the only shovel—compliments of one wise, old man who somehow had *known* things would come to that point, but the others used their hands to help.

When it was done, Kracke did his best to disguise the grave with grasses and leaves. Then he motioned the others up and toward the right. Their night had only begun.

The length of Cynthia's "night" depended entirely on their success.

# THIRTY-FIVE

KRACKE STOOD, RIGID, TENSE, SENSES PROBING. Most of what surrounded him remained in darkness; meager light spilled from the Future's parking lot, and while not far away, that was below him and helped little.

He had entered an altered state, as he had done before when the need had arisen. Kracke would have grimaced—and grinned—had anyone used the term *altered state*, but he *was* divorced, separate, from that he or anyone else considered "normal."

Never had he liked the feeling; always he was thankful for his ability to embrace it.

He was beyond having hope or giving up hope. Such concepts were alien to him at that time. They belonged . . . elsewhere. He was . . . different. He welcomed that.

Kracke's face showed the change; it was totally unexpressive. His eyes were deep, penetrating. He swiveled his head in a slow, seeking, purposeful manner. He looked, sought, waited.

For the enemy.

Few people, anywhere, at any time, had seen him in such a state. He, in a way, prided himself on that.

It was a state of total ruthlessness, of disregard for anything or anyone other than as they affected his ability to attain his goal. To others he could, he knew, be frighteningly inhuman.

Yet, without that ability, he would long before have been dead. Without it at that moment, he and Brandes and Sarah and the others would be dead. Never did Kracke forget that the others included the man for whom he worked—and for whom he held great admiration—and a young boy.

*Still, they might become—be—secondary . . .*

Nothing moved in the woods apart from his own group.

They are changing, too, he thought. *They are more quiet, more efficient. They understand more, feel more . . . feel less.*

Soldiers could not be far behind, but they could not be very near him yet, either. He had minutes. Maybe quite a few minutes. Perhaps as many as ten, but that was unlikely.

An insectlike sound built steadily as he swept his eyes across the forest. Then the sound was louder—and for Kracke unmistakable.

*Lawrence has air support.*

Kracke, seeing the inevitable, felt a wave of despair. They could not win, even without Cynthia's body could not hope to cross the mountain.

He looked up. Mountain, he thought. *We have been calling it that, but it's no more than an age-eroded ridge. High, steep. Yes, high enough.*

*High enough to stop us from reaching Andy's great-grandson.*

*And if they have a chopper, even reaching the truck will not matter.*

But almost immediately, he regained that single-minded goal orientation. He, Brandes, Wismer, had weapons. Hit right, the chopper would fall.

*Still*, then, there was a chance.

The sound came closer—and then moved away, to his right. The *whump-whump* of dual blades was apparent then, not only to him but to the others. Everyone was looking toward the source of the sound.

The sound simply passed them by, the helicopter itself still not visible because of the trees. Then it dropped lower. Kracke recognized it immediately.

Painted mostly white with red highlights, it definitely was not military. It was an Agusta-Bell Jetranger II, he saw. His recognition of the type, of the model, was instantaneous and instinctive, but for several seconds he was even more confused.

Then he understood.

Dorfman's serum was being delivered to the Futures lab.

Without thought, it seemed, he knew what he had to do. He shouted, "All of you. Run. Toward that chopper. *Now*. No fucking questions. Just *run*."

There had been a quality in Kracke's voice that neither intimidated nor frightened the others into obeying. It simply reached deep inside them and *made* them move, virtually tugged at their arm and leg muscles. As one, the group scrambled down the hill close behind the agent.

Kracke paused for a few seconds and waved the others toward the dense brush bordering Futures' parking lot. He waved to Wismer as he passed; the older man slowed, waited.

Kracke reached for the CB radio again. He did not know what to say. "Gerry," he asked, "I just realized I don't know Andy's great-grandson's name. What is it?"

Wismer looked surprised. "Andy," he said. "They're a tight family." Wismer's face, Kracke thought, was drawn and tired, and it had twisted as he'd answered. He had seen death before— in quantity and too frequently—but the sound of the rifle fire that had killed Andy had taken strength from Wismer. He would regenerate that strength, Kracke knew. People like him always did, always had to. It was not a matter of choice.

It was time simply to save one young life.

"Andy," Kracke said into the walkie-talkie. "Can you hear me?" He hoped desperately that the mountain—or ridge— would not interfere. It didn't.

"Yeaah, sirrr."

"Andy, get out of there. We won't need you."

"Sir, I was told to stay here."

"For as long as you were needed and then to help us with the truck. I know." Kracke paused. He didn't have time to convince the boy. "Everything's all right now. Just get out of there, okay? And thank you. Thank you very much."

"Well, I'd feel better if I heard from Gramps."

"He's out of range now. I'm relaying for him."

"Oh," the voice brightened. "Okay, then. Good luck, sir."

"Same to you, Andy. Thanks again."

A straight approach relying on force was out of the question, Kracke had thought. Too many things could go wrong. The vacated lab parking lot was large enough that men running with rifles would be seen far too quickly.

He had known those in the helicopter would not be expecting violence, of course. They had no reason. But the sight of armed men could quickly upset anyone, Kracke knew.

So, instead, he had used Brandes.

Brandes knew his nervousness did not show. He was far too scared and had been pushed by—things—too far to show outwardly how he actually felt, how close he felt to emotional, if not physical, collapse. He simply did as Kracke said.

"I'm Dr. Brandes," he shouted as he approached the helicopter, just touching down. He hoped his clothing would not seem too outrageous; he doubted anyone aboard could hear him, but he was certain they had seen his mouth move.

*Show the normal signs of friendliness,* Kracke had said. *Talk, Wave your hands. Make yourself visible.*

*Something* worked. One of the two doors on his side of the helicopter opened, and the pilot leaned out. By then he had cut engine power and the rotors' thwacking was decreasing both in frequency and intensity.

Brandes continued his approach. Only residual wind from the downdraft ruffled his hair by the time he could be heard.

381

Brandes stood only feet from the pilot, who was busy removing his headset.

"What?" the man shouted.

"I'm Dr. Brandes."

"Oh. Look, I don't know names. I guess he does." He pointed next to him. A man, dressed in a jacket and a mercifully lightweight turtleneck knit, sat there looking as though he had not enjoyed his flight. Brandes assumed—correctly—that he was Dorfman.

"Oh," Brandes said. "Please come with me."

"Can't," the pilot said. He turned to the other man and spoke in loud but more or less normal tones after having himself removed Dorfman's headset.

Brandes heard him tell the scientist he'd arrived.

Dorfman wasted no time. He opened his door, reached behind his seat for a small steel case, and stepped out onto the ground. He began to walk around the front of the helicopter, obviously heading toward Brandes.

"You, too," Brandes said to the pilot.

"Can't," the man repeated. "My instructions were very specific. I walk out there, I'm part of it and I . . ."

He stopped.

As if from nowhere, Kracke had arrived at the door Dorfman had left open, had climbed aboard, and had placed the muzzle of his handgun against the pilot's neck.

The pilot simply turned into a statue. No one had to explain what was pressing against his flesh.

Dorfman, rounding the front of the helicopter had not yet seen anything. When he reached Brandes, he was greeted with a weapon pointed at him and, too, froze granite-still.

Kracke spoke to the pilot, but Brandes could not hear. Both men got out on Brandes's side, and all four walked toward the lab building.

"This is—" Dorfman began, his voice shrill. Kracke just told him to shut up, and he did. The pilot never said a word.

They approached the goose, Peter's outsized tank of salt water. The struts supporting it provided ample shade from the parking lot's lights.

Soundlessly, wordlessly, Brandes and Kracke bound and gagged both men, as Wismer led Sarah and Linda from the brush bordering the parking lot.

Everyone met at the helicopter, and within less than thirty seconds had boarded, Brandes and Kracke in the front.

Kracke showed no hesitation as his hands played over the controls.

"I take it—" Brandes began.

"Yes, I know how to fly it."

Within seconds the rotors began to swing around, faster, then faster still. The ground jerked away as Kracke tilted the Jetranger at an outrageous angle, gaining at the same time altitude and distance from the lab.

Brandes felt himself relax. Even when, a few minutes later and with the ground below just an occasionally lighted dot-in-darkness, Kracke cursed over the fuel situation, Brandes continued to feel better than he had thought he ever would again.

Perhaps better than he ever had.

Perhaps, he thought, better than he should.

"We can't go all the way," Kracke said. "Damn thing hasn't enough fuel."

"Well," Brandes said expansively, "we'll think of something."

Kracke was familiar with Brandes's type of behavior. Brandes felt as if he had won, as if all problems had ended. Kracke himself had to fight feeling the same. It was a natural reaction. But he knew that their problems were still some distance from truly being over.

Kracke believed they had eluded Lawrence. He doubted the colonel had authority to shoot them down, even if he could find them.

But in retrospect, he thought, Lawrence never had been their

383

major obstacle. It seemed odd to think that so soon after what they had just been through, but it was true.

They still had to get to Allenberg and Jason—and then to those ultimately behind the Lyle tragedy. They had to get back to Cynthia within the next several days.

And with everything thus put into perspective, there was one more thing: I don't have enough fuel to get us to New Jersey and to Allenberg.

# THIRTY-SIX

TANGO PATROL CALLED ITS HEADQUARTERS EIGHT and one-half minutes after the commandeered helicopter had taken off.

Lawrence was not a man to admit defeat easily; neither did he give it a euphemistic name.

The situation, for the most part, he thought, was not beyond salvage.

That his career might suffer at first seemed inevitable. But that was not the proper, the profitable, way to think. Now, he thought, was a time not to avoid losses but to minimize them.

He called his superiors and told them what had happened.

He suggested that by staging a "miraculous" cure for Lyle they not only could support their own positions but undermine anything the others might say—if they indeed escaped and if they even intended to release the information they had.

There was, to Lawrence, a strong possibility that they would not. He knew of the workings of agencies such as Kracke's.

It was difficult to anticipate what would happen. Should his own superiors prove as well connected, as powerful, as they always had seemed, he himself might leave the entire incident relatively unscathed.

*Relatively. If they chose to allow that . . .*

He had felt himself grow cold in an instant, though, when instead of being reprimanded, his superior simply had told him that "things would be taken care of."

*Things.*

At first he'd felt relief that the whole matter—except for that remaining in Lyle (thank God they'd left him the Dorfman serum and two trussed-up men!)—no longer would be his responsibility.

Then he began to wonder, and he felt cold.

He began to wonder if he would be one of those "things" to be "taken care of."

Allenberg looked at his grandson, who was deeply asleep only a few feet from him on a sofa. A very wide-awake and alert man also was in the room.

Allenberg did not know his name. Fitch had not referred to any of the guards by name, but Allenberg took no hope from that. A willingness to remove masks, to become . . . too friendly . . . on the part of criminals usually to Allenberg had meant that no witnesses were to survive.

Fitch, though, was in a different league. Fitch's men were not protecting their identities because Allenberg and Jason would be allowed to live. Their identities were being protected because it was the *professional* thing to do.

Fitch, his organization—however powerful and well distributed that might be—would not allow them to live. Could not.

Allenberg grasped at no illusions.

Allenberg looked at Jason and felt fear for him. The boy slept from the type of exhaustion brought on by too little activity.

Oh, they had used the boy to make lemonade during the day and coffee at night and in the morning, but most of the previous day for both captives had been spent sitting, waiting, watching.

Jason—God, how he loved him!—had not lost his belief that all would be well.

*He* firmly believed that someone would rescue them, or,

barring that, that his grandfather would think of something. *And,* barring *that,* that *he* would think of something himself.

Allenberg's eyes were moist as he looked at his sleeping grandson.

He was proud.

"Ten minutes," Kracke said.

Brandes heard him through the headset, but not well. The constant rhythmic *thrumping* of the rotors penetrated even the headset's insulation.

The euphoria Brandes had felt after the escape had drained from him. He now knew what Kracke had known all along—danger still lay ahead.

And they were nearly out of fuel.

"What are we going to do?" he shouted, despite the fact that it was only the microphone near his lips that had to "hear" him.

"Land," Kracke said.

*So simple.*

Kracke spun the Jetranger around suddenly and began to descend. The lights of an all-night Pathmark supermarket below beckoned. At that hour, he knew, there would be room enough to land. Then he would hot-wire one of the cars in the lot and, with luck, get all of them on the road. If he was fast enough in the theft, he contemplated, they could get away with the stolen car before anyone knew what was happening.

Still, Kracke recognized that they could not make their assault on the New Jersey farm that night.

*Dawn. Dawn will have to do.*

They might as well find a small roadside motel and sleep a few hours. After, of course, he had made a phone call that would draw together the team he would need.

The farmhouse would not be easy. His team would not approach in camouflage jackets and berets or such nonsense. They would be mailmen, mechanics, farmhands—whatever he could think of that would get them close enough to neutralize the kidnappers' force without endangering the hostages.

It could be done, he knew.

He pushed those thoughts aside and, through the headset, began to explain to Brandes what would happen and what he would have to do as soon as they touched down in the supermarket parking lot.

They dropped the final few hundred feet swiftly.

Kracke left the helicopter as soon as he was sure it safely had touched down. He left the engine running, the rotors turning at an idle. The noise still was sufficient to create confusion, diversion.

The helicopter had been positioned carefully between the building and the small knot of the parked cars.

Quickly, Wismer and the women left the helicopter on Kracke's side, blocked from view by the helicopter itself.

Only Brandes remained. His job was simple enough, and it might not even be necessary.

Brandes flipped a switch Kracke had indicated and waited. His microphone was connected to a public-address system.

"Make up something," Kracke had told him. "Tell them it's a medical emergency—it's close enough. Improvise.

"Just tell them to stay away until I get a car over on the other side of the chopper."

Brandes was nervous, but, he thought, not greatly so.

*My nerves are getting used to this. They're numb.*

It took a while for people to come out of the store. Apparently, the sound had gotten their attention, all right, but the swift, crashlike descent had kept them *inside*. Even when they saw the helicopter had landed safely, they approached at a slow walk.

Brandes made sure he had the switch in the right position. Still, the people, two of them wearing the long white coats common to lab technicians and grocery clerks, were a hundred yards or more away.

The Jetranger surprise had bought the group more time than they had anticipated.

Then the shoppers were close enough.

Brandes cleared his throat; the sound rumbled across the artificially lit parking lot like thunder, and everyone approaching suddenly froze.

Brandes himself, who had not expected a volume that would greatly overpower the engine noise, was momentarily stunned. He recovered, drew a breath to say something.

The medical emergency sounded good enough, he thought.

He didn't need to say *anything*, Kracke shouted.

Brandes swung quickly. A station wagon was parked on the far side of the chopper.

Brandes didn't wait, but just for good measure growled into the microphone—cringed at the sound—and tore off the headset. Vismer, Sarah, and Linda were in the back of the car. Brandes leaped in the front.

Within five more seconds, Kracke floored the accelerator and the wagon bounced onto the road outside the parking lot.

Suddenly, as Kracke continued to increase his speed, the agent started to laugh. Then he stopped and looked at Brandes. "I haven't had a hell of a lot to laugh at in the past few hours. I like to when I get a chance," he said. "You know," he said, "that helicopter, now that it's on the ground, probably has enough fuel to sit there and idle for another hour or more." He giggled again.

"Hell of a diversion," he said. "They're probably still stalking the damned thing. They might not even notice the car missing for a while."

"We have to get Adrian and Jason," Kracke said.

Suddenly, a strange feeling enveloped Brandes. He asked a question he had not considered he ever would be capable of asking.

"Why?"

Kracke turned his head. Sharply. No one else made a sound. Brandes continued.

"We have to tell people in authority about what is happening in Lyle," Brandes said. He paused and stared back at Kracke. Total silence reigned, except for the sounds of the road, the occasionally squawling of tires, the occasional thrusts of an engine overworked against inclines.

Brandes regretted, more than he ever thought he could regret, what he might have done to Sarah by what he'd said.

Her father.

Her son.

Could he explain what was in his mind? More importantly . . *could he get Kracke to explain what* he *found so difficult?*

Kracke answered in a perfectly calm voice. "It might look like we're wasting our time," he said. "I agree."

He paused, wanting to say to Brandes, "You've changed." He didn't.

"But there has been something going on that *I* don't understand." Kracke went on in a low, throaty voice.

"I didn't mean that to sound like I always *do* know what's going on. But this is different. Adrian and I . . . we go back a ways. Whatever he hasn't told me, and *I know there's something,* is vital. I'm convinced of that.

"What would happen, Alex, if we went as high as we could and reported—and then found out that the people we talked to were the worse choice?

"Adrian knows something, Alex. Something important. That's why we go for him first. All right?"

"Of course," Brandes said. He felt his face flush. He turned and said, "Sarah . . ."

"Alex," she interrupted. "Don't try to explain. I wanted to know myself."

Brandes turned back, faced the windshield, was aware only of very occasional lights illuminating the secondary road.

"Where to now? Right there?"

"No," Kracke said. "I don't think Lawrence can easily touch us right now. Our only danger is that whoever Fitch has in Lyle will notice we're gone and will report."

"It's more likely," he said, "that they'll guess we're trying to do just what Alex suggested. Report in ourselves. There's no way they can know that we know about New Jersey."

"So?" It was Sarah.

"So," he said, "we find a place to rest a few hours. Somewhere near the farm. I'll make my calls. We could use the rest, and then we'll have until dawn for the team to assemble and meet us."

Not even Wismer offered a suggestion, Brandes noticed. They drove in silence. Kracke's plan was accepted.

A few hours must pass before they could rest, Kracke knew. Then another few hours . . . then one way or another, they would win. Or they would lose.

The neon sign of the motel not only lit the road, it was impossible to miss because of its buzzing.

Every time *Vacancy* flashed on, it made a noise like a hive of bees.

Kracke pulled into the parking lot of the motel. It suited him fine. He directed the others and walked alone to the office, where he rented three adjacent rooms. He would occupy one by himself. Wismer and Brandes would share another, Sarah and Linda the third.

There were, he guessed, two dozen units in the motel. A central outdoor alley separated the complex, divided it in half. In that corridor were the public telephones, the ice machine, the soda machines, the machines that dispensed cheese and crackers and half-melted Hostess cupcakes.

"We must be ready about an hour before dawn," he said. "We'll get to the farm about dawn. Let's get some rest."

"I'm thirsty and hungry," Linda said.

"Okay," Kracke nodded his head. "No feast, but go to the service area where the machines are." He pointed, vaguely, and then reached into his pockets. "As a matter of fact," he added, "it wouldn't do any of us any harm to have something in our stomachs." He handed her quarters and looked around.

Wismer found a few quarters in his own pockets, as did Brandes.

Linda nodded and left.

Kracke went to the office, paid a sleepy clerk, and returned with keys. He went immediately to one of the rooms. The others followed.

Kracke dropped down onto his bed.

The silence was profound. There seemed little need for anyone to talk.

"I've got to make that call *now*," Kracke said abruptly and levered himself from the too-soft motel bed. As he opened the door, he saw Linda returning, her arms balancing cans of soda and cellophane packages of snacks.

"You want any?" she asked.

"Just a soda," Kracke said. "Some crackers if there are enough."

Kracke left for the telephones. Brandes had no difficulty imagining what Kracke was thinking.

*Will I be talking to someone I can trust?*

*Will the team be assembled in time?*

*Will it work?*

"We can win out through this." The voice surprised everyone.

It was as though no one expected anyone else to say a word. Wismer continued. "I know the type of people Jim is calling. They are dedicated people," he said. "They will be dedicated to Adrian, if nothing else." He looked toward Sarah as he said those last few words.

"I'm not going to thank you for that, Gerry," she said. "People thank other people most often when they know they've been lied to. You see, I *know* something of my father's people.

"I *know* you're right."

She paused, then grinned and added, "I do thank you for reminding me, though."

Everyone grinned. It relieved the tension.

"I guess we ought to be getting to our own rooms," Brandes said. Wismer nodded. No one moved.

"I guess," Sarah said, "we'd better wait for Jim, right?"

That time the tension was really broken. Everyone allowed a soft laugh.

Kracke came back.

"Dawn," he said. He looked straight at Sarah. "We'll get them at dawn."

# THIRTY-SEVEN

THE SOUND OF SMASHING GLASS AT FIRST SEEMED to Brandes just part of a dream.

Brandes could not immediately place why breaking glass should be in his dream; he had been on a dark, very arid, very lonely plain—a desert—and certainly there had been no glass, had not been anything like glass for miles around.

He twisted on the bed; the shattering-glass sound persisted; in a spasm of need to make the jigsaw-puzzle pieces of his dream fit, he saw on that plain a service station with large plate windows that were falling to pieces . . .

He had not undressed and was face-down on one of the two small, narrow beds in the room he and Wismer had taken.

*The sound was not part of any dream.*

He heard it again, and then he heard the sound of men grunting—the sounds passed easily through the thin-sheetrocked walls.

Brandes began to swivel on his hips, to try to place his feet on the floor.

The nearly musical, always threatening, cacophony of breaking glass, he realized, was real—and it was near.

The sound of . . . other people . . . also was real.

Brandes then woke as fast as he could, but the hours of stress and uncertainty, of danger, had claimed a toll. He could not help but take seconds to shake his head, to clear his eyes, to realize that he was *not* dreaming and that the sounds he heard were real, were actual—were *happening*.

Wismer already was sitting on his bed, his feet on the floor, his face confused but uncannily alert, illuminated only by the dim light that filtered from the road and from the motel's neon sign through gauzy curtains.

"What?" Brandes began.

"*Ssshh*," Wismer cautioned.

The sound was coming from Kracke's room.

But there was no need for any more silence.

Everything happened too quickly—certainly too quickly for Brandes to react in any useful way.

The door to their room crashed open and a silhouette pirouetted once and then fell dully and heavily to the floor.

It was Kracke.

Brandes tried to rush forward, to grab at the falling body. He failed, and when he did, a metal object struck him on his left temple, knocking him nearly senseless and causing him to fall half across the semiconscious form of the agent.

Brandes had no idea of what was happening; he knew only that he was frightened. That things had gone wrong. That the man who had come to represent strength, ability, was prostrate beneath him.

Thinking of Kracke in that light made Brandes's own fear more justifiable to him, more human. If Kracke were gone . . .

*Let that not be* . . .

In that instant he felt more helpless than he had since the night had begun, since the running from Lawrence, since Andy's death, since the digging of Cynthia's grave.

*The digging of Cynthia's grave!*

*No!* something shouted inside him.

*That* cannot be.

Cynthia cannot be allowed to awaken, as had . . . as Peter had awakened . . .

No, he thought. Cynthia cannot die like that.

*I may die, but quick, clean . . . Not that either.*

A calmness settled over him, at least it temporarily overlay his desire to strike out, to hurt those who would hurt him and the others, the persons who would allow Cynthia to die clawing uselessly at the weight of soil above her.

*Soil I helped put there.*

His mind raced backward.

Brandes thought of her and wanted desperately to fight—yet, at that point, he did not know what he would be fighting.

*Too fast. Too fast.*

Without at that time realizing it, he had learned. From Kracke, from Allenberg. From everything. *He* could strike out blindly at that point and probably guarantee himself that clean, quick death—it would help no one.

*Certainly not Cynthia.*

Brandes had learned to wait, to think.

He heard Kracke make a small, painful sound.

*Kracke! God, no. Not you. Not you.*

Brandes looked up and saw a dark figure standing above him, his hands holding a rifle that seemed like one of those he and Kracke had taken from the soldiers in Lyle. The barrel of that rifle had been the metallic object that had crashed into his head, he knew.

The fear was tangible, a tangible presence for him. He wondered if Kracke ever felt such fear, or if he—Alex Brandes, alone—were subject to such fear.

*I am afraid.*

Another man joined the one who had hit him. He, at first, also was backlit in the doorway. Then came still a third man.

The second moved Wismer against the far wall, reaching across the narrow bed, his hands flat on the beige-painted wall.

Pain inched, then lanced, through his head as he tried to move. He was aware of Kracke moving beneath him.

He tried to stand, to remove his weight from Kracke.

Again he was hit; again he fell.

"Just stay there," a voice said.

Several more moments passed, and the same voice said, "Okay, now. You. Now. Up. On the bed. Sit. On the bed." The voice was accompanied by a prodding from the muzzle of the rifle. Brandes got to his knees and felt Kracke tense as he moved.

*No, Jim. Not now. There are too many of them. Please don't do anything . . .*

The steel again pushed into his ribs. He finished getting up, sat on the bed.

Suddenly the lights came on, and he saw he faced four men, one of them still just outside. His vision was blurred, but he could make out the contours, the outlines.

*Lawrence? How? How?*

But they were not dressed in uniforms . . .

He watched in silence as Kracke, too, was half lifted, half prodded, to the edge of the bed. Brandes was very glad that the agent did not do anything to antagonize their captors, whoever they were.

Two more persons entered.

One was Sarah.

She did not look at all disheveled, Brandes thought, by her recent nap nor by her even more recent encounter with rifle-laden men. She looked, Brandes thought, furious.

Then he saw why.

Sarah was half-tossed on the bed on which Wismer eventually had been allowed to sit.

Linda stood in the doorway, a pistol in her right hand.

She gave instructions to the men.

They listened.

"This time, Alex," she said, turning toward Brandes. "This time *he*"—she gestured at Kracke—"won't help you."

God, Brandes thought, we never guessed. Yet it all made sense.

She must have been, he knew then, the diminutive second cyclist.

*God, I hate her.*

He thought of Peter.

*Truly, I can hate.*

# THIRTY-EIGHT

CHILL PERMEATED THE FARMHOUSE. EVERYONE felt it in one way or another.

Fitch, his men, felt it just as a phenomenon of the weather, of the early morning, of temperature.

Brandes—and the others who had accompanied him—felt it more deeply and, in a sense, quite differently. They felt it as weariness, as loss, as defeat.

Kracke straightened in his chair, stretched.

The ride from the motel to the farmhouse had been long and uncomfortable. Brandes, Wismer, Kracke, and Sarah had been loaded aboard the flatbed of a truck and been covered with a canvas sheathing. No thought had been given to their comfort.

None had been expected.

*Loss.*

*This is loss. This is what it feels like to lose.*

Brandes thought about his sense of loss briefly when his turn had come to be loaded onto the truck. Loss was as suffocatingly unreal as it was so terribly, terribly apparent and unavoidable.

For several hours the truck had lurched over secondary roads before it had stopped with a finality that shook some central core in Brandes.

"We're going to the farm," Sarah had said about fifteen minutes before the truck had stopped. Part of Brandes wanted desperately to be clever and to say, "Well, that's where we *were* going . . ." and perhaps give her hope. He could not.

They had arrived at the New Jersey farm and brusquely had been led from the truck to the house. Night still had covered their movements; in the darkness, Brandes, and, he suspected, Sarah, tripped a few times over hummocks and in small holes dug by the field's animals. Their transfer, though, quickly had been completed.

Brandes never before had been to the farmhouse. Kracke had been, but mostly on short visits when he had had to bring situations to Allenberg's attention.

The entire progression was like a speeded-up film in Brandes's mind. Events were compressed . . .

They walked onto the wooden porch and then into the building. Allenberg sat on a sofa, his back straight, his eyes threatening but impotent.

Jason stood next to him.

"Ma!" he shouted as Sarah entered. He began to run toward her, a young child in need of a caress, of an embrace, of hope.

He stopped in two steps and simply looked at Sarah.

"Yes," she said to him. "They've got us, too."

That seemed to say most of what could be said. The boy then did continue to approach his mother, but quietly and calmly, and no one interfered.

"We'll get out of this," he whispered into her ear. She only smiled. Then she reached out, hugged him.

"Sit down," a man said.

Two armed men motioned toward the sofa and to other leather-upholstered chairs near it. Brandes, Kracke, and Sarah moved toward the sofa at once, and a short confusion followed. Finally, Sarah sat next to her father, who gently placed his left hand on her leg, squeezing with a reassurance he did not feel. The nondescript men withdrew, leaving only two other persons, one armed.

Brandes sat further down on the sofa. Kracke exchanged a brief look with Allenberg and then took a chair.

"I take it . . ." Allenberg began.

"Shut up," one of the men said.

Everyone looked; next to him stood Linda. No one wanted to look directly at her; none seemed able to resist.

All knew what had happened.

While she had gone for soda and crackers, she had made a telephone call.

Simple.

One incredibly vital and disastrous telephone call . . .

Kracke silently cursed himself for allowing her—or anyone, for that matter—out of his sight.

The so-far silent man looked relaxed and confident.

"My name is Fitch," he said. "I truly feel it unfortunate that you all came here to join my other two guests. As you'll understand, it was not of my choosing."

No one responded.

"I am not a man to gloat or to torture," he said. "You all will be moved within the next two hours. No one will be harmed—unless you cause me or my people to cause you harm. All of you then will spend a few weeks as our guests and then you will be released."

Brandes stiffened.

*Tell him about Cynthia?*

No one, he noticed, relaxed at Fitch's calm and soothing reassurances.

He decided to say nothing for the moment. Still, Cynthia was uppermost on his mind.

"By then," Fitch continued, "my organization will have accomplished its purpose. There will be nothing you can do. Really! Not a damned thing *then* could be done by *anyone!* So, then you can just go home.

"Hell," he said expansively, "for all I care, you all can go out to dinner and get drunk."

He eased a pistol from his jacket.

"Just to keep you honest," he chuckled. With it, he gestured toward the weapon so calmly held by Linda Denard.

He looked carefully around him.

Fitch did not expect any attempt at resistance, but if he could forestall one by promising them safety he would do so. Mixing in a show of potential force was good technique.

He knew, he had learned, that people in such situations—even when they *know* their captor is lying—*want* to believe in their eventual safety. For several seconds he looked at the faces of his prisoners and began to wonder if his calming technique would work, would guarantee him placid obedience.

To his surprise, it was Allenberg who relaxed first. The strain had left his face, the tension retreated from muscles too long taut with expectation of sudden and violent movement. He never would have thought . . .

*I can't be sure. Not with him.*

"Tell them, Adrian," Fitch said.

"There is nothing to tell them," Allenberg said. "Not if you really intend to let them go."

His eyes then took on a smoldering but still vibrant flame as they caught Fitch's, centered on them, transfixed them.

"Wrong point of view, Adrian." He felt his own reaction to Adrian Allenberg's eyes, to Adrian Allenberg's truth. He had to push forth *his* truth—though only for a short while.

*But until then, keep them occupied, "happy."*

"We don't have to kill to keep our secrets to ourselves any more than does Uisce Beatha. That"—he looked at the others—"is the organization Adrian represents. I'm sure Adrian will have a wonderful time explaining Uisce Beatha to all of you; I doubt he's done that with any of you up until now. Anyway, it isn't violent—and, unless it's vital, neither is my organization. We simply have different goals, different ways of looking at the world and at what might be done to help it.

"We're both, in a sense, patriotic, if being concerned about the whole planet can be considered 'patriotic.' We view what that means differently."

"Not violent?" Allenberg raised his voice just slightly. "What

401

do you call murdering Peter Brandes? What about Lyle? The people dying there?"

"No excuses, Adrian," Fitch said. "An explanation, of sorts, maybe. No excuses. If Peter Brandes had created *just* what he was contracted to create, the people of Lyle would not be suffering."

"And Peter?"

"We even would have left Peter alive. We might even have given him the grant he wanted." When Fitch said that, Brandes's insides twisted.

"When he told us that the substance was ready—but with a small alteration—we could not afford to do either. No alterations. You can understand that, Adrian."

The lies were fluid, Fitch thought. He remembered that the decision to kill Peter Brandes had been made almost at the same time the man had agreed to work for Fitch's group.

*And that bastard never did tell us just what he'd made . . .* He remembered that Linda had reported that *something* odd had been going on, but she hadn't actually figured it out. Then came time for Rachek.

*Maybe we did kill Peter too soon. Hell, no matter now . . .*

For Fitch, Lyle's tragedy was just that. Something tragic. An unfortunate incident.

Fitch grew expansive.

"Let me tell them about Uisce Beatha, Adrian . . ."

"Not necessary," Allenberg snapped. "I'd be more than willing to tell them. While I've been a director of Uisce Beatha, it never has ordered a killing."

"*You* never have ordered a killing, Adrian. I don't think the entire organization is as naïve as you. But then you really aren't that naïve otherwise, are you? As head of your own agency you would order a termination without a second thought. Interesting."

"We don't . . ."

"Oh, shut up, Adrian," Fitch said suddenly. "For four decades Uisce Beatha has thought it was savior of the world—and a civilized savior at that.

"Don't you think there might be people who disagree with you, Adrian? People who believe what *they* believe as much as you believe what you do?

"Don't *you* start getting on some soapbox, Adrian. You least of all." Fitch turned suddenly toward Brandes. "Ever heard of a man named Hoeckle?"

He didn't wait for an answer. He turned to Kracke and paused. "No use saying anything to you, is there, Mr. Kracke? You're agency, that's all. You probably don't even know what we're talking about.

"Didn't fill in your department, did you, Adrian?"

He spun again, faced Sarah. She was looking quizzically at Linda, and Fitch caught her gaze.

"Looking for something in Linda, Miss Allenberg? Don't believe she was the one who told us Peter was . . . taking a new tack, so to speak. She's been with us since the beginning." He paused. "I am sorry," he said, and almost sounded convincing, "that you and your son have become involved."

He brightened.

"But, as I said, in another few weeks we'll have the production mechanism set up—and you won't be able to do anything. So, then we'll let you go."

A small, coarse, uncharacteristic laugh escaped Sarah. Fitch raised an eyebrow; Linda lifted her pistol.

"Don't believe me?" Fitch asked. "You should learn more of the dynamics of the world."

He turned again.

"Jason," he said, "how about you get your mother a cup of coffee? In fact, make your usual potful. Maybe two." He faced Sarah. "He really makes good coffee."

Brandes had listened in a semi-detached stupor; then something happened. He felt that detachment fade—no, sharpen . . . He was very aware. The barb about Hoeckle had not gone past him.

*Incredible. Years thinking of little else. Hoeckle is now so small, so unimportant . . .*

*God, for the right reason, I might kill Hoeckle myself.*

For several seconds he felt lost in those thoughts; he had to will his mind back to his present situation. To their present situation. To Cynthia.

Fitch was not necessarily the key, he thought. He was there, and he was armed. So was Linda.

*Bitch.*

*But what had Fitch said? Two hours. A few hours.*

Brandes then realized that he had not fallen victim of a vast, unreasoning, inescapable, and impenetrable governmental network.

*Lawrence doesn't know we're here! I'd bet on it.*

Brandes did not look to the army for help—Lawrence had more reason to want him and the others dead than did Fitch and his mysterious organization. But, if Lawrence had not been involved in their capture . . . *What the hell is Uisce Beatha?*

*Two ways of looking at this . . .*

*More than one enemy wants me—or, my enemies are not working together.*

Brandes preferred the latter—and it did make sense. Only Linda's call had alerted Fitch and his people. There had been no emergency transmission from Lawrence.

Still, that did not mean their position was materially different, Brandes thought. He looked at Kracke, who sat motionless except for small movements of his head. He looked at Wismer. His former high school teacher sat, back not quite rigid yet certainly not slumped, next to Kracke.

Brandes stood suddenly and said, "I take it I can go to the bathroom?" He bumped brusquely into Jason as the young boy also stood, intending to go to the kitchen to make coffee for the captors and their captives.

The boy looked up abruptly; their eyes met. Brandes reached out to steady the boy; finally both straightened. Still their eyes locked.

Brandes wanted very much to say something. He hoped his eyes managed some communication of their own.

He also wanted to tell Jason that things would be all right. He

404

new better. Just that brief glance into the boy's eyes told him
ever—should that chance ever present itself—try to con the
id.

Brandes kept walking a few paces and then stopped at a casual
ut authoritative gesture from Linda.

*Linda. Armed Linda. Bitch.*

"With help," Fitch said. He glanced at Linda, who finally
estured him toward a small corridor that led from the living
om.

No one was speaking when he returned. He had searched the
ntire bathroom for *anything* that might be useful, that might be
weapon. Useless.

There had been a very limited supply of toilet paper.

Brandes slowly walked back, sat.

Brandes considered the room, the people. He considered what
e had learned and had been told. He considered what he might
e able to do.

If the army is not involved, he thought, Fitch will have to rely
nly on men from his own organization.

And what of those called by Kracke? From *his* agency?

Brandes lifted his face, and even as he thought that, he saw
racke twist his left hand to look at his watch.

No, he thought. Kracke may be looking forward to their
rival.

*I think I've gotten even more cynical than he.*

Linda, after all, had been privy to their discussions during their
pparently useless flight from Lyle and Lawrence.

*There will be no team. Or it will be too late.*

"No need to check your watch, Mr. Kracke," Linda suddenly
aid. Kracke looked up, innocence scrawled over his face. "Your
eam will not get here."

Another question answered, Brandes thought.

"You see, some of our people, like Mr. Allenberg there, have
nore than one allegiance. Some of them owed Colonel
awrence. Actually they owed Colonel Lawrence's bosses.

405

Colonel Lawrence, of course, owes everybody. No team at dawn, Jim. Nothing."

Kracke did not change his expression, but *something* about the man changed. Brandes could feel it. From Sarah, too. There was a wave of loss that swept through their number.

"What happens in a few hours?" Wismer asked, as though he was prepared to believe the answer.

The question caught Fitch offguard—apparently, he had somehow accepted that none of his captives really believed him. But then, he thought, people do reach out, do grasp.

What pretenses we carry, perpetrate, Brandes thought. Even in such circumstances. *He says something and hopes we believe it. We don't. When we act as though we do, he's surprised. What a game, what complex rules. How without apparent purpose.*

"Well," Fitch said, recovered, "we put you on a van that's coming here. You'll be taken to a house not any bit less comfortable than this.

"Then, you'll wait. My people by then will have practically set up the machinery to remove the gold from seawater. Then, of course, Uisce Beatha will have a few problems to work on, won't it, Adrian?"

"A commercial process to extract gold might hurt some countries," Allenberg said. "Maybe South Africa, Canada to a degree—Australia, maybe. Maybe even Northern Ireland. It won't do much else."

"Not generally released, Adrian," Fitch said. He paused when he heard a sound from the kitchen, a banging. Linda straightened immediately and started to walk that way when Fitch realized from where the noise had come.

"It's all right, Linda," he said. "Kid's passing out the morning coffee to the men."

She relaxed; he resumed.

"No, not generally made available. But what if we play a little, Adrian? What if we quietly give gold to Argentina, to Chile, to Mexico, to Ethiopia, to the Sudan? What if supplies of the stuff are made available to all the up-to-their-eyeballs debtors?

"One damn good thing, I'll tell you. Colombia won't have to depend on cocaine income anymore."

"Oh, you hero," Allenberg mocked. "Saving all those schoolchildren . . ."

"Don't knock it," Fitch snapped. "Of course, that's just a byproduct, anyway."

Here it is," another voice called, breaking the tension.

Jason walked in with a tray loaded with a large pot and numerous cups and saucers. His entrance, Brandes saw, allowed both Allenberg and Fitch to retreat slightly into themselves, to probe for their own weaknesses, to worry. Brandes didn't. He didn't give a shit, he told himself, if *tons* of gold were taken from the oceans.

*All that is too . . . far away. Too distant. I care about me, about Sarah and Gerry and Jason. About Cynthia. Chile's debt is somewhere else.*

Brandes realized he could listen to Allenberg and Fitch argue world politics and never come to a conclusion about who was right. For all he knew, Fitch might be.

What he *did* know was the mechanisms Fitch used. His brother's murder. Trying to stop investigation of a disease that was decimating a town . . . Those things, Brandes thought, said much about Fitch's politics.

Jason sat down after he finished serving coffee to everyone. Fitch and Linda also had cups; Fitch had scoured the kitchen before he had allowed Jason to become their supplier of lemonade and coffee.

No rat poisons, no kitchen cleansers.

The worst, he'd said, the kid could do was make everything salty. And he hadn't.

"But more importantly, Adrian," Fitch continued, sipping delicately, "it undermines your 'one-world' program.

"The governments of the world no longer will—well, for a while anyway—be dependent on each other the way they were.

407

We'll unwind in a few months what took you forty years to put together."

"You'll have massive financial collapses in every industrialized country in the world."

"Goddamn it, Adrian!" Fitch shouted. "Do you really have to shovel *me* that damn pompous, self-righteous shit? Do you think my organization *has* to be less intelligent than yours? All of this will be carefully controlled."

"As carefully as you control Uisce Beatha? How the hell can *you* be so pompous not to think that some finger of Uisce Beatha is not already in *your* pie?"

"That is impossible." Fitch's face was hard, then softened. "That is impossible."

"Of course."

"Where is this other house?" Wismer asked suddenly, putting his own black coffee down on a small table.

Again, Brandes thought, the make-believe. He looked around the room, watching expressions. When he got to the young boy, he smiled. Jason did not smile. He nodded his head fractionally as if he knew what Brandes was doing, and Brandes thought he felt something melt inside him.

The others were . . . attentive.

"Virginia," Fitch said. "Nice country. I understand you like horses, like your boy," he spoke to Sarah.

"I'm not as good a rider."

"Well, maybe you'll have time to practice. Like I said, nice country down there. Good horses."

Fitch reached into the kitchen and pulled a chair through the connecting doorway and sat down. Linda looked sharply at him, seemed snubbed, and did the same.

"How many weeks will we be there?" Wismer again.

"Oh." Fitch fiddled with his triangular lapel pin with his left hand and then let the hand drop into his lap. "Maybe two. No more than three. The process really is very simple once you have the organism."

408

"What," Brandes asked, "are you going to do with the organism's other . . . characteristics?"

Linda cleared her throat, taking several seconds. "You mean," she asked, "what about the Lyle disease?"

"Yes. You do remember that I have another reason for asking about that."

"Oh!" she exclaimed and coughed into her hand. "Yes, of course. I've already reported about Cynthia. She'll be taken care of."

Brandes said nothing. He just looked at Linda, at Fitch. His eyes moved from one to the other.

Fitch rested the hand holding his pistol in his lap. Brandes watched him, and after hearing Linda's comment, did not feel a shred of sympathy for the man.

"You may as well give me that," Brandes said to Fitch and pointed toward the gun.

Automatically Fitch raised it and aimed it at Brandes, his motions slow, the barrel moving in a small circle without end as he tried to hold it still.

Brandes stiffened, looked toward Jason. The boy nodded.

"Linda," Wismer said, catching some of the byplay and following along without really understanding, "give me yours."

She coughed, raised her weapon. Her eyes shone, glistened.

"What?" Fitch asked and coughed, the deep wracking causing his aim to drop.

"The coffee," Jason said suddenly. Everyone looked at him.

"We checked that kitchen," Linda said, her words interrupted now and punctuated by coughing and gasping. "He said we did. There was nothing . . ."

"There wasn't!" Fitch aimed his comment at her, as if in defense.

"There is now," Brandes said. "Why don't you give us those guns?"

"Are you out of your fucking mind?" Fitch roared. His hand seemed steadier to Brandes.

*Bluff it then . . .*

"Not at all. Oh, you can shoot us. You can too, Linda. You'd do better to shoot yourself."

"You see, we're walking out of here, and you're going to let us."

"Sit still, shut the hell up," Fitch said. "I don't know how or what—I know I don't feel like I'm going to pass out right now. And this gun takes little effort to fire. I'm quite healthy enough to kill you, you son of a bitch."

"And kill yourself?" Brandes quickly asked.

His heart slowed slightly when Fitch did not fire; the others looked at him.

"Jason put some of the Juliet crystals in your coffee," he explained simply. "I slipped them to him before. He's very bright. You've both ingested the actual virus. Virtually an immediate effect. No real incubation to speak of this way."

"Silly," Fitch said. "We have men," he paused, looked at Jason and nodded. "Okay, forget the men. The kid got them first. But you can damned well see we're far from helpless, Brandes. Linda, get some rope. We can tie all of you up. We *could* shoot you."

Linda rose shakily to her feet to obey; Brandes waved at her to sit down, but she ignored him.

"You'll do neither, Fitch. You won't kill us. You won't tie us up.

"Let me tell you what you *will* do after I tell you what would happen if you tried either of those things.

"You, that bitch, and your men would be dead. *Dead*. And dead in a way you can't even contemplate. Not really." He looked at Linda, and he felt blood pounding in his temples as he thought of her, of his brother, of her betrayal—of Peter's death, of the *way* he had died.

He realized he was enjoying himself. He didn't even find that surprising.

"You'll be found 'dead' by your own people, Fitch. Linda, hear that? We'll either be tied up or shot. I promise you this, you

410

bastards, if we're tied up we won't tell one living soul that you two and your men are *not* dead.

"Think about that, Fitch. You, too, Linda. You think about it very hard. Think about what Peter went through. Buried. And then in three days . . . *alive*. Or maybe they'll make this whole area a quarantine zone, just like Lyle. Maybe Lawrence will come and burn both your bodies."

He stood up and walked forward and gestured to the others. Slowly, singly, they also stood.

"And if you're real lucky, Linda, you won't be waking up just when they're lighting the fire. Think about it."

He waved the others toward the door. They moved slowly.

"Jim," he said in a very low voice to Kracke, "the men outside will be pretty sick but still dangerous . . ." He trailed off as Kracke nodded.

"You see, Fitch, you're going to let us walk out of here because we are the only people on this earth who will know in half an hour you are *not* dead. We're the only ones who can prevent someone treating you as if you were.

"You want to die scratching at a coffin lid or screaming on a garbage heap, Fitch?" He pushed the others out. Kracke already had gone. Fitch and Linda tried to keep their weapons lined up, but their heads were slowly sinking, their eyes blurred and lids heavy.

"How about you, Linda? You want to go that way?"

"Bastard," she wheezed. "You fucking bastard."

"From you," he began, stopped, smiled.

"You'll tell them, then? Tell them we're not dead?" Fitch asked.

Brandes's face firmed into granite as he looked at them, one and then the other.

"Probably a few hundred people, good people, died in Lyle," he said finally. "My brother died. I don't give a shit about your gold and your international money plots, but I care about those people. I should let you rot.

"Then, maybe I'm just not like you," he said finally as he turned to follow the others out on to the meadow.

Outside, Sarah, Wismer, and Jason were hugging and embracing. Brandes walked up to them and gravely took Jason's hand.

"Thank you," he said.

"Thank *you*," Jason replied, and that subject was dropped.

"It's all right," Kracke said as he came around the corner of the porch. "They got their doses a little earlier, thanks to you"—he tousled Jason's hair—"and now they're sleeping very nicely. What next?"

Brandes was surprised to find the question directed at him, and was even more surprised to find that all the others were looking at him, awaiting an answer.

*Changes. In me, too. Changes.*

"We get someone to get Cynthia," he said without hesitation. Kracke nodded, took Wismer by an elbow, and moved into the house to make telephone calls.

"Go ahead, Alex," Allenberg said and smiled.

"From here on it's more your field, Adrian."

"Really?"

He grinned and took Jason inside with him.

"Will you tell her again?" Sarah asked. Brandes blinked once, then knew what she meant.

"I don't know," he said. "Things are different. A lot different. Maybe they're different in a way that it *would* work. Maybe in a way, it couldn't possibly. I do love her, Sarah. But—" he hesitated a second—"I love you, too."

He caught her chin in the palm of his hand and captured her eyes.

"Give it time, Alex. Maybe all three of us will know what we want. Eventually. We're not in high school. We don't need our lives all sorted out before the prom."

"Maybe," he said. "I've got some things to learn about me first, I think. In a while, I'll go back to the *Seige*, but not right away." He paused, leaned over, kissed her delicately yet deeply. "I'll talk to you," he said.

412

"I know," she said and walked inside.

As she did, she held open the door for her father. Allenberg walked onto the porch and stood next to Brandes, who by then had leaned his forearms on the railing and was looking out over the meadow and the purplish-blue hills toward which they stretched.

"You've changed, Alex," Allenberg said.

Brandes nodded. He was surprised by the depth of kinship he felt with the other man—the one he had all but hated only days before as he played a pinball game on Fire Island.

"What now?" Allenberg asked.

"I don't know."

"Going back to the sea?"

"Not for a while, Adrian. I think I'll go back to Lyle for a few months, maybe help Jonathan put that place back together. If that's possible."

"Good idea," Allenberg agreed. "You're the perfect person for the job."

"And you?"

"Same as always. For all of us, I guess. I've learned something about involving your family in—"

"Things they not only are able to handle but are just plain needed to do."

"Yeah," Allenberg looked slightly surprised. "I guess I hadn't looked at it that way. Anyway, Jim and I will go back to work. Of course, Jim will need some time off. There's that Colonel Lawrence, you know." He cast his gaze sideward as he said that, but Brandes only nodded without expression.

*He has changed*, Allenberg thought.

"What about them?" he asked Brandes.

"Who?" Brandes asked, honestly not understanding.

"Fitch and Denard. What about them?"

"What do you mean? Why ask me?"

"You're the only doctor around here, Alex." Allenberg stopped, looked hard into Brandes's eyes. "People will be getting here soon. None of us will differ from your opinion.

"Hell, you're the doctor! Are you going to tell those people that Fitch and the others are alive, Alex?"

They stared at each other for several seconds, then Brandes turned again to look out over the waving, wind-caressed meadow. Finally he turned back to Allenberg.

"I don't know, Adrian," he said.

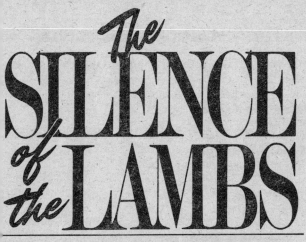

# The SILENCE of the LAMBS

## THE ELECTRIFYING BESTSELLER BY

# THOMAS HARRIS

" THRILLERS DON'T COME ANY BETTER THAN THIS."
### —CLIVE BARKER

"HARRIS IS QUITE SIMPLY THE BEST SUSPENSE NOVELIST
WORKING TODAY." *— The Washington Post*

# LANDMARK BESTSELLERS

# FROM ST. MARTIN'S PAPERBACKS